VE
LULLABY

DR WHO – THE MISSING ADVENTURES

Also available:

GOTH OPERA by Paul Cornell

EVOLUTION by John Peel

VENUSIAN LULLABY

Paul Leonard

First published in Great Britain in 1994 by
Doctor Who Books
an imprint of Virgin Publishing Ltd
332 Ladbroke Grove
London W10 5AH

ISBN 0 426 20424 7

Cover illustration by Alister Pearson
Venusian based on a sketch by Jim Mortimore

Typeset by Galleon Typesetting, Ipswich
Printed and bound in Great Britain by
Cox & Wyman Ltd, Reading, Berks

This book is dedicated to the memory of my father

J. E. HINDER

writer and critic

Acknowledgements

First and foremost, thanks must go to Jim Mortimore, without whom I would not be typing acknowledgements today, largely because it was his idea that I should write a *Doctor Who* novel in the first place; also because of his endless advice, criticism, copy-editing, loan of books, videos, etc., plus of course his incredible drawings of Venusians (see front cover). I must also thank Craig Hinton for extremely useful comments on the text; any nice pieces of continuity you notice will almost certainly be due to him (and if not, they'll be Jim's). Thanks also to my mother for letting me use her telly to watch the above-mentioned endless *Doctor Who* videos; to Chris, Barb and Nick of the Bristol Community Writers' Group for support, advice and general writers' chat; to the Bristol SF group, i.e. Brian, Chris (again), David and Dalva, the two Matthews, Peter-Fred, Richard, Tim and others too numerous to mention, for lots of free ginger beer and stimulating – if occasionally radioactive – conversation; and finally to Anna, Ann H, Helen, Nadia, Anita and Joe, Patrick and Martine, and all at BT for support and encouragement, cash loans, Xmas pressies, good food, cups of tea, etc.

They were waiting.

They were waiting for permission.

They were waiting for permission to remember.

They had known there was food in the rocks whirling around the little yellow sun. But they had made a mistake. Misled by the blue oxygen sky of the third planet, they had pounced on it, hungry and eager; but they had found only chemistry. True, it was complex, helical chemistry; it metabolized in the muddy pools, it replicated, it mutated. It might one day be Mind. It might one day be edible. But for now, it was nothing.

Disappointed, they had licked the salty scum from their fingers and returned to their ship.

Then the second planet had moved into view, dark around the limb of the star. They had smelled its heat, tasted the fear in the Mind living there, the unmistakable flavour of imminent death. They had probed that Mind, sought out the juices and sinews of its culture until they found a way of getting what they needed: a mind that was willing to admit them. A weak, individual mind; a mind ready to grant permission.

But they would have to wait. The permission, they were told, could only come with a death. This was acceptable to them, and they said as much. It was more than acceptable: it was poetry, truth.

For they had been predators, long before they had travelled the stars. Once, with long legs and long teeth, they had lived on the brown plains under a russet sun. They had run after their prey, brought them down with claws and teeth in the ancient, honourable way. There had been permission then, the permission granted by the weakness and fear in the eyes of the prey.

Killing had never been done without it. When there had been no permission, there had been waiting and hunger, and games with death in the years of drought.

And here, amongst the rocks whirling around the dwarf yellow star, there would still be waiting, there would still be hunger, there would still be games with death. The final permission was still required.

They were not resentful, they were not impatient: they enjoyed the game. There was nothing of it that they did not enjoy. The searching, the mistakes, the waiting, the eating that was soon to come, when they would rend the flesh of the second planet with their teeth, fill the emptiness of their minds with its juices –

Oh yes, they were happy.

They were happy to wait for the feast.

They were the happiest creatures in the universe.

Prologue

Dying

Dharkhig knew that he was dying when the parade of his grandchildren began.

One after another they entered his bedchamber, neat and quick in their young green skins. Some said nothing, some muttered, 'Honoured sire.' One tried to talk about a language he was learning, another politely admired the moss-tapestries growing on the walls. Each one would stay for a few minutes, visibly uncomfortable, their eye-stalks waving about in five different directions, lifting one leg after another to inspect the new goldenwood shoes woven around their hooves.

Dharkhig watched them and concentrated on breathing.

When they realized that he wasn't going to speak, each one would solemnly open all five mouths and turn slowly around in the full ceremonial greeting for a leader of the clan. Dharkhig eyed those politely gaping orifices, the fields of young, white teeth with only the occasional gleaming chitinous filling, and imagined the quick young tongues tasting the foul air exuded by his mouldering body. He knew they were glad to go.

When he spoke at last the child who was with him jumped, her five legs drawn up beneath her as if she were fleeing a ghost. She landed again with a solid thud, her eye-stalks at full extension, all five eyes staring at Dharkhig.

'Thought I was gone already, did you?' he asked.

'No – no, grandfather, honoured sire – er – '

So well schooled they can't speak any more, thought Dharkhig irritably.

'Then do as I say and move me to the window,' he said aloud.

The child – Zidifghil, was it, or Midharkhij? – moved hesitantly towards the trolley-chair.

'The watcher-for-death – awk! – that is, the honoured Trikhobu – she said you were not to be – '

Dharkhig closed three of his eyes, felt the terrible weakness returning.

'Just move me, child,' he breathed.

Unwanted fluids rose in his throats, tasting of bitter death. He swallowed with difficulty: his belly heaved, and a cloud of tiny silver dust-flies danced somewhere inside his brain. Dharkhig watched them for a while.

'Grandfather – sire – oh!'

Dharkhig forced open his east eye, saw the discomfited child hovering over him, her skin flushed blue with effort. He opened his other eyes, one by one. His trolley-chair was by the window. She had moved him: he had slept, or fainted, through it.

'Only sleeping, child,' he managed. With a supreme effort, he reached out his east arm and touched the young one's quivering lips. She flushed even deeper, and Dharkhig was sure her belly quivered with pleasure inside its straps and wrappings.

Moments like this made him doubt all that he had worked for: children like this, surely, should be given hope, not told to wait placidly for the end of the world.

But what else could I do, child? he begged silently as he lowered his hand. What choice was there?

He forced himself to think no more of it, and turned three of his eyes to survey the scene outside the window.

The sun was high, he saw; higher than he had hoped. It would be many hours until sunset. Even through the layers of tinted glass the light was barely endurable, the glare of a roaster's oven rather than that of a living world. The heat rose in visible streams from the chitinous roofs of the city, turbulent rivers of air chasing themselves into the sky. Even the sun rippled, as if an ocean was storing itself in the upper atmosphere.

Which it is, Dharkhig reminded himself. He looked at the old harbour, dry as an abandoned nightfish-pot, stranded far above the coast and the new harbour – and, looking down, those too seemed dry and empty, the sea an evaporating mud-pan in the afternoon heat.

'I will not live to see the night.'

The sound of his own words startled Dharkhig; they startled the child even more. Her hooves clattered on the wooden flooring as she moved to stand over him again.

'No – I am sure – that is – you will be better soon – will live many days – er – years – '

'I will not live to see the night,' repeated Dharkhig. Suddenly he was aware that the words he had spoken were true. He would never again see the sky darken, feel the cool land-wind on his belly, know the sense of joy that comes when the sun, the enemy, is gone below the world and living things can start to live once more.

'Bring me paper, child,' he said.

The child hesitated, then fetched a pad of green paper from one of the grey long-pouches hanging on the walls. She silently pressed it into Dharkhig's west hand.

Slowly, painfully, Dharkhig pulled back the flesh of his writing-finger to reveal the sharp, grooved claw. Blood seeped into the groove: old, purple blood. Balancing the book on his north and south hands, he wrote on the first page:

'Jofghil *goi*-Dharkhig, Presidor of the Night Council of Bikugih – my son: eat, remember. Dharkhig.'

He tore the page loose, and handed it to the child. With his north eye, he watched her read it and shiver slightly.

'The others should be here,' she said. 'I will fetch them.' Her manner had aged in a moment, the way a child's does. She was turning to go before Dharkhig could react.

'WAIT!'

Somehow, Dharkhig found an echo of that voice that had once commanded a quarter of the world: the voice that had sent his people into the inferno that had been Cracdhalltar to bring out the bodies of the dead for remembering; the voice that had mourned when the Isles of the Ancients had died; the voice that had made his people accept that their entire world was dying and that they must face the inevitable end with courage and peace, not as mindless animals.

The child turned.

Dharkhig forced his eye-stalks to twitch upwards in the ghost of a formal acknowledgement-of-duty.

'I will not forget anyone,' he said. 'I have known for many years who I would invite to my funeral.'

He wrote a second invitation and a third; a fourth, a fifth. Soon he lost count as the names and the ranks spilled from his blood-memory almost without conscious effort. Once he stopped and crossed out a name as he remembered that its owner had preceded him to Dhallgohidhall, the Land-which-is-no-land; once he added an extra pair of names, new children who must be honoured. Once he paused and felt a wave of giddiness rise into his brain as the slight strength he had found drained away from his limbs.

He swallowed, shut all of his eyes for a moment.

'No,' he muttered. 'Not yet.'

There was one more guest to invite. He squeezed one last drop of blood from his flesh, opened his eyes to write.

But the light had changed.

He twitched his stiff, corroding eye-stalks towards the window.

The city was no longer there. Nor was the sun. Instead, a frightening, lifeless plain curled upwards and dissolved into a dull yellow sky.

Dharkhig twitched his east eye towards his granddaughter. She was crouched by the medicine-table, carefully counting and arranging the funeral invitations.

The sunlight shone on her folded lip-cloths, glinted on a blue jewel that hung from one of her eye-hoods.

The sunlight. But there was no sun –

'Child,' he called, 'what do you see outside the window?'

Her west and north eyes extended curiously, then her lips rippled with puzzlement.

'Nothing, grandfather, only the city – and the sea.'

Dharkhig nodded, suddenly recalling a long-ago garden, a childhood companion, a forgotten sadness. He had so wanted to be a Philosopher, then: he had tried so hard to see the mysteries that Mrakdihig had seen amongst the twisting vines of Kidheghall. He had fasted, he had denied himself water, he had stood for hours in the terrible heat of the sun: all in vain. The lights of the future, the gift-motes of the past, both were denied him. Politics and leadership had been second best – all his life he had failed to achieve the one thing he truly desired.

'And now I see a vision,' he muttered. 'Now.' He tasted the bitter irony, mixed with the bitter death, deep in the pit of his throats where his five tongues met.

'Open the window, child,' he said.

She stared at him.

'But grandfather – honoured sire – it is afternoon. The heat – and you are so ill – '

'Just open it,' he said quietly.

His north and east eyes watched her as she struggled with the bolts and chains, then folded back the first, the second, the third pane of protective glass. His other eyes watched his hand move, writing almost of its own accord.

The time, day and year of tomorrow's dawn.

A name which was no name.

' – my friend: eat, remember.'

He signed it with his full clan-name.

The last window was open. The vision was still there, the vision that the child could not see: the stony desert waiting under the yellow sky. Dharkhig could feel the heat of it searing his mind. It was far beyond any ordinary heat;

it was beyond even the heat of Cracdhalltar when it had died. It was the heat of fire itself, the heat of death. The air tasted of sulphur, and thunder boomed endlessly.

Nothing moved on the bare stones. Nothing lived, anywhere.

Dharkhig knew then that this was a vision of the future.

'Is this all that will remain?' he asked at last. 'Will there be no monuments, no words, no music? Will no one know that we ever lived?'

In the vision the thunder boomed, empty of meaning.

With his last strength, Dharkhig stretched out an arm into the inferno. The hand holding the invitation quivered, the paper curled.

He let it go.

For an instant he heard another, more alien sound, roaring louder than the thunder.

The invitation vanished.

Dharkhig closed his eyes for the last time, felt death stir in his belly.

'Remember us, Doctor,' he breathed. 'I beg of you, remember us all.'

Book One

The Purple Cloud Hour

1

Remembering

'Well, Doctor – now what?'

Ian's voice made Barbara jump. She forced herself to look away from the scanner, where a blank greyness had replaced the picture of Susan's bewildered face.

Ian was standing by the console, leaning forward slightly in that way of his: intrusive, almost aggressive, as if he were ready for a fight. Any second, she thought, he's going to ask the old man to take us home. Again. For all the good that asking will do us.

Barbara glanced at the Doctor who was hunched over the controls of the TARDIS, apparently oblivious to everything except his own thoughts. Quickly she got up off the *chaise longue*, trying to ignore the tiredness in her legs; she hurried over to Ian and put a hand on his arm.

'Leave him alone, Ian,' she said quietly. 'Can't you see he's upset?'

The Doctor's head snapped up: he stared fiercely at Barbara for a moment across the console.

'I'm not upset,' he snapped. 'Not at all upset. I've always known that Susan would leave us. Ever since I first – ' He broke off and his face contorted slightly. He looked down for a moment. Barbara became curiously conscious of the steady motion of the time rotor, the strange, pulsating hum of the TARDIS in flight. Then, with a visible effort, the Doctor pulled his head upright and grasped the lapels of his jacket. 'Susan is a grown woman now. It would no longer be right for me to detain her. I have released her to live in a way of her own choosing.' He hunched over the controls once more and flicked a few switches. Barbara was almost sure that the switches didn't do anything.

She propelled Ian towards the inner door of the control room.

'I don't know about you, Ian, but I'm hungry,' she lied. 'Did you ever work out how to make the food machine produce a spaghetti bolognese that doesn't look like a stick of Brighton rock?'

Ian frowned briefly, glanced back at the Doctor.

'What does he mean, he "released her"? He locked her out, didn't he?'

Ian had a point there, Barbara thought. But she didn't want to discuss it now, with the open door behind them. She gestured at the food machine.

'Spaghetti bolognese?'

'Oh – KD/NB, I think.' Still frowning, he prodded at the curious coloured dials on the machine; it blinked and squawked a few times and produced the usual slabs of anonymous-looking substance, this time in an iridescent green. Ian handed her one.

Barbara held it up, sniffed. 'Smells OK,' she said. She nibbled at it: at once her mouth filled with creamy, stringy pasta and the rich, slightly bitter sauce. And it was *hot* – a comfortable mouth- and stomach-warming temperature. She chewed, swallowed, sighed.

'You know, Ian,' she said, 'the only time I had Italian food as good as this back home was when I got the job at the school. Father took me out to celebrate.' She paused. 'The restaurant was called Vincenzo's. They had red-and-white check tablecloths made out of – what's that new plastic stuff? Fablon? – and straw flasks hanging on the walls.'

Ian didn't appear to be listening; he was staring at some space beyond the console room door, the stick of food in one hand, the other fingering his Coal Hill School tie.

'Not eating?' prompted Barbara.

He shook his head, sighed, then took a small bite and

wrinkled his nose. 'I'm still not sure I like Italian.'

Barbara grinned. 'Could do with some Chianti to go with it. I don't suppose – ?'

Ian examined the controls. 'There's a code for wines,' he said. 'But I'm not sure what it is.' He prodded a button cautiously: the machine squawked, but produced nothing.

'Chianti, did you say?' said the Doctor's voice behind them.

Barbara turned. The Doctor was advancing towards the machine with a mischievous expression on his face. 'What vintage would you like, my dear? And would you prefer it barrel- or bottle-aged? A *rufino*, or perhaps a *classico*?'

Barbara looked at Ian and raised her eyebrows hopefully; Ian shrugged.

'I think ordinary Chianti will be fine, Doctor,' he said. 'Just make sure that it comes from Earth.'

The Doctor turned the dials, prodded the machine with a finger. Two bright purple slabs emerged from the dispenser. Barbara picked one up and took a bite: wine came alive in her mouth, light, clean, slightly astringent.

'I don't know how you do it, Doctor,' she said. 'It's marvellous.'

The Doctor beamed at her. 'No trouble, my dear young woman. No trouble at all.'

'Well, Doctor, we've got food and wine,' said Ian. 'All we need now is a candle-lit table for two and the evening will be complete.'

Barbara couldn't repress a giggle, but the Doctor appeared to take Ian's remark with complete seriousness. He flashed his eyebrows, gestured vaguely.

'A table? Follow me, follow me.'

He led them down the corridor that passed their sleeping quarters.

With a jolt, Barbara realized that the door to Susan's room was gone. Not just closed – gone. She stared at the blank roundels on the wall for a moment, wondering if she could be mistaken, then hurried to catch up with the others. She opened her mouth to say something to Ian, but thought better of it.

They turned left into a long corridor that Barbara somehow thought should have led back towards the console room – but it didn't. Instead it passed several doors, all open, all leading into a vast hall filled with the buzzing and clicking of electronic machinery; then it curved downwards, ending in a set of double doors. The Doctor opened the doors, revealing a room about the size of the assembly hall at Coal Hill School, decorated with the ubiquitous roundels and filled with chairs.

There were high-back chairs, armchairs, basket chairs, deck-chairs, sofas, high chairs, easy chairs, revolving chairs; chairs on their sides, chairs jammed against each other, chairs stacked up, chairs covered in dust sheets; chairs with broken legs, chairs with no backs, chairs with holes in the seats; a ring of wood that might once have been a seat fitted around the trunk of a large tree; chairs with castors, chairs with wheels, a chair with what looked as if they were small silver rockets attached; and a big shiny red chair with six incredibly short legs and a back about sixteen feet high, which Barbara doubted was intended for any human person at all.

'Now, if you two would like to help yourself to chairs,' said the Doctor, 'I think I can find a table.'

He strutted into the room and looked around for a moment, then strode off. He prodded at a blank section of wall with his cane and, to Barbara's astonishment, it started to fold down into the room with a whirring of motors and a loud metallic clicking sound. Attached to the inside of the displaced wall was an enormous wooden table, complete with a four-foot candelabrum which was evidently screwed to the surface. Barbara held her breath, but the section of floor underneath the descending table was miraculously clear of chairs.

The table hit the floor with a thud.

Ian, frowning, walked across the room and began

examining the legs of the table, which were flush with the floor. Barbara could almost hear him thinking: what happened to the wall?

Don't ask, thought Barbara. She walked across to join him, picking up a couple of light wooden chairs on the way. She set them at the top end of the table, opposite each other.

'Now, a candle – ' muttered the Doctor. He began to rummage in his pockets, produced in quick succession a ball-point pen, a thermometer (household) and the oil cap for a car, still with some oil on it. He handed the last to Ian who looked at it for a moment, glanced at Barbara, then put it down slowly on the corner of the table.

Meanwhile the Doctor had resumed the search. Two handkerchiefs appeared, both of bright red silk, followed by a green piece of paper with some odd-looking pictograms sketched on it. He stared at them for a moment and muttered, 'I really must get around to that. Most remiss of me.' Holding the paper in one hand, he put the handkerchiefs back in his pocket and finally, with an expression of triumph, produced a stubby yellow candle about an inch long and a box of matches. Smiling gleefully, he stretched up and put the candle in the top of the four-foot holder, struck one of the matches and lit it. The air instantly filled with the scent of lemons.

'It's everlasting, you know,' he said.

'The candle as well?' Barbara couldn't quite bring herself to be surprised.

The Doctor nodded and blew out the match. 'Of course, of course. Now if you would excuse me – '

'Aren't you joining us?' asked Ian, gesturing towards a handy armchair.

The Doctor shook his head. 'I have things to do, you know. Many things to do. And – ' he beamed at them ' – I'm sure you two have a great deal to talk about.' He turned and left. Barbara noticed that the green piece of paper was still clutched in his hand.

She sat down at the table and smiled slightly at Ian, but he was staring fixedly after the Doctor. She cleared her throat.

Ian seemed to shake himself. He sat down and began eating, but in an abstracted, mechanical way; it was clear that his mind was somewhere else.

Barbara cleared her throat again

'Sorry, Barbara. It's just that I – ' he began, then paused, looking at her.

Barbara took a bite of the spaghetti, a nibble of wine. Waited.

'It would be past Christmas by now,' he said at last.

She remembered the calendar on the wall in his room, the days crossed off in neat school ink. Nodded.

'The second Christmas,' Ian went on. ' A whole year gone from our lives. If we ever get back – even to the same time – we'll still be that year older.'

She nibbled at the wine again, leaned back in her chair. Her eyes strayed to the tall red chair; she noticed that it had a faint zig-zag pattern inlaid into the glossy surface.

'We've seen things no one else in our time has seen, or will ever see, she said. 'Ancient man; the Aztecs; the French Revolution; Skaro; Marinus. We'll have that time, those memories.'

Ian met her eyes for a moment, made his best ironic smile.

'Oh yes, it's had its charms. Who would want to go through the whole of their life and never meet a Dalek?' He stood up, bit at his food, then started to pace up and down the length of the table. Barbara noticed for the first time that the ceiling of the room was a dome, patterned with the same roundels that covered the walls. About a third of the way up, a small chair hung from a spike, looking very much as if it had been hurled up there in desperation when somebody had run out of space on the floor.

'We have to do something for ourselves, not just rely

on the Doctor,' Ian said suddenly.

Barbara stared at him, puzzled.

'To get back home? But what can we do? The Doctor is the only one who knows anything about the TARDIS. We can barely even work the food machine.'

Ian leaned forward. 'Yes, but are you sure he's doing everything he can? I've been thinking about it a lot. We don't have any way of checking on him.'

'Are you suggesting he's deliberately keeping us here? Oh, Ian, after all we've been through – he's tried and tried – '

'I don't know what I'm suggesting,' Ian broke in. 'I just think we should try to learn something about how the TARDIS works. Then we'll know what to think.'

Barbara shook her head. 'I can't believe that the Doctor would deceive us about something so important.' She paused, aware of the frown on Ian's face. 'Why do you think he's so upset about leaving Susan? He could go back and see her any time he liked if the TARDIS was working properly.'

But Ian was frowning. 'I don't see that the Doctor's particularly upset,' he said. 'He told Susan he would be back, remember. Maybe he can visit her whenever he likes. Maybe he could take us back to London, 1963, right now if he wanted to. I'd just like to know.'

He stood up and walked swiftly out of the room.

Barbara half-rose, then sat down again, sighed, closed her eyes. She remembered Vincenzo's, the restaurant she had told Ian about. Her father's face, proud and beaming and slightly drunk, and the plump little waitress with her green, white and orange necklace, and the traffic grumbling in the street outside, and somewhere there were parks and brick houses and red buses and nightingales and walking by the Serpentine and the smell of chalk dust and rainy Sundays and honeysuckle –

She swallowed, put a hand up to her eyes, discovered they were wet.

'Yes, I would like to go home, Doctor,' she said aloud

to the empty room. 'I really would like to go home soon. If you can possibly manage it.'

'Give me the reading on the neutronium counter, Chesterton.'

Ian peered at the dial. The needle was waving about wildly. 'Er – about seven,' he offered. 'No, make that six.'

'Too high, too high. Far too high. Really this is most inconvenient. I do wish – ' The Doctor broke off, crouched down and reached under the console. Rattling and banging sounds followed. The TARDIS swayed to one side; the time rotor stopped briefly, seemed to shiver, then resumed its steady motion.

The Doctor's muffled voice issued from beneath the console: 'The neutronium counter, Chesterton, the neutronium counter!'

Ian looked down. The needle was motionless.

'There isn't a reading at all, Doctor.'

There was a loud metallic bang from within the machinery, and the TARDIS swayed again. The needle twitched.

'Oh-point-five,' read Ian.

The Doctor reappeared, clambered upright, straightened his jacket.

'Well done, young man. Now tell me if the reading changes.'

The Doctor flicked a few switches: nothing very much happened.

Keeping his eyes on the dial, Ian said, 'What I was hoping, Doctor, is that you would be able to show me how to – well, how to pilot this thing.' From the corner of his eye he saw the Doctor glance up; he felt the old man's piercing gaze on the side of his face. He ignored it and carried on: 'I realize that it's not a simple task, but I'm sure it would help if I had some idea – I mean, there have been times when it would have been useful – '

The ship started to shake violently. Ian realized that the needle in front of him was rising.

'Counter reading one-point-five, Doctor.'

The Doctor nodded. The TARDIS ceased to vibrate.

'Two-point-five.'

The familiar roaring sound of materialization began. From the corner of his eye, Ian saw Barbara enter the console room; he risked a glance up at her, made a tiny shrug. The reading on the dial slowly mounted; as Ian called out the numbers, the Doctor seemed to get more and more pleased with himself. He rubbed his hands, chuckled, seeming ready to do a little dance.

'I really do think that this time we might manage it!'

Ian felt a sudden leap of excitement.

'Doctor, are we going back to 1963?'

The Doctor glanced at him, frowned.

'1963? No, no, no. Far too unstable, young man. It never works. Goodness knows, I've tried it often enough. But this far back in time, it should be possible to stabilize – closer to the origin of the Universe you see – '

Ian had a sinking feeling.

'This far back? How far back, exactly?'

'Oh, about three billion years I should think. Now then – '

He flicked a switch: the TARDIS shuddered slightly and the time rotor stopped moving. After a moment, the materialization noises ceased. The Doctor briefly scanned the controls, nodded. Pulled out a silver fob watch from his waistcoat pocket, glanced at it, sighed.

'Not bad, I suppose,' he said. 'But we're almost an hour late. The Venusians will be very annoyed, I'm afraid. They regard punctuality as a particular virtue, especially at funerals.'

'Venusians – ?' began Barbara, but the Doctor had already pushed open the outer door of the TARDIS.

'I did do my best,' he said – apparently to someone outside – and was gone.

Ian looked helplessly at Barbara. 'So what do we do now?'

'I suppose we'd better go to the funeral.'

'Are you sure we're invited?

Barbara giggled. 'We'll find out soon enough if we aren't. Come on.' She slipped through the door.

Ian went to follow, but instead almost collided with Barbara coming back in. She was pale and her body was shaking.

'What is it?' he asked, pushing her behind him in a protective gesture that had become almost automatic.

'The Doctor,' said Barbara, her voice quavering, 'is being strangled by something about the size of a rhinoceros, with snakes growing out of it.' She took a deep breath. 'There must be a thousand of them out there.'

Ian peered around the door. It was dark outside, but the light from the TARDIS was sufficient to show the huge being towering over the Doctor, its body mottled yellow and green. Something that did indeed look like a giant snake stretched out from the top of its body and was wrapped around the Doctor's neck. And – yes – there were hundreds more of the creatures, slowly shuffling down a dimly lit slope towards the TARDIS. The air was hot, humid and smelled slightly of ammonia.

So much for funerals and punctuality, thought Ian. He almost swore aloud, then remembered there was a lady present. But why did the Doctor always have to land them in this sort of situation?

'Doctor!' he hissed. 'I'll distract it – if it lets you go, get back in the TARDIS, quick.' He cupped his hand to shout, looked for a handy rock or something to throw at the monster.

The Doctor turned, his face pale in the light from the TARDIS door. He smiled mischievously.

'Ah, Chesterton! You must meet one of my oldest friends. This is Jilet Mrak-ecado of the clan Poroghini – Mrak-ecado, this is Ian Chesterton, male half-imago of the budling Susan.' He nodded, and beamed at both of them. 'Our custom is to shake hands rather than to grip the neck,' he added helpfully; it was a moment before Ian realized that this remark was addressed to the alien.

Ian stepped out slowly, saw huge pillar-like legs, each ending in a splayed, star-shaped hoof, and a tangle of the snake-like things twisting and rolling in the air above the body. Some of the latter ended, startlingly, in eyes, which peered at Ian with evident interest.

The being squatted down as Ian approached, and extended one of the thicker snake-limbs – which Ian supposed he must call an arm, since it ended in a star-shaped organ with a vague resemblance to a hand. At the same time, a huge Y-shaped gap opened in the alien's body, just below shoulder height; the gap was filled with teeth. Ian had the uncomfortable feeling that his head would fit in there just nicely.

The Doctor made a curious nodding, beckoning gesture.

Ian extended his hand, touched the alien flesh. The hand closed itself over Ian's, the petal-like fingers reaching almost to his elbow. The surface was quite dry and rough, more like tree-bark than skin.

'I greet you, Ian Chesterton of the Doctor-budling Susan,' said the alien. 'I hope that your birth-pains have faded.'

Ian opened his mouth, drew a breath, then realized that he hadn't the faintest idea what the alien was talking about.

He glanced at the Doctor, who merely beamed and said, 'Oh yes, Susan divided well.' He raised his voice slightly. 'Barbara! If you'd like to come out, you can meet my friend.'

Ian swallowed and looked over his shoulder.

'It's safe – I think,' he called, acutely aware of the cool birchbark-skin of the alien still closed around his right hand.

Barbara's face appeared around the door. She walked slowly out, her eyes fixed on the vast spider-like bulk behind Ian. A second alien arm snaked past Ian, the star-shaped hand splayed wide. Barbara jumped back.

'It's OK,' Ian said. 'He's just shaking hands.'

'And this clanswoman is – ?' asked the alien. Ian became aware of a curious hissing, popping sound behind the words, as if something were being fried in deep fat.

'Barbara Wright, female half-imago of the budling-Susan,' supplied the Doctor, and introduced Mrak-ecado to Barbara in turn. 'Go on, Barbara, shake hands,' he urged.

Barbara's eyes searched out Ian's.

'Not until you let go,' she said.

Ian frowned. 'Why – ?'

'Let it go!' Barbara's voice was shaking.

Ian pulled his hand out of the alien's grasp. It shifted uneasily, the tips of the petal-fingers twitching, then withdrew.

Very slowly, Barbara reached out her own hand. She touched the alien skin briefly, as if testing a cooking hob to see if it was hot; then, satisfied, she warily gripped the tips of the petal-fingers from the outside, giving them no chance to grip her own hand. She let go almost at once. Ian nodded to himself. She was right. He wished he'd been as cautious.

Barbara looked across at him, her face flushed with anger.

'I thought it had hypnotized you both – or something – I thought I was going to have to fight it – '

He reached out and took her shoulders, squeezed them gently.

'It's all right,' he said. 'I'm quite un-hypnotized, I assure you.'

She managed a smile. 'Just be more careful next time, will you?'

And then the Doctor was there, awkwardly patting Barbara's arm. 'My dear young woman, there's absolutely nothing to worry about. I've known Mrak-ecado for two hundred years, on and off. He's one of the most respected Philosophers on Venus.'

Ian jolted upright, let Barbara go. 'Venus?' He looked up into the clear sky, which was a deep ocean-blue in colour. A single star twinkled near the horizon. Ian had an awful suspicion that it was the Earth.

The Doctor had put on his reproving expression.

'Of course Venus, my dear Chesterton. Where else would you meet Venusians? Were you not listening to me just now?'

'But Venus is covered in cloud,' spluttered Ian. 'That probe they sent last year measured the surface temperature as nine hundred degrees – it must be uninhabitable – '

The Doctor put a finger to his lips. 'Shh-hh! Tact, young man, tact!' He lowered his voice to a whisper. 'I remind you that we're a long way in your past. A very long way indeed. Venus is quite habitable at the moment and will be for – let me see – ' he pulled out the silver fob watch once more and examined it closely ' – another fifty years at least. Now, do please, both of you, remember we're at a funeral and try to behave appropriately.'

Ian stared at Barbara who, rather to his surprise, was grinning.

'Well,' he asked her, 'how do I behave at a Venusian funeral?'

Barbara, still grinning, slowly shook her head.

Behind them, they heard the Doctor explaining to Mrak-ecado in a loud voice, 'I'm really terribly sorry, you must excuse them. You see they were only born last week.'

Barbara raised her eyebrows. 'I think that's another thing we're going to have to ask him about,' she said.

Barbara had never seen a more peculiar funeral. It was taking place on an open hilltop, an uneven patch of ground covered in small grey pebbles. Spiky weeds about the size of thistles sprouted at wide intervals. There was no building nearby, nothing that might have been a church or a chapel; there was no sign even of a coffin. No one seemed to be in charge. The Venusian mourners – at least she assumed they were the mourners – squatted on the ground in the half-dark, variously waving their long, thin arms or stamping their hooves. Some walked, scuttling across the ground with apparent purpose, but they never seemed to arrive anywhere; they would stop suddenly or reverse their tracks. Barbara had once seen a film of starfish, sea urchins and other rock-pool fauna: this scene was similar, except that she was in the middle of it, and the fauna were about three times as big as she was. Every time she approached one of the huge, dimly lit forms she shrank back, afraid that some random movement would knock her flat.

The Doctor seemed unconcerned by it all; he walked ahead with Mrak-ecado, deep in conversation, occasionally striking at the weeds with his cane. Odd words and phrases drifted back to Barbara: 'tangential, undoubtedly tangential' – 'fifth sphere of harmony' – 'lines of *antiunometric* force, my friend.' But as they climbed further up the slope their quiet voices were buried in the din emitted from the other Venusians: gurgling, popping sounds, bony clicks, the clatter and splash of hooves on the pebbles. They passed a Venusian standing high on legs, his hooves contracted to points, his body stretched up so that his eye-stalks were almost ten feet above Barbara's head. He was shouting at the top of his voice: 'I say NO! It is here in the ruins of a once-great city that we must remember the past, yes, but also accept the future – ' A little further on, at what seemed to be the highest point of the hill, another Venusian leaped up and down on the spot, calling out, 'One gate, two gate, three gate, four gate, five – ' Her five hooves clacked together at the top of each jump.

'Surely they don't let their children play skipping games at a time like this?' she murmured to the Doctor.

The Doctor gave her a sharp glance.

'She's not a child and she's not playing.'

Barbara looked at Ian, who shrugged.

'Sit down and eat,' said the Doctor impatiently. 'Then you'll understand.' He sat down on the rough ground, pulled his legs up in front of him. Mrak-ecado squatted next to him, belly to the ground, legs hunched so that his knees were higher than his eyes. Even in this position, he was taller than Barbara.

Uneasily, she sat down. The ground was rough and pebbly.

'You'd think they could provide cushions,' she said.

'My dear Barbara, a cushion suitable for a Venusian would be far too big for you to sit on,' said the Doctor. 'Now eat, please do.'

Barbara noticed a Venusian hovering around behind Mrak-ecado, its body silhouetted against the deep blue of the sky. It carried something in its hands that looked like a model Chinese pagoda; at a gesture from the Doctor it reached down and put the object on the ground, then withdrew. Barbara saw that the pagoda was a stack of plates, each plate separated from the next by five stumpy legs. The Doctor picked one up and helped himself to something that looked like a segment of fruit, or possibly cheese. When he saw Barbara looking, he proffered the plate to her, smiled. 'Ladies first, eh?'

'Are the young ones going to eat and remember, then?' rumbled Mrak-ecado. Something in his tone made Barbara hesitate, her hand above the plate.

'I don't see why they shouldn't join us,' the Doctor replied. 'It won't hurt them. Besides, it would be a courtesy to my old friend – ' He was looking at Barbara now; she nodded and took a segment of the food.

It was spongy, and slightly sticky, and extremely sweet. It reminded Barbara of the honey pancakes her grandmother had used to make her when she was a little girl, except that – oddly – in the centre, there was something meaty and slightly bitter. She turned to Ian who was still standing, suspiciously examining the contents of the next plate, and grinned.

'Just as well we didn't have dessert in the "restaurant",' she said. 'This is delicious!'

Ian took a segment, sniffed, nibbled at it and shook his

head. 'Too sweet for me, if you don't mind,' he said politely.

'Courtesy, young man – ' began the Doctor; but before he could finish there was a loud *thud* and a Venusian landed between Barbara and Mrak-ecado. Her eye-stalks were waving wildly, her whole body heaving up and down as gusts of air moved in and out of her lungs.

'My old friend! Your journey has been successful!' she wheezed at the Doctor. 'And congratulations! These two young people must have been Susan?'

Ian and Barbara looked at each other in total bewilderment; it occurred to Barbara that she hadn't yet understood a thing that any of the Venusians had said. Just when you thought you'd got a grip on the meaning, the speaker would add another phrase, or another sentence, that made all of it into nonsense. The Doctor, however, seemed to have understood perfectly.

'Yes – quite so, quite so. Last week. An easy birth, so they tell me.' He clapped his hands and beamed broadly at the newcomer, introducing her to Barbara and Ian as Trikhobu, daughter of Dharkhig.

Trikhobu did not shake hands, but leaned over towards Barbara and Ian, extending an eye-stalk to inspect each of them. The eyes themselves were human-like, although about three times too big; but there was a flap of flesh around the eye which was uncomfortably reminiscent of the hood of a cobra. Barbara tried not to flinch.

'Most interesting – highly divergent – and only two of everything,' concluded Trikhobu. 'Tell me, Barbara, do you remember my father yet?'

Barbara opened her mouth to reply, then realized she hadn't understood the question and had nothing to say. Desperately she looked at the Doctor.

'Only Barbara is remembering,' he said, still beaming broadly. 'Ian thought it was too sweet.'

Barbara looked at Ian, who grinned and said quietly, 'Gibberish must be infectious.'

She grinned back, but shushed him, muttering,

'Venusians have very good hearing.'

'How do you know?' he asked.

A good question, thought Barbara. How did she know? She didn't recall the Doctor mentioning it. Perhaps Trikhobu had told her; she relied on her daughter for most things these days.

No – hold on – Trikhobu is *Dharkhig's* daughter, she thought. She closed her eyes, shook her head to clear it. Heard a thunder of hooves and hastily opened them again, to see two Venusians rushing past them at a full gallop. One was shouting, 'We must get them out of the fire! We must remember them!' Barbara looked around, but could see no fire. Trikhobu and Mrak-ecado seemed unalarmed. And there was no taste of smoke in the air, as there had been at Cracdhalltar.

Where?

Barbara jerked upright, clenching her fists. *What had she been thinking?* She had never heard of Cracdhalltar, but the name brought a clear image to her mind: a cloud of smoke the size of a mountain, the lake boiling, a searing impossible heat, screams of pain and terror –

She shuddered.

A hand fell on her shoulder. Barbara jumped, then realized it was only Trikhobu.

'You are remembering now?'

'I'm – a little confused,' admitted Barbara.

'Don't worry, I'll watch for you,' said Trikhobu courteously.

'Is Barbara all right?' asked Ian.

Barbara tried to look at him, then realized she had to turn her head to do that. What had happened to her eye-stalks? She put her hands over her face, felt the alien bones there, shuddered again.

'She's remembering,' explained Trikhobu. 'She ate a piece of my father.'

'Bit-loop neurotransmitters,' said the Doctor, adding, 'Wlloop! Wlloop! Wll-lloop!' He began making swimming motions with his arms.

'May you have bright water,' said Barbara politely: then wondered why she'd said it.

'Look, I want to know what's going on.' Ian's voice. 'Barbara, what's the matter with you?'

She made the effort to turn her head at last, saw the concern and fear written on Ian's face.

'I – don't know,' she said. 'I should know – ' she added.

Eat, remember. Ian's face swam in the dim light. Two of everything, and his eyes stapled to his head like that – how could he hope to understand?

'I'm remembering,' she said. The words sounded strange in her mouth, shrill and musical, like the song of the *ghifghoni* when they rested their rotor blades at sunset. 'Remembering,' she repeated.

'Remembering what?' Ian was almost shouting. 'Doctor! What's happening? *Doctor!*'

'Wll-lloop! Wll-lloop!'

Eat, remember. Eat. And remember.

Barbara could see the *bosifghal* forest now, dull green in the evening sun. She picked her way delicately between the thick boles of the trees, her leather-shod hooves silent in the leaf-litter. Five sleeping tailor-moths stirred as she passed; idly, she followed their paths through the air, an eye to each one, until they vanished into the gloom. They all flew upwards, and she took it as an omen: her speech to the Night Council would be a success.

'The culmination of evolution is a civilization which can accept the end of its existence,' she murmured, rehearsing not so much the words as the emotion contained in them. 'Without animal fear, without chaos and panic, but in calm and in acceptance until the very last moment.'

From somewhere, a voice interrupted her rehearsal. 'Barbara?' Her body was being shaken. She pulled up her belly and hissed angrily, tensed her legs to kick the aggressor. 'Barbara! Please! You've got to snap out of it!'

Then the voice faded and she was standing in the fiery

sunlight on Hidarateg Peak, overlooking the vast Bikugih plains. The horizon was soft, grey, smudged by the mist of evening; the sky was blue.

'We cannot fight the end,' she said, declaiming aloud to her people, three-mouthed in harmony. 'All such fighting is animal, futile. We must accept – accept, and die with our minds aware and our eyes to the light.'

Yes! The feeling was right: the speech was ready. The Night Council would be convinced, beyond doubt. Gaping all her mouths wide in triumph, Barbara turned her five eyes towards the sun.

2

Requests For Assistance

Ever since his eyes had opened and he had ceased to be the same person as his sister, Kantihif Havteg of the clan Rimikugih had been afraid of bipeds. He remembered too well the long cold minutes as a child, drifting in the blue-green underwater of his child-pool, five eyes watching the tiny black spots of a stickwalker's foot-pads as it moved around on the surface above; he'd been terrified that he would run out of breath and have to go up before the horrible thing flew away. Once, Havteg had run out of breath, and the stickwalker – probably as afraid as he was – had jumped onto one of his eye-stalks. Havteg's screams had raised his bud-mother's entire household; she had put nets over the pool after that.

Now I have to go up again, he thought. And I'd better not scream this time.

The alien was walking up and down the lower slopes of the Funeral Ground, quite near to its ship; but it made no attempt to enter the craft. Instead it seemed to be studying the ground – at least, that was where the part of its body containing its eyes was pointing. Occasionally it would turn so that its eyes faced up the slope to the main funeral party; when it did this it would mutter something and ram one bunched-up hand into the palm of the other.

Havteg wondered whether the alien was remembering or thinking: whether it could see him or not.

He edged closer to it, zig-zagging so that anyone who noticed him would think that he was remembering with the other guests. The alien ignored him. As Havteg grew closer, the resemblance to a stickwalker seemed to increase: the fuzzy cloth bindings were like the fuzz on a walker's chitin, while the lack of wings, the missing eyes and mouths, only made the alien look deformed. Havteg struggled to control the tightening in his throat and to remember his duty.

This may be the only chance we get.

He reached into his east lip-pouch and fingered the cool goldenwood of the dart gun. He felt faintly unsafe, and faintly ridiculous. He didn't even know if the darts would work on the alien. It would probably be better to threaten to bite one of its limbs off, thought Havteg; but the notion made him feel sick.

'Just a rumour,' Barjibuhi had said. 'That's all we have. The Acceptancers may be trying to mislead us – but we can't take the chance of ignoring it.'

The only chance.

The moment felt too insignificant for that, Havteg decided: he felt too insignificant. A clansman afraid of forked animals. It was ludicrous that the fate of an entire civilization was to be decided by an irontip dart that might not work, by whether any of Dharkhig's guests saw Havteg and guessed what he was trying to do.

He was walking almost parallel with the alien now. Suddenly it turned and faced him.

'What have you done with Barbara?' it asked. Its mouth was tiny, horrible. Havteg fingered the gun once more, then decided it could wait. But he kept his hand in the lip-pouch, ready.

'I am Havteg,' he said. 'Are you remembering? I will watch for you.'

The being repeated the strange punching motion of its hands. 'Look, I don't want remembering or watching, I just want Barbara and the Doctor back alive, sane and in one piece, thank you very much.'

Havteg felt his skin tighten with despair. This was going to be much more difficult than he had expected. He had been told that these aliens were rational; surely they must be, to build a ship that could move between worlds. But the words the stickwalker spoke made no sense.

'The Doctor?' he replied cautiously, repeating the only name that he recognized. 'You are the Doctor?'

'I – ' The alien hesitated, as if it were not entirely sure who it was. But that was normal, of course, if it had been remembering. 'If I am the Doctor,' it said finally, 'what do you want with me?'

Havteg flattened his eye-stalks in bewilderment. Had he understood correctly? How could the alien's identity depend on what he, Havteg, wanted?

'You are either the Doctor or not the Doctor,' he began, then broke off, realizing that he couldn't even be sure of that. This was, after all, an alien.

With his north eye, Havteg could see two of the funeral guests looking on. Obviously they were no longer remembering. At any moment they might decide to come down the slope and have a closer look at the alien themselves.

The only chance.

Havteg decided that there was no more time to worry about details.

'I would like to see the inside of your ship,' he said quickly, quietly. 'I am curious as to how you travel between the stars.'

The alien turned its single, giant eye-stalk for a moment to point its eyes at the small blue box. Somehow the eyeless part, with its obscene decoration of fibrous matting, was even more disturbing than the seeing part. It looked like a fungus growing on the corpse of an animal.

'The TARDIS?' the alien said after a moment, turning back to Havteg. 'I can't get inside it, the Doctor has the – ' It paused for a moment. 'All three of us have to be here before the door will open.'

Havteg felt his skin slacken a little; at least that made sense. Use of the device required the consent of the whole clan. So the alien wasn't – totally alien. It might be able to help them after all.

To the west, one of the guests was speaking; as Havteg watched, they started down the slope towards him.

The only chance.

Havteg took a step closer to the alien and whispered, 'We need your help. We cannot follow Dharkhig. We cannot accept the End. We have prepared everything: we have food, animals, plant seeds enough for a thousand colonists. But we cannot master the building of a rocket ship. They fail, they explode – ' Havteg broke off, suddenly aware that he was gabbling, giving away secrets to someone who was not a Rocketeer, was not even of his species; then realized it was too late, he had committed himself, and went on: 'If we could use your ship, or if you would let us copy it – even a simple copy, a simple ship, just enough to get us to the third planet – we would be grateful, we would cherish your memory in the heart of our bones – '

The alien was staring at him fixedly with its tiny, sunken eyes.

'The third planet?' it said.

Havteg gestured into the western sky, at the pale blue star still shining there against the growing silver light of dawn. 'Yes. That one, there. We have examined it with special instruments; it is a world like ours, we think we could live there. Do you know? Can you tell us?'

But the alien was backing away. 'You're talking about the Earth,' it said. Its voice was louder now. 'You're going to invade the Earth, aren't you? You're just like the Daleks. No wonder you drugged – '

The guests were still strolling down the slope, almost within earshot now. Desperately Havteg pulled the gun out of his lip-pouch; to his horror, he fumbled and dropped it on the ground. With three hands he scrabbled after it, got it against his west hip where it would be hidden from the approaching couple by his body. He held the barrel to cover the deadly iron *chink* of the dart loading itself against the spring, pointed the gun at the alien. The being took another step backwards, both its eyes focused on the weapon.

'Please, no further,' begged Havteg. 'You must find a way to help us. Please. Or I will have to kill you.'

Barbara woke up feeling sick. She tried to pull up her belly, to squeeze the juices out of her stomachs, but it only resulted in a dry gulping in her throats. She tried to move, to test her balance, but her muscles felt strange, as if they were linked together in the wrong places. She opened two of her eyes, saw flame-coloured mosses growing on a ceiling above her, matted in the *unsharhijih* pattern; they looked familiar. And the roof-window, in the centre of the dome – the cross-hatch pattern of the panes –

Trikhobu. She was in the writing-room of Trikhobu's house in Bikugih.

She tried to open her other three eyes, but nothing happened. She tried to move the two eyes she had, but they wouldn't budge. With an effort she craned her whole body upwards – her legs were horizontal – and – *by fire!*

She sat back again, gasping with shock.

Alien. She was *alien*.

An arm – *her* arm – with its deformed hand, waved in front of her face as if it were trying to wipe something away; when it touched she felt slimy, humid skin. She cried out and heard a thin animal squeal issuing from her mouths – no, mouth, she only had one mouth open – by fire, she would choke like this –

Gasping, she pulled at the skin around the top of her body, trying to force open her other mouths. But it was no use. They weren't there. There was only that smooth, slimy flesh. She squealed again, breathing hard, beat her fists against the rough fibres of the sleeping-mat.

'Barbara? Are you all right? Are you still remembering?'

Trikhobu's voice. Barbara almost sobbed with relief.

A star-shaped hand descended towards her face. Two

dry green fingers touched her lips. Shakily, Barbara reached out with her heavy, deformed arm to return the gesture. She had to turn her head to see Trikhobu squatting by the sleeping-mat; her hand wavered towards Trikhobu's nearest mouth and clumsily made contact.

'The Doctor said that perhaps the dose was too high for your metabolism,' observed Trikhobu with one of her other mouths.

The Doctor . . . ? An old man; long, silver hair, Edwardian clothes – and those eyes – watching, weighing –

Barbara nodded, made herself sit upright.

'I'm Barbara,' she said aloud. 'I live in the TARDIS.' Console, hat-stand, the gilded clock – the strange machine that cut and set her hair – Ian's calendar –

She looked down at her body again: this time she felt less shock. Contradictory thoughts chased themselves around her mind: legs cut off – no, both of them are OK – where are my arms? – one, two, all there. But something wrong, something wrong, something *wrong*.

'I had – a dream,' she said. 'Or maybe I was remembering.'

'You were remembering a part of my father's life,' said Trikhobu. 'You don't have to tell me about it. Only very close friends do that.'

'But you're my – ' began Barbara, then stopped, realizing how she had been going to finish that sentence: 'daughter'. Deeply loving Trikhobu, greatly laughing Trikhobu, absolutely trustworthy Trikhobu –

But no, those were Dharkhig's memories. She – Barbara, who lived in the TARDIS – barely knew Trikhobu. They weren't even the same species.

'One of your hooves fell off,' said Trikhobu suddenly. 'How long will it take to grow back?'

Barbara glanced down and saw that she had indeed lost a shoe. 'It won't grow,' she said. 'It's a made thing – look.' She slipped the other shoe off, slithered round on the rough matting to pick it up, waved it in front of Trikhobu's eye-stalks for her to see.

'Oh! Oh dear!' said Trikhobu. 'I didn't know! I put it with the garden rubbish.'

Barbara stared at her for a moment, noted the tightened skin, the wildly waving eye-stalks. Then she began to laugh.

'It's all right, Trikhobu, the Doctor can get another one from the TARDIS.' She paused. 'Talking of which, where is the Doctor?'

'The Doctor is with Jilet Mrak-ecado. There was a recital.' Barbara knew that Trikhobu meant a recital of philosophy; more of Dharkhig's memories. Trikhobu went on: 'Ian has gone for a walk somewhere. He was upset, I think.'

Barbara stared at the *unsharhijih* of flame-moss on the wall. Remembered Ian's voice calling her name in panic, remembered his hands shaking her. He hadn't eaten any of the funeral meat; he had said it was too sweet. So he wouldn't –

'Upset!' she said. 'I should think he was upset! Did anyone think to tell him what was really happening?'

Trikhobu's eye-stalks waved uncomfortably. 'We tried, but he wouldn't listen. The Doctor said he would come round in time, and that I should look after you.'

'Trust the Doctor!' said Barbara, mostly to herself. 'Why does he always think I'm the one that needs looking after?' She stood up. 'Come on, Trikhobu, we've got to find Ian.'

She looked at her one shoe, which she still held in her hand, then glanced down at her stockinged feet.

'Do you think there's any chance of getting my hoof back?' she asked.

Jilet Mrak-ecado of the clan Poroghini touched the third pentave strings of his seventy-five string guitar, adding a thin, air-carried harmony to the melody he was plucking on the fifth pentave underwater. The music rippled softly across the cool green water of the bud-pond; the air-harmonies lost themselves amidst the grey moss-shaggy trunks of the *binihabeg*. Above, clinging to the branchless spires of the trees, *ghifghoni* preened their rotor membranes, their skins glinting blue and violet in the early morning sun.

The Doctor lay on his side, his body sloping down the bank towards the bud-pond, half his head under the water so that one of his strange, sculpted ears was beneath the surface and the other above it. Both of his eyes were closed, and his mouth was twisted into a gentle curve which Mrak-ecado recognized as a smile.

Mrak-ecado wondered how much his old friend actually heard of the music, with only two ears. He must miss many of the finer harmonies, yet he seemed to enjoy it as any Venusian would – more than most, in fact. Mrak-ecado touched the thirteenth pentave, both above and below the water, and listened to the harmonies dance.

From the corner of one eye, he noticed the middle-plate of his timer change from brown to pale blue. Time, he knew, was running out. Reluctantly he damped down the vibrations of the major pentaves, leaving only a faint, rubbed harmony from the thirteenth. It was the traditional invitation to talk.

'Your skill in playing has not decreased, old friend,' said the Doctor after a while.

'Neither has your skill in listening,' said Mrak-ecado politely.

There was a pause. A solitary *ghifghoni* set out on a stiff practice flight across the garden, its rotors rattling in the still air.

'You will be wanting to return to your bud-children?' asked Mrak-ecado eventually.

The Doctor lifted his head out of the water, shook the drops out of the fine white fungus growing on his head.

'You know, I had almost forgotten them,' he said. 'Without Susan, it seems – ' He broke off, shook his head again.

Mrak-ecado, puzzled, let the guitar echo into silence.

'This must be one of the differences between your

species and ours,' he said. 'Our budlings do not see, are not active out of water as Susan was. When Susan divided, it must have seemed like a death, even as Barbara and Ian were born.'

'It's not like that, exactly – there are other differences – ' Again the Doctor didn't seem able to say any more.

Mrak-ecado pushed the guitar up to float in its rest position, spread out like the petals of a hand-in-water, then walked out of the pond and squatted on the brown moss beside his old friend.

'Barbara and Ian are parts of Susan,' he said. 'They have her memories between them. That should be precious to you. And, new-born as they are, they need looking after, just as much as she did.'

'Memories?' The Doctor seemed bewildered for a moment. 'Oh – of course. In your terms, yes. And it's true, Barbara and Ian need looking after. Not only are they young, their species is young.'

It was Mrak-ecado's turn to be bewildered. Their *species*? Surely Barbara and Ian must be the same species as their bud-parent? But some instinct stopped him from voicing the question aloud; the answer, he knew, would take too long.

He glanced at his timer again; the top-plate was now charcoal-black. He began sloshing his way out of the bud-pond, heading towards the villa; as he'd hoped, the Doctor politely rose and followed.

'I will arrange a *kigfih* carriage to take you to Trik-hobu's villa,' he said, adding after a moment, 'I will ride with you.'

The Doctor nodded distractedly, as if his mind was still elsewhere.

Strips of golden sunlight lay across the brown chitin dome of the villa; as they walked towards it, *ghifghoni* took flight from the stone guttering, whirled down across the moss-beds, hunting the scuttling *minifih* of the soil.

There was a movement behind the screen of *dafarji*

bushes to the east of the path. Mrak-ecado turned an extra eye to follow it and was surprised to see a clansman in cheap orange belly-wrap squeezing between the knobby stems, eyes curled towards them. He was weighed down by coarse white ankle-bags and heavy leg-pockets, and his arms were thick from regular manual work. He cut across the *triohrihil* moss-bed without care, his hooves scattering the delicate gossamers.

'Take care!' called Mrak-ecado, irritated. 'I value those plants!'

Then he saw the gun.

It was a heavy-duty dart weapon of the type used by the military. The stranger pointed it at Mrak-ecado.

'I am Kinjiju Jignivi of the clan Presonil, who are of the Below the Sun Believers,' he said. 'We require the assistance of the alien in a matter of grave importance to the Venusian People. You must allow him to depart with me at once.'

3

Further Requests

The city of Bikugih, Ian had quickly decided, was not like the other alien cities he had known. Morphoton, the Sense-Sphere and even, in its own unpleasant way, the Daleks' city on Skaro: all of them had possessed a sense of design, as if a single architect had taken a single set of plans and commissioned a single builder to execute them. Ian had taken this to be the mark of an advanced culture.

If that was true, then the Venusians weren't very advanced. Once Havteg and Ian had left the great avenue of trees where the TARDIS had landed, Ian had seen little that indicated order or centralization; there were houses, that was all. Most of the houses were roughly dome-shaped, but otherwise they had no regularity. Some were of brick, some of crude stone, many appeared to be made of mud. They were laid out apparently at random, often overlapping like soap-bubbles. There were no regular streets between them, just strips of ground, some paved, some unpaved, some little more than tunnels between the high walls of the larger buildings.

It was still barely light and Ian had trouble seeing where he was going; he kept stepping into muddy pools or bumping into the low pentagonal tables that the Venusians seemed to like to keep outside the doors of their houses.

Havteg talked continuously, with one arm wound around Ian's body and the pear-shaped wooden object he called a gun pressed against Ian's armpit. The chief subject of his commentary was rockets. He talked about Mark-4 types and Mark-7 types, winglets and tail fins, solid and liquid fuels, nose-cones and impact velocities and energies of movement and movements of stress, until Ian's head was spinning with it.

As they walked, they gradually acquired an entourage of Venusian children, ranging in size from squeaking toddlers no bigger than piano-stools to boisterous, shiny-skinned youngsters as high as Shetland ponies and probably twice as heavy. They jumped up and down, craning their eye-stalks at Ian, shouting, 'Clansman Rocketeer! Clansman Rocketeer! Is there going to be a launch? Is the alien going to help you launch the rockets?'

'I hope so,' Havteg replied. 'It's most important that he does.'

By the time this had been repeated a few dozen times, Ian was beginning to feel that perhaps it *was* most important. It was only with an effort that he reminded himself that these people were planning to invade the Earth, and that he must not co-operate with them.

Finally they arrived at a tall enclosure made of what looked, at first sight, to be gold. As they got closer, however, Ian realized his mistake; the walls were made of the same highly polished gold-coloured wood as Havteg's gun. He could see the grain of it, the blue-green moss growing in the gaps between individual planks. As they got closer still, he noticed that the wood was warped in several places and there were gaps in the wall where parts of the planking had rotted away.

'It doesn't look as though the invading-the-Earth business is making you a lot of money,' commented Ian. 'Why don't you offer embroidery classes instead?'

Havteg stared at him with three large red eyes, and blinked sorrowfully.

'I do not understand,' he said after a moment. 'In what way does cloth-patterning with the hands help in achieving a successful launch? And what has money got to do with it?'

Ian decided that, if it wasn't for the gun being pressed against his armpit, he might have felt rather sorry for Havteg. Idealists were obviously the same everywhere.

They had reached a tall gate which stood half-open and entirely unguarded. Havteg waved fiercely at the children and told them to stay outside and keep watch, then ushered Ian through. Inside was an expanse of greenish mud, in which stood about half a dozen dilapidated-looking buildings. They resembled log cabins, except that on a second look they proved to be pentagonal rather than rectangular. One had a side missing; another was a complete wreck with no roof and only skeletal walls. In the middle of the compound stood a wooden gantry about fifty feet high; Ian presumed this was where the rockets were launched. He noticed as they walked closer that the wood was blackened and several of the struts were broken.

There were about a dozen Venusians around, and they were all staring at Ian. Havteg shouted, 'Fritifhil! Get Barjibuhi – now!'

The order was unnecessary. There was a *thud* of wood and a Venusian galloped across the mud, slipping and sliding, to slither to a stop in front of Ian. He was big even by Venusian standards; not so much tall as extremely wide. His legs were like pillars and his hooves sank several inches into the mud. Wisps of steam rose from his skin, which fell in folds around his mouths and hips.

'Well done, Havteg!' he gasped. 'You've brought him!' He opened the mouth facing Ian and went on, 'Doctor! I've heard so much about you. I'm so glad you've decided to help us.'

'He says that he won't – ' began Havteg, but Barjibuhi was already squelching his way back across the compound. Havteg marched Ian after him.

'The Mark Five Hundred And Twenty Three exploded, I'm afraid,' said Barjibuhi. 'But I'm sure if the Doctor has a look he'll be able to give us some ideas.'

He jumped up through a doorway into one of the

buildings. Ian hesitated: the doorway was at least six feet off the ground, but Havteg lifted him up with one arm and pushed him through with a knee in the small of his back. Ian fell, winced as his hip caught some object lying on the floor. Havteg jumped up behind him, stood blocking the entrance. It was almost dark inside.

'It's a shame,' said Barjibuhi's voice as Ian scrambled to his feet. 'We were very much hoping to get this one off the ground, but I fear the pressure from the explosive powder may have been too great.'

Ian took a cautious step forward. As his eyes adjusted, he could make out two large, dark objects, roughly cylindrical in shape. One had fins sticking out of it: Ian counted five. The other ended in a dome-shaped nose. Between them were scattered several smaller pieces, mostly black in colour. There was a familiar smell in the air; after a moment Ian recognized it as wet charcoal, the smell of a bonfire the morning after Guy Fawkes night. At the same time he realized what he was looking at. The smaller pieces weren't just black, they were blackened – in fact, charred. Other pieces were splintered. The nose-cone was polished and elaborately carved. Helplessly, Ian started to laugh.

The rocket had been made entirely of wood.

Vivojkhil had never expected to see an alien, not unless one came to see the end of the world. When she'd asked about it, her bud-mother had told her that aliens only visited the gentry, they would never bother with *echilikhig* like us.

Well, bud-mother had been wrong.

The alien was standing in the corner of the clan-childfield, half an *ojotti* from the *cog-o-cog* maze. It was talking to a clansman in labourer's wraps, an *echilikhig* if ever there was one. The alien was one of the two-legged sort, with a single eye-stalk – the sort that the books called a *monopedocular biped*.

Vivojkhil had read all the books; she had borrowed

them from her uncle Jopestiheg, who would be her father when she came of age.

Dry-mouthed with excitement, she edged a couple of steps closer, keeping her body behind the cover of the big dodecahedral boxes that the children used for architecture practice. Only her eye-stalks were showing, all five of them flat against the purple chitin. The alien and the clansman obviously hadn't seen her; they just carried on talking. The white fungus on the alien's eye-stalk twitched in the wind.

Vivojkhil hadn't realized from the books how little the aliens were. This one wasn't even as tall as the pillars of the *cog-o-cog* maze. And there was something else, too, that she didn't get from the books; a sense of difference, of alienness. Vivojkhil had been twice to the memorivivium to see the models of ancient creatures now lost from the world – the monstrous shaghorn, the two-headed klakkluk, the pattifangs with their harpoon-like beaks. But none of them had seemed as strange as this being, with its two thin legs and its single, lopsided eye-stalk. However did it stand up?

Perhaps, Vivojkhil thought, that was why the clansman had one arm wound round its body like that. But surely wherever the alien came from, there weren't Venusians to hold them up all the time? Or perhaps they kept Venusians as servants? Perhaps the clansman was the alien's servant, and had travelled between the worlds with it.

Vivojkhil wished she knew. She wished she dared walk up to them and ask.

They were talking in very loud voices; if Vivojkhil hadn't known that nobody ever, ever argued with aliens, she'd have thought they were arguing.

' – tell you I have absolutely no interest in your absurd and impossible plans!'

That was the alien's voice, high and squeaky. The clansman said something she couldn't hear; she caught the word 'beg'.

'That is neither here nor there, young clansman. I

remind you that I was brought here against my will. I refuse – ' The rest of the sentence was lost to the wind.

Vivojkhil felt her belly tighten as the meaning of the words went home: 'brought here against my will'. In all the stories Vivojkhil had heard, aliens were supposed to kidnap Venusians, not the other way around. How could the clansman possibly – ?

Before she could think about it any more, she heard hooves approaching from the north, *click-click-a-click-a-clickclick*. Only one person she knew walked like that; she curled an eye around to see if she was right.

Yes. It was Anaghil, trotting along the stone path across the childfield, the new green ankle-jewel that she was so proud of glinting in the sun. The youngest clan-sister, Podsighil, was with her, bouncing from side to side of the path in the wet moss, kicking up trails of dew-drops with her small hooves.

'Hisst! Anaghil!' whispered Vivojkhil, and made a frantic hand signal.

All Anaghil's eye-stalks shot upwards as she saw the alien. She grabbed Podsighil two-armed and hauled her up on to her back, clattering over to join Vivojkhil in the cover of the dodie-boxes. She knocked one in her haste, and the big, hollow box rocked back and forth a couple of times.

Vivojkhil saw the clansman glance over curiously. He relaxed, but kept an eye-stalk curled in their direction.

'He's seen us!' hissed Anaghil.

'It's your fault!' replied Vivojkhil crossly.

'Why are we hiding anyway?'

'Because I think the clansman has kidnapped the alien and we ought to find out more.'

'Don't be ridiculous! You're just scared.'

Vivojkhil hesitated. She was acutely aware that what she'd just said did sound ridiculous. But it was also true. She realized that she had to convince Anaghil of that, and quickly. 'I heard them talking – ' she began.

At that moment Podsighil spotted the alien. She jumped

into the air, landed with a thud on top of the dodie-box.

'It's an alien! Look! Look! It's an ALIEN! LOOK!'

Anaghil jumped up after her. The dodie-box fell over, rolling them both up against the first pillar of the *cog-o-cog* maze. Podsighil started to wail. 'My leg hurts! It hurts!' Vivojkhil, exposed, saw the clansman turn three eyes towards them.

'Leave us, children!' he shouted, three-mouthed. 'The alien and I are discussing matters of vital importance.'

Vivojkhil expected the alien to yell for help then, to say it had been taken here against its will, but it only said, 'Yes, yes. Matters of vital importance. It would be best if you left us alone.'

With a surge of relief, Vivojkhil realized that she must have misheard or misunderstood the conversation. She felt the tension in her belly relax.

Then she saw the gun.

It was tucked against the alien's belly, almost hidden by the clansman's hand. But there was no doubt that it was a gun.

Vivojkhil's own belly heaved, and she was almost sick. She had to get away. Go to her bud-mother, better still to Uncle Jopestiheg, who was the clan's squadsman. And Anaghil and Podsighil had to go too. Quickly.

She took a step northwards, away from the alien and his kidnapper. Then another. Then another. Tensed her legs to gallop.

Anaghil and Podsighil were rolling themselves upright, the little one still wailing faintly about her leg.

'Come on!' said Vivojkhil. 'We've got to – '

There was a sound of galloping hooves on the moss to the north. Turning an eye to look, Vivojkhil saw a clanswoman in a sea-blue belly-wrap in the act of leaping off the ground. As she flew through the air over Vivojkhil's eye-stalks, she shouted, 'Alien! I wish to speak to the alien!'

She landed almost on top of Anaghil and Podsighil, causing the little one to dive into her sister's belly-wrap, cheeping with terror. The stranger ignored them and galloped around the maze, shouting as she went:

'Alien! You must show us how to grow gills! It is of vital importance to the future of Venusian civilization!'

The alien turned its button eyes to stare at her.

'Gills! I have no more idea how to provide you with gills than – ' it began, but the kidnapper put a hand over its mouth and swung his gun to cover the new arrival.

'Leave us, Frefotengu. I have first claim to the alien's knowledge. He is going to teach us how to live beneath the surface of the sun.'

'You are wasting the visitor's precious time with that piece of idiocy! Really, Jignivi! You know perfectly well that the temperature on the sun is such that there can be nowhere habitable, and anyway – '

'Your scheme is supposed to be practical? What is the use of learning to live beneath the sea when it will all boil away in less than ten generations?'

'The ocean circulation is such that the End will be much delayed if we can open links between the northern and the southern – '

'That theory is simply not valid! Whereas it is proven that there are holes in the surface of the sun, lending access to much cooler verticalities – '

'Not cool enough!'

'How do you know that? If we could explore – '

'Meanwhile burning to death – '

'Which we will anyway if you – '

'You can't even get there!'

The alien, Vivojkhil noticed, had somehow freed itself from Jignivi's arm; it was turning its peculiar single eye-stalk so that its eyes could examine first one, then the other of the clansmen. Slowly, it began stepping northwards through the *cog-o-cog* maze. It didn't surprise Vivojkhil that, even though its eyes were facing the wrong way, it negotiated the complex pattern without fault.

When it had reached the exit, it turned its eyes to face her. The flesh around them and around its tiny mouth creased up in a peculiar way and it began making little snorting noises; it was strange, alien, but Vivojkhil wasn't afraid. She had a feeling that the alien was laughing.

Abruptly it seemed to see her, and its flesh smoothed out.

'What's your name, child?' it asked.

'Vivojkhil, honoured one.'

The alien began to rummage around in the complicated buttoned wrappings it wore around its belly. At length it pulled out a red piece of cloth.

'If I give you this, Vivojkhil, will you let me ride on your back to the Presidor's apartments?'

Vivojkhil wasn't sure about the Presidor's apartments; it was a long way.

'It might be better to go to my clan-uncle – '

'No!' interrupted the alien. 'Not your clan-uncle. I must see the Presidor.'

He waved the cloth in front of her, which Vivojkhil thought was silly, because she could see he was in trouble and she didn't need to be given a present to help him.

'I'll try,' she said.

'I'll go with you!' said Anaghil suddenly, emerging from behind the dodie-boxes with Podsighil on her back. 'I can help if you get tired.'

Vivojkhil jumped; she had almost forgotten her bud-sister was there.

The alien turned its eyes to face them.

'Yes, you had all better come with us,' he said.

All? thought Vivojkhil; then spotted the two fives of eye-stalks flattened against the purple tops of the two northernmost dodie-boxes.

Durfheg and Kigihij. Of course. She might have known her clan-brothers would be around somewhere. But she was the biggest. She would be the one to give the alien a ride.

The two would-be kidnappers were still arguing:

' – impossible to regulate the hydroluminous thermal distribution – '

' – measurements are completely invalidated without any definite particulation gradient – '

Vivojkhil lowered her hands to make a step for the alien; he scrambled up onto her back without difficulty, found sensible places to put his hands and feet.

'Go!' said Vivojkhil to her clan-siblings. She jumped over the dodie-boxes and hit the ground at a gallop. Behind her, she saw Podsighil jump from Anaghil's back to Durfheg's, from Durfheg's to Kigihij's. She obviously thought it was a game.

They were almost at the other side of the field before Frefotengu and Jignivi realized what was happening and leaped after them.

Barbara leaned on the goldenwood rail of the Tower of the Night Council and looked out at the view of the sea. The sun was just above the horizon, reddened by mist. Its size alone was frightening, reminding Barbara how much closer she was to it on Venus than she had been on Earth. Its heat was small as yet, a coal-fire warmth, but Barbara knew that it would be strong enough by mid-morning to shrivel unprotected Venusian skin. She wondered what it would do to human skin.

'Violet,' called Trikhobu.

Barbara glanced down at her watch, peering at the tiny second-hand inset into the dial. 'Three minutes and thirty-five seconds,' she said.

Trikhobu's hooves clicked across the marble flooring. 'We should be able to work it out from that,' she said. 'The red-to-violet is equal less one-seventeenth to the violet-back-to-red, any child knows that, and the cycle is repeated in the five other shades, plus one one-hundred-and-twenty-second part for the middleplate to trigger. Now you said there were sixty seconds to a minute – how many to a day?'

'Sixty minutes to an hour, twenty-four hours to a day,' explained Barbara patiently, looking at her shoes. The right one still had bits of reddish leaf adhering to it from

Trikhobu's rubbish heap. She reached down and picked at them, but they wouldn't come off.

It had been Trikhobu's idea to try and work out the ratio between the length of Earth's day and that of Venus; her curiosity had been triggered by Barbara's remark that the sun seemed to be taking a long time to rise. Barbara herself was less curious. What mattered more to her was that it was twenty past midnight by her watch, but only just past dawn local time, which meant she was completely out of synchronization with her surroundings – again. She'd only just got over having to put her watch eleven hours forward to cope with twenty-second-century London. She sighed, and wished the Doctor had let them get a good night's sleep before suddenly deciding to rush off to a funeral.

Trikhobu had unsheathed the writing-claw on her north hand, and was scribbling figures on a notepad.

'Eighty-six thousand four hundred,' she concluded. 'Which means – ' She began scribbling again. Barbara watched as the smallest plate of Trikhobu's time-crystal changed from yellow to amber, then almost immediately from amber to red. After a long pause the middle plate changed from dawn pink to a mossy green, then the small plate began its cycle again, red-to-amber, amber-to-yellow: it would go all the way to violet and back again in five cycles of differing colour intensity. There was a third, large plate, about the size of a Venusian hand, whose five colours signified the hours of the day; at the moment it was a rich, blackberry-juice purple. The three plates were linked by fine pipes of glass, stained in several apparently permanent colours.

Barbara decided that it was a very beautiful way of telling the time.

'Four-hundred-and-seventy-nine two-hundred-and-thirty-firsts,' announced Trikhobu. 'To the third approximation.'

Barbara blinked. 'About two?'

Trikhobu crossed a few numbers out. 'Yes, that's the

first approximation,' she said. 'Of course, it's getting longer all the time; by one one-hundred-and-sixteenth of its length every thirty-three years.'

Barbara blinked again. 'Why's that?'

'I don't know,' said Trikhobu. 'Some people think it's to do with gravity and the sun; others say it's the upper air mixing with the interplanetary ether. But I think it's just that the world's getting tired and old, and doesn't want to turn any more.'

There was a pause. Barbara peered over the rail, felt the cool breath of the dawn wind on her cheek. Five hundred feet below, Venusians scurried between the chitin and marble domes of the five Grand Avenues of Bikugih, some still carrying their green or violet night-lamps. She walked around the platform, scanning the broad streets carefully, looking for any sign of Ian; and frowned when she saw nothing.

'Are you sure they would come here?' she asked Trikhobu. Barbara still didn't really believe that Ian, upset as he had been, would have agreed to let some strange Venusian take him on a guided tour of Bikugih; yet Trikhobu's clan-cousin Fifijkil had sworn she'd seen him leave the funeral ground arm-in-arm with 'a clansman with a loud voice who was saying he'd show him around Bikugih'. And Fifijkil had had no reason to lie.

'It might take a while if they were walking,' said Trikhobu, 'especially since you walk so slowly.' She paused. 'Don't worry, they'll be here. No one would show a stranger around our city without visiting the Tower. It is the only building that remains from the time of the Goldenworkers – '

'I know,' said Barbara simply, tapping her head to signify the presence of Dharkhig's memories. But she almost wished she didn't know – that all the Venusian clutter in her brain would just go away. It would seem more normal, somehow. Some of the memories were remarkably specific: for example she knew the exact height of the tower, eight Venusian *ojotti*. Others were vague: ghosts of night-storms, echoes of sea voyages, shadows of mountains. She turned back to the rail and walked around the platform again, her eyes following the star-shape of the streets. Ian still wasn't there.

After a moment she asked Trikhobu, 'Will I always have this piece of your father with me?'

Trikhobu said, 'It will dilute in time.'

The dawn wind gusted again. Suddenly Barbara felt terribly, terribly tired. 'Let's go down,' she said. 'I can't watch the streets for ever. And Ian's bound to go back to the TARDIS if he can't find us.'

Trikhobu twitched her eye-stalks in agreement. 'I know a good *juldihaj* on South-west Grand Avenue,' she said.

The word *juldihaj* triggered a memory of legs and belly soaking in cool, scented water, of three tongues lapping at a bitter-sweet drink from marble bowls. It all seemed like a very good idea to Barbara.

She followed Trikhobu down the stairway which wound between the outer and inner walls of the tower. The individual steps were ten feet high; Trikhobu jumped each one, landing with a sharp click of hooves. Barbara, of course, couldn't do that, and had to use the winding slope of the ramp on the inside, intended for small children and cripples. It was steep; she needed to grip the wooden rail with both hands in order to keep her balance. Trikhobu stopped every third or fourth step to let her catch up.

At last they were out, on South-west Grand Avenue. Barbara's nose filled with the familiar yet alien smells of a Venusian street: *bosifghal* smoke, roast *grifharji*, *juldha*, and a delicate rose-like scent that she couldn't find a name for. Venusians clattered by, mostly on foot, some in carts drawn by *kigfih* – many-legged animals which reminded Barbara of nothing so much as giant beetles. Most of the Venusians turned an eye or several in Barbara's direction as they passed, but only a few of the bright-skinned children actually came up to her. One rather timorously extended a hand to touch Barbara's neck. She managed not to shrink from the gentle grip, and returned the formal greeting, squeezing the folded flesh at the base of the Venusian's eye-stalks.

'They seem fairly used to aliens,' she commented to Trikhobu. 'More than my people would be, anyway.'

'We do have occasional alien visitors,' said Trikhobu. 'Most of them are like the Doctor: they just wander around, give us a little help now and then. We've learned not to worry about them.'

They had now reached the end of South-west Grand Avenue; ahead, the sun had caught the domes of the Presidor's apartments, blazoning them with gold. Barbara noticed a few Venusians squatting on the low wall around the gardens, their legs apparently tied down with ropes.

'What are they?' she asked, finding no clue in her Venusian memories. 'Prisoners?'

Trikhobu peered with a couple of eyes. 'No, protestors. It's a new stunt; they've tied themselves to the wall. Probably one of the anti-Acceptancer factions – you know, the Rocketeers, the Below the Sun Believers, the Magnetologists, the Water-breathers, the Volcano People, the Cave-makers. They're all jokesters really – strange machines, holes in the ground.'

Barbara probed Dharkhig's memories with regard to anti-Acceptancers, but could only come up with a sense of confusion, of enmity.

'I suppose you can't blame any of them,' she said cautiously. 'The end of the world isn't a pleasant thing to contemplate without any hope of escape.'

'Is it better to blow up half the world, as the Volcano People would like to do?'

It was one of Dharkhig's phrases; Barbara recognized it as her own. She suddenly realized that Trikhobu, too, would be thinking Dharkhig's thoughts for much of the time.

Barbara made a struggle to use her own, human reason. 'And you don't wan't to escape?' she asked.

Trikhobu stopped walking, flicked all five eyes away from Barbara. Her belly quivered. Barbara knew instantly that she'd made a serious mistake. Trikhobu was hurt at least, possibly angry. She opened her mouth to apologize, but Trikhobu spoke first.

'We're here,' she said, pointing at a low, chitin-domed building with sandstone walls. 'The best *juldihaj* in Bikugih.'

Barbara wasn't sure what happened after that. There was a sudden movement near the wall of the Presidor's apartments; a pounding of hooves on stone; a small, black object flying through the air. A Venusian voice shouted, 'Power to the magnetic field!'; then a searing light seemed to come from everywhere at once. Something hit Barbara very hard, and she felt the ground fall away beneath her.

4

Battering Ram

Vivojkhil had been running for so long that her legs were shaking. She had run all the way up Piniheg Hill and along Ehilijihig Street; she'd zig-zagged through the slums, leaping over pools of sewage and ruined walls and beggars; then she'd climbed Brehigu Hill, darting off into the alleys when Jignivi and Frefotengu had threatened to get within clutching distance.

Now she was running between tall grey walls that dripped water and grew strange, deep green shadow-mosses. Anaghil, still carrying Podsi, was close behind; but the orange-clad form of Jignivi was also visible, struggling a little on the narrow path, but getting closer. Vivojkhil tried to run faster, but she couldn't: her mouths were foaming, her lungs were heaving, and the alien was a dead weight on her back.

She had a horrible feeling that she was lost.

The alien had only spoken once, when they were in the slums. 'Poverty,' he'd muttered. 'Poverty on this scale – what has become of Bikugih?' Now he spoke again, pointing at the east wall with his wooden stick: 'Down there.'

Vivojkhil saw a gap in the wall, dived through it. She looked wildly around and saw a mossy bank sloping down to a wide, clattering thoroughfare of *kigfih* carts and high clansfolk in fine-weave belly-wraps. Chitin domes rose on the far side, and the air was full of the scent of *juldha*. Vivojkhil scrambled down the bank, dodged carts and strolling pedestrians alike, scurried for a while under the shelter of the broad-branched *chedhanhig* trees that lined the centre of the street, then dived through a gap in the traffic for the far side.

'We've got an ALIEN!' bawled Podsi, somewhere behind her on Anaghil's back.

'Shut her up, Anni!' shouted Vivojkhil. 'We've got enough trouble as it is!'

She saw Jignivi and Frefotengu emerge further down the street, eye-stalks waving. Any moment they would see –

'That one,' said the alien suddenly, gesturing once more with his wooden stick. Vivojkhil saw a narrow entrance between a *juldihaj* and a diamonder's.

She turned, her hooves skidding; jumped over a startled passer-by; bounded down a steep flight of stone steps between high walls. There was a pool of water at the bottom of the steps; she jumped over it and paused for a moment to catch her breath. Behind her, she saw Anaghil's shadow in the entrance, heard the clatter of her hooves as she jumped down the steps.

'Alien's here! Alien's here!' shouted Podsighil.

Thanks, Podsi, thought Vivojkhil. She ran on, following the curve of the alley to the west. It began to slope upwards. She caught a glimpse of the familiar domes of the Presidor's apartments above them in the light.

'We've got an alien! We've got an alien!'

There was someone ahead, standing at the entrance, a guard perhaps. Vivojkhil braced herself to jump over him.

Two hooves lashed out, stopping her dead. Four arms locked with hers, to hold on with a painful grip. A fifth arm, she noticed with a shock, carried a gun.

But the stranger was no Presidor's squadsman: his belly-wrap was plain white, stained with greenish mud.

'Kantihif Havteg of the clan Rimikugih,' said the stranger. 'I have matters to discuss with the alien. Matters of supreme importance to the future of Venusian civilization.'

'Oh really, this is quite ridiculous,' said the alien. 'What piece of nonsense do you want my help with?'

A hoof stamped on the ground. 'Our scheme is not nonsense! We have done all the necessary research. We merely require your technical assistance for a short time.'

'Dear me! Does *everyone* on Venus who requires technical assistance demand it at gunpoint?'

As the Doctor spoke, Vivojkhil noticed Anaghil behind her gently lower Podsighil to the ground. The youngster made a little *wheep* of protest and tried to cling to Anaghil's leg; Anaghil pushed her away, whereupon she attached herself to Vivojkhil's ankle.

Vivojkhil saw her clan-sister brace herself to jump.

' – have already built both solid- and liquid-fuelled propulsion systems – '

Anaghil flew up over Vivojkhil, over Havteg. The clansman reached up for her with a couple of arms, but he was too late. Anaghil was gone.

There was a crash and clatter of hooves on stone, then Vivojkhil heard her clan-sister's voice calling, 'Help! Help! The alien has been kidnapped!'

Havteg jabbed a hoof into Vivojkhil's hip.

'Run! Run now!'

Vivojkhil flattened her eye-stalks. 'No.'

'You have to co-operate!' Havteg's hooves pushed at her body; his gun arm circled until it was pointing at her flank from a hands-width away.

Shaking, Vivojkhil stood her ground. He wouldn't shoot her, surely. He wouldn't shoot a child.

'Alien, we already have Ian of your clan in our keeping. If you do not make this child co-operate, then you will be remembering him tomorrow.'

Before the alien could reply, there was a thudding of hooves on the muddy alleyway behind them. Vivojkhil saw Frefotengu and Jignivi appear, breathing hard; Jignivi had Kigihij, the smaller of the two clan-brothers, half-smothered against his hip. Durfheg was following behind, shouting, 'Don't kill my clan-brother, honoured clansman! Please don't!'

Podsighil, still clutching Vivojkhil's leg, made a startled *wheep* and clung on harder.

The alien sat up on Vivojkhil's back.

'Nobody is going to kill anyone,' he said fiercely. 'Jignivi; Havteg; Frefotengu; what has happened to the honour of your clans, that you dare threaten little children in this way? I demand that you let all of them go, at once. Then I will consider meeting all of your demands, as far as I possibly can.'

There was a moment's absolute silence. Vivojkhil could hear the faint echo of *kigfih* hooves from the street, the sound of water dripping on stone.

'Perhaps we should come to some compromise – ' began Frefotengu.

A shadow passed over the entrance to the alley-way behind Havteg. There was a frightening series of metallic clicks. Havteg seemed to shrink down into the ground.

Terrified, Vivojkhil caught a glimpse of a glossy black belly-wrap, the sharp edge of a cuttershell.

'Legdhitreb Brignontojij of the clan Rastwet,' said a clipped, angry voice. 'All adults present here are under restraint of movement, by order of the Presidor.' The voice paused. 'On pain of death.'

'What a shame,' murmured the alien. 'And just as we were about to come to an arrangement.'

Barbara didn't want to go to school today. Her shoulder was hurting and she would rather stay asleep and dream. It was a nice dream: she was standing on a tower overlooking the whole of London with her daughter Trikhobu, who was copying Barbara's map of the Underground with coloured crayons. For some reason Trikhobu's hands were little and pink, instead of big and green like they were supposed to be, but that was all right. She could draw better like that.

But Barbara couldn't go on sleeping. Her mother kept shaking her, and Trikhobu was shouting now: 'I'm sorry to wake you, Barbara, I know you are hurting, but something has happened to Ian.'

Ian!

Barbara sat bolt upright, wincing at the pain that shot through her shoulder, up her neck and into the recesses of her skull. She remembered everything at once: the jolting ride on the *kigfih* cart, the old yellow-skinned Venusian prodding at her head and muttering to Trikhobu about concussion and sleep.

'Ian,' she said aloud. She turned her head to face Trikhobu, and winced again. She was in the evening-room of Trikhobu's villa. Brilliant sunlight was streaming in through the east window, silhouetting her friend's squatting form.

'He's been kidnapped,' said Trikhobu miserably.

As her eyes adjusted to the light, Barbara saw that the Venusian's skin was tight with tension. She reached out and touched her friend's lip. Trikhobu returned the gesture, relaxed slightly.

'There was a heliograph message,' she said. 'Mrakecado sent it.'

Somehow Barbara had known all along that something had happened to Ian. Something always did. But because she hadn't been able to prove it, hadn't been able to do anything about it, she had pushed it to the back of her mind and had followed Trikhobu tamely around the city.

'Who's kidnapped him?' she asked.

There was a pause. Trikhobu's eye-stalks waved vaguely. Barbara had a bizarre notion that her friend was going to ask her to guess.

But she said, 'The Doctor was kidnapped by the Below the Sun Believers and the Water-breathers, but then he escaped and was kidnapped by one of the Rocketeers who told him that they were holding Ian before they were all arrested.'

Barbara blinked. She'd thought she'd had an eventful few hours, but it was evidently nothing to what had been happening to her friends.

'The Rocketeers are quite mad, of course,' Trikhobu went on. 'But they're not like the Volcano People. They're not dangerous.'

'That's what you said about the protesters outside the Presidor's apartments,' said Barbara, rubbing her injured shoulder and glancing down at the scorch-marks on her clothes. She made an effort to roll off the sleeping-mat, had to grab one of Trikhobu's arms for support.

'It was only a firecracker!' protested Trikhobu. 'They were trying to get you away from me, so that you would help them. I don't suppose anyone thought it would actually hurt you.'

'And Ian had gone off on a sightseeing tour, according to you,' observed Barbara, letting go of Trikhobu's arm and walking over to the window. She felt rather than saw the Venusian's skin flush blue with embarrassment behind her; so hastily added, 'Sorry, Trikhobu, but you're just too nice for this world.'

Even as she spoke, Barbara had a feeling that this was one of Dharkhig's sentiments. Well, so what? She agreed with it, didn't she?

She peered out of the window, but could see little against the glare of the sun. Her shoulder still hurt; she leaned against the window frame, felt the polished wood press against her palms.

'What do you suggest we do now?' she asked. 'Have we any idea where Ian has been taken?'

'No. The Doctor has gone to Jofghil to get help.'

Barbara noticed that the tendrils of the moss-tapestry on the wall were undulating gently where the sunlight fell on them, bringing the *unsharhijih* pattern to life.

'I suppose we'd better go and see this Jofghil as well, then,' she said, half to herself. 'Who is he, anyway?'

Trikhobu drew herself up proudly. 'He's my eldest clan-brother, one of Dharkhig's sons. He's the Presidor of the Night Council.'

Jofghil. Of course. Dharkhig remembered, where Barbara didn't.

But Dharkhig's memories spoke in her mind, as clearly as if the old clansman had been whispering in her ear: 'Jofghil is a fool.'

Even now, squatting in Jofghil's office, Mrak-ecado found it hard to believe that his clan-nephew was really Presidor. Little Jofghil, Jofghil of the delicate hands, who had played with his goldenwood dolls in the shade of the sunset wall? Surely it had not been so many years ago? Yet here was Jofghil, no longer little, although he retained a wet green glow to his skin reminiscent of youth; Jofghil, wearing the starched lip-cloths of office, his black belly-wrappings marked with the yellow pentagon of the Night Council. He was talking, as usual.

'I'll tell you what we're going to do! We're going to raid those burners – raid them now! I will not tolerate this!'

One of Jofghil's eyes was fixed on the Doctor, who sat quietly on the floor, his legs straight out, his back against the wall; another three watched Havteg, Jignivi and Frefotengu who squatted in separate corners, arms and legs roped, hooves shorn away. The remaining eye wandered between Mrak-ecado and the two security guards who watched the door of the office. The eight of them made the room crowded; the heavy, mossless panelled ceiling seemed lower than Mrak-ecado remembered it.

'I'll be honest with you, uncle,' Jofghil went on, speaking with the mouth facing Mrak-ecado. 'I've been looking for an excuse to get these Rocket people for some time. We know where they are – we know what they get up to. But they've been very careful up till now – never done anything illegal.'

Jofghil took a step towards Havteg; the prisoner stirred uneasily.

'But now we've got you!' he spat. 'Kidnapping – and an alien, no less. Before the first day of morning's over there won't be a plank of your precious "launch complex" left standing.'

Havteg said nothing. Mrak-ecado remembered that when Jofghil had talked to his wooden dolls like this, they had begged for mercy in squeaky voices issuing from one of Jofghil's other mouths. He wondered if there was some way he could signal to Havteg and the others, warn them that begging for mercy might be a good idea.

The Doctor spoke up.

'You must do as you wish with these people, Presidor. That is your right and your duty. But I must ask you to consider my companion's safety.'

'You suggest we give in to them? That we let them use your space-and-time ship, as this miserable *nijij* has suggested?'

'No, not that. But we could be a little more – discreet. Until Ian is returned to us.'

'If you come near us in force, we will kill him at once,' urged Havteg. His voice was hoarse, as if from shouts of pain. Mrak-ecado imagined that Jofghil's guards hadn't been gentle with him when they had cut off his hooves.

There was a moment's silence: the moss on the walls, ancient, honourable greens and blues, stirred in the filtered sunlight. Mrak-ecado realized that he was feeling slightly sick: it must be the shock, he thought.

'You see what I mean?' Jofghil was speaking with the mouth facing the Doctor. 'There is only one way to answer these people. Lighibu!' One of the guards snapped to attention, her mouths gaping in salute. 'Tell Brignontojij to bring up three squads of harpoonists and a squad of cuttershell throwers. To await my direct orders.'

'I really don't – ' began the Doctor, but Jofghil didn't let him finish.

'The decision is made. I have every faith in the abilities of my clansmen.'

The Doctor twisted the muscles of his face, then turned his stapled-down eyes towards Mrak-ecado. 'What do you think about it?'

Uncomfortably, Mrak-ecado took a step towards the window. He stared with three eyes through the filters at the dim shapes of guards patrolling the lawns, the batteries of catapults entrenched behind the walls.

'I don't know, my old friend,' he said. 'This is not the city of my youth; it is not the world of my youth. Everything is harsher now, so near the End. There are many who are desperate, many who are starving, who will do anything for a piece of bread or meat. Or a piece of hope. These clanspeople – ' he gestured at Havteg, Jignivi and Frefotengu ' – are not to blame. No one is to blame. The decline is as inevitable as the End which will follow.' He paused. Outside, there were shouts as Jofghil's orders were relayed to the guards' quarters: hooves clattered on stone. 'I do truly wish that my clan-brother Dharkhig's dream of Acceptance were possible – I wish I could see it happen, all the millions of us marching in peace and in order to our deaths. But I know it cannot be that way. I know it cannot be.' Mrak-ecado became aware that his body was trembling. He broke off, opened a different mouth, said quietly, 'I'm sorry, Doctor. I think Jofghil is right: we need to act as swiftly as possible.'

He moved away from the window, squatted briefly out of courtesy to Jofghil's rank, then pushed past the guards into the low, white corridor outside. He strode on unseeing, barely noticing the swift young squadsmen with their harpoons and guns rushing past him in obedience to his clan-nephew's orders.

Let me have no part in this, he thought. Let me go home. Let me have no part in it.

Except for the Venusians squatting in it, the room could almost have been a space-mad little boy's bedroom back in England in 1963. Wooden models of rocket ships hung from the ceiling on pieces of string, were attached to the walls, lay scattered about on the floor. True, a close examination of the models revealed a level of detail not usually found on a child's toy; some were cut in two, showing double-walled fuel chambers supported by curved buttresses, and cabins filled with tiny images of five-legged, five-armed aliens; but if Ian half-closed his eyes, let the five walls blur into four, let the undulating mosses decorating them become brightly coloured wallpaper, then he could almost be visiting his kid cousin John, talking to him about the possibility of life on other worlds. He could almost be home.

'And you're sure the Earth is uninhabitable? Even now? There is not some part that we could live on?'

Reluctantly Ian opened his eyes. Barjibuhi was squatting in the middle of the floor, a chart of the solar system spread out in front of him, the corners held down by model rockets. Ian had seen enough of the chart to know that it was totally inaccurate: the orbits weren't even elliptical, but consisted of strange patterns of circles with smaller circles on their rims. Chains of pentagons connected the orbits to the sun.

'Not a chance of it, I'm afraid. We were on Earth earlier today.' Ian glanced at the guard squatting by the door: the strange pear-shaped gun was still pointing his way. 'You wouldn't last a month.'

Ian had been telling a lot of lies about the Earth. Taking his inspiration partly from Marinus and partly from Skaro, he had described the petrified forests, the deserts of brown rock, the mountains of blue glass. He had described the burning heat of the day, the unbearable cold of night. He had described the chimerins, the great dust-storms that blew in the winter, shredding everything in their path. He had described the miserable existence of the few remaining Earth-people, buried in salt caverns underneath the remnants of seas. He had done such a good job that Barjibuhi had started asking about Mars as an alternative destination. Ian had told him that it was pretty dry there, too.

Now, with his eyes waving around desperately above the chart, Barjibuhi asked, 'And I don't suppose that Jupiter, or Saturn – ?'

Ian shook his head. 'Too cold. Too far from the sun. And the atmospheres are poisonous, anyway.'

'Then the Acceptancers are right. There is no hope. Everyone will die when the flames come.'

Ian was beginning to feel sorry for the Venusians. It wasn't their fault that their planet was dying: as far as he could understand from Barjibuhi, it was a natural process, caused by the steadily lengthening day. He remembered the messy squalor of Bikugih, the stinking rubbish heaps, the stagnant pools.

He stood up and paced over to the small, shuttered window.

'There must be something you can do,' he said. Three of Barjibuhi's eyes turned to look at him.

Ian twisted one of the thin wooden slats of the blind so that he could see out; then winced at the glare of the sun. He became aware of a low, regular, scraping noise and imagined a Venusian with a knife made of flint and quartz, patiently shaping a piece of wood. Barjibuhi had said that, even with the help of the slum children for rough labour, it could take a year and a half to build a rocket.

For the first time Ian felt doubt. It was becoming increasingly obvious that the Venusians were not at all like the Daleks; their 'invasion' was no more than a desperate attempt at escape. And he was, after all, three billion years in the past; if the Venusians went to Earth now, they would find no life more complex than single-celled organisms – possibly no life at all. Perhaps the Venusians had *brought* life to Earth, in which case –

In which case, someone was going to have to help them. They were hardly going to get there in wooden spaceships.

He turned to Barjibuhi. 'Are all free metals poisonous to you?'

Barjibuhi's eye-stalks twitched. 'All except gold, and to some extent platinum, titanium – but these substances are very rare, and the Acceptancers will not allow us access to them. It is the same with every endeavour: they find reasons for stopping us. They won't even let us try.'

Ian tried to think of a way you could use gold, with its relatively low melting-point, in a rocket. Perhaps if they could manage to make some sort of platinum alloy – but without metal tools they could handle, how would they work the metal?

'You need an insulator,' he said. 'Something that will keep you and the metal apart whilst you work with it. Do you have anything you could make high-temperature gloves from?'

Barjibuhi pushed two of his hands together, then pulled them apart with a loud popping sound.

'Yes, but it wouldn't help. The metal fumes would be fatal to the workers after a while. And there would be broken pieces – accidents – '

Ian realized that Barjibuhi must already have considered this problem and decided that there wasn't a satisfactory answer. He thought for a moment what it would have been like if the only working metal available on Earth had been uranium: poisonous, radioactive, dangerous. He doubted that humanity would ever have progressed beyond the uncomfortable existence led by the Tribe of Gum in 100,000 BC. The Venusians, all things considered, had done very well.

'Do you think we could – ' began Barjibuhi, but he was interrupted by a pounding of hooves outside the room, a scratching at the door.

Barjibuhi snapped. 'I said I was not to be disturbed!'

A muffled voice replied: Ian heard the words 'urgent', 'alien', 'Presidor's guards'. Barjibuhi opened the door, revealing a small, distressed Venusian child.

'Are you sure?' asked Barjibuhi. Then: 'Mrithijibu! Guard the alien – do not let him leave the room.' He left with the child, to be at once replaced by a squat Venusian with black lip-cloths and a missing eye, whom Ian assumed was Mrithijibu. The newcomer produced one of the now-familiar pear-shaped guns, and pointed it at Ian.

There was a long silence. Ian peered out of the window

again, but could see nothing against the glare of the sun. There were shouts in the distance, and wooden banging noises which could have been anything. Then there was a huge thud, making the floor quiver. A Venusian child squealed: a long, frightened noise.

Barjibuhi rushed in. 'They want the alien,' he said to Mrithijibu. 'They are breaking down the walls.' He seemed dazed; his eye-stalks waved around randomly, as if he wasn't really looking at anything. 'The explosive powders are ready. I am sending all the children away.'

There was another ground-shaking thud.

'Shall I kill this one?' asked Mrithijibu, gesturing to Ian.

'We'd better, I suppose,' said Barjibuhi.

Ian felt a cold, horrifying shock. Barjibuhi was a scientist, an inventor; he had seemed reasonable, even compassionate. Now he was gazing at Ian, three eyes like cobras ready to strike. Mrithijibu's gun issued a metallic click.

'At least let me talk to the people attacking you!' cried Ian. 'If it's me they're after, I might be able to persuade them to let you go – '

Barjibuhi flashed a palm at Mrithijibu, clearly instructing him to stop; then seemed to think for a moment.

'I could still be useful to you alive,' Ian pointed out.

There was another thud and an awful splintering sound.

Barjibuhi dashed out of the room, shouting, 'Take the alien!'

Mrithijibu lifted Ian bodily in three arms, set off at a trot through darkened wooden corridors. As they reached the courtyard, there was another splintering sound. Ian could see the wall swaying under the blow.

Barjibuhi's voice came from somewhere: 'Light the fuses! Quickly, before it is too late!'

Then Mrithijibu was pounding down a curved ramp into a dimly lit stone cellar. Ian saw wooden bowls containing white powder. With a shock, he recognized rope fuses trailing from the bowls, smelled the gunpowder smell, realized he was looking at crude bombs.

The fuses were smouldering.

Barbara clung hard to the base of Trikhobu's eye-stalks even though she knew that the tight grip must be hurting her friend. Trikhobu was at full gallop; her body rocked from side to side like a small boat in a storm. Barbara could see the mud track jouncing ahead of them, the mess of hoof-marks, the ruts left by the *kigfih* carts. Her nose was filled with the ammoniacal stink of Venusian sewage.

'We're nearly there,' gasped Trikhobu. She used one of her two free arms to point at a wall of goldenwood, glowing in the morning sun. Over the gales of the Venusian's breath, Barbara heard a distant thud of wood on wood.

Barbara and Trikhobu had arrived at the Presidor's apartments to find clansmen everywhere, everyone excited, people jumping over each other in the confusion. The protestors on the wall had vanished: under arrest, a young guard had told them cheerfully. 'There's a raid,' he'd added. 'Jofghil's leading it himself.'

When they'd found out exactly what was being raided and why, Barbara had felt a lurching sensation of panic. All her acquired Venusian instincts told her it wasn't going to work; firmness but negotiation was the method, Dharkhig seemed to say. She'd started to shout at one of the guards as if she herself were Dharkhig, ordering them to stop the raid; the aliens had stared at her in amazement. When she'd realized they weren't going to obey, Barbara had started punching their thick tree-bark hides with her fists, shouting, 'You're wrong! You're wrong! They'll kill him!'

It was then that Trikhobu had lifted Barbara onto her back, said quietly, 'Come on, we'll run after them. I'll carry you.'

Now, as they climbed the steep slope towards the wall

of logs, Trikhobu was plainly all but exhausted: she was trembling, and gusts of steam were issuing from her mouths. Ahead, Barbara could see a gang of Venusians in the black belly-wraps of Jofghil's guards, carrying a tree-length of golden wood tipped with a pointed black stone the size of a car. As she and Trikhobu approached, the gang charged forward. Peripherally, Barbara noticed the half-demolished dome of a mud hut behind them, possessions scattered on the ground, an elderly Venusian waving an impotent hoof in the direction of the attackers.

There was a vast splintering sound as the battering ram met the wall. Staring in dismay, Barbara saw the planking topple forward, the gang jump back. Then the rest of the wall buckled and fell inwards. The attackers sprang forward again and jumped over the remains, cheering.

'Too late,' she muttered, mainly to herself. 'War's already started.'

Then she saw the Doctor, standing with a Venusian in a black-and-yellow belly-wrap whom she knew must be Jofghil. The Doctor was shaking his head. Barbara jumped down off Trikhobu's back, ran through the mud towards him.

'Doctor!' she yelled. 'You've got to stop them!'

'My dear young – ' began the Doctor, then stopped.

Barbara saw the movement out of the corner of her eye and spun round to look. For an instant, she thought that the wall was merely being pushed back upright by the defenders; then she saw the orange spurt of flames behind it. She started to run forward, but stopped when she saw a log hut rising into the sky, breaking apart into white fire. Burning logs flew through the air as the first wave of heat hit her. She staggered, her shoes slipping on the wet ground.

The second shock knocked her off her feet. Sitting in the cold mud, she stared in disbelief as a third, then a fourth fountain of fire and fragments rose from within the compound.

'Ian!' she shouted. A burning lump of wood landed a yard from her outstretched arm. 'Ian!' The air was rapidly filling with smoke and ash; the heat from the huge columns of flame was enough to burn her face.

'Ian!'

Book Two

The Green Leaf Hour

5

Searches, Escapes, Predictions

Afhighid Kontojij of the clan Siridih woke feeling uneasy, and wondered if the feeling was significant.
He didn't remember having any dreams, but he knew that he ought to check; now, before he did anything else. He took two deep breaths, five-mouthed, five-lunged; felt his mind slip into the *geheron* state with the ease of a lifetime's practice.

Nothing happened. The rough stone wall of his sleeping-room stared back at him; the old, cracked writing-table with its clutter of inkmoths, shells and notepads remained real and unwavering.

No dreams, then. Nothing within reach, anyway. But Kontojij continued to feel uneasy.

He curled an eye towards the inner doorway of the sleeping-chamber, the one that led into the laboratory where he kept his apparatus for looking into the future. Perhaps he should make the reading early today, he thought.

He unfolded his legs from beneath his body, felt the usual stab of pain from his bad hip as he did so. He stood up, trying to ignore the continuing ache in his hip and smaller twinges and clicks from other joints. He swayed from side to side and waved his arms in the *izhih* pattern until he felt the prickle of returning circulation in his hands and ankles. When he judged that his body was ready, he crouched and made the jump up through the doorway.

In the laboratory, white, fierce morning light shone through the outer door and the narrow slot windows, making Kontojij blink. Everything seemed quiet: the predicting-crystal was dark and silent on its stand between the wooden calibration frames, the *nijij* in their glass tank seemed to be asleep. On the ceiling, the *fehiliju* mosses he had planted almost thirty years ago waved slowly, peacefully.

Kontojij advanced towards the predicting-crystal, stopping when his hip stiffened abruptly.

No, he decided. Exercises first, then breakfast. Then he would be able to concentrate. Anyway, the *huyaot* apparatus was more sensitive later in the day; if there was anything to find, that was when he would find it. He tensed himself carefully, rubbed his aching hip, jumped up through the outer doorway.

Outside, the heat made his skin sting. The sun itself was hidden by the massive red and white rocks of the Dhallijall ridge, which rose like the crest of a breaking wave to the south and east, blotting out a third of the sky; but the heat still found a way. Heat was reflected from the yellow desert of the plains below and, to a lesser extent, from a few of the mountain peaks that had caught the sun; it was refracted from the glaring blue-white sky; and a gusty, fire-hot convection wind ascended the slope from the desert, full of dust and grit. Kontojij wondered how much longer he could survive, even here, in this carefully chosen place. Probably for as long as my hip lasts, he decided.

He walked to the edge of the rocky platform on which he had built his living quarters, stared five-eyed down at the plains. Hooding his eyes against the glare, he could just make out the Y-shaped black smudge which had once been the city of Cracdhalltar.

'Good morning, fair city,' he said, three-mouthed in harmony, as he had said every morning for thirty years.

Once the words had been a statement of mourning for the dead city, an expiation of his sense of loss. But Kontojij had the awful feeling that they had become no more than a habit.

He shuffled down the path which led to the place where the visitors left his food. Thirty years ago, when he'd fled from Cracdhalltar, he'd taken what he thought would be enough: dried *grifharji*, *pekatisi*, *merihini*, four cartloads-worth up the long slope. He'd reckoned without the drying-out of the mountain, the death of every living thing, even at this once-temperate altitude. If it hadn't been for his visitors and the seemingly endless stores they kept in their warrens under the world, Kontojij would have died of thirst after the first two years.

The box was in the usual place, a cool hollow in a flat grey rock, the same place where he had left the report of yesterday's *huyaot* the previous night. He prised off the *binihabeg*-wood lid and saw that it contained the usual things: water, a box of *pekatisi*, tongue-bread, a couple of rashers of nightfish, a bag of *kirimbi*-nuts for the *ghifghoni*, a wad of paper. He lifted the box awkwardly, two-handed, and walked back up the slope. His hip complained, grinding and sending little stabs of pain down his leg.

From long habit, Kontojij put the box down inside the doorway of the house, though there had been no scavengers around to steal his food for years. He took out the *kirimbi*, hooked the bag over an ankle-claw and set off towards the *ghifgihonij*, which was at the north end of the house, down amongst the shelter of the rocks.

The *ghifghoni* stirred and creaked as they heard him approach. Serapihij, the youngest, poked her long jaws and eye-cluster out of the narrow slot window of the hut and hissed; Kontojij hissed back, knowing that the little creature understood the sound as a greeting. He heard the sound of rotors slapping eagerly against the wood.

As quickly as he could manage with his bad hip, he jumped down the three steps at the bottom of the path. The air in the rocky hollow was cool, miraculous, like the long-ago mornings of his childhood. There was even a little moss growing here and there; the last, he suspected, anywhere south of Conorihib.

'A little water, air, and the absence of sunlight,' he

muttered to himself, glancing at the fire-bright shields of the mountain peaks above.

He unbolted the heavy wooden door of the hut and the *ghifghoni* scrambled out, a confusion of violet and blue and green, twirling and *chff*-ing and squawking. Miraghoni was last as usual; the heavy old flyer only made a few token turns of his rotors, enough to push himself up on to the steep, chitin-tiled roof of the *ghifgihonij*, where he settled and began to preen his membranes.

Kontojij watched the others until they became no more than spots against the glare of the sky. He envied them, up there, in the cool thin air above the tops of the mountains.

He looked up at Miraghoni, who squawked and tilted his eye-cluster to watch him with five bead-like green eyes.

'They'll be back for their breakfasts, don't worry,' said Kontojij.

At the mention of the word 'breakfast', Miraghoni squawked again, launched himself into the air and, spinning gently, drifted down to land on Kontojij's back. He opened his jaws.

'*Chff*-rrrr,' he commented.

'Yes, yes, breakfast,' Kontojij replied.

He reached down and took one of the nuts from the bag which he'd hooked onto his ankle-claw. He was just about to feed it to the flyer when he noticed something blue and gleaming protruding from his belly-pouch.

He picked it out, thinking it might be a piece of broken rotor membrane, that the old flyer might be shedding. But when he took it in his hand it was hard and cool.

Glass. Blue glass. One of the others must have picked it up in the mountains yesterday, he thought, and Miraghoni must have scavenged it off them. Funny I missed it last night.

He examined it closely, wondering what it had once been part of, but it was hard to tell. Erosion had sculpted it into a lens shape; it almost reminded him of –

– the lens-grinder's eyes were a deep, deep blue, magnified and enriched by the polished glass of the lenses he had fitted over them. Kontojij watched the happy, confident movements of the clansman's arms, the colours on his skin dancing as he juggled with prisms, lenses, goblets, crystals. 'I sell light,' he had said. 'I am the rainbow-seller,' as he dropped the prism into Kontojij's hand. Later, in the darkness of the huyaot*-room, the visions in the crystal, the visions that were not rainbows: the stone towers of the city, burning, the goldenwood carvings along the High Main, burning, the bubble-arched balconies of the Hif-Cracdhall, burning, everything, burning, burning, burning, burning –*

Kontojij returned the present with a jolt, breathing hard.

'You old fool,' he said aloud, startling Miraghoni who jumped up and flew into the *ghifgihonij*, squawking, a nut in one of his pairs of jaws. Ignoring the flyer, Kontojij set off at a gallop along the path to the laboratory.

For thirty years, he had kept the art of *huyaot*, the sacred art of Cracdhalltar, alive. For thirty years he had traded trivial predictions about the weather and the fall of governments for food and water from the people who lived in the warrens. And now, when the feeling was back, the same feeling that had driven him into the streets of Cracdhalltar willing to spend all his money on the best, the most sensitive *huyaot* apparatus, the feeling that the End was near, he hadn't recognized it for what it was.

Gasping, his skin burning, his bad leg dragging behind him, he reached his living quarters and the entrance to the laboratory. He jumped down, looked around, began making preparations for the *huyaot*.

But a nagging feeling in the back of his mind was telling him it was already too late.

Most of the smoke had cleared, but the air still smelled of gunpowder and charred wood. Barbara stood up and wiped the tears from her cheeks. Part of her wanted to curl up on the ashy ground and go on crying for ever; but she was determined to ignore the feeling. She knew that they had to recover Ian's body, get back to the TARDIS, get away. She knew, too, that they were going back to Earth, 1963 – if she had to get down on her knees in front of the Doctor and beg him to do it. Ian was going to be buried at home.

She bit her lip to stifle a renewed attack of sobbing, and looked around her. Jofghil's squadsmen were scuttling around the ruins of the compound like huge spiders, picking up pieces of charred wood and depositing them in a steadily accumulating heap just outside the wall. The wood was carved into strange technological shapes; one of the pieces looked like the tail-fin of a rocket. A few shiny-skinned Venusian children were hanging around the heap, whistling and calling to each other; when one of the squadsmen appeared with a new piece they would shuffle away, hissing like cats.

Barbara suddenly realized that the Doctor was nowhere to be seen.

The last time she remembered looking, the old man had been standing right beside her; Jofghil had ordered both of them to stay away from the wreckage until his people had pronounced it safe.

'Don't you go missing on me too!' she muttered, feeling a rising sense of panic. Then she caught sight of Trikhobu limping towards her. One of the Venusian's legs had been caught by a fragment of burning wood; a piece of skin was hanging loose over her knee, and the flesh was swollen and blue. Barbara knew her friend ought to have accepted Jofghil's offer of a *kigfih* ride to a healer, but Trikhobu had refused to leave Barbara, and Barbara had refused to go anywhere until Ian's body was recovered.

Now Trikhobu approached with three arms extended, eye-stalks erect.

'Barbara!' she exclaimed. 'I think there is some hope for Ian.'

Hope? Of course there wasn't any hope. What was

Trikhobu talking about? Barbara felt tears start again.

The big Venusian took Barbara's neck in two hands for a moment, a gesture which Barbara vaguely realized was supposed to be reassuring.

'There aren't any bodies,' she said. 'Not one. And the Doctor found this hole in the ground.'

'A hole?' asked Barbara. A soft, sourceless light dawned somewhere inside her brain. 'You mean Ian got away? He's alive?'

'He could be. The Doctor thinks – '

But Barbara had already started running. She could see the Doctor now, the familiar upright figure with his walking cane and silver hair, standing on top of a heap of broken timbers and pieces of stone. He saw her, beckoned with his free hand.

'Doctor! What have – '

He stopped her with a raised palm, pointing with his cane at a cluster of Venusians, filthy with ash, who were levering at a pile of rocks with long sticks made of grey chitin.

'That pile isn't just rubble,' said the Doctor. 'The rocks in it have been broken for a long time – look at the eroded edges.'

As Barbara looked, there was a clatter of stone and some of the rocks fell away; she thought she saw a dark gap behind them. She started forward, but the Doctor took her arm.

'I think the whole thing may have been deliberate. If someone lives in continual fear of arrest – as the Rocketeers must have done – they will usually make plans for a safe escape.'

Barbara looked at the Doctor. In the strong Venusian sunlight the lines on his face had softened; but somehow that didn't make him seem any younger. She wondered for a second how old he really was, how old Susan had really been. What he thought about her obvious concern for Ian, whether he had seen it all before.

'They blew their base up deliberately?' she asked.

'They are likely to have other bases. I imagine that Ian will be taken to one of them.'

There was another clatter of falling rocks below; looking down, Barbara saw that there was definitely an opening in the ground behind the rocks. She shook off the Doctor's gentle grip and ran across to investigate.

'No one past this point!' shouted a burly Venusian, moving to block her way.

'He's my bud-brother!' yelled Barbara.

The Venusian hesitated. Barbara heard Jofghil's voice: 'Let her through, but – '

Barbara pushed past, scrambling over scattered rocks. From somewhere behind her she heard the Doctor calling out for her to be careful.

The entrance was a simple hole in the ground, still more than half blocked. Peering through it, Barbara saw a dimly lit tunnel sloping downwards. The floor was covered in rubble.

'Ian!' she called. Her voice echoed slightly, but there was no other response. She began to push her way through the gap; she instinctively tried to withdraw her belly, Venusian-style, until she realized that the action wouldn't make much difference to the shape of her human body, and crouched down instead. A sharp pain ran through her shoulder and neck, reminding her that it was only a few hours since she had been concussed by the Magnetologists' 'firecracker'.

She heard the click of the Doctor's cane behind her.

'My dear young woman,' he said, 'you should be more careful – '

With a final heave, Barbara was through. She half-rolled, half fell onto the stone floor. A large rock teetered, then started to tumble after her; she scrambled upright just in time to get out of its way.

The Doctor, crouching, followed her through the now slightly enlarged entrance. He had a wide, mischievous grin on his face.

'You see, all you needed to do was wait for one more

rock to be removed and you could have walked through.'
He did so, then slithered awkwardly down the slope. Barbara held out a hand to help him. He took it, briefly. Looked back over his shoulder.

'Take great care in clearing out the rest of the rocks,' he shouted, then started off down the tunnel at a fast walk. Barbara followed.

'Where do you think this – ' she began to ask, only to be interrupted by a vast thud behind them. The ground shook violently, tipping Barbara off her feet; she flung herself against one wall, covering her head with her hands. The Doctor was shouting something, she wasn't sure what.

There was a clatter of rock on rock and something hit Barbara's back hard enough to knock the wind out of her. Blinding waves of pain moved behind her eyes. When they had gone, everything was silent, and all trace of daylight had faded.

When they had made Ian get in to the box at the end of the tunnel, they had told him it was made for a *dihilrahig*. Ian didn't know what a *dihilrahig* was, but he guessed it was a lot less high than it was broad: he could wriggle several feet in any direction he liked, but there wasn't enough room inside for him to so much as sit upright.

He examined the view through the slats again. It hadn't changed for several hours. Dim grey light. Shadowy objects that were probably other crates. There were sounds of creaking timbers, the occasional banging of wood on wood. A smell of ammonia. Ian thought he might be on a ship or a barge; but he had heard no sounds of water when they were loading him aboard.

He returned his attention to the heavy piece of wood that held the lid of the crate in place. Using two or three fingers squeezed through the narrow slats, Ian could just get enough leverage to shift it. It had been a slow job: the wood was splintery and uneven, and it often jammed. Ian's fingertips were raw, weeping blood, and the muscles of his hands and upper arms were stiff with pain. But there were only a few inches to go.

Wincing every time he pushed, he resumed the job. The bar shifted half an inch. Sweat ran down Ian's sides, giving a fresh soaking to his already sodden shirt. The bar shifted an inch – a half inch – another half. Then stuck. Ian pushed until the blood ran from his fingertips again, but it was no use. He rolled his body from side to side, kicked at the roof of the crate; heard something move. Pushed again.

Still nothing.

He lay back, breathing hard, clenched his fists. There had to be a way.

Suddenly the light brightened, and Ian heard the boiling-fat sounds of Venusian voices.

' – be all right if that's all the goods he wants.'

'So if there's extra?'

'I'll want more. I have my costs to cover.'

Hoof-steps approached across planking.

'I don't think – ' the voice broke off, perilously close. Ian held his breath. 'Hinifghil! The bar has fallen off this *dihilrahig* cage!'

The crate thudded.

'No!' yelled Ian in sudden fury. He pushed up against the lid with his arms and legs together.

Perhaps because the Venusian had moved the bar, perhaps because of the strength of Ian's anger, the lid lifted. Ian found himself sitting upright, free. A Venusian was staring at him, all five eyes wide.

Ian froze for an instant, then leaped out of the crate, then froze again when a horrible roaring sound broke out behind him.

It was the Venusian, screaming: 'Hinifghil! Help me! There is a giant stickwalker – an alien beast – '

Ian started running. He was in a large wooden hold full of crates of varying shapes and sizes. Grey daylight entered from an open hatchway; clambering over boxes, Ian headed towards it. Somewhere behind him, there were shouts, the thudding of hooves.

There was a ramp ahead, leading to the hatchway; Ian ran up it.

At the top, he found himself on a curving wooden deck, surrounded by Venusians. Hooded eyes curled towards him; red, yellow and blue irises, large black pupils. Mouths opened, arms waved around like angry pythons. A babble of voices began.

'We did not know there was an alien – '

' – might be dangerous – '

' – can't have been on the cargo list – '

' – should put it under restraint.'

Then, louder and more authoritative: 'It is an alien belonging to my group. We have obtained it for research purposes. It is dangerous and should be restrained.'

Ian recognized Barjibuhi, advancing towards the crowd down the steeply sloping deck. Behind the Venusian, a crenellated wooden tower supported a tall mast fully rigged with white sails. Ian looked over his shoulder and saw an even taller mast the size and girth of a large tree. It stood on top of a wall of wood covered in huge wooden pipes and sloping ramps.

If he could reach the cover of those –

The Venusians around him seemed to have backed off after Barjibuhi's warning; there were a couple of gaps in the crowd. Ian ran for one, hoping that none of the Venusians were feeling very brave.

They weren't. One leaped into the air with a terrifying scream which sent Ian swerving to one side; but it was only getting out of the way. The others scattered.

He heard Barjibuhi shouting, 'Stop the alien!' Ian glanced back to see Mrithijibu, a gun in every hand, leaping through the air, his hooves drawn up to clear the eye-stalks of the milling passengers.

The deck was sloping upwards now; the wooden wall of what Ian assumed was the deckhouse was very close.

Then, with a shock, Ian realized the wall was moving.

He stopped, looked at it again, looked at all of it, realized how his eyes had been fooled.

He was looking at the top part of a vast wheel, perhaps a hundred feet across, surrounded by a framework of ramps and pipes. The ramps led up to a high platform behind the wheel where the mast stood. The forward part of the mast deck overlapped the top of the wheel, creating the illusion of a deckhouse with a flat top.

'Kill the alien beast.'

The voice was remarkably casual, and too close. Before Ian could react a rain of small wooden darts fell from somewhere above his head. One embedded itself in his arm. Ian watched the blood flow from the wound for an instant, then looked up and saw several Venusians craning over a wooden railing, doing something that looked very like reloading guns.

'Fire further shots as necessary,' said the same calm voice.

'No! Don't kill it!' Barjibuhi's voice. 'We need it for – '

'The overriding necessity is the safety of the passengers on this globeroller,' the calm voice replied.

Ian ran. The curving deck narrowed, sloped upwards more steeply, led him closer to the wheel. Two Venusians in brightly coloured belly-wraps jumped out of his way and scuttled up a ramp. But behind him, Ian heard the heavy thud of hooves in pursuit.

Ahead, the deck stopped at a high rail. Beyond it, about six feet away, Ian saw the slowly turning outer surface of the wheel. It was coated with a white, rubbery-looking substance several feet thick and scored with a pattern of deep grooves. There was no trace of water anywhere on the wheel, but there were black stones embedded in the wood and fragments of crushed leaves stuck to it.

Ian frowned, looked behind him, saw a brilliant green canopy of leaves drifting slowly past the deck rail fifty yards away.

Then we're not at sea, he thought. Which means –

He remembered the calm voice: 'globeroller'. Roller. And now he could hear it: the slow, deep hiss and crackle of the wheel turning on stone.

There was a thud of wood and a shout: three Venusians, all dressed in white belly-wraps, came into view around the corner of the deck.

Ian climbed on to the rail, jumped for the surface of the wheel and pushed his hands and then his feet into two of the grooves. He slipped once, fell a few feet, his hands burning on the rubber. Then he managed to find a grip, and sailed up past the deck again. He heard shouts: 'Fire at will! – 'No! Please! We need it for – '

Scuffles, thuds. Darts thudded into the rubber surface. Ian kept his face turned away to protect his eyes. Clinging on grimly, he was carried in only a few seconds under the shadow of the topdeck, out and astern. He had a brief glimpse of sunlight gleaming through the gaps between sails, of black minarets, shiny like a beetle's back, with refraction colours sliding across their surfaces as he moved. A glimpse of the deck, of Venusians running, dangerously close. A shout. Then darkness, followed quickly by a dimmer light. The strain on his arms and legs increased as his body became closer to horizontal; he felt like a spider clinging onto a ceiling.

He looked over his shoulder, saw the ground approaching amazingly fast. Twenty feet – ten – five –

He flung himself off the wheel and away from the vehicle, landing awkwardly in a hail of pebbles. He scrambled to his feet, glanced up at the wooden belly of the globeroller but saw no trace of pursuit. On either side he saw sun-bright stone, and beyond that the thick green-yellow trunks of the trees he had seen from the deck. He ran towards them, slipping and sliding on the greasy, blackened surface of the road. There was a low bank of gravel at the edge of the forest; Ian scrambled over it, lay flat.

He noticed a strong smell of petrol.

The dart was still sticking out of his arm. Ian pulled it

out; it had an iron tip which was covered in blood, and blood had stained the sleeve of his jacket. He looked closely at the dart, wondered if it had been poisoned. If so, it didn't seem to be having any effect on him. Yet. Well, he would worry about that in a moment.

He peered up over the gravel, watching the stern of the globeroller move past, two tall masts in full sail and the decorative black minarets glinting in the sun. The vehicle showed no sign of stopping, but ground on, tilting slightly as it disappeared from view. Ian waited until he could no longer hear the sound of the huge wheel on the road, then stood up and looked around him.

The road stretched out, a hundred yards wide, shimmering in the heat of the sun. Behind him the forest was yellow-green trunks, coiled leaves, the same in every direction.

Ian realized that he had no idea where to go.

The predicting-crystal was almost fully powered up. It glowed in Kontojij's darkened laboratory, faint images of possible futures forming and dissolving within it. The pale blue light was just sufficient to show the notched wooden sticks of the calibrating frame, the strips of leafribbon hanging from the marker points. Below the crystal on its tripod the *nijij* twitched in their heptagonal glass tank. Wooden hoops held down their seven pulpy legs and small, tasty worms hung just out of reach of their flailing tentacles. Their hunger and frustration sent a glitter of power through the gold *anteyon* receivers suspended above their exposed brains.

Kontojij sucked in a deep breath through his north mouth, to exhale it in a long, worried hiss. This was his third attempt at a reading. The first two had shown only insubstantial ghosts, faint patterns of lines in the crystal that might have been arms or legs or trees or mountains. But the *feel* of the *huyaot* had been of pain – fear and pain: enough of it to persuade Kontojij to make the difficult decision to cut away the *nijij*'s skull-crests. It was painful for the little creatures and they wouldn't live long now; but it meant more power was available to the apparatus.

This time he should be able to *see*.

He shifted his weight, wincing as the pressure momentarily fell on his bad leg. It had remained immobile, and agonizingly painful, ever since his panicky gallop up the path; Kontojij had a feeling he had dislocated it. He suspected that he might not be able to walk properly for some days, perhaps never; but somehow that didn't seem to matter.

The crystal had reached full power; he could feel the faint pressure of its *anteyon* force on his brain. The light was bright enough to reveal the painted diagrams on the walls of the laboratory, the chitin shutters over the windows and door. But still the images remained vague, well below the range of calibration. Kontojij stretched towards the apparatus, bringing four eyes to bear on it, trying to focus better. Not for the first time, he wished he had taken up an offer, made many, many years ago in Cracdhalltar, to have a magnifying lens ground to fit in the hood of one of his eyes.

No use worrying about that now, he thought. It's far too late for that –

Abruptly the images in the crystal sharpened to become recognizable scenes. A strange, curved cavern – a lake – fields of *beghi* – and –

Kontojij felt his belly tighten with fear.

Clansmen were dying. Their legs and arms convulsed, their eye-stalks stretched out rigidly as violet blood and black vomit gushed out of their gaping mouths. As the images came closer Kontojij *felt* their deaths: pain, terror, the sensation of life being irrevocably sucked away, without hope of remembering. The force of the terror was so great that Kontojij had to back away from the apparatus. As he did so, he noticed the calibration frames. The leafribbons were curled back to their fullest extent.

Unwanted thoughts filled his brain: for it to be that

powerful it would have to be everyone, everyone in the world dying –

Kontojij's belly heaved; bile filled his mouths and for a moment he couldn't breathe. With an effort he swallowed, brought his body under control. For longer than the interval of red-to-violet he remained frozen, eyes shut, breathing deeply, slowly. To take his mind away from the fear he made a calculation: the height of the tank was about eight-hundredths of one *ojotti*, the longest radius of the predicting crystal was one-hundredth of one *ojotti*.

'The transfinite ratio of the fraction to the whole, multiplied by the circular fraction, divided by the square of the radius ratio, all divided by three,' he muttered. 'Then multiplied by Rifghil's constant.'

He did the calculation in his head; to the first approximation, the answer was three-quarters of a day. There was no need to think about the probability: at that kind of range, with this kind of signal strength, it was as near to certainty as made no difference.

He opened his eyes again, stared at the tiny images in the crystal, five-eyed, wishing they were an illusion. Knowing that they could not be.

Before the next sunrise, barring a miracle, his entire species was certain to die.

6

Deaths, Voluntary and Otherwise

The squad was tired. The snap of their hooves on the loose stone of the road had taken on an irregular rhythm, displeasing and inharmonious; the arms holding the packs against their backs twitched, shifted, shifted back again. They glanced back too often at the carts that rumbled and clicked over the ground behind them, the rough wood painted with the yellow colour of death. They screwed up their lips at the smell of death that blew from the carts on the low, hot wind. Hakih Gwebdhallut listened to them, watched them but said nothing. He was tired himself. It had been a long night's work and they wouldn't be finished until noon.

Too much work, he thought. Too many fields going to the desert, too many people going to be remembered.

Fragments of broken rock were scattered by the sides of the road, several of them big enough to hide a sniper. Hooding his eyes against the glare of the sun, Gwebdhallut watched each one that came into range. Nothing moved.

A faint whistle from ahead: his lieutenant, Sesifghall, had seen something. Gwebdhallut sped up to a trot, unconsciously touching the goldenwood barrels of the five guns he carried strapped to his legs. He caught sight of Sesifghall crouching behind a rock. She didn't need to make the hand-sign for 'barrier'; Gwebdhallut had guessed as much from her whistle and her movements on the rough ground. There was something to be said for having your bud-sister in the squad, however much the authorities in Inarihib disapproved of it.

He advanced cautiously. A crude gate was set across the track just before the ridge top. The box by its side was unmanned, but Gwebdhallut whistled the approaching squad to stop nonetheless, signalled them to fan out around the gate so that they could approach the blind ridge on a broad front. The carts waited behind, the *kigfih* waving their eye-stalks uneasily.

Gwebdhallut advanced to the gate alone. It was a single wooden bar, cracked and charred with age; one kick would have broken it. But Gwebdhallut waited in front of it silently, having signalled his spread-out squadsmen to ensure that they had stopped.

'Villagers of Lijonallall,' he said aloud, three-mouthed in harmony. 'We ask that you receive your last visitors in peace.'

The regulations required him to say it, of course, but he would probably have said something like it even without the regulations. Gwebdhallut believed in respect.

He pushed the gate softly, one-handed; it swung back without resistance. Alone he advanced to the ridge, his squad crawling forward, rock-to-rock, on either side of him. His hearts beat hard, his belly tightened painfully. At last he reached the top and could see into the valley of Lijonallall.

The village wasn't much: a few mud-domes in the brown sand, most of them ruined. Around it, a few withered *konji* plants died slowly in fields whose soil was turning to powder. One *bosifghal* trunk still stood, bare of leaves or moss, the wood scourged by the sun and the wind until it resembled stone. Heat rippled around everything. There was no sign of movement.

Gwebdhallut signalled to the squad for maximum caution, began to walk slowly down the slope. The carts rumbled on after him, their yellow paintwork gleaming in the sun. About half-way down, he saw a single, yellow-skinned old clanswoman step out of one of the huts, flatten her eye-stalks briefly, then squat politely, tipping her body in Gwebdhallut's direction. Her legs were painfully thin. As Gwebdhallut watched, other villagers slowly emptied out of the huts, formed up in loose ranks behind the old one. Most were visibly starving.

Gwebdhallut felt his belly relax, his skin loosen. It looked like this was going to be one of the easy ones. He beckoned the squad in, began walking a little faster. As he came close to the first huts, the old clanswoman shuffled forward so that they would meet out of hearing of the others. A gust of hot wind moved across the desiccated fields, blowing brown dust over them.

The clanswoman reached out with a skeletal arm, gripped the neck of Gwebdhallut's eye-stalks. He could feel the bones through the flesh of her fingers.

'Taven Frinallenegu of the clan Onnallall-Jehigibi, bud-mother of Lijonallall. You are the Inspector?' Her eyes were scanning the silent squadsmen, the line of carts with their yellow paint.

Gwebdhallut returned the greeting. The old clanswoman's skin was brittle, flaky. Vitamin deficiency, he remembered.

'Hakih Gwebdhallut,' he said briefly. 'We are here to ensure that you will be remembered.'

Frinallenegu made a slight squatting motion. 'We are grateful.' She seemed to hesitate, then said, 'It was a wise decision. The land is dead around us.'

'You have lived as well as you could,' said Gwebdhallut formally. 'Are your people ready?'

Again Frinallenegu seemed to hesitate.

'There are only sixty-one now. Mrijil Parenagdehu has died and been remembered.'

With his south hand, the one that Frinallenegu could not see, Gwebdhallut signalled to Sesifghall. A hand twitched in discreet acknowledgement.

Frinallenegu started to walk towards her clanspeople. Gwebdhallut followed. The squad spread out slightly; Sesifghall and one other seemed to drag their hooves, then quietly slipped off into the fields. The carts stayed where they were.

Close to, it was obvious that the villagers were indeed starving. Several had collapsed onto their bellies in the hot sun, unable to support themselves on their shrivelled legs. Mouths gaped, revealing ulcerated tongues. Hammer-flies burrowed into the weakened clanspeople's skins.

'I have to take the names,' said Gwebdhallut quietly.

Frinallenegu gaped politely, said nothing.

Gwebdhallut took the roll from his pocket, stretching it out flat between three hands. He hated this bit most of all; although, officially, it was what he was here for.

Recalling what Frinallenegu had told him, he drew out his writing-claw and crossed the name Mrijil Parenagdehu off the list, then began to read the other names.

One by one, the villagers raised a hand. Gwebdhallut noted their position, the colour of their ragged belly-wraps, any distinguishing marks. When he had finished, the squadsmen – who had surrounded the villagers without seeming to – moved in, politely issuing the little wooden sticks with the deadly iron on their tips. Gwebdhallut wrote, 'Sixty-one irontips issued', in the space provided on the roll.

There was a silence. Another gust of wind blew, rattling the flimsy shutters on the huts. The burrowing flies made faint clicking noises. Gwebdhallut always felt he should make a speech at this point: praise the courage and selfless sacrifice of the villagers, assure them they would be remembered until the bones of time were cracked. But he knew that there was no point. He was nothing to do with these people: he didn't know them, wasn't meant to know them, wouldn't even be one of those who remembered them. There was nothing he could rightfully say.

But when the silence stretched, he murmured, 'Take your time. If there's anything you feel you need to do first, do it; we will wait.'

Frinallenegu, with a sudden, startling movement that had half of Gwebdhallut's squadsmen reaching for their guns, pushed her irontip into the thick vein on the top of her north leg. Her mouths gaped; her eyes widened, glazed; with a shudder, her body collapsed on the floor. A stench of excrement filled the air.

Gwebdhallut gaped, stood to attention; the other squadsmen instinctively did the same. Other villagers began dying, most of them quickly like Frinallenegu, a few slowly when they missed the vein. The latter kicked feebly like crushed dust-flies, breathing in shuddering gasps. Some were helped by their neighbours, who gave them a second shot.

Suddenly there was a shout: 'Yonidhallu! No!'

A young clansman had sprung upright. He leaped across the fallen bodies towards a young clanswoman with her irontip poised against her leg. He was too late. She either didn't hear him or ignored him; she was dead when he reached her side.

Gwebdhallut didn't need to look at the list of names to know: bud-brother and bud-sister. It could so easily have been us, he thought; Sesifghall and Gwebdhallut.

The brother, trembling, had pushed all five eye-stalks towards Gwebdhallut, and was now crouched to spring. For some reason, Gwebdhallut was unable to move, even to signal to his squadsmen.

'Burner!' swore the villager. 'You smouldering *burn* – '

Four dart-guns popped: one dart skittered away across the dry mud, the other three found their mark. The young clansman convulsed once, then collapsed onto his belly, dead.

Gwebdhallut felt the bile churn in his stomachs.

The other villagers, trembling, used their irontips: one called out weakly for help.

'I'm frightened,' she said. 'I can't – ' She gestured with the irontip.

Gwebdhallut signalled to one of the squadsmen, who quietly walked over and, murmuring reassurances, killed her before she knew what was happening.

When the last one was finished, the carts rumbled forward, and the squadsmen went to work loading. Limp legs and arms waved loosely as the bodies went aboard; hammer-flies scattered, blundering angrily through the air. Gwebdhallut carefully checked the bodies against the information from his roll, then labelled them with the appropriate name using a paste-brush. When he had finished, Sesifghall materialized by his side, brown dust covering her belly and legs.

'Nothing,' she said briefly. 'No tracks.'

Gwebdhallut's eye-stalks twitched acknowledgement. If Mrijil Parenagdehu had gone, then he had gone carefully, and he had gone a long way. Perhaps he had thrown himself on the mercy of another village – or perhaps he was really dead.

Gwebdhallut hissed faintly. It wasn't his problem. The rememberers would find out when they ate the bodies. He signalled to the carts, and the drivers kicked their hot, sleepy charges into movement. Gwebdhallut closed his eyes, savoured the relief of the moment.

'One more village, my friends,' he said aloud. 'One more today, then we're going home.'

'Can you hear it?'

The Doctor stopped dead in the half-dark of the tunnel, forcing Barbara to do the same. She rubbed at her right hand where a falling stone had bruised it, wondered how many aches and pains she could accumulate in one day.

The Doctor spoke again: 'Yes, most definitely. Traffic.' The lines on his face were back now, waving and dancing in the light from the flame of the everlasting match he held in his hand.

Suddenly he blew the match out. Barbara began to shout a protest, then saw the light ahead. After a moment she became aware of the sound that had caught the Doctor's attention: the clatter of hooves on stone, the deep rumbling of the wheels of *kigfih* carts. She hurried after the Doctor, who was striding towards the exit as if an ambush was a distant possibility rather than – as Barbara felt it was – a distinct likelihood.

She caught up with him at a wide grating made of varicoloured chitin, through which could be seen daylight and a stone wall.

'Ingenious,' muttered the Doctor. He was prodding at one side of the grating. 'See – hinges, concealed amongst the scrollwork.'

Barbara looked, but could only see vague carved shapes. She pushed at the grating, but it didn't budge.

'I wouldn't worry about that,' said the Doctor in a warning tone. 'Remember what happened at the other end, eh?'

He crouched down and, with an agility belying his appearance, crawled through a gap at the bottom of the grating. Barbara followed.

'Designed to stop Venusians, not humans,' said the Doctor in a self-satisfied tone, dusting himself off.

Barbara looked around. They were in a pentagonal stone pit about eight feet deep. Barbara could hear the sounds of hooves and carts above, but the walls were vertical, and there were no steps.

The Doctor stretched upwards; he was unable to even reach the lip of the pit. Barbara tried it, but her hands too fell a few inches short. She tried standing on the chitin bars of the grating, but it was set several inches into the wall and she found it impossible to keep her balance.

'Designed for Venusians to get out of, not humans,' she said, with an exasperated glance at the Doctor.

The Doctor tsked a few times; then reached upwards with his cane; the end of it projected about a foot above the top of the pit. He tapped it loudly, several times, against the stone.

There was the sound of hooves approaching; then three hooded eyes peered over the edge of the pit. Recoiled. There was shouting from above; Barbara heard the word 'stickwalker'. After a moment, more eyes appeared.

'Well don't just stand there,' grumbled the Doctor. 'Help us to get out.'

Four long Venusian arms unravelled themselves and reached down; Barbara and the Doctor grabbed two each and were hauled upwards.

Barbara found herself in the middle of noise and confusion. Venusians hurtled about, shouting, hand-signalling, jumping over each other and over the crush of *kigfih* and hand-drawn carts. Straight ahead was a vehicle which seemed to consist mostly of a huge, yellow-painted vertical wheel, about seventy feet in diameter and perhaps thirty feet across. A five-sided wooden deck adorned with sculptured minarets was fitted around the equator of the wheel; five masts flying blue and grey sails sprouted precariously at the corners. A vastly taller mast, with the sails reefed, stood just forward of the wheel; Barbara had to crane her neck to see the top of it.

Globeroller, said Dharkhig's memories. But having a name for it didn't make it any the less impressive.

Venusians were bounding towards the globeroller in great frog-jumps; some were clinging to platforms that were already being raised up its sides. A Venusian squatted in a pentagonal wooden contraption with five trumpet mouths, yelling, 'The last boarding for Conorihib! *Dawnwind Rider* to Conorihib, the last boarding is now!' over and over again.

Barbara stared for a few seconds, then turned to the Venusian who had pulled them out. Dharkhig's memories recognized her as a loader, not an important person.

'Is Ian on that thing?' she asked.

The loader stared blankly.

'Ian – an alien, like me. Is he on the *Dawnwind Rider*?'

The loader pushed two of her hands together in a gesture of puzzlement; they came apart again with a popping sound. Behind her, Barbara heard a loud crack of sails filling. Looking round, she saw the boarding platforms drawing up, the sails unfurling, the globeroller starting to move.

'There were some people,' said the loader at last. 'They wanted a box for an animal – they had it under a belly-wrap, but it had two legs, like you. They left on the *Accepter of the Wind*, bound for Inarihib. But that was before the purple hour changed.'

Barbara glanced around and saw a tricoloured timepiece hanging from the corner of a distant shed. She read the three coloured plates, worked out that Ian had been gone for at least two hours.

Well, that followed; the Rocketeers would hardly have hung around waiting for them.

Other Venusians were crowding around now. Barbara glanced at the Doctor, but he was searching in his pockets for something, a frown on his face.

'When's the next globeroller to Inarihib?' asked Barbara of the loader, with a glance around her: several rollers of various sizes stood in the distance on the brown stone paving of the port, loading goods and passengers.

Another blank stare. 'Well, not till next sunrise, of course.'

'Next sunrise? But we have to go after him!'

The loader stared blankly yet again; an expression she was rather good at, Barbara decided.

'The wind only blows the right way in the morning,' she said at last, slowly. 'And they have to get over the hills before the petrol forests start burning.'

'Petrol forests?' Dharkhig's memories drew a blank: Barbara glanced at the Doctor, but he was standing on a block of chitin with a mirror in his hand, peering over it as if he were sighting it on something.

'You know, the ones that burn down every morning,' the loader insisted. 'The petrol forests.' She glanced up at the distant clock. 'They'll start burning any time now.'

The laboratory was silent except for the faint scratching of the *nijij* in their tank as they fed. The sulphurous light of mid-morning shone through the windows and the open doorway, glared off the polished surface of the writing-bench. The heat was all but unbearable.

Kontojij normally spent this part of the day asleep in

the cellar-pool, trying to dream of his budlinghood. Today he knew he didn't have that choice.

He read through the message he had prepared again. It seemed to make sense. Firstly he stated that the message was important, and must be read at once; then he described the *huyaot* officially, its parameters, its degree of predictivity, the likely time of the indicated events; then he described what he had seen. Before ending the experiment, Kontojij had forced himself to go back, to observe closely, to fill in the background behind the deaths: the upward-curving ground, the stickwalker-like beings with their eyes stapled to their heads, the blue box with the flashing white light. All these details were noted in the message. Kontojij could only hope that at least one of them would provide a clue as to the nature of the threat. He rolled the paper tightly, pushed it into a cylindrical chitin pod and put the pod in his lip-pouch with the other five.

One for each *ghifghoni*, he thought sorrowfully.

He turned his attention to a glass beaker full of greyish-white paste. He lowered an eye over it, surveyed the surface for a moment, dipped the tip of a finger in and took a tiny sample to taste.

Normal. Good.

He took the beaker, jumped up out of the laboratory, four-legged, his fifth leg still dragging painfully.

The bag of *kirimbi*-nuts was where he had left it. He crouched down, pulled a nut out of the bag and ran it across the surface of the paste so that the greyish substance accumulated in its grooved surface. When he had completed the process with all the nuts, he returned them to the bag.

He started to walk down the path to the *ghifgihonij*. The *ghifghoni* were lined up on the roof of their quarters; at Kontojij's approach they went into a frenzy of squawking and *chff*-ing, jaws open, beating their rotors up and down against the chitin tiles. Kontojij took the bag of nuts in his hand and rattled it.

'Late breakfast today, my friends,' he said, scattering the nuts on the ground. With a clattering of rotors and a lot more squawking, the little flyers dived from the roof and started scooping up the nuts, flying virtually upside-down to do so. As Kontojij had hoped, they were too hungry to worry about the paste smeared over their food.

He took the message-pod out of his lip-pouch, noticed the blank address label, abruptly realized that things might have changed in the thirty-five years since the memory powder had been prepared. The *ghifghoni* would fly to the right place; but his old friend need not necessarily be living there any more.

Kontojij unsheathed his writing claw and scrawled, 'To Jilet Mrak-ecado, or any other Competent Philosopher of Bikugih.'

For a moment Kontojij saw a clear picture of the brown chitin dome, the *triohril* beds, the *binihabeg* trees around the bud-pool. He wondered if it were his own memory, or whether the tiny sample of paste he had tasted had found its way into his brain.

The *ghifghoni* were getting restless now, glancing at the sky, glancing at the *ghifgihonij* that was rapidly becoming unfamiliar to them. Kontojij's eyelashes fluttered with sorrow. He knew that some of the flyers would die before they reached Bikugih. Perhaps all of them.

'First the *nijij*, and now you,' he muttered, but he knew he had to try. By the time his visitors arrived tonight to collect the report, it would be too late. And he had little chance of finding the entrance to the visitors' cave, stumbling about half-crippled on the slope in the full heat of day. Too late, he wished he'd taken up – just once – their invitation to visit the warrens. All his scruples about not getting involved in their possibly dangerous plans suddenly seemed no more than an old clansman's foolishness, now that his pets were going to die because of it.

Quickly, before he could change his mind, he crouched and picked up Serapihij. He clipped the message pod into her egg-pouch, patted the little creature's belly and put her down again. She squawked fiercely, tried to bite him, then took off into the air with a sudden explosion of sound. She circled the *ghifgihonij* once, as if getting her bearings, then headed out to the north. The other flyers jumped, flapped; Kontojij swiftly gathered them up, clipping the messages to them. One by one they followed Serapihij, rotors twirling.

Kontojij watched them go until they were no more than dots over the mountains, then climbed slowly back up the path to his quarters.

Ian was thirsty.

He was trying not to think about it. He was trying to keep his concentration locked on putting one foot in front of another. On avoiding the frequent ankle-deep holes in the ashy soil. On keeping a constant bearing on the sun so that he would not wander round in circles. But the feeling kept coming back: a painful dryness in the throat, an inability to swallow: I'm thirsty, I'm thirsty, I'm *thirsty*.

There were no streams in the forest. Ian had only found marshy places, full of purple, mushroom-shaped things that reared up and spat seeds at him. Some of these were still clinging to his jacket, trying to germinate, white roots waving feebly in the empty air. He had tried picking some of the fruit that clung in gelatinous clusters to the green trunks of the trees, hoping the clear fluid they contained was water; but when he had burst them the fluid had stung his hands, and the stink of petrol had made him feel sick.

The marshes stank of petrol too; Ian made a mental note never to strike a match in this place.

He wondered how far it was to Bikugih. The road was some distance to the south of him now; perhaps, he thought, he should have stayed on it, despite the risk of running into another globeroller. He might not be headed for the city at all.

And even if he was, what would he do when he got

there? Go to the TARDIS? Would Barbara and the Doctor be there? Who had kidnapped them? Had they escaped?

'Questions, questions,' he muttered aloud. 'Trouble is, no answers.'

The only thing he knew for sure was that he was alone and more or less lost on an alien planet where everyone was his enemy, walking in a forest which stank of petrol and had no water, and the sun glimmering through the leaves was almost hot enough to burn his skin and he was *thirsty*.

There was a sudden crashing sound in the leaves above him. Startled, Ian jumped to one side. Something black and about the size of a cat dropped out of the branches and hissed at him. Three green eyes on stubby stalks examined him; the other two waved at the foliage above, where there were further crashing sounds.

Ian stepped back. The creature was small, but it might be poisonous.

A second creature dropped from the tree, then a third. They hissed loudly, unfolding long, spade-like claws.

Ian retreated another step. He heard a crash of branches and a hissing sound behind him.

He dodged sideways, started to run.

More of the creatures dropped out of the trees ahead. Ian swerved to the left, but there were yet more of them already on the ground, their spade-like claws extended.

Ian froze, breathing hard. Sweat trickled down his face; his injured arm throbbed.

The creatures lowered their claws to the ground and began digging. In a surprisingly short time they had all disappeared beneath the soil, the only trace of their presence tall black spoil-heaps and a haze of dust in the air.

Ian stared for a moment, then began to laugh from sheer relief. 'Attacked by a pack of rampaging moles!' he said aloud. He rubbed at his arm, began walking, dodging the spoil-heaps until he reached clear ground.

In the distance he heard a dull thud, as if something heavy had been dropped on the ground. He stopped again, held his breath, listened.

There was a low roaring sound, gradually getting louder; other thuds and bumps. It sounded like a heavy vehicle moving. Was he nearer to the road than he thought? Then he saw movement, deep inside the forest. Something flickering, amber-coloured –

Fire!

Ian looked around, saw flames spreading on every side, advancing at a terrifying speed. He turned and ran, ran south towards where the road might be, where there might be an open space, some kind of safety.

He realized his mistake when he saw the flames ahead, the tree-trunks exploding.

For a moment Ian felt sheer animal panic. He *couldn't* die this way –

A column of thick black smoke obscured the sun; the heat from the flames burned the back of his neck. The fruit that Ian had been trying to eat a few minutes ago started detonating. He was pelted with a hail of black, smouldering seeds. He pulled his jacket up around his face, which was already scalding in the heat. He felt the skin of his lower arms burning through the thin material of his shirt.

It shouldn't burn for long, he thought. If I can just survive for a few minutes –

His jacket and trousers were beginning to smoulder: the air was so hot he could barely breathe it.

The moles, he thought. The moles must survive somehow. That's why they were digging – they heard the fire coming.

He turned and ran towards where he thought the moles might be, gasped with relief when he saw the spoil-heaps through the flame-lit tree trunks.

He stumbled towards them, wondering if he could cover himself in loose soil until the blaze was over. He started digging at the nearest spoil-heap with his hands.

He realized that this was his second mistake when the heap exploded in his face, throwing him to the ground and setting fire to the trees around him.

Barbara watched the middle plate of the clock change from cinnamon-brown to pink, and sighed. She wiped the sweat from her face and stared at the heat shimmering from the pale stone of the rollerport. A full middlechange; more than half an hour. And still no sign of Jofghil.

'I still say we should go after Ian with a pair of runners,' she said.

The Doctor was sitting in the shade, his back propped against the pale blue chitin wall of a storage shed. He looked up at Barbara, shook his head.

'Jofghil has the resources, my dear. You must remember that we have very little Venusian money – ' he held up the single dice-like coin that he had been able to find in his pockets. 'Jofghil can organize an official search; probably he has already started one.'

'Then why isn't he here?' Barbara had little faith in Jofghil: Dharkhig's judgement still sounded in her head every time the name was mentioned. His performance with the Rocketeers hadn't increased her confidence. She wasn't even sure that the Doctor's improvised heliogram had been understood by the Presidor; the Doctor had admitted he wasn't sure whether the heliographic code he had sent meant 'Ian has been taken to Inarihib' or 'a five-winged snake has been seen in the eastern marshes', and the reply had consisted merely of, 'Acknowledged: will act'.

The Doctor fished the mirror out of his pocket again.

'Very well. I will see if I can find him with this.'

Barbara's patience with the old man suddenly ran out.

'Doctor, is there any reason why we can't use the public heliograph facility?' She waved at the distant wooden tower, clustered about with slowly moving mirrors. 'At least they'll know the proper codes.'

The Doctor had moved into the sun and was sighting

over the mirror once again. 'We don't know where we'd be sending the message,' he pointed out. 'The set-up people would get most confused, I fear.'

Barbara opened her mouth to object but was distracted by a distant shout. She turned and saw a procession of *kigfih* carts making its way across the rollerport. With relief, she recognized Trikhobu in the lead cart, riding with Jofghil and a squadsman who shouted, 'Make way for the Presidor' through a three-mouthed wooden trumpet. Very few Venusians did make way: the carts swerved back and forth, the *kigfih* jittered, curses were exchanged.

The Doctor jogged her elbow. 'You see?' he said. 'You should have more faith in the Venusians. They are an old and respectable civilization – much older than, for instance, your own.'

'It's not the Venusians I don't have faith in, it's – ' began Barbara; but the carts were almost within earshot, and she decided it would be best if she shut up.

As the carts drew up, Dharkhig's memories recognized the squadsman at the speaking-trumpet as Brignontojij of the clan Rastwet. Barbara greeted the officer with the nearest she could manage to a proper salute. He gave her an odd look with two of his eyes, said something to Jofghil. Barbara opened her mouth to explain but thought better of it.

Trikhobu jumped down from the cart and squeezed Barbara's neck.

'We came as quickly as we could. Jofghil's sent a heliogram to Inarihib, asking them to look out for Ian. Everything should be all right.' She had a notepad in her hand, covered in purple writing. 'If my calculation about the wind speeds is correct, Ian should be three-hundred-and-forty-nine four-hundred-and-twentieths of the way there, to the second approximation.'

Barbara blinked.

'Yes, but can the Inarihibi be trusted?' she asked. She had a feeling from Dharkhig's memories that relations between the cities of Inarihib and Bikugih weren't too good, but she couldn't remember why, and didn't know whether the information was current. And all the Doctor had seemed to know was that the Inarihibi were famous for their Alabaster-Age granite temples.

Trikhobu's eye-stalks flattened.

'In this matter, probably. They will expect something in return, of course.' Trikhobu must have guessed that this would make Barbara anxious, for she added quickly, 'Jofghil will agree to it, whatever it is. Don't worry.'

She curled an eye and a finger towards her notepad and began scribbling more calculations.

Perhaps, Barbara thought, she was trying to calculate the reliability of the Inarihibi government. Or Jofghil's reliability.

She looked around, saw Jofghil, Brignontojij and another squadsman talking to the loader. The latter suddenly started shouting, 'I'm no traitor – I didn't know it was an alien! They said it was an animal!'

'No one could be so stupid!' Jofghil yelled back. To her astonishment, Barbara saw the two squadsmen step forward and lift up one of the loader's legs. Brignontojij began chipping at her hoof with a stone chisel.

She ran over, shouting, 'Brignontojij! Stop that! There are no grounds for arrest!'

Everyone stared at her, even the Doctor; she realized she was speaking with Dharkhig's voice again. Eventually Jofghil spoke.

'This is a matter of government. I know best how to proceed.' His skin was blue with anger.

'You really must learn to control your alternate personalities,' said the Doctor quietly to Barbara. 'It can become very embarrassing, believe me.'

Barbara felt her face flush with blood. For a moment she wasn't sure who she was, even whether she was human or Venusian. She only knew that arresting the loader was stupid, and that Jofghil was doing it to cover the fact that he wasn't doing anything else. She tried a different tack.

'I don't want you to arrest this clanswoman, Jofghil,' she said. 'It isn't necessary. I just want Ian back. I appeal to your mercy as the Responsible One of the Night Council.'

Jofghil's skin remained mottled with blue blood. 'I've done what I can,' he hissed. 'The Inarihibi authorities have been informed. It is now necessary to follow up other lines of enquiry.'

Barbara glanced at the Doctor, who frowned and shook his head, but said nothing. To her surprise she noticed Mrak-ecado standing behind the old man, paying off a *kigfih* cart driver with one arm, and watching her and the Doctor with an eye each.

Suddenly the sun went out, and the rollerport was plunged into shadow.

At first Barbara thought it was a cloud, albeit a sudden and very dark one; only when she turned back to Jofghil, and saw the Venusian staring five-eyed at the sky, his belly contracted with obvious terror, did she look up.

Half the sky had disappeared; in its place was a vast shield of grey rock, pitted with craters and cracked by long shadows. Looking wildly around, she saw that it was so large that only a thin line of light was visible between it and the northern horizon.

'Doctor, what is it?' she asked, trying to keep the fear out of her voice. 'Is it falling?'

The old man was balancing his walking cane horizontally on one finger. He peered at it, measuring the length on each side of the balance point with spans of his other hand.

'No tidal effect,' he said after a moment. 'Whoever lives in that rock, they've got it under perfect gravitational control. And – ' he cocked his head to one side for a second, as if listening for something ' – no atmospheric displacement, either. Not a whisper of it. How very odd.'

Mrak-ecado stepped forward, four eyes on the sky, one on the Doctor.

'Old friend, is this your doing?' he asked.

The Doctor shook his head. 'Mine?' How could it – '

He was interruped by a voice. The voice sounded to Barbara like a radio announcer: calm, professional, in control. Only afterwards did she realize that it had not spoken aloud, that it had been neither male nor female, that its tone had been cold, alien, something completely *other* than human – or Venusian.

'Venusians of the city of Bikugih,' it said. 'We, the Sou(ou)shi, greet you. Please do not be concerned by our presence here. We are visiting you purely for the long-term benefit of the cycle of life throughout the universe. We offer your species an opportunity to leave your world before the final collapse of the ecosystem. We assure you that you will be provided with accommodation suitable to your needs. We regard it as a privilege to be allowed to assist you in this way, and we promise that, for as long as our own species survives, each of you and all of you will be remembered.'

Book Three

The Yellow Moss Hour

7

Differences and Decisions

Someone was singing.

The voice was deep; orchestra-deep, sea-deep. Tones swam and mixed in its depths like fish.

> 'Close your north eye, my little ones, and fold your south leg under the belly of your wishes.
> 'Close your west eye, my little ones, and fold your east leg under the belly of your hopes.
> 'Close your east eye – '

Ian's hands hurt. It was a steady, throbbing pain, like a burn. Funny, that: he had been dreaming about fire. A forest full of petrol. Funny what you dreamt about.

> ' – little ones, and fold your south-west leg under the belly of your dreams.'

Ian opened his eyes. There was a Venusian sitting over him, a dark ammonia-smelling shadow in a dimly lit room. And the forest had been real. He sat up, looked down at his hands, saw lobster-red skin shining under a coat of oil.

He cautiously touched his left hand with his right. Winced.

'Don't do that.'

It was the voice of the singer: rich, warm, perfect. Ian had the bizarre notion that she would do rather well at Covent Garden.

'The salve will help your skin mend itself, if you let it.' She moved slightly, stretching an eye-stalk towards him. 'I am Efhil Jellenhut, bud-mother of the clan Onihinallall.'

'Ian Chesterton, teacher, of the clan Earth.' His voice was hoarse and his throat hurt. When he had finished speaking, he coughed. He started to extend a hand, then thought better of it. 'Thank you for – ' He paused to look around him. He saw a dome-shaped room with dark, cloth-covered walls; more cloths in every possible colour were draped on frames around the room. Sunlight, filtered by a green curtain, glowed softly in a doorway. 'How did I get here?'

He remembered the flames, the spoil-heap exploding: then nothing.

'My bud-brother Henefenhut found you in a tree-mole nest at the edge of the petrol forest. He said you were asleep.'

Ian frowned. Asleep? But there had been flames all around him!

– his clothes on fire –

Yes, his jacket was scorched. And there was a hole in his trouser leg – burned through – and burned skin underneath, coated in the oily salve.

'The soil had collapsed. You must have fallen through into the nesting chambers,' said Jellenhut.

'But how – surely they must be deeply buried – it's not likely – ' Ian could think of a thousand objections.

'Don't question miracles,' said the Venusian softly. 'They happen. Would you like something to eat?'

The shuttle descended in silence, the only source of light in the darkened sky. It was wingless; two vertical white cylinders decorated with coloured lights. As it grew nearer, shadows formed, multiple and multicoloured: shadows of Venusians, of *kigfih*, of the long masts of the globerollers. The shadows moved, lengthened, and the shuttle became real, vast, an illuminated skyscraper standing on five sturdy pillars. It was only when Barbara looked closely that she realized there was still a small gap between the pillars and the ground.

Still the shuttle made no sound. For some reason

that worried Barbara. Spaceships were supposed to be noisy, violent. This gentle, inexorable descent seemed unnatural, somehow, almost unreal.

The Doctor clearly shared her unease: a deep frown was on his face, and when he caught Barbara's eye he shook his head, beckoned.

'It looks like a Venusian budling,' he murmured when she was close enough to hear. 'Consider it: five-fold symmetry, and those flipper-like projections at each end. It's obviously designed to reassure the Venusians. But if they wanted to reassure them, why not – ?'

He broke off as Jofghil approached. The Presidor had barely moved since the Sou(ou)shi ship had first appeared: it had been left to Mrak-ecado to order Brignontojij and the other squadsmen to clear a space for the shuttle to land. Even now Jofghil seemed to be moving in a trance of fear, his eye-stalks trembling, his mouths sealed tight.

'You will speak to the aliens,' he said to the Doctor.

'I?' The Doctor tapped his chest and frowned again. 'But – '

'You are alien, they are alien. That should be sufficient.'

The Doctor gave Jofghil his sternest stare. 'Don't be ridiculous! I don't know anything about – '

He was interrupted by shouts from the Venusians standing around them. Turning, Barbara saw that a door had opened in the shuttle, perhaps fifty feet off the ground. Lights moved, then –

Barbara gasped. A giant Venusian with wings drifted out over the rollerport. The wings, glittering red and gold, were curved above the body as if sheltering it. The body glowed a deep sea-blue as it descended in silence towards the ground.

'Theatre, pure theatre,' muttered the Doctor. 'Look at the spotlight up there.'

Barbara looked and decided that 'theatre' was too small a word for it; the 'stage' was about a thousand feet high.

The landing-craft touched down near the shuttle, then rolled forward through the circle of watching Venusians. As it came nearer, Barbara realized that there were three human figures sitting in it – no, not quite human. Their faces were too pink, their eyes too round, and their bare torsos were coated with a fine, golden fur. They looked ahead, smiling. The smiles were identical, as were the faces. Barbara shuddered.

The craft rolled up almost to Barbara's feet, stopped just as she was about to jump aside. Three pairs of Sou(ou)shi eyes stared into hers.

She glanced wildly at the Doctor.

' "Take me to your leader",' he muttered. 'Only they forgot to ask who the leader *was*, first; which implies of course that they already knew. Hmm.'

One of the Sou(ou)shi spoke:

'Kintibi Jofghil of the clan Poroghini Presidor of the Night Council.' It was said all in one breath, as if the title and the name were the same thing. 'We request this one to speak with us.'

Barbara stepped aside: Jofghil, facing the aliens, swayed backwards, his eye-stalks waving in confusion. The Doctor looked at him, pointedly raising his eyebrows.

'You are Kintibi Jofghil of the clan Poroghini Presidor of the Night Council?' asked the Sou(ou)shi. Barbara wasn't sure which one had spoken or whether it was the same one that had spoken last time, and had the impression it didn't matter.

Jofghil finally twitched assent, added aloud, 'I am.'

'We bring you greetings. We have, as we have stated, come to save your entire species. As we understand your city to be the most important place on your world, we have come here first. We need to confirm that you are satisfied with our intentions before we proceed to arrangements.'

Jofghil's eye-stalks flattened against his body. For a moment, Barbara almost felt sorry for him.

'I – that is – I must consult – '

He made a frantic hand-signal to Mrak-ecado, who stood quietly behind him.

'The Sou(ou)shi are offering us an almost inconceivable boon,' said the Philosopher. 'And we must thank them. But I do think – and I'm sure that the Night Council would agree – that we should make some attempt to confirm that they can do what they say, and that there is a place where we can go and be welcome.' He paused. 'Do you not agree, Doctor?'

'Yes, yes, most definitely.' The Doctor did not turn to look at Mrak-ecado: he was still staring at the Sou(ou)shi. 'And also – '

'We can settle these questions,' said the Sou(ou)shi – again, Barbara was not sure which one spoke. 'There is room for a population of one hundred and twenty-six million Venusians aboard our ship for a period of two tendays. We will take you to the nearest habitable but uninhabited world; that is, the third planet in your own system.'

Barbara heard the Doctor mutter, 'No, no, no.' Then she realized:

'The *Earth*?'

Both Jofghil and the Sou(ou)shi ignored her.

'The third planet?' asked Presidor, with the mouth facing Mrak-ecado. 'Isn't that where those Rocket people wanted to go? Can we be sure this isn't some kind of stunt that they've – ' He stopped suddenly, perhaps realizing the ridiculousness of the suggestion.

The Sou(ou)shi began talking again. The Doctor drew Barbara aside and muttered, 'There's something very odd going on here.'

Barbara glanced at the Sou(ou)shi in their vehicle, the three pairs of eyes and the three identical smiles pointed at Jofghil. She nodded.

'They're not taking them to Earth,' the Doctor went on.

'How can you be so sure?'

The Doctor raised his eyebrows. 'Have you ever seen a

fossilized Venusian in one of your museums?'

'Fossilized – ?' said Barbara. Then she remembered how far in the past they were.

'We need to get aboard their ship,' the Doctor was saying. 'Then we might be able to find out something more.'

Barbara looked up at the spaceship, at the dim landscape of its underside, now barely visible in the glare from the shuttle.

'I don't see how we can do that unless the Sou(ou)shi let us.'

'Neither do I.' The Doctor too was looking upwards. 'It's a shame Chesterton isn't with us. He might have been useful.'

He spoke in a casual, offhand manner. It reminded Barbara of the way he would speak during a game of chess: 'It's a shame I don't have my white bishop.'

'It's not a game, Doctor.' The words were out before she had considered them. 'Ian could be dead.'

'Oh, I shouldn't think so. He's pretty resourceful, you know.' But the Doctor was still gazing at the spaceship, his interest in Ian abstract.

Barbara felt a flare of anger. 'Don't you care about Ian?' she asked fiercely.

The Doctor turned, stared at her. He seemed puzzled.

'I'm as concerned about the young man as you are, believe me,' he said, taking her arm gently. 'But don't you think that the fate of a whole planet full of sentient beings is more important than the fate of one person?'

'It depends on whether you – ' began Barbara, but the Doctor would not be interrupted.

'My dear Barbara, the Sou(ou)shi ship is the heart of the mystery here, and I insist that we investigate – '

Suddenly Barbara had had enough. She snatched her arm away from the Doctor's.

'I don't care about mysteries! I just want to find Ian and get away from this place!' She looked around, saw Trikhobu standing near the shuttle amongst the Presidor's squadsmen, four of her eyes on the shuttle, the other on Jofghil and the Sou(ou)shi. Barbara waved, her fingers unconsciously approximating the Venusian hand-sign for need-to-speak. Trikhobu understood, and replied in kind. Barbara started towards her.

' – would allow a small delegation to make a preliminary visit – ' the Sou(ou)shi were saying.

'Barbara!' called the Doctor. She heard his footsteps coming after her; he grabbed her arm. 'Barbara, I think that we may be allowed to see the ship.' He tried to pull her back towards the aliens.

Barbara stayed put.

'I'm sorry, Doctor, but I think I ought to do something to help Ian. I'm going to ask Trikhobu if she'll help me get to Inarihib.'

The Doctor stared at her for a moment. 'But what could you do? You've seen what the Rocketeers are like. They're dangerous people. You might end up being kidnapped yourself – you might even be killed.'

'I'm going to do something!' Barbara started to walk away again, then realized the Doctor wasn't following. She turned and shouted at him: 'You don't care about anyone, do you? Everyone's just a – a chess piece, to you, now that Susan's gone. Ian, me – '

'My dear Susan – ' began the Doctor.

'*I am not Susan!*' bawled Barbara. 'Nor am I a piece of Susan, whatever you've told the Venusians. Neither is Ian. We're people – people who are travelling with you, and through no choice of our own. You have a responsibility to us. If you can't get us home, very well. But at least you can look after us in the meantime. Or if you won't – if you're too busy with your "mysteries" – ' she waved upwards at the omnipresent darkness of the Sou(ou)shi ship ' – then we'll just have to look after ourselves.'

The Doctor stood for a moment, then turned quickly and walked back towards Jofghil and the Sou(ou)shi visitors, his cane clicking on the ground. Barbara stared, her lungs heaving, her throat dry from shouting, until she saw him speaking to Mrak-ecado; then she, too, turned away.

She blundered straight into Trikhobu.

Dry Venusian hands gripped awkwardly at her shoulders; Barbara buried her face in a wall of hard Venusian flesh.

'I used to shout at Dharkhig, sometimes,' rumbled Trikhobu. 'He didn't like it either.'

Gantohi Ruribeg of the clan Esinallihall looked at the mountain floating in the sky. Through the secondary prism of the mossocular it became a bubble of rock floating above a bubble-shaped city, linked by the linear rainbows of the exposure measurements. Somehow, it looked less improbable that way than it did to the unaided eye.

A vision of Dhallgohidhall, he thought. The land-which-is-no-land, the land floating in the sky.

But it was not Ruribeg's job to feel awe, or wonder, or to question the nature of things. It was his job to make measurements. To produce evidence. To report.

Satisfied with the exposure rainbow, Ruribeg carefully unscrewed the main cap of the mossocular and stowed it in a wooden pouch. He jiggled the glass plate in the back of the machine to make sure it was true, then locked it in place and waited for the picture to germinate.

A little bunch of children stood around him on the dusty road, watching.

'Do you know what it is, clansman Ruribeg?' asked one of them quietly.

Ruribeg gaped at the child. He had a reputation in the area for knowing things: in his position, that was inevitable. But this time he didn't know, and thought it safer to admit it.

'I'm just gathering evidence.'

'Will you take the evidence to a Philosopher?'

'Well – ' Ruribeg hesitated. 'To a sort of Philosopher, yes.' It wouldn't be sensible for the children to know where he would really be taking the evidence. Even now.

Especially now.

The craft that had dropped from the belly of the rock down to Bikugih rollerport was rising again, bright white in the deep shadow, like a flying lamp bigger than a building.

The timer on the mossocular read amber-of-cherry-pink. Less than twenty-five per cent. Good: there should be a clear trail exposure showing the track of the mysterious craft. More evidence.

Ruribeg waited, the sun burning the skin of his sides. Occasionally he exchanged a remark with one of the children; once, his house-neighbour passed, hooves clicking on the road, a bucket of water in each hand. Her heavy body swayed from side to side, slopping the water in the pails.

At last the timer told Ruribeg that the exposure was complete. He took a flask of fixing-poison from his ankle-bag, poured a small amount into the funnel at the top of the mossocular. At the same time he capped the prism with another hand.

He waited a little longer, for the moss on the plate to die, then brought it out into the light and gaped with satisfaction. A perfect exposure: even the rock formations on the surface of the object were visible, and the light-craft showed up as a clear, bright streak. Only by bringing his eye almost in contact with the plate could he see the individual filaments of moss which had grown in response to the light focused through the machine.

He let the children see the picture, crowding round him, pushing at his back; when they had seen enough, he began to pack it away, carefully unscrewing the joints and packing the legs and body into separate ankle-bags.

'You should take another one!' shouted one of the children.

Ruribeg flattened his eye-stalks.

'There are calculations I must make,' he lied.

He set off at a canter down the road, leaving the

bewildered children behind him. No doubt they would wonder why he was leaving such an interesting object behind without further study. Perhaps they would even resent him for deserting them.

But this time, he couldn't worry about what the children thought. About the possibility of suspicion. About the damage that his strange action might do to his carefully established persona.

The matter was too urgent for that. The world had changed, changed for ever, and the Volcano People needed to know about it.

Dinner was still wriggling.

Ian stared at it, trying to fight back his instinctive disgust. The *nijij* were skewered by their legs to a goldenwood plate about six feet across. Sunlight, concentrated by a sheet of curved glass, glared off the wood: when Ian put his hand there, it was as hot as any oven. His skin stung under Jellenhut's salve.

'They're best eaten whilst they're still alive,' said Jellenhut. She reached in, extended a long claw from one of her hands and neatly ripped open the flabby central body of one of the animals. She reached in to the steaming juices, yanked out a pinkish object about the size of a golf-ball, offered it to Ian.

'The brain,' she said, when Ian just stared. 'It will help your nerves to regenerate after the shock you've had.'

Ian looked at the twitching limbs of the dissected animal, felt the gorge rise in his throat.

Jellenhut said, 'Don't worry, it's quite tasty – almost sweet when it's not overcooked. Not like *cajingu* brains.'

'I – er – we don't eat brains on my world. It's – well, we don't.'

Jellenhut turned three eyes on him for a second, then said, 'Sorry, I didn't realize,' and popped the dripping brain into her mouth.

'I'm not really hungry,' said Ian hastily, before she could offer him any more pieces of dismembered flesh. As he said it, he realized it was true. 'I think it must be the shock,' he added, not wanting to offend his host.

Jellenhut gave him another three-eyed stare, then pulled two brick-sized pieces of wood from one of her lip-pouches and began to clack them together.

Before Ian could ask what this meant, the answer became obvious: he and Jellenhut were surrounded by a crowd of shrieking, bouncing children. The smallest – standing no higher than Ian's knee – began bouncing around Jellenhut, yelling, 'Meaties! Meaties!' The larger ones helped themselves to the feast, long claws scissoring out of their hands. Their eyes were level with Ian's chest, and they must have weighed as much as horses; as they pushed and shoved at each other to get the best positions by the sun-oven, Ian was kicked in the leg. Wincing, he retreated.

'Be careful of the alien!' said Jellenhut belatedly. 'He is hurt.'

Standing at a safe distance, Ian could see that there were fewer children than he had thought; five of the larger children, and two small ones jumping around Jellenhut.

'Are all of these your children?' asked Ian.

'Of course they're mine!' replied Jellenhut, with the only mouth that wasn't occupied in hissing, whistling and scolding at the children. 'I wouldn't be feeding them otherwise. Now feast, children – *feast*, not squabble,' she continued with another mouth. 'You must do honour to the beasts you are eating by conducting yourselves in a civilized manner at their deaths.'

The youngsters organized themselves and began stabbing at the *nijij* in what looked like strict rotation. Each had a couple of eyes on Jellenhut, as if hoping she would go away and leave them to squabble again. Ian had to smile.

Jellenhut opened the mouth facing Ian again.

'Children! I suppose they are much the same on any world.'

'All the ones I've met, certainly,' he said. 'And I've met quite a few.'

'You have the honour of being a father, then?' asked Jellenhut, stepping away from her brood.

'No, but I'm a teacher.'

Jellenhut's eye-stalks flattened. 'A teacher? What has a teacher to do with children?'

Ian frowned. 'We – well, we teach them things.'

Jellenhut's eye-stalks remained flat. 'But if you teach children you must be their father, surely? Or are you a mother?'

Ian blinked.

'No, I'm just a teacher. Barbara's a teacher too.' He remembered that Jellenhut didn't know who Barbara was, so added, 'Barbara's my travelling companion.' He stopped then, thought of Barbara and the Doctor, drugged and incoherent at the funeral, and now in the hands of goodness-knew-which group of Venusians. He tried to clench a fist in frustration, but only hurt the burned skin of his hand.

'You're a sort of uncle, then?' asked Jellenhut, evidently oblivious to his distress.

Ian hesitated. He suddenly wanted, very badly, to get back to Bikugih. He looked up and down the length of the village. The mud-dome houses blurred into each other, shimmering in the heat; in the distance, a few Venusians worked in the fields, coloured sunshades raised above their backs. The scene was *alien*, alien down to the dry, blobby plants that weren't quite grass growing around the edges of the huts.

If he was to survive, if he was to get back to Bikugih and help his friends, he needed to know more. And Jellenhut was the first Venusian who hadn't tried to drug him, kidnap him, shoot him, or put him in a cage. He supposed she counted as a friend.

He turned back to face her.

'Tell me about the way you bring up children,' he said slowly. 'Tell me from the beginning.'

'Well, as soon as they're born, the midwives bring them to me from the bud-pond. I look after them, feed them, clothe them and clean them until they are old enough to look after themselves. Then they're assigned a father – '

'But what about the natural parents?' Ian interrupted. 'Don't they mind having their children taken away?'

'They aren't being taken away!' exclaimed Jellenhut. 'I am the mother; they are with me!' She paused. 'I think that you must have very different customs.'

'Our children stay with their father and mother – with their natural parents.'

Jellenhut's eye-stalks twitched. 'I think I see what you mean. Each mother has a child. But how is it decided which children stay with which mothers?'

'They stay with the ones – well, the woman who gave birth to them and the man who is her husband.'

'Her what?'

Ian tried again. 'Her mate.'

'You mean each clanswoman only has one mate? You do not all mate together, at the bud-pond, each year?'

'No, we – er – mate separately.'

'Each one on your own? But how could you possibly do that?'

Ian felt his face going red: he was beginning to lose his anthropological detachment. When he had joined Coal Hill School, he had never expected to have to explain the birds and bees to a nine-foot alien whose idea of sex was an annual mass orgy.

'No, Jellenhut,' he said. 'Two of us mate together. We stay together for life. And the children are brought up by that pair, exclusively.'

But Jellenhut's eyes were waving about wildly.

'I don't understand. How can a male and a female alone be fertile together? Surely there must be at least two females?'

'At least two – ?' began Ian; then stopped. If the Venusians all mated together, perhaps that was because they had to. In which case –

'There must be a *biological* difference! Look, Jellenhut, in our species a male and a female constitute a fertile union, on their own. Each one makes a genetic contribution to the child – '

'But how does the male do that?' Jellenhut's bewilderment was evident.

Helplessly, Ian started to laugh. 'Never mind how he does it, that's how it is!'

Jellenhut's eye-stalks steadied a little. 'That is your clan, then? This one male and one female and their children?'

'Yes, that's our clan,' said Ian, triumphant. At last they had understood each other.

'But such a small unit would be subject to intense psychological pressure,' mused Jellenhut. 'It must be very difficult for you. Do you only have small ponds on your world?'

Kintibi Jofghil of the clan Poroghini had liked being Presidor of the Night Council, until today. He had liked being at the centre of things, he had liked making decisions, he had liked the busy schedules and the fact that he had no time for anything but his duties. It had made him feel important; necessary to his clan, his city and his world.

Now he knew that he wasn't. Wasn't necessary at all, for anything.

He looked across the wide blue plain that the aliens had built inside their spaceship, picked out again the five lakes, the wide stripes of *bosifghal* forest, the *beghi* paddies covered with grey water, and knew that everything he had ever done was irrelevant. Venusian civilization was saved.

Jofghil squatted down on the hard stone of the observation balcony and felt thoroughly miserable.

'We hope we have selected the parameters correctly,' said one of the three Sou(ou)shi, its large black eyes turned towards Jofghil. 'Some of you will have to live in this environment for up to fifteen days, whilst the embarkation proceeds.'

Jofghil looked at the alien: the pale blue belly-wraps hanging about its middle, the goldenwood hooves fitted to its misshapen feet. It was ugly, he thought, but at least it was making an effort to look Venusian – unlike that other alien, Mrak-ecado's friend, with his spiky cloth coverings and that bolt of white fungus on top of his eye-stalk. Jofghil shuddered. It made him feel a little better that it wasn't the Doctor's people who were going to save them.

'We repeat: are you satisfied with the parameters of your provided environment?'

Jofghil glanced around at the other members of the Night Council: Ketenehi, the Eldest, in her purple wrap of office, the others in a mixture of clothes. Some of them still looked half-asleep.

'Are *you* satisfied, my fellow Councillors?'

Jofghil had often found it a useful tactic to put questions he couldn't answer to the floor; it had the effect of making uncertainty look like consultation.

This time it didn't work. Eye-stalks twitched uncertainly. Ketenehi muttered something. From behind them, the squadsman Brignontojij cleared his throats, a deep low rumble.

A cool, almost cold gust of wind blew against Jofghil's skin. He looked around for Mrak-ecado but the philosopher was nowhere in sight. He realized that he would have to say something himself.

'It could be a little warmer.'

The words hung in the air for a moment; another cold gust blew across the balcony.

One of the aliens asked, 'How much warmer?'

Jofghil felt his skin flushing slightly.

'About as warm as the dawn wind,' he said quickly. 'I think most of us would be comfortable then.'

The Sou(ou)shi paused again, their three pairs of eyes focused on Jofghil.

'It will take one-tenth of a day to do,' they said, speaking in unison.

'Do it,' said Jofghil.

He flicked a hand-sign at Ketenehi; its literal meaning was 'I win this game'. And Jofghil did feel he had won: he was still Presidor, he could still make decisions.

The Sou(ou)shi twitched their heads from side to side. 'It will be done. Are you otherwise satisfied?'

Jofghil stared at the view for another few moments. Should he ask something else? But what? He looked for Mrak-ecado again; saw, with some relief, the old Philosopher slowly climbing up the earthen bank below the observation platform, his pet alien in tow.

'I am satisfied,' he said.

The Sou(ou)shi made a curious twitching gesture with their heads, then spoke in unison: 'We are grateful for your acceptance, Kintibi Jofghil of the clan Poroghini Presidor of the Night Council.'

Jofghil squatted formally in response. He felt happier about the Sou(ou)shi now that they had given him some role in their rescue operation.

The Doctor and Mrak-ecado had started up the stone ramp that led to the platform; the Doctor, Jofghil noticed, was using his third leg – the thin, wooden one that he attached to the end of his arms – to balance on the steep slope. He could hear the Doctor's squeaky, alien voice.

'All we need to do to prove my theory correct, old friend, is to ask the Sou(ou)shi one simple question.'

'But they *can't* be monopsiopsychosemiotic! I would have noticed it from – '

'We will ask them, anyway. I don't see how it can give offence.' The Doctor was at the top of the steps now; breathing heavily, he approached the three Sou(ou)shi, who all whirled round to stare at him.

'Take me to your leader,' he said.

There was a slight pause.

One of the Sou(ou)shi said, 'We have no leader. But you may speak with this-one-who-is speaking.'

The Doctor turned to Mrak-ecado and hissed, 'You see?' He turned back to the Sou(ou)shi, his hands grasping the tips of the spiky cloth that grew on his body. 'Well, this-one-who-is-speaking, do you have a name?'

'I can have the name Pown(ow)ri, if that is acceptable to you.'

'Pown(ow)ri, hmm, yes. Pown(ow)ri. Quite a good name. Tell me, Pown(ow)ri, do you make a practice of rescuing doomed species?'

'We are happy to save their energies for the greater good of all.'

'But don't you want anything in return?'

Jofghil stared at the Doctor, horrified. Payment was the last thing he wanted discussed: what could Venusians possibly give to a people that could move entire civilizations between worlds? He opened a mouth to protest, but the Sou(ou)shi spoke first.

'We do not expect payment. Kintibi Jofghil of the clan Poroghini Presidor of the Night Council has not mentioned payment. However, if any Venusian wishes to gratify us, we will accept gifts of works of art.'

Jofghil's belly dropped against the ground with relief. Art, he thought; that could be managed.

But the Doctor hadn't finished. Craning his strange, spiky body forward, he pulled at the glass objects that hung around his neck, and placed them over his eyes. Jofghil wondered if the objects helped him to focus his psionic powers.

'But where do you put them all?'

'Habitable but uninhabited planets are found. They are used to fertilize.'

The Doctor's face twisted into an incomprehensible pattern; Jofghil was reminded of how alien this being was. He wondered if the Sou(ou)shi, with their similar physiognomy, understood this twisting of the flesh.

The Doctor walked around the Sou(ou)shi and approached Jofghil. The Sou(ou)shi turned slowly, following his movement with their whole bodies.

'You should be careful with them.' The Doctor waved his wooden stick-leg in the air near their hosts. 'Don't agree to anything until you understand everything.'

Jofghil felt his skin flushing with annoyance. How dare the Doctor insult the aliens openly like this? He turned an eye to Mrak-ecado, who stood silent at the top of the steps. The old Philosopher gave the slightest of hand-twitches: 'too far'. The other members of the Night Council, too, looked shocked: Ketenehi's mouths were sealed in a rigid line of disapproval.

Jofghil decided he'd had enough of the fungus-head's interference. He took a stride forward.

'Doctor,' he announced, two-mouthed in disapproval. 'I order you to be silent. The Night Council desires to conclude its negotiations with the Sou(ou)shi without further interference from you.'

The Doctor's face stretched, the strips of fungus above his eyes rising across the top of his head. He seemed about to speak, but Mrak-ecado placed a warning hand around his neck.

'We cannot risk offending the Sou(ou)shi, old friend. Surely you can see that.'

The Doctor glanced at the Philosopher, then turned and walked away, his third leg clicking on the polished stone. Mrak-ecado hesitated, then squatted briefly to Jofghil and went after the alien.

Jofghil turned to the Sou(ou)shi.

'I beg that you will excuse the alien. I foolishly assumed that, because of the physical similarity between you and the Doctor, he would be able to assist our negotiations. I ask you now to ignore him. He cannot speak for the Night Council or any Venusian.'

'Do not be concerned.' The Sou(ou)shi spoke in unison. 'We are not offended. We will arrange to neutralize this difficulty for you.'

Jofghil gaped with relief.

Another gust of wind blew. Jofghil noted with satisfaction that it already seemed warmer.

* * *

One by one, the others died.

Serapihij watched it: she watched their rotors slow, their flight dip. She watched their temporary recoveries, their long, final falls to the ground. To say she felt sorrow would be to assign her feelings a *ghifghoni* could not, quite, feel; but she felt a wrongness, perhaps bewilderment.

Home had always been near. Now it was very far away. So far that the others were dying.

Perhaps she too would die.

The air swirled with heat; heat and hot dust. The orange plain stretched below, radiating an implacable heat; the sun blinded her upper eyes, burned her back and the delicate blades of her rotors. Serapihij was thirsty, thirsty to the point of panic, but there was no trace of water visible.

Except, far ahead, a faint haze on the horizon.

A haze that might be water-mist.

That might be a city.

That might be home.

Serapihij forced her rotors to turn, again and again and again.

Even in the cabin of the land-yacht, the heat had been stifling; on the deck, in the sun, it was unbearable. Barbara had found the shade of the long sail and was staying in it. Trikhobu, too, seemed happy to stay put; she squatted on a deck-rug, her legs sprawled, seemingly half asleep. Her notepad was open under her west hand, and she scribbled occasional, dreamy, calculations.

Barbara watched the two-Venusian crew moving about, adjusting the sails, cranking the masts up and down, steering. Every few minutes one of them would plunge into the cabin and splash into the pool of water there.

To that part of her brain which had absorbed Dharkhig's memories the routine was familiar and reassuring. The creak of ropes and cloth, the banging of hooves on wood, the rumble and clatter of the big wheel on the road, even the yellow-and-red fields drifting slowly past the rail; they all meant that she was going somewhere, that she could leave the action to someone else and think for a while.

Barbara had taken advantage of the land-yacht's facilities to wash and change. One of Trikhobu's spare belly-wraps served, with the addition of a few strategic wooden pegs, as an excellent sari; it was certainly cooler and more comfortable than what she had been wearing. And, examining herself in the cabin mirror, Barbara had decided she looked very fetching. Ian ought to be pleased when he saw her.

If he was still alive.

Anxious again, she stood up and peered forward, saw bare yellow hills rising above the fields, their slopes shimmering in the heat. The road forked not far ahead; a little shack marked the habitation of the Wayfinder. At the sound of the approaching vehicle, she shuffled out of cover and called, 'North road to Martahig, south road to Inarihib.'

Barbara grinned to herself, and wondered why the Venusians had never invented the concept of a signpost.

Gejenihu, the senior of the crew, called out an acknowledgement and asked if the Inarihib road was clear yet. The Wayfinder replied, 'Hot and smoky, still burning in places. The Martahig road's safer.'

Well, there's your answer, thought Barbara. Signposts don't tell you about the state of the road ahead.

'Which route?' shouted Gejenihu.

There was a short pause. Barbara realized the question was addressed to her. She looked at Trikhobu, who stirred herself and began scribbling on the notepad.

'Wind speed – atmospheric clarity – Tonengu's formula – won't be a moment, my friend – '

Gejenihu spoke: 'The only way from Martahig to Inarihib is by river barge, so that will be slow; but if we go on the direct road we may get becalmed in the petrol forests, which is even slower. And very hot, dangerously so.'

The other crewman, a Philosopher by the name of Nohik-imaden, had pulled the sail in; the land-yacht was slowing for the junction. Barbara knew she had to make a decision quickly.

Trikhobu was still scribbling. 'Three-hundred-and-twelve five-hundred-and-sixty-sevenths – won't be a moment – '

Barbara turned to Gejenihu.

'What do you think?'

The Venusian pointed with three arms to Martahig, with two direct to Inarihib. Barbara recognized the gesture: a two-fifths chance. She closed her eyes for a second, nodded.

'We go south,' she said. 'Inarihib.'

The crew both jumped to the sail and whipped it round; Nohik-imaden yanked at the rope that turned the front axle. Barbara felt the land-yacht shudder and sway as they turned.

Trikhobu looked up, three-eyed.

'Our chances of being becalmed are nine-hundred-and-five sixteen-hundred-and-eighty-thirds,' she said. 'I hope you have made the right decision, my friend.'

Barbara stood, looked ahead at the road winding between the bare hills, the smoke haze hanging over the horizon.

'So do I,' she said.

Gwebdhallut knew that something was wrong as soon as the squad had entered the village. The villagers in the fields had neither welcomed them nor hidden from them; they had simply hissed in disapproval, as villagers usually did when the Death Inspectorate passed through.

'They're not expecting us,' he murmured to Sesifghall as they approached the dusty space of the budling-ground.

His bud-sister did not turn even one of her eyes from her constant examination of the mud-huts surrounding them.

'That's no reason for not carrying out our duty,' she said.

'I wonder if there might have been some mistake.'

Sesifghall spared him a single-eyed glance. Gwebdhallut knew what that glance meant. She might as well have said it: you're afraid, you're looking for excuses.

Sesifghall had always been the leader, the active one; he had been told that she had been the larger split of the budling when they had been born. Gwebdhallut often wondered why he had been promoted over her.

They had reached the bud-mother's hut now. The bud-mother herself was squatting in the doorway, apparently half asleep. She sat up suddenly at their approach, belly shrinking with alarm.

'What is your business?'

Gwebdhallut glanced at his bud-sister.

'I believe you know,' he said quietly.

The bud-mother jerked upright.

'No! We appealed –'

'There is no appeal any more,' said Sesifghall. 'That has been stopped.' She was already pulling out a gun.

'But we are controlling our population – we have only seven children in the whole village – '

Gwebdhallut lowered his eye-stalks. 'I'm sorry, bud-mother, but these facts do not alter our duty.' He flicked out a hand-signal to Sesifghall: permission to kill.

The bud-mother leaped into the air, rolled sideways and away to the south-west, bawling, 'Henefenhut! *Henefenhut!* They have come to kill us!'

Gwebdhallut started to trot after her, but Sesifghall restrained him with a touch on the arm, gestured at the bud-hut.

'The children will be in there,' she said. 'I will deal with them; the bud-mother will not resist after that. You take the rest and sweep the fields, with my Five innermost.'

Gwebdhallut twitched his eye-stalks in acknowledgement. Sesifghall always knew what to do in a fight. He started to signal to the squad, then saw a two-legged alien jump down from the doorway of the bud-hut, its two tiny eyes swinging from side to side on an oversize stalk.

'You'd better kill that ugly thing as well,' he said to Sesifghall. 'Whatever it is.'

Sesifghall twitched acknowledgement, raised her guns, fired twice. The darts struck the alien cleanly. It gave a startled squeak, jumped sideways, began to run around the curve of the hut.

Gwebdhallut stood, paralysed with shock. He recalled something he'd been told many years ago, in training: some species of alien are immune to the effects of iron-tips.

Sesifghall was following the alien.

'Be careful!' said Gwebdhallut. 'It could be dangerous, if we can't kill it with the darts.'

'I'll kick it to death if I have to,' said Sesifghall. She leaped after the alien, firing again from mid-air.

The dart hit the alien in the leg, and this time it fell at once. It rolled, twitched its legs a few times, then was still. Sesifghall prodded it once with a hoof, then trotted back to Gwebdhallut, gaping with satisfaction.

'Got the burner!'

Must have hit the vein this time, thought Gwebdhallut. Relieved, he cantered away to join the rest of his squad.

8

Battles for Survival

Jofghil couldn't count the lights: he couldn't even begin to estimate their number. Topaz, vermilion, emerald, saffron, aquamarine, violet; they covered the walls, floor and ceiling of the gallery – and the gallery seemed to stretch into an infinite distance.

Brihilohu, the Arts and Psionics Councillor, was clearly unable to decide which mouth to speak with.

'It's won– ' he began with one; then interrupted himself with, 'The sense of colour is – ' and at the same time, 'The harmony of the whole!' His arms flailed with awe.

'It is one of our favourite pieces,' admitted the Sou(ou)shi modestly. 'The Philotirians spent the whole of their stay with us completing it: they even wanted to stay longer, though we could not see how the work could be improved.'

Jofghil was beginning to get used to the golden aliens. Although still bemused by wonders, he could quite accept that the Sou(ou)shi were capable of carrying out their promise, just as they had done for other peoples in the past.

Mentally the Presidor drew up a memo for Brihilohu, instructing him to commission all the mandated artists in Bikugih to prepare a piece for the Sou(ou)shi to add to their collection. In addition there should be philosophy recitals, healing chorales, gymnastic competitions – anything the aliens would appreciate. Venusians should not be outshone in generosity, he thought, not even by a whole spaceship's cargo of pretty lights. Yes, that was a nice turn of phrase – perhaps he could use it in a speech –

'Kintibi Jofghil of the clan Poroghini Presidor of the Night Council.'

His reverie broken, Jofghil looked at the strange golden-fuzzed skin of the Sou(ou)shi addressing him.

'You will now need to prepare your people for embarkation. We must visit the other cities of your planet.'

Jofghil had to think for a moment before he realized that the aliens were telling him that the delegation's visit was over.

'Of course, of course,' he said hastily. Then, with an eye on thc other members of the Night Council, he said formally, 'We are all agreed, then, that we will work to implement our side of the Sou(ou)shi's plans?'

Twenty-three quiet 'ayes' were voiced in response; lights glimmered around, above, beyond the speakers, lending a sense of magic to the occasion.

'We thank you for your acceptance, Night Councillors of Bikugih,' said the Sou(ou)shi, all three together.

Jofghil squatted in appreciation of the courtesy, and the other Night Councillors did the same.

There was a clatter of hooves on the stone floor of the Philotirian gallery. Jofghil saw Mrak-ecado, his skin strobing with varicoloured light as he hurried towards them. There were two Sou(ou)shi with him, and he looked worried.

'The Doctor's staying behind!' he shouted.

Jofghil's first reaction was relief. The fungus-head would be out of the way for the next few days, so he wouldn't be able to interfere.

Then he thought about what the Doctor might say to the Sou(ou)shi.

Mrak-ecado had obviously thought of that too. 'I tried to talk him out of it – I told him that this was a Venusian matter – that he didn't understand – but he insisted – '

Jofghil had never seen his clan-uncle so distracted and upset. Even when Jofghil had failed his First Nomination for the Night Council, all those years ago, the Philosopher had kept his detachment, his calm demeanour.

'Don't concern yourself,' he said quickly. 'It's not your fault. I only hope the Doctor doesn't put any obstacles in the way of Venusian–Sou(ou)shi friendship.'

One of the Sou(ou)shi – or perhaps all of them – spoke.

'There will be no difficulty. Be assured of that. The Doctor was merely curious about our ways and our history. We always appreciate curiosity, and give it its appropriate response.' A pause. 'The Doctor too can be used to fertilize.'

As soon as he was reasonably sure that the big Venusian was out of sight, Ian opened his eyes. He sat up slowly, pulled the two darts out of his arm and a third one out of his leg.

'Ian Chesterton, the human pincushion,' he muttered to himself.

But at least he was still alive. Pretending to be dead had worked; the big Venusian had stood over him for a moment, prodded at him – Ian had heard the hissing sound of her breath – but then had walked away, hooves crunching on the dry soil.

He stood up, cautiously, wincing as he put his weight on the injured leg. The dart must have caught a muscle, he thought.

From inside the bud-mother's hut there was a loud thud, a terrified squeal. A sickening *snap* of bone.

Ian looked around for something that would serve as a weapon, then remembered the darts. He picked them up off the ground and trotted towards the doorway of the hut.

He stopped when he saw the children's bodies.

They were in a heap outside the hut, legs and arms stiff, contorted, the eyes filled with milky fluid, the mouths gaping flaccidly open. As he stared, blankly, another small, twitching body rolled out of the doorway and into the heap. Ian heard its bones snap as it rolled across the ground.

Ian's head filled with helpless thoughts: *I should have, why didn't I –*

There was a sound from inside the bud-mother's hut: a metallic click.

'Jellenhut?' asked Ian.

There was a movement in the doorway. Ian caught a glimpse of a red-and-black chequered belly-wrap, saw two huge legs curl back, the hooves contracting into killing points.

She's not going to use the gun this time.

Without stopping to think, Ian hurled all three of the darts he held in his hand at the shadowy form inside the hut. He saw the Venusian rear up, but she was too late. One of the darts caught her on the ankle.

She kicked once, then slumped forwards, her five hooded eyes wide with an almost human expression of astonishment. Then she was dead, her skin steaming. A stink of ammonia filled the air.

Ian looked around, saw two more Venusians a hundred yards away along the dusty track between the huts. They were wearing the same red-and-black belly-wraps as his attacker.

'Sesifghall! Sesifghall is dead!' shouted one. The other fired a gun; a dart skittered across the mud at Ian's feet.

Ian crouched down, found the dart, hurled it back. It fell short.

The Venusians halted, signalled something to each other with their hands. Then they both charged, one veering to the left, the other to the right. Their hooves thudded on the dry soil.

Ian scrambled back over Sesifghall's body and through the doorway of the bud-mother's hut. One of the dead Venusian's arms trailed through the entrance, and Ian saw a pear-shaped gun in her hand. He bent down and tried to prise the gun from between the stiffening fingers.

He was still trying when the walls of the hut burst open and the two Venusians, eye-stalks waving, reared up on either side of him.

* * *

Barbara wasn't sure whether she'd been asleep. She half-remembered strange, two-eyed dreams, all the time anxiously staring ahead . . .

She stretched, feeling the blood run into her muscles and into her brain. She noticed Trikhobu had woken up; the Venusian was sleepily moving her eyes around, taking in her surroundings.

'No wind,' she mumbled.

Barbara glanced up at the sail; it flapped, once, then fell limp. The land-yacht teetered, tipped slowly sideways.

Gejenihu flung the support boom out. It hit the ground with a shock that almost knocked Barbara off her feet.

'Tie it!' shouted Gejenihu, hurling a coil of rope along the length of the deck. Nohik-imaden caught it four-handed and hurled it lasso-style around a couple of short, stubby bushes. To Barbara's amazement, the rest of the coil flew back into the crewman's arms, in obvious breach of the laws of gravity and momentum.

While Barbara stared, Gejenihu jumped over the white arch of the wheel, landing with a complicated five-hooved thud in front of her.

Two of his eyes followed the direction of her stare, then he gaped.

'Quite handy having a magic-user as second, sometimes.'

Of course. Magic. Nohik-imaden. The long vowels, the visions. Mrak-ecado, once Mrakdihig, was a magic-user. Dharkhig – no, Dharkhig had an unconverted name. But he had always wanted –

'Sorry, we're stuck. No wind at all,' Gejenihu went on. Barbara looked up, focused on the young clanswoman with difficulty. Gejenihu made a wriggling gesture with her arms: apology, dissatisfaction. 'I should have realized – I've done this route often enough. The day is not of the right kind for a successful passage; it's too hot.'

'Don't apologize,' said Barbara gently. 'Today has been enough to confuse anybody.' She looked around. The rocky plain seemed white in the actinic Venusian sunlight. In the distance, a village straggled along a dry slope, the huts like dark blisters on burned skin. The shadows were still quite long, even though it was nearly noon; with a shock Barbara recalled, via Dharkhig, that Bikugih was almost seventy degrees north of the Venusian equator. If this was the Arctic, she wondered what the equatorial districts were like.

'We should get help from that village,' said Gejenihu. 'With any luck they'll pull us all the way to Inarihib, if you promise to buy them some food.'

Trikhobu searched in her ankle-bags, all five at once. Barbara grinned at the human-ness of the gesture. A collection of wooden shapes, like children's playing-blocks, clattered onto the deck.

'Four pyramids, nine dodecs and a couple of dozen cubes,' she announced, examining them with various eyes. 'Should be enough to feed a towing crew.'

Barbara knew that this was quite a lot of money, that Trikhobu was being incredibly generous. She wondered if the Doctor would have some sort of currency in the TARDIS that could be used to pay her friend back.

Then she remembered that she'd quarrelled with the Doctor, and scowled. She glanced at the huge bulk of the Sou(ou)shi spaceship, rearing above the northern horizon like an oversize mountain range, and hoped the old man would be more reasonable when he'd finished investigating his mysteries.

Nohik-imaden and Gejenihu had jumped down from the land-yacht and were banging chocks under the wheel.

'Are you coming with us?' shouted Nohik-imaden.

Barbara looked over the rail at the ground, twenty-five feet below, glanced at Trikhobu. Her friend squatted down, pressed her belly against the deck, tilted the top of her body in Barbara's direction.

'You'd better ride, I think,' she said.

Barbara would have preferred to go on her own two feet, but she knew that she would be more of a burden walking than she would be riding. She could only walk half as fast as the Venusians: their skins would be burned black before her slow legs had reached the village. She levered herself up onto her friend's back and sat cross-legged as she had before, with two of Trikhobu's hands in her own and a third on her back, bracing her.

Trikhobu jumped, and for a moment they were flying. The sun's light hit Barbara's face with the force of a blow; it was as if she'd jumped into the jet of a giant flame-thrower. The shock when they hit the ground was gentle by comparison.

The three Venusians set off at a fast trot. Barbara had had hopes of being cooled by the air as they moved, but it seemed to be hotter than she was. Within a minute she was soaked with sweat.

They were about half-way there when Gejenihu stopped, crouched down, signalled to the others to do the same.

'Something's up,' she said, her voice a low rumble. 'Inarihibi Inspectorate, I think.'

Trikhobu's body shifted beneath Barbara. 'But it can't be – the spaceship – '

'They wouldn't necessarily know about the spaceship,' said Nohik-imaden. 'Not if they've been out on patrol.' He gestured to the north, where a ridge of hills had risen, hiding most of the ship from view. What was left could have been mistaken for cloud, if you didn't look at it too closely.

Gejenihu spoke again.

'Definitely the Inspectorate. I can see the bodies.'

Barbara, from her perch on Trikhobu's back, peered forward at the village. But without the Venusians' hoods to shield them from the glare, her eyes could only see the dark spots of the huts – and other dark spots –

'Four dead in the street, at least,' said Gejenihu, cautiously craning her eyes upwards. 'And there's some more in the fields. Funny, I can't see any of the Inspectors. They must be finishing them off in the houses.'

'What's happening? Is the village under attack?' Barbara could find nothing in Dharkhig's memories about the Inarihibi Inspectorate, or why the name had made Trikhobu shudder.

'The Emergency Council of the City of Inarihib,' said Trikhobu, 'believes in killing people when they're not useful any more.' The anger was evident in her voice, in the stiffness of her free arms.

'You can't blame them too much,' said Nohik-imaden. 'The city would have starved by now without the policy.'

'Better starvation than murder,' rumbled Trikhobu.

The reality of the situation suddenly dawned on Barbara.

'You mean that the villagers are being killed? Because they're not useful?'

' "Uneconomic" is the word, I believe,' said Trikhobu.

'That's horrible!' Barbara glanced at the dark sliver of the Sou(ou)shi ship visible over the hills. For the first time, she realized how necessary the aliens' offer of rescue was, to a people whose only options were murder or starvation. For the sake of the Venusians, she hoped that the Doctor's evident suspicion of the newcomers was unfounded.

Dharkhig's memories muttered a protest, whispered the virtues of acceptance. She ignored them.

Aloud she said, 'We ought to tell them about the Sou(ou)shi. Then they'll stop killing the villagers.'

Gejenihu issued a prolonged, low, bubbling sound. It was a moment before Barbara realized it was a laugh.

'Inarihibi Death Inspectors aren't noted for their imagination, only for their rigid adherence to given orders. They'd probably just kill us. If we were lucky, they might tell us we were liars and spies, and then kill us.'

'But we have to do something!' Barbara's eyes were becoming accustomed to the glare; she could see movement in the village. 'People are dying for no reason!'

Trikhobu suddenly sprang upright, almost throwing Barbara off her back.

'You're right,' she said. Before anyone could reply she

had set off at a gallop towards the village.

Barbara clung on tight to Trikhobu's hands, and hoped that her friend knew what she was doing.

It took a moment for Ian to realize what was happening.

The first Venusian dropped, arms flailing, his eyes turning milky with death. The second one raised an arm, facing away from Ian, to fire a gun with a metallic twang.

Ian saw another Venusian standing in one of the ragged gaps in the wall left by the attackers, its body silhouetted against the bright sky. It leaped into the air, screaming, 'Child murderer!' The scream choked off, the body dropped to the ground, slid across the floor of the hut, crushing the cloth-covered frames.

Ian stared at it for a moment, then turned to face the surviving attacker. If he could get the gun out of the dead Venusian's hand –

But his assailant just stood there, quivering. After a moment he slumped slowly onto his belly, twitched once, and died. Ian stared, then saw the dart lodged in his arm.

Behind the body, a familiar green belly-wrap was visible through the broken part of the wall.

'Jellenhut!' he called.

There was no response.

'Jellenhut!'

Was she dead too? Ian started towards the gap in the wall, dodging the steaming bodies. He saw a gun on the floor, stooped to pick it up. It was bigger than he had thought, almost too big to hold in one hand.

Cautiously, he stepped outside.

Jellenhut was standing, quivering, in the full sunlight, all five of her eyes curled down towards the tangled bodies of her children.

There was a movement behind one of the other huts. Ian saw a red-and-black chequered belly-wrap, an arm reaching around the dried mud wall. He raised the gun in his hand, although he had no idea how to fire it. The arm withdrew.

'Jellenhut,' he said softly. 'We ought to get inside.'

The bud-mother said nothing.

There was another movement, down amongst the long dried mosses of the fields below the village. Further away, Ian saw a Venusian dart from the cover of one hut to the next.

He raised the gun, looked frantically for something that might be a trigger, found a curious depression in the wood which moved slightly when he pushed it with a finger.

He held the gun two-handed, aimed at the last place he had seen a movement, pressed the spot hard with both thumbs.

The gun jolted in his hand, and a dart flew along the track, skipping on the ground once, to halt with a clatter against a rock.

There was a scuffling sound, a patter of falling stones.

Jellenhut hadn't moved.

'Bud-mother – ' said Ian.

A single eye twitched towards him.

'We deliberately limited the numbers,' said Jellenhut at last. 'We hoped that with just a few of them, they would be able to lead the life of our ancestors, they would remember us until the End. We even thought – ' She broke off, and Ian realized that her whole body was shaking, vibrating, as if there were a machine inside it. 'They could have been happy, just for a while. For a few years.'

Suddenly she sprang forward, pulled a dart covered in purple blood from the hide of one of the children, plunged it towards her leg.

Ian jumped forwards, grasped her arm. 'No!'

Jellenhut pulled against him for a moment, then froze, quivering. The point of the dart was touching her skin. It occurred to Ian that if Jellenhut died now, she might easily kick him in a death-spasm. He imagined lying in the mud amongst the bodies, his ribs broken, waiting for the attackers to close in.

'Jellenhut,' said Ian, keeping his voice calm and slow.

'You are the first person on your world who has shown me any kindness. I want to show you kindness in return. I don't want you to die.'

Five eyes swung to stare at Ian. The lashes twitched from side to side, making a tiny clicking noise.

'It is an unkindness to persuade me to live,' said Jellenhut. 'Now that my children are gone – now that I have failed in my duty – '

Her arm began to pull against Ian's again, driving the point of the dart against her skin. Ian wrenched it back.

'You have a duty towards me,' said Ian, slowly, carefully, considering every word. 'I need you to help me stay alive. I'm alone on this world, and I don't know what's happened to my friends. If you will look after me until I find them again, then I will help you to be revenged for the deaths of your children.'

There was a long silence. Jellenhut's body began to tremble.

'I don't need revenge,' she said. 'But you are right. You are my guest. I should not leave you to – *them*.'

Inch by inch, the hand holding the dart moved upwards. Ian noticed the depression in the skin where the point had made contact. At last, Jellenhut's hand opened and the dart clattered to the floor.

Ian saw a flash of black-and-red out of the corner of his eye. Turning, he saw one of the attackers out in the open.

Ian hefted the gun he had used, aimed it, squeezed the firing button.

Nothing happened.

'Jellenhut, how – ?' he began, but he had no chance to finish the question.

With a splintering of wood and crash of falling soil, three Venusians erupted from the cover of the three nearest huts and charged towards them.

Vivojkhil watched the grey landscape of the ship hovering above her.

It *was* a landscape, she thought: there were the mountains and the circular seas, and those dark cracks might be rivers –

'I wonder if you *need* a whole world, to travel between worlds,' she said.

Anaghil shifted from the green-and-white by yellow-and-pink position in the *cog-o-cog* maze to the rainbow centre.

'I win,' she said.

Vivojkhil's eye-stalks flattened.

'Anni, I don't know how you can think about *cog-o-cog* with that – that mystery in the sky.'

Her clan-sister's eye-stalks flattened in turn.

'But it makes it nice and shady!' she complained. 'I mean, we wouldn't normally be able to play this late in the morning, it would be too hot. I say we make the most of it.'

Vivojkhil looked around the clan-childfield. Durfheg and Kigihij were piling up the dodie-boxes in some kind of formal pattern – Vivojkhil thought she recognized the *asidhallall* – as if architecture was the most important issue of the day.

For the first time in her life, Vivojkhil felt inclined to go and join the adults of her clan. Surely they would be discussing the ship and its all-important message?

She looked up at the sky again and saw something moving against the dark landscape there. She brought a couple of extra eyes to bear and realized that it was nothing to do with the ship: it was a *ghifghoni*, a big blue one of the sort that people used for long-distance messages. It was flying slowly, weaving in the air, as if it were lost or very tired.

Vivojkhil whistled to it but it took no notice.

Anaghil followed the direction of Vivojkhil's gaze.

'I think it's hurt,' she said.

As she spoke the *ghifghoni* plunged towards the ground, tried to right itself, failed and landed awkwardly on the grass.

Vivojkhil set off at a gallop towards it, with Anaghil close behind her. As they drew closer, she could see that the little flyer was seriously ill. It was limp against the ground, rotors twitching, eyes drooping.

'It's almost dead!' gasped Anaghil. She picked the *ghifghoni* up with two hands and crooned at it for a moment, then gently put it in one of her mouths. It began to lick at the sugary saliva pooled under her tongue.

'There's a lump,' said Anaghil after a moment, with a spare mouth. 'I think it's got an egg.'

She lifted the flyer carefully and pulled out a shiny object from its belly-pouch. The little creature wriggled, nipped her hand, fell out of her mouth and flopped on to the grass, gasping.

'It's a message,' said Anaghil. 'Look!'

Vivojkhil took the capsule, curled an eye close to read the writing engraved on the seal.

'"URGENT and IMPORTANT – to Jilet Mrakecado, Philosopher of Bikugih",' she read aloud.

Anaghil was silent.

'"Philosopher of Bikugih"! And "URGENT and IMPORTANT"!' Anni, we've got to take this to the clan, we've got to deliver it – '

'The *ghifghoni* is dead,' interrupted Anaghil. She reached down and touched the little creature with a finger; it rolled over on the grass, limp.

Anaghil's eyelashes blinked quickly, time after time. 'It had better be an important message,' she said.

By the time they reached the first houses Barbara could see the bodies for herself. Two of them lay amongst the stubble of *konji*, toppled together as if they had been trying to protect each other. Another was stiff, splay-legged in the centre of the main street, foam still drooling from its mouths. Trikhobu slowed down to a walk as they passed. Barbara felt her friend's body shudder.

'Irontips,' said Trikhobu, gesturing at the two small

darts sticking out of the corpse. 'The burners. Scorching, incinerating – ' She broke off, to begin again with another mouth. 'How can they do this to their own people? How can the Inarihibi go on voting for Councillors who kill in the name of survival? What promises – '

Trikhobu broke off again, pointed with an eye-stalk.

'Barbara! Is that – '

Barbara looked and saw two Venusians galloping across an open space, perhaps a hundred yards ahead; a third rolling, arms flailing, dying; and, crouched by a pile of bodies outside a part-ruined hut, an alien, two-legged, two-armed –

Not an alien.

'*Ian!*' she yelled.

A dart thudded into the ground somewhere near Trikhobu's hoof. The Venusian pulled up short, shied like a startled horse, dived into the cover of a crumbling clay wall.

Barbara let go of her friend's arms and slid down off her back, landing amidst the short, knobby stems of a *dafarji* plant.

'You'd better stay here, Trikhobu,' she said. 'Or better still, go back and fetch the others. You'll be safe there.'

'I don't understand – ' began Trikhobu.

'There's no time for a debate, just go!' Barbara tapped her friend on the lips, then started down the track at a run.

But when she got to the place with the pile of bodies and the half-ruined hut, Ian was gone. A fresh Venusian corpse lay on its side against the wall of the hut, legs twitching feebly, but there was no other movement.

'Ian! It's me! Barbara!' she shouted.

Her voice echoed from the distant hillside.

A Venusian jumped from between two of the huts, hissing like a vast snake. Barbara stared for a moment at the approaching green bulk, the gaping mouths and the waving eye-stalks, then turned wildly to the left, down towards a patch of spiky *konji*. The sound of the hooves got closer.

'Barbara!'

Ian's voice.

There was a terrifying roar, and the sun vanished. Barbara realized that the Venusian had jumped; instinctively, she dived for the ground. Too late. She felt a shaft of pain run through her shoulder into her skull; the shock half-blinded her for a moment.

When her vision came back, she was flat on her face on the hard dirt. She sat up, saw the Venusian sprawled out next to her. His mouths were gaping, his lips twitching; his eyes were filling with the milk-of-death.

'Barbara!' She turned her head and saw Ian running towards her. 'Barbara, are you all right?'

Movement to her right: two Venusians were moving in.

'Ian! Look out!'

She saw him turn, clumsily lift his gun. One of the Venusians leaped sideways for cover, the other carried on.

Ian was fiddling with a dart, trying to load the gun.

The attacker jumped.

Barbara cried out, 'Ian!', but she knew it was too late.

A heavy shadow jumped out of the doorway of the half-ruined hut, met the squadsman in mid-air. The two bodies fell to the ground in a flailing heap. Ian jumped clear, still awkwardly trying to load the gun.

Without conscious thought Barbara turned, crouched down by the dead squadsman at her feet and unstrapped the gun from his leg. Cradling it awkwardly in her alien hands, she turned to face the fighters. The squadsman had the advantage now, and was driving repeated kicks into the clanswoman's belly. Barbara saw the soiled wraps of a bud-mother, felt a sense of outrage at the barbarism of it.

Carefully, she took aim.

The dart hit the soft part of the hip-joint, precisely over the vein. The squadsman dropped instantly.

Still without thinking, Barbara turned again to the corpse. She unbuckled a quarrel of darts from the leg, pulled out a dart, reloaded, buckled the rest around her waist. She started to unbuckle a second belt of ammunition, then heard a squeal of pain, turned and saw Trikhobu struggling between two squadswomen.

She ran across the square, vaguely aware of Ian shouting behind her. If only she'd had her five eyes intact –

A hoof landed on Trikhobu's east arm; Barbara heard the sound of splitting bone. She brought the gun up as she ran, stopped, found a target, fired.

One of the attackers dropped; the other jumped back, screamed and fled up the street. Her blood up, Barbara ran after her, reloading as she went, but after a couple of *ojotti* she realized it was hopeless in this feeble two-legged body, and stopped. Her lungs were heaving and there was a regular, painful pounding in her head. Sweat dripped off her hands.

A dart thudded into her side. She pulled it out of her robe, hurled it at the attacker without looking, then turned, dived towards the squadswoman, fired.

Hit.

The squadswoman dropped, screaming. She carried on screaming, and kicking, but Barbara knew she would die.

There were another couple of Fives of them in a huddle between two half-demolished huts. Several bodies, squadsmen and villagers, lay on the dry mud around them.

Barbara waited, until she was within dart range, then reloaded the gun, raised it.

'Inarihibi! You have disgraced the honour of our people and our world! Leave this place at once or die!'

It was only when she felt the rawness in her throat that Barbara realized she was screaming at the top of her voice.

The squadsmen began to retreat, shuffling up the slope, then beginning to run. But one stopped, his eye-stalks lowered in the *highir*, the position-of-servitude.

Barbara aimed the gun.

'Sesifghall was my bud-sister,' said the clansman. 'Please – I must take the body for remembering.'

Barbara didn't move. Slowly, his body shaking, the clansman withdrew. Barbara – just – resisted the temptation to fire anyway, to let him join his bud-sister in the land-that-is-no-land.

When she was sure they were all gone, she turned and walked back to the square. She could scarcely keep her balance on two legs any more, and there was a strange humming sound in her brain. She saw the injured bud-mother arming herself with darts from one of the corpses. Ian was running across the budling-ground towards her. Trikhobu squatted in the middle of the square, her injured arm cradled between its two neighbours. Barbara ran up to her, concern and anger equally mixed in her five hearts.

'My daughter! Why are you here? How dare you disobey me?' she yelled, and fainted.

The taste of the Doctor's mind was odd, as if there were structures in it more complex than could be accounted for by his appearance. Long corridors of memory took sudden, impossible turns, and vanished; chains of thought rolled around similar hyper-dimensional corners, and returned elsewhere in the pattern, subtly altered. Pown(ow)ri, disconcerted, withdrew the psi-probe.

The Doctor glanced at him, one sharp, almost painful glance, then returned his attention to the slow, bright-coloured crystals of the sculpture in front of him.

'Definitely a very late work,' he said after a while. 'See there – ' he gestured with his cane ' – and there.'

Pown(ow)ri looked, but he couldn't see what it was that the Doctor was referring to. The mm'x crystals didn't seem to have any fixed shape or pattern; but they didn't appear to change shape either, unless you counted the soft play of colours across their faces. When Pown(ow)ri tried to look at a single crystal it was impossible to say whether it was a cube, a dodecahedron, a sphere, or some more elaborate, less regular shape; each crystal flowed into, was a part of, the surrounding matrix, yet had its own separate, undeniable identity.

Pown(ow)ri remembered the Aveletian sculptor who had made this work, the taste of his mind, the way he had died. Yes; there was a similarity. But the Doctor's mind was larger, the pattern stranger.

He wondered how the Doctor would die.

The Doctor gestured again, this time at a gloomy spread of violet that hung over the body of the sculpture like a dying sky, ever-darkening without ever getting dark. 'This work suggests to me an ending. A completion. Don't you agree?'

'I agree,' said Pown(ow)ri, carefully. 'The Aveletians were truly perceptive.'

The Doctor seemed to think for a moment, then said, 'It's a great shame the Aveletians didn't survive longer.'

'Their sun was dying; they lacked space-going capability.'

'A pity you didn't save them, as you are saving the Venusians.'

The Doctor was staring straight at Pown(ow)ri. His eyes were hard, unmoving, yet somehow in flux, as if, like the mm'x crystals, shape or colour was not of importance to them. Pown(ow)ri felt that the Doctor knew exactly what he was thinking, though he could feel no trace of a psi-probe.

With a conscious effort, he damped down his thought processes and said quietly, 'We did save the Aveletians. Their energies are within us now.'

The Doctor seemed unsurprised. He tapped the floor with his cane, and sniffed in what Pown(ow)ri suspected was a gesture of superiority. Pown(ow)ri felt his fur bristle with indignation.

'So, you consumed their mind-energy. And their bodies were used to fertilize?'

'You are correct. The planet we chose for them is now developing independent life based on the pattern of their genetic code. In a similar way, we will eat the bodies of the Venusians, and use the resulting detritus to fertilize the Earth. We are not lying when we say that we will take them there.'

The Doctor paused and seemed to meditate, stroking his chin. Pown(ow)ri waited, his mind quiet, his psi-shields up.

'Makers of worlds,' said the Doctor at last. 'By means of betrayal and excrement.' His tone was loaded with disgust.

'We destroy; we create,' said Pown(ow)ri. 'That is our function.' He spoke calmly enough, but his hands stretched in a gesture that would once have unsheathed claws.

'I wonder how my human friends would react to the idea of their creator as a species of psionic vampires?' mused the Doctor, adding, 'You're not related to the Great Vampires, by any chance?'

Pown(ow)ri had never heard of the Great Vampires. He said nothing, tried to think about his claws ripping out the Doctor's throat, slitting his belly. It felt good.

The Doctor looked up sharply.

'And what if the Venusians don't want to be destroyed? What then, eh?'

Pown(ow)ri was ready for this question.

'But they have given their permission. We have it on record.'

The Doctor frowned. 'Their permission? How? They think they're going to be – '

'We will do everything we have promised,' said Pown(ow)ri softly. 'We promised to accommodate them here. We promised to take them to Earth. We promised to remember them.' He paused. 'They have indicated, through the person of Kintibi Jofghil of the clan Poroghini Presidor of the Night Council, that they are satisfied with these promises.'

'But that is an outrageous deception! How dare you treat a civilized people in such a way?'

'How else would we get their co-operation?' Pown-

(ow)ri was genuinely puzzled. The Doctor had not seemed stupid, but it was clear that he was not familiar with even the most basic principles of diplomacy. 'Our method of communication is such that we are incapable of telling a lie, Doctor. We merely shield people from those parts of the truth which they might find uncomfortable.'

'It's still outrageous! I – I – '

The Doctor seemed lost for words. He turned his back, and for a moment Pown(ow)ri thought he was going to walk away down the darkened, winding passageway.

'May I take it that you are opposed to our plans?' he asked the alien.

He could already feel the stirring in his belly that meant his body was beginning to Change.

'Of course I am opposed!' The Doctor didn't even turn round.

Pown(ow)ri felt the muscles of his arms tense, felt the long-ago claws come into being on his hands, the long-ago teeth growing in his jaw.

'Then I regret, Doctor,' he growled, 'that we have no alternative but to kill you. I take it we have your permission?'

9

Remembering the Children

Suddenly, the sun was shining.

Vivojkhil stared up at the sky, startled; every other Venusian in the crowded street did the same.

The air was blue, clear, the eye of the sun near its midday height.

'The ship's gone!' said Anaghil.

'I can see it's gone,' said Vivojkhil.

'Got to hide from the sun!' shouted Podsighil, dancing around from hoof to hoof on the white stone of the roadway as though it had already heated up. 'Got to hide! Got to hide!'

'All right, Podsi,' said Vivojkhil, pulling the little one into the shadow of her belly. 'You'll be safe there for the moment.' She continued examining the sky, wondered where the ship had gone.

'I wonder what the reward will be,' mused Anaghil.

'Reward?' asked Vivojkhil, confused, her mind still in the sky.

'For bearing the message to the Philosopher.'

'I hadn't thought about it,' said Vivojkhil, truthfully. She put a hand in her lip-pouch, felt the smooth shape of the pod they had taken from the dying *ghifghoni*. 'A cube or two if we're lucky, I suppose.'

'A cube or two!' piped Podsighil from somewhere close to Vivojkhil's belly. 'A cube or two for me! A cube or two for me!'

Curious adult eyes curled towards them.

'I told you not to bring Podsi!' hissed Anaghil, flushing blue with embarrassment.

'You started it,' rejoined Vivojkhil crossly, then quickly changed the subject before her clan-sister could start an argument. 'Look! There's not far to go now – just down to the trees, there.'

As she spoke, she saw a clansman in the blue belly-wrap of a Philosopher pacing in the shade of the tall *binihabeg* trees.

She picked up Podsi and accelerated to a canter, ignoring Anaghil's protests. Somehow she felt she really had to get this message to Jilet Mrak-ecado as soon as possible. After all, the *ghifghoni* had died trying to deliver it.

'Philosopher!' she called as she reached the gate. The clansman was out of sight now, behind the gleaming brown dome of his villa.

'I'm busy!' came the irritable reply, echoing around the chitin and stone. 'There are many matters about which I need to have debate with myself. I have no time for children.'

Anaghil came up, hooves clattering.

'What have I missed?' she asked.

'Nothing,' hissed Vivojkhil. Then, three-mouthed: 'I have an urgent message for Jilet Mrak-ecado! Delivered by *ghifghoni*!'

There was a pause, the sound of hooves on soil, then the Philosopher appeared. He was heavily built, with long eye-stalks, his skin here and there turning to yellow.

'You are Jilet Mrak-ecado?' asked Vivojkhil timidly.

The Philosopher's eye-stalks twitched in assent.

'We found this.' She fished the pod out of her lip-pouch.,

Mrak-ecado took it, examined the seal.

'Afhighid Kontojij!' he muttered. 'I'd thought he was long dead.'

He broke the seal, pulled out the scroll.

Vivojkhil politely looked away, letting her eyes rove the crowded street. She noticed two clanswomen in uniforms of the Presidor's office quietly examining everyone who passed. Both had an eye firmly fixed on Vivojkhil and her clan-sister.

She felt her belly tighten a little.

'Thank you,' said Mrak-ecado suddenly. 'You were right to bring this message to me privately. If you could leave now, I would be grateful.'

'Leave?' asked Anaghil. 'But there's a reward if – '

Vivojkhil literally jumped in front of her sister's mouth.

'I'm sorry, honoured one, I had to bring her,' she stuttered. 'She is young and did not mean – '

But Mrak-ecado merely waved an arm at each of them, then strode away into the shadow of his villa.

'He doesn't have to give us a reward, clan-sister,' hissed Vivojkhil furiously.

'But – '

There was the sound of a heavy door closing somewhere in the villa.

'I think we ought to stay around and see if he gives us a reward later,' said Anaghil.

'And I think that would be rude,' said Vivojkhil. 'We were asked to leave.'

She pressed Podsi firmly against her belly and set off up the hill. After a while, Anaghil followed her.

'I need your help,' said Jellenhut.

The Venusian was standing somewhere behind him. Ian could see her bulk in the corner of his eye. But he didn't look away from Barbara's flushed, unconscious face.

'I need you to help me remember my children,' Jellenhut went on. 'Is your clanswoman well enough to be left on her own?'

Ian glanced up, but still kept the damp cloth pressed against Barbara's forehead. His first impulse was to say no. Barbara hadn't stirred since she'd collapsed after the battle; Ian and Jellenhut had lifted her body into the shade of the hut, and Jellenhut had provided a bowl of cool water and a cloth. But although Ian had splashed enough water on

Barbara's face to leave her hair dripping wet, he could still feel the unnatural heat of fever on her skin.

'What do you want me to do?' he asked.

A pause. Ian felt the warm sweat running down his own face, and wondered if Barbara simply had heatstroke.

'Trikhobu has told me that your people cannot eat large portions,' said Jellenhut. 'But I would be honoured if you felt able to eat perhaps a couple of the smaller children. Their memories would be as happy in your clan as mine, I am certain.'

Ian stared at the alien, standing half in, half out of the sunlight, four of her eyes fixed on him in obvious expectation. Around her was the brassy silence of the Venusian noon, the violent heat rippling up from the ruins of the mud huts.

'You want me to help you *eat your children*?'

Jellenhut's eye-stalks twitched.

'How else would we remember them?'

Ian recalled the funeral. Barbara and the Doctor eating the sweet pancakes.

Eat, remember . . .

And Barbara, who had a fever and seemed to think she was a Venusian.

'We do not eat all the body,' said Jellenhut into the silence. 'Just the memory-parts of the brain.'

Ian thought for a moment, then said quietly, 'Jellenhut, I respect your customs, but I think that it might be dangerous for me to – '

'You don't understand.' Barbara's voice, interrupting him.

Startled, Ian looked down, saw that her eyes were open. When she saw him looking, she smiled.

'Hello, Ian. It's all right, I'm me again now. Where's Trikhobu?'

'Gone to get help – from the land-yacht, she said.' He paused. 'How do you feel?

'Hot, and I've got a rotten headache.' She pushed his hand away from the cloth on her forehead, began rubbing her face with it. When she sat up, she winced and grabbed Ian's arm for support. She stared at his burned hands. 'What happened to them?'

'I got stuck in a burning forest. Jellenhut reckons it's a miracle that I got out. What happened to your shoulder?' He could see the bruise, green and purple, spreading up her neck.

'I got blown up by someone representing – oh, I think it was the Magnetologists; then I was standing in the wrong place when a tunnel collapsed.'

They looked at each other, and both grinned broadly.

'Pretty much as usual, then,' offered Ian.

'Well, at least we're both still alive,' said Barbara, pushing herself upright. She winced again, then spoke more seriously: 'We should help the bud-mother now.'

She started towards the door of the hut, into which Jellenhut had silently withdrawn at some point in the conversation.

Ian stared after her.

'Are you sure it's safe? To – eat them, I mean.'

Barbara stopped, turned, frowned at him.

'Of course it's safe! Venusians have been doing it for thousands of years.'

Ian got up, but his doubts must have shown on his face because Barbara said quietly, 'It hasn't hurt me – in fact, it's helped me survive. And we still need to get back to Bikugih, find the Doctor – '

'Yes, what has happened to the Doctor?' asked Ian. 'Why isn't he with you?'

He looked around, half-expecting to see the old man striding across the empty village, swishing his cane and frowning at the scattered bodies of the dead. But nothing moved.

'We – uh – had a row,' Barbara was saying. 'He didn't want to – that is, I – '

Ian turned back to Barbara and discovered she was blushing. He raised his eyebrows. What had the Doctor said that she was so embarrassed about?

'He wanted to go on the spaceship,' said Barbara, looking down.

Ian frowned. 'I didn't think the Venusians had any spaceships. Not any that could fly, anyway.'

'It isn't Venusian, it's Sou(ou)shi. They've come to rescue the Venusians. Fly them all away.'

Ian stared at her.

'Who are the Sou(ou)shi?'

'They're a sort of alien. Like big monkeys. They say they're something to do with – ' she hesitated ' – the cycle of life. I think that was it.'

'And they're going to fly the Venusians away in a fleet of spaceships?' It sounded wildly improbable to Ian; he wondered if Barbara had been hallucinating.

'One spaceship. It's about the size of a biggish mountain.' Barbara's voice was matter-of-fact enough. 'You could see it, over there, if the hills weren't in the way.' She gestured towards the north. Ian stared, seeing nothing but the bone-dry ridge rising against the sky.

'Actually, I didn't think much of the Sou(ou)shi,' Barbara went on. 'They were creepy, if you know what I mean. I think that the Doctor thought so too – that's why he wanted to go and have a look.'

Ian took Barbara's arms, turned her to face him, looked into her eyes.

'Look at me, Barbara,' he said. 'Are you sure about all this?'

She returned his gaze steadily. 'I'm not mad, Ian. And this is nothing to do with Dharkhig's memories. The ship is there. The Doctor got on it. Ask Trikhobu.' She paused. 'We need to get back to Bikugih, quickly, and find out what's really happening. And you need to remember a Venusian before we go, otherwise you're not going to be able to cope.'

Ian swallowed. He was suddenly aware of his hands hurting where they gripped Barbara's arms.

'You have to trust me,' said Barbara.

The silence lengthened. At last it was broken, by a

rich, deep, Venusian voice:

> 'Close your last eye, my little ones, and fold your last leg into the belly of your sleep, of your endless, endless, sleep.'

Jellenhut was singing the lullaby to her children for the last time.

Ruribeg watched as Bismar Mrodtikdhil of the clan Esinallihall, Commander of the Volcano People, looked three-eyed at the picture taken by the mossocular, and wondered what his clan-uncle was thinking.

The old clansman didn't say anything, which constrained Ruribeg to be silent. Occasionally Ruribeg heard him scribble something on a writing-pad on the other side of his body, out of sight.

Ruribeg waited, one eye on the Commander, the other four wandering around the *dihilribi* mosses on the walls of the stone room, the golden flames of the *brakud*-oil lamps hanging from the ceiling, the pattern of lava flows carved into the polished wooden legs of the Commander's five-sided desk.

'And the entire Night Council of Bikugih went up in this – ' he pointed at the streak on the mossoculograph ' – this "light craft"?'

'They did,' said Ruribeg, adding, 'according to the public heliogram.' He paused, wondered if his clan-uncle considered that he should have gone to the rollerport and checked it for himself.

'And what exactly did the aliens say?'

Ruribeg repeated it, word for word, from his notes. He felt an obscure pride that he had managed to take any notes in such a sudden and confusing situation; though at the time it had never occurred to him to do anything else.

When he had finished reading, the Commander thought for a while in silence, his eyes in the *kirhi* position. Finally he said, 'The intervention of these aliens may be of great benefit to the Volcano People. They may even enable us to realize our plans at last. But we need to be sure.'

The Commander was silent again for a while, but this time four of his eyes were staring directly at Ruribeg. Discomfited, Ruribeg shifted from hoof to hoof, trying not to commit the impropriety of hiding his eyes.

'Gantohi Ruribeg,' said the Commander at last. 'There is something you need to know. But it is of the highest confidentiality.'

Ruribeg swallowed, then gaped in formal acceptance of the burden of secrecy.

'We possess a means of looking into the future.'

Ruribeg stared. 'But I thought – '

' – that the Art died with Cracdhalltar? No. Not quite. There is one clansman left who knows the Art of *huyaot*. His name is Afhighid Kontojij. He has been invaluable to us; his advice has often prevented the interference of the city-dwellers in our plans.

'I think you should visit him immediately.'

The Doctor gazed at the marble building with its low, silver dome, took a deep breath of the *jetheru*-scented air, and wondered if he ought to have accepted Pown(ow)ri's offer of death. The silly, growling creature had looked so disappointed when he'd said no. He stretched out his hands in front of him, looked at the deep wrinkles, the knobby irregularities of the knuckles, and thought about pain. He looked up at the *mereon* again, wished that he hadn't seen its like before, a hundred hundred times, somewhere else, somewhen else, wished that it still had the power to move him.

Slowly he walked up to the building between rows of pink and green *jetheru*; across the marble bridge over the tiny, utterly clear stream. The Sou(ou)shi, he reflected, had spared no cost in keeping this gift of art in its original setting. He approached one of the sixty-four silver doors that were set in the marble wall. He looked at the almost-human, but dwarf-sized, figure moulded in bas-relief there. Its eyes seemed to darken as his shadow passed over it.

He looked at the drooping ears, the shadowy third eye in the high forehead, the lines that bisected the cheeks, and tried to feel it: *sorrow, sorrow, we are leaving home, we will never return.* But the words remained words, the action of intellect upon perception.

He wondered how Susan was getting on, though he – of all people – should know how idiotic the thought was. Susan wasn't 'getting on' *now* at all; she *would be* 'getting on' in about three and a half billion years' time. But still the Doctor found himself thinking: a day has passed, two days, she will be with David, they will be planning a wedding in some half-ruined church, choosing a place to live –

And then –

'How will you tell him, my dear?'

I can't bear your children, David, my people and yours are not cross-fertile –

Maybe they would adopt a child, one of the many orphans of the terrible war; or more than one child. He imagined Susan, happy in the middle of her huge family, teaching her children Earth-things, half-forgetting her own inheritance. And David growing older . . .

Would she try to disguise it? Dye her hair, perhaps? Put something on her skin to make it dry and wrinkled? How long would it be before she had to admit the truth?

I won't grow old, David, not for hundreds of years. My people are – different. But I'll put flowers on your grave, David, flowers on your grave . . .

The Doctor swiped the air with his stick, felt it slash into a *jetheru* bush he hadn't even seen. Petals scattered onto the granite paving; some eight-fingered thing native to the world of the *mereon*-builders chittered and scurried away, invisible under the leaves.

Yes, thought the Doctor, surveying the rows of flowers through misted eyes, maybe the Sou(ou)shi way was for the best: a few seconds of terror, and then the end. Better than all this stitching and patching and mending of history, the good intentions that go astray, the misery that can never be prevented, the child deprived of her inheritance by an old man's whim of rebellion and curiosity.

'I have my duty to my friends.' That was what he had told Pown(ow)ri, when he had refused the alien's offer. To his surprise, the Sou(ou)shi representative had merely nodded, and told him that in that case he would have to be confined on the ship until the 'energy-saving operation' was over.

But –

'My duty.' What was his duty to the Venusians? To save them from the Sou(ou)shi, and thus condemn them to fifty or a hundred years of struggling on in ever-increasing misery until the fire came down from the mountains and swallowed them all? And Ian and Barbara?

He stopped, blinked. Ian. And Barbara.

What had Barbara said? 'I am not a piece of Susan.'

But that was what he had told his old friend Mrakecado: that Susan was still with him, albeit in two parts. He realized now that he had half-believed it himself.

'You must make your own life.' He had told Susan that, but he himself had failed to break the bond.

As he must do. Now.

How old was Barbara? Twenty-five years?

'And how old am I?'

The Doctor swished his stick again, gazed at the little stream running between the bushes, the marble bridge.

'Old enough to know better,' he answered himself. 'Old enough not to leave my friends on an alien planet while I wallow in self-pity up here. Old enough to know evil when I see it, and try to put a stop to it.'

He wiped his eyes, pulled at the lapels of his jacket, and set off purposefully down the path.

There was a job to do.

The memory part of Inikhut's brain was the size of a saucer, and about an inch thick. It was whitish, pale in the dim light of the hut, lined with purple blood vessels. Jellenhut held it in three hands, offered it to Ian.

'Eat, remember.'

Ian took the slippery piece of flesh awkwardly, almost dropped it. He held it in his hands and glanced at Trikhobu, whose eye-stalks twitched. Behind her, Nohik-imaden made a soft bubbling sound and muttered, 'Mi-ma! Mii-i-ma!'

'Go on, Ian,' said Barbara softly from the doorway. Her face was in shadow against the glare outside. Ian couldn't see her expression.

Barbara and Gejenihu had been chosen to keep watch while the others remembered; having seen Barbara handle a Venusian gun, Ian had to agree that it made sense. But, even though Trikhobu had confirmed Barbara's story about the Sou(ou)shi ship, Ian wasn't convinced that Barbara was entirely normal after her dose of Dharkhig. She didn't ordinarily run around killing people, for example. Not even alien people.

He brought the flesh to his mouth and bit off a tiny piece. It didn't taste sweet at all in this raw condition; it was fatty and slightly salty, like melted cheese. Looking around the hut, he saw that Trikhobu and Nohik-imaden were also eating, five-mouthed, whole portions at once.

'Can you eat more?' said Jellenhut with the mouth facing Ian.

It was a simple question, not a request. Ian was very tempted to say no. But Barbara was still looking down at him from the doorway. She needed someone to trust her, Ian realized; she was isolated, afraid, in her half-Venusian state.

He took another bite of the – he tried not to think of it as brain; of the food. Cheese. Yes, he thought, I'm eating cheese. It's a bit runny, a bit mushy here and there, but not bad. And it would be rude to refuse a gift. He swallowed, took another mouthful, another. Somewhere in the middle of the fourth mouthful he noticed Barbara relax; she nodded at Jellenhut and stepped through the doorway into the glare outside.

Feeling a little dizzy, Ian turned his eyes away from the door. Jellenhut took the piece remaining in his hands and quietly put it in one of her own mouths.

'The effect is less without the preparation,' she noted. 'But Trikhobu is right. I should not expect you to risk too many memories in your small brain.'

Ian nodded, but secretly wondered why his mother was trying to protect him. He was seven now: quite old enough to eat funeral meat. His brain wasn't that small! Then he smelled the blood, looked around the hut, saw the stained cloths, the strange adults, the guns. There *was* something wrong.

'Who died, mamma?' he asked.

But before his mother could reply, there was a commotion outside the hut: thuds, squeaks. A strange animal screamed. Frightened, he ran up to his mother, huddled against her belly.

The animal screamed again. 'Ian! Help me! IAN!' There was something familiar about the sound.

'We should help – ' he heard his mother rumble. But Ian clung to her tighter in a fresh surge of panic, refusing to let her go.

He had just realized that three of his eye-stalks were missing.

Gwebdhallut whirled in mid-air and felt his hoof connect solidly with the stickwalker, the deadlier of the two, the one that they had left on guard. It cartwheeled in the air, landing with a limp thud next to the still-twitching body of the dead Venusian guard.

Gwebdhallut paused for a moment, not even breathing, listening for sounds from inside the hut.

The repeated thuds of someone jumping. An adult voice calling 'Meat-ies! Meat-ies!' with an oddly childish inflection. Nothing that indicated any alarm. They were remembering the dead, as he had known they would.

Good.

Up till this moment, Gwebdhallut had wished the rest of the squad was with him – to provide cover, or to provide a diversion. Now he was glad that the cowards had gone home; he would be able to take his revenge for Sesifghall alone.

He wheeled again, leaped over the body of the Venusian and into the doorway of the hut. As his eyes adjusted to the dim light, he saw the other alien – the one that had killed Sesifghall – crouching against the bud-mother's belly. The bud-mother was unarmed, eyes hooded with remembering.

The alien began to sing in a thin, high voice, 'Close your eyes – or three of them at least – '

The lullaby. Gwebdhallut paused for an instant, wondering what the alien was remembering. Then he moved in for the kill.

Kontojij woke with a start, staring blearily at the rough walls of his sleeping-room. What had woken – ?

A rustling sound. A clatter of chitin on stone.

There was something in the laboratory.

The heat prickled on Kontojij's skin. He tried to get up, yelped as his bad leg refused to support him. Balancing awkwardly, four-legged, he remembered the *huyaot*, the aliens, the killings.

The rustlings from the laboratory continued.

I'm going to die, thought Kontojij. They've come to kill me. And: at least I got the message away first.

Rustle-rustle. Click. The ticking of small feet on the stone floor of the lab.

'*Chff*-rrr?'

Kontojij's belly almost fell to the floor in relief.

'Miraghoni!' he called.

The sound of hurrying little feet, a single clicking sound. The little flyer appeared in the doorway, his rotors slowly whirling.

'Rrr-rrr-rrr!'

Kontojij hobbled across the floor, reached up to pat the

ghifghoni and received a nip on the fingers for his pains.

'So you decided to stay behind, then?'

'*Chff* – rrr!'

Kontojij allowed a couple of his mouths to widen in a gape. Miraghoni must have missed out on breakfast altogether, and thus missed eating the memory paste – that was why he was still here. The flyer was hungry.

'I'll see what I can find for you,' he said.

It occurred to Kontojij as he went for the box that he hadn't had his own breakfast. He wondered whether he ought to eat something now; but he didn't feel hungry. He picked a rasher of *pekatisi* out of the box for Miraghoni, wondered why the flyer hadn't helped himself. A lifetime's habit of laziness, he supposed.

He hobbled back to Miraghoni, who had hopped up on to the writing-desk in the sleeping-room. Kontojij noticed the bulge in the flyer's belly-pouch where the message-pod was lodged. He wondered whether he should take it out and save himself from having to write another copy of his report to leave for his visitors tonight. Then he wondered whether there was any point in struggling down the slope with it anyway, with his leg so bad: surely it would be too late by then for the warning to be of any use.

He decided to think about it later, tore the *pekatisi* rasher into strips and fed it to Miraghoni.

'*Chff-chff*. Rrr,' demanded the little flyer when all the pieces were gone.

'Greedy!' scolded Kontojij, but his hearts weren't in it. The world might end tonight. What did it matter how much Miraghoni ate now, if it kept him happy?

There was the sound of splashing water from the lab.

Kontojij's eye-stalks flattened. He jumped up through the doorway and looked around. The *nijij* were stirring and thrashing in their tank, bumping against the glass.

Kontojij's earlier sense of unease returned. He shuffled closer to the tank, saw that one of the star-shaped animals had somehow got loose from its shackles. It was blundering around in the cloudy water, setting the *anteyon* receivers swaying.

Kontojij reached into the water with his north hand, trying to catch the slippery creature; and was rewarded by a crooked wrist as one of the legs wrapped around him with the convulsive strength of panic. He dragged the *nijij* out of the water, but he was too late. Its exposed brain burst open, sending jets of purple blood across his arm, the sides of the tank and into the water.

Cursing, Kontojij lifted the twitching body out of the tank, started across the lab to the doorway with a vague idea of throwing the body outside.

Then he stopped dead. A pale blue glow was coming from the predicting-crystal.

But he wasn't in the *geheron* state – the effect prism wasn't in place –

On the other side of the laboratory, there was a clatter of chitin on stone as a window-blind fell into place, shutting out some of the afternoon light. A second blind fell; then the outer door swung shut. The blue glow from the crystal brightened, seemed to spread out, flakes of blue light dancing in the air.

The words 'manifestation of psi-force' trickled through Kontojij's head, as if he were contemplating making a written report on the subject. He dropped the dead *nijij* on the floor.

The water in the *nijij* tank darkened and filled with purple blood. Small objects rose into the air, tumbled, whirled: inkmoths, the glass beaker still dirty with memory-paste, pieces of leafribbon. Some of them began to glow.

Kontojij felt something brush his south leg; he watched splinters of blue light whirl around him. His belly tightened with a sudden lurch of panic that brought bile to his throats. He knew that he had to get out. But as soon as he moved, hands grabbed his legs – no, they grabbed *inside* his legs, yanking at tendons, twisting at bone. He took a chance on it being an illusion and stumbled forward, then howled with pain as he discovered his mistake.

A shape began to form around the predicting-crystal and the bloodied ruins of the tank. An alien shape, two-legged, only partially symmetrical. It glowed a fierce, painful blue. The shape took a few strange, bipedal steps towards him.

'Who are you?' he asked, trying to ignore the pain now coursing through every part of his body. 'Why are you doing this?'

But Kontojij's time for asking why was over. The alien reached out its two glowing arms, as if to touch his lips. But the glowing arms moved on *through* his skin, bringing unbearable pain, as if he were being burned from the inside. Kontojij felt bones and membranes snap, twist, crush. He tried to scream, but his throats were filled with blood.

His last coherent sensation was of alien hands, like sun-hot *anteyon* receivers within his body, feasting on the terror radiated by his dying brain.

Pown(ow)ri watched the Doctor walk into the shuttle bay with an immeasurable sense of relief. The alien had stayed so long in the *mereon* gardens that Pown(ow)ri had begun to wonder whether he might actually keep to the terms of the agreement, and thus remain alive; but clearly he had merely been planning his escape, or perhaps trying to lull any watchers into a sense of false security.

Either way, it wouldn't be long now.

Pown(ow)ri leaned against the metal shelf of the observation bubble and touched a control which lensed the one-way glass to give him a close-up view of the alien. The Doctor walked slowly through the huge space, looking around him, taking in everything. He ignored the big, showy, wingless shuttle that had been used to ferry the Venusian delegation to and from the ship. Pown(ow)ri had not expected him to do otherwise; it was obvious from the view through the glass windows of the bay that they were now in high orbit. A non-manoeuvrable shuttle was not likely to be of much use. The Doctor similarly ignored a couple of square, burn-scarred freight shuttles that had been left by the Signortiyu people; perhaps he thought they looked too battered to be safe. Finally he chose a small, aerodynamic shuttle with delta wings and clean titanium power units, a recent gift from the Gowenn people. He walked around it once at a distance, then examined it more closely, as if checking for booby-traps. Then, with a curious shaking of his head, he tapped his stick against the cabin door.

It didn't open, of course.

Pown(ow)ri waited.

The Doctor tried talking to the door; then he found the coded panel and punched in a few codes. None of them worked. He paced up and down for a while, shaking his head from time to time; then his face brightened, he gave an exclamation, and moved towards a point at the rear of the shuttle.

There was a sealed hatch, and a large purple button. The Doctor pressed the button.

The hatch opened with a thud of explosive bolts; it almost hit the Doctor on the head. He hesitated for a moment, then scrambled up through the new entrance. Inside, Pown(ow)ri had no cameras. But the shuttle's on-board computer reported that the Doctor cracked the code for the launch sequence in record time, using an 'unknown sonic device'.

Pown(ow)ri's respect for the Doctor's powers increased.

The shuttle began to move, rolling on a magnetic track towards the bay doors. The Doctor had omitted to enter the unlock code for the doors – perhaps he didn't think there was one – so Pown(ow)ri helpfully entered it for him. He had, after all, promised the Doctor that he would not be harmed as long as he stayed on the ship.

The shuttle moved through the doors. Zooming the observation bubble lens to maximum power, Pown(ow)ri caught a brief glimpse of the Doctor sitting in the control seat of the shuttle, cheerfully pulling at levers. Perhaps he thought he was really piloting it; perhaps not.

The shuttle began to accelerate, riding the same gravity-controlled pathway that the larger shuttle had used to reach the planet's surface. It shrank to a silver cross, then to a star drifting through the thin reaches of the Venusian upper atmosphere.

Then the pathway ran out.

The safety buffers had been switched off, of course; no Sou(ou)shi had any intention of using a shuttle while they were so far above the planet's surface. As the thin air caught it, the shuttle twitched and bobbed like a piece of discarded wood floating on rough water. A trail of vapour emerged from one of the power units. For a few seconds, Pown(ow)ri had the impression that the craft was flying. He imagined the Doctor wrestling with the controls, struggling to stabilize the re-entry at this impossible angle.

The shuttle began to glow red, then orange. The power unit shut down. The craft made one last frantic twist in the air before it split into several parts. Pown(ow)ri watched the scatter of sparks fall through the atmosphere until they had either burned out or were too faint to see. Then he moved his face in a pattern he had copied from the Doctor.

He smiled.

Book Four

The Grey Water Hour

10

News

Kintibi Jofghil of the clan Poroghini looked around at the vast crowd and allowed all five of his mouths to gape in a smile. He supposed that Dharkhig in his heyday might have drawn such a large crowd as this, but he was sure that his clan-uncle could never have presided over such a happy one. From his position on the Presidor's speech-podium, in the middle of the lawns, Jofghil could see them packed into the gardens of the Apartments, arm-against-hip, ankle-against-belly, eyes craning up at him, bodies swaying in appreciation even though he hadn't yet said a word. Beyond, where the shadow of the buildings ran out, there were sunshades up against the noon glare: pink, purple, green, grey, yellow, black, blue, orange, red, white, they spread out over the lawns, spilled over the walls, flowed up the slight incline of South-west Grand Avenue – and, Jofghil had been told, down Marhipil Avenue and Dharkhig Avenue, and Brehigu Street and the Cracdhall, though of course they couldn't see him from there. Sunshades covered all the high chitin domes and the older slate-gabled roofs of the ancient city; even the top of the Tower of the Night Council was smudged with colours. It was as if giant flowers had sprouted everywhere, careless of the killing noon sun.

It was a noisy crowd; they were cheering at nothing, foot-juggling with household ornaments, or chanting random phrases from favourite recitals, from dance-chants, from lullabies – any sound or movement which could be used to express joy. Children were running around, rattling wooden *behi-behi*, beating clackers together, shouting or leaping up into the lower branches of the *chedhanhig* trees; others were tearing cloth into small pieces and hurling it from the roofs. It fell in coloured clouds, disappeared under the feet of the crowd. Jofghil wondered whether anyone would bother to clear up the mess, or whether they would leave Bikugih forever tonight with a hoof-deep litter of cloth in its streets.

Leave. Forever. Tonight.

The thought was like a cold shock in his belly: most of these people would be on the Sou(ou)shi ship by dawn tomorrow. Many of them would never see another sunrise on Venus. It was impossible, unbelievable.

But it was true.

He bent an eye down to look at his notes, blooded a writing-claw, scribbled, 'never see another sunrise – seems impossible – but *true*.' After a moment's thought he drew a ring around the new words, and a line to indicate where he should say them: after item three on Mrak-ecado's carefully prepared list of points.

It had always been like this throughout Jofghil's career. Mrak-ecado had prepared the agenda; Jofghil had provided his own unique, emotive flourishes to help sell it to the crowds. They worked well together.

Jofghil took one last look around the crowd, then drew himself up, curved his eyes into the *didhabhir*, or position-of-speech-making: a perfect five-pointed star. An expectant hush spread across the crowd. Juggling stopped, children were silenced.

Then Mrak-ecado came into the sight of Jofghil's south eye, hurrying along the path between the lines of guards. The old Philosopher's skin was blue with exertion; he made frantic, repeated need-to-speak signs, three-handed, towards Jofghil.

Confused and a little irritated, Jofghil stepped off the podium and descended the wooden stairs. The crowd began making puzzled murmurs.

Mrak-ecado drew up, gasping for breath.

'I have news,' he said. 'Urgent news. For you alone,

old friend.' He waved his arms at the guards, the press of curious bodies and craning eye-stalks beyond.

'It can wait, surely?' asked Jofghil. 'These people are expecting a speech.'

Mrak-ecado's eyes darted around.

'No – no. The speech is less important than what I have to say.'

They were speaking quietly, but not quietly enough. Whispers were spreading in the crowd.

' – something's happened – '

' – news of the aliens – '

' – I knew it was all a – '

Jofghil hastily ushered Mrak-ecado down the stone path between the lines of guards, and in through the ceremonial doors of the Apartments. They crossed the high, ceramic-tiled porch, passed the guards on the inner doors and entered the great hall.

'Well, old friend?'

Jofghil's voice echoed from the galleries and balconies and benches, the high wooden tables, the long slots of the shuttered windows.

Mrak-ecado seemed to hesitate for a long time, then said, 'I have some new information about the aliens.'

'Which ones?' asked Jofghil.

Again the long hesitation.

'I believe – my old friend the Doctor. He has somehow become – involved.'

'Involved in what?' Jofghil tapped a couple of hooves impatiently. 'I think I should ask you to get to the point, old friend. The people are waiting for my words.'

'Let me tell you what happened. I have received a message by *ghifghoni* from my old friend Kontojij, the last of the Cracdhalltari. He keeps alive the art of *huyaot*, of looking into the future.'

'I have heard of it,' said Jofghil doubtfully.

'He performed a *huyaot* this morning. He saw many people being killed – perhaps everyone in the world. And in the place where they were dying, he saw – '

Mrak-ecado broke off. For a moment his voice echoed, then silence.

'What did he see?' asked Jofghil.

Mrak-ecado seemed to shake himself, finding his concentration with an obvious effort.

'A blue box with a white flashing light. That's what Kontojij said. The Doctor's ship. He saw it in the *huyaot*, though he has never seen it in life. He saw it destroy something that looked like the inside of the Sou(ou)shi ship, though he has never seen that either. And all the people in the world were aboard.'

Mrak-ecado's legs began to jerk uncontrollably, little proto-kicks of anger and distress.

'I don't want to believe Kontojij, clan-nephew. But I have to. The Doctor is already aboard the Sou(ou)shi ship; we have no knowledge of what he may be doing there.' The Philosopher took a breath, then declaimed formally, three-mouthed, his belly tight with pain: 'Presidor, it is my duty to inform you that the Doctor is planning to kill us all.'

Jellenhut looked at the sky. It was shining like a sheet of poisonous yellow metal; dark streaks of cloud were forming on the northern horizon. The light reflected from the wood of the land-yacht's deck; from the planks of the central pentagonal cabin; from the polished chitin of the rail, making each look as if it were made from some alloy of iron: ugly, and dangerous. Beyond the rail, the dry stalks of wild *konji* twitched and rustled, disturbed by random puffs of wind. In the distance, the hills were black.

'A storm is coming,' Jellenhut said quietly to Nohikimaden.

The young magic-user twitched an eye-stalk in response. Three of his arms were working to let out the green cloth cradle of the cargo winch; the other two were slowly uncoiling the rope.

'Looks like a bad one,' he replied, surveying the clouds

with a spare eye. 'The wind will be pulling west soon; it would be easier to go to Inarihib.'

'But hardly wise.' Jellenhut gestured at the distant village. 'News of our – ' she hesitated ' – resistance may have reached the city by now.'

'Hardly wise to risk the Bikugih route either.' Nohik-imaden finished laying out the winch cradle, patted it flat, let it slip over the side. 'The road's almost certain to flood.'

'We can't stay here.'

'It would be less risky.'

'The Death Inspectors may come back. We couldn't fight all of them.'

'After the fright that Trikhobu's alien gave them, I would think the chances of their return are a lot less than the chances of being washed out on the road.'

Nohik-imaden began winding the winch out. The cogs made faint groaning sounds, like an animal in pain.

Jellenhut felt a surge of irritation at the complacent young magic-user. He might be too young to understand how she felt in the face of the massacre of her children and her people, but he could at least show some response of his own to the killings, or to the loss of his crew-sister Gejenihu, instead of this mechanical detachment that she supposed he called 'Philosophy'.

'Okay! I've got it!' Trikhobu's voice came from the ground below where she was waiting with Barbara. Jellenhut leaned over and peered down with two eyes, saw Trikhobu gently lifting the alien on to the winch cradle.

No one was sure how badly Barbara was hurt. She hadn't moved or made a sound since they'd found her; she was breathing, a little, but Venusians who were breathing like that were invariably being remembered by the following day. She had lost a lot of blood before Jellenhut had bound her wound; it stained Trikhobu's belly-wrap an incongruous bright red.

The winch began groaning again, a longer and more agonized sound, as Nohik-imaden lifted Barbara aboard.

'Can you sail?' he asked suddenly. 'With two there would be a much better chance of keeping control if there's any trouble.'

Jellenhut spread her arms helplessly. 'I am a bud-mother; my only duty – '

'I can sail!' piped Ian from the shade of the cabin. His voice still carried the inflections of Inikhut's; for some reason, the remembering had given him the temporary impression that he was Inikhut, rather than merely sending him to the fields of the past. His every word made Jellenhut wince. 'I went sailing with Henefenhut last – last – ' But the child in Ian trailed off, confused, his sense of time broken by death. Jellenhut closed her eyes in pain.

It hadn't been easy to kill the Death Inspector. She was a bud-mother, sworn to protect life, trained to nurture it. Even with her children dead, and Ian clinging to her leg screaming for protection with Inikhut's voice, it had taken all Jellenhut's willpower to drive the spent dart into Gwebdhallut's leg. Watching his death agony had been like feeling her own.

It would be easy for her to die now; but she had her duty.

'Bud-mother – ' It was Nohik-imaden.

Jellenhut opened her eyes, saw Ian curled up on the deck, arms flailing in distress. She ran to him, put three of her arms around him, drew him against the hard bone of her hip.

'Mii-ma,' squealed Ian. 'Mii-i-ma! Hurr-rr-ts!'

His soft body, thought Jellenhut. His alien body. I can't even comfort him.

She held on as best she could, three of her eyes on the darkening sky.

Five hundred *ojotti* to the north-east of Bikugih, at a point on the coast called Sisikhigu's Beach, an alien biped about one tenth of one *ojotti* tall was stuffing crystals into its pockets. The wind blew out of a grey sky, across a grey sea, ruffling the white fungus which grew on the biped's single eye-stalk. It was rubbing its hands together, perhaps in satisfaction.

'Lucky they had these crystals on their ship,' it muttered. 'And luckier still that they didn't know anything about their uses!'

An *ojotti* or so behind the biped, the wind whistled and echoed strangely around the corners of a metal and glass artefact, clearly also alien. The artefact was covered in long gouge-marks and burn-scars. Just in case any watching Venusian should be foolish enough to approach the poisonous object, a large chalked notice had been written on each side of it, saying DANGER: METAL! in the three most common Venusian languages.

The crystals which the biped sought were scattered across a couple of *ojotti*s of the beach to the south of the metal artefact. They stood out against the grey, rounded pebbles because of their colour, the soft glow they emitted, and their angular shape – though exactly what shape they were was impossible to describe, since not all of it was visible to three-dimensional eyes.

'Save them for a rainy day,' the alien muttered, grabbing another handful and stowing them away. The pockets of its jacket seemed to be remarkably capacious; within a short time it seemed to be satisfied that it had cleared the beach of crystals. It stood up straight, winced, massaged its back for a moment.

What the biped muttered next couldn't have been understood by any Venusian watcher, for it wasn't spoken in any language native to Venus. Nor could anyone from that civilization which would one day exist on the third planet have understood it, for the language was not native to Earth either. Nor could it be translated with precision into any language of Venus or Earth.

To translate it approximately, the alien was calculating aloud a quotient for energy absorption and multi-dimensional displacement, taking into account the simultaneous differential equations of chronon decay in each of the three thousand or more crystals which it had used to buffer its re-entry in the shuttle's emergency pod, the thermal energy of atmospheric friction having been dimensionally displaced: in other words, it was trying to work out where it was, and also when it was. But it was also, as part of the same soliloquy, within the very same words (for the language it was using was as ancient and subtle and complex as the geology of a world), wondering whether any of the Aveletians – who had, after all, made the crystals – had made their escape from the Sou(ou)shi in the same way that it had.

'I doubt it,' was the grim conclusion in English, and to the more mathematical part of its mutterings, 'Not far in either direction.'

Meaning time and space, of course, not left and right.

These conclusions reached, it glanced at the sky, frowned, then set off purposefully along the beach in a south-westerly direction through space and a forward direction through time, its cane clicking on the stones.

It had not been walking long when there was a crack of thunder from the darkening sky and, as if on cue, the rain started to fall, the huge drops almost hot enough to scald human skin. The biped tutted a few times, tapped its cane irritably.

'I really must remember to carry an umbrella,' it muttered. 'At all times. You never know when you're going to need one.'

Ruribeg closed two of his eyes, took three deep breaths. He *would* make it to the top of the slope. He *would*. He looked at his companion, Alitihi Nefkhil, striding firmly upwards ahead of him. If she could do it, he could.

The heavy water-carapace slopped and shuddered around Ruribeg as he started moving again over the rough ground. The exposed parts of his body – his ankles and eye-stalks – were blistering in the heat despite the salve on them; and even the water in the carapace, drawn from cold springs only a few hours before, was beginning to get uncomfortably hot.

‘How does the old hermit manage to live out here?’ he asked Nefkhil.

‘He keeps to his shelter most of the time. Especially this time of day. Save your breath, you lose coolness by talking.’

Ruribeg twitched his eye-stalks in acknowledgement: the skin cracked painfully as he moved it.

He looked to the south, where a wall of yellow vapour rose into the sky. It was the Steamwall, the physical manifestation of the End; the ocean boiling away into the sky. Ruribeg was sure that it was closer than it had been the last time he had seen it from these latitudes, over a year ago. He could make out individual ripples, like the rough surface of a fungus, and city-sized whitish bubbles moving slowly upwards beneath a dirty gauze of mist.

The sight of it filled him with a sense of urgency. He found himself hurrying, suddenly heedless of the heat and the stinging grit in his eyes. If the Sou(ou)shi don’t get us, the Steamwall will, he thought; and didn’t wonder at the surface-lubbers’ willingness to accept the aliens and their huge ship at face value.

But the Commander, his clan-uncle, was right. The Volcano People could afford to take no such chances.

‘This is the place where the messages are normally left,’ said Nefkhil suddenly. With one gauntleted hand she pulled up a flat stone in the shade of a boulder. There was nothing there.

Ruribeg looked at her, four-eyed.

‘We’d better get up to the shelter,’ she said. ‘He won’t like it: he’s an ill-tempered old burner.’ Her eyes blinked rapidly.

‘If he hasn’t done the *huyaot* yet, the Commander’s orders are that he should begin – ’

‘I know, I know. We’ll see about that.’ She paused. ‘Let me do the talking.’

Ruribeg twitched acknowledgement; his cracked skin stung.

They pushed on up the slope, following a well-worn

path to Kontojij's living quarters. Nefkhil, in the lead, stepped around the heap of rubble that the hermit used to keep the evening sun off the walls.

'Old master!'

No reply.

Ruribeg became aware of a strange taste in the air. It reminded him of his childhood, of when he had worked in the bloodhouse, before he had trained as a messenger.

Nefkhil advanced to the doorway, curled an eye-stalk inside.

'By fire!' she muttered.

Ruribeg was by her side in an instant, two eyes curled through the doorway. For an instant he saw nothing but sun-dazzle, then his eyes adjusted.

The bloodhouse.

It was everywhere: hoof-deep on the floor, splashed across the walls, pooling on the pentagonal workbench. Blood. Blood, mixed with fragments of glass and chitin and bone and flesh. Blood, dripping off the moss and strips of peeled skin that clung to the ceiling. Blood, in a puddle with a single staring eye floating in it.

For a moment, Ruribeg couldn't find his breath. When he did, e managed a faint, inarticulate cry. He felt Nefkhil's hand on the base of his eye-stalks, wordless comfort.

A voice sounded from somewhere inside the building.

Nefkhil and Ruribeg exchanged a glance, then the old squadswoman blundered in, hooves squelching in the mess of flesh and blood on the floor.

Ruribeg waited until he heard Nefkhil's dry laugh.

The other voice spoke again.

'*Chff*-rrr? Rrrr?'

A *ghifghoni*. Of course. Kontojij kept them. Nefkhil had mentioned it before they started out. He was supplied with *kirimbi*-nuts for them.

There was a clatter of chitin, a muffled squawk, and a stubby green flyer emerged from the doorway, rotors whirling. It settled on Ruribeg's hip, trembling.

'Rrrr?'

'Come and look at this!' called Nefkhil.

Ruribeg took a step inside the doorway, then heard Nefkhil's gasp.

'By fire!'

A voice inside Ruribeg told him that he should go and see what Nefkhil had seen, what Kontojij had seen, that he should collect the evidence that he had been sent to collect.

Another voice told him he should *run, run now.*

There was another clatter of chitin within the laboratory. The *ghifghoni* squealed and dug its five stubby feet into Ruribeg's flesh.

Ruribeg took a step forward.

'Nefkhil!'

There was a blue light glowing from one of the inner doorways; it seemed unnatural. Ruribeg couldn't remember any phenomenon from his training that could cause a light of that kind. He jumped down into the laboratory, called once more.

Then Nefkhil screamed:

'Ruribeg! Get away from here! NOW!'

Ruribeg hesitated, then saw the blue light flow like lava through the inner doorway, flecked with blood.

Nefkhil screamed again.

'Get away. Away!'

The blue light grew brighter. Ruribeg jumped back up through the outer doorway.

Behind him, Nefkhil screamed again, this time utterly incoherent. Ruribeg ran, promising himself that he would bring help for Nefkhil, that he would come back with a hundred of the Commander's best squadsmen –

But for now, he ran, with the *ghifghoni* clinging to his shoulder. Behind him, the air was shredded with screams.

Ian had always liked the rain, but it felt different now.

When he was little he'd splashed around in the deep, muddy puddles around the bud-mother's hut, rejoicing in the lovely slimy soaky feel of water on his skin. Later he'd learned to tip his body back and drink the raindrops as they fell, rinsing one mouth after the other with the luscious clean wetness. But now –

Now the water felt hot and itchy, and his skin was hanging heavily on him as if he were about to shed it.

And something else was wrong. Something appalling had happened.

He peered through the heavy grey downpour, trying to work out what. He could only see forward – was that unusual? He tried to remember whether he'd been able to see out of the back of his head when he'd been fighting the Daleks in London. There had been that moment in the mines when –

No. He wasn't sure.

He glanced down at his wet hands, realized they were scalding in the hot rain. He would need more of Jellenhut's salve soon.

He looked around, trying to see the bud-mother, but saw only grey shapes at the far end of the deck.

The deck –

He looked up at the sail, sluicing water, and saw the support-boom lashed to the cabin wall. Were they on Henefenhut's land-yacht?

But Henefenhut was dead.

Which meant –

If only it would stop raining! The water was soaking his jacket, his trousers, his shirt. It ran in streams across the deck of the land-yacht, cascaded off the sail, puddled against the rails.

His shoes squelching, Ian walked slowly towards the big rubber wheel, wondering if he ought to jump on to it like he had last time.

No –

Concentrate on the facts, Chesterton.

Who had said that? Never mind. The facts.

He counted his hands: one, two. His feet: also two. Right. When had he used to have five?

In the village –

– when the big clansmen had come with their red-and-black chequered belly-wraps and the darts oh no the darts and dying I can't I'm only seven dying no –

The deck came up to meet Ian and he moaned in terror. His stomach heaved but there was nothing to bring up. He coughed, retched, then sat gasping, suddenly cold despite the hot rain.

There was a thudding of hooves on the deck: 'Ian! Are you all right?'

Trikhobu. Barbara's friend.

Barbara – !

– *'Help me! IAN!!'* –

Ian stared at Trikhobu. One of her arms was tied in a sling, a sling made of red and black chequered cloth. Water dripped from it.

'I've got to help Barbara,' he told the alien. 'Where is she?'

Trikhobu gestured to the cabin.

Ian dived through the entrance, fell, landed awkwardly on his two feet. Pain shot through his ankle. He ignored it.

'Barbara?'

There was no reply, but as his eyes adapted to the darkness he made out a white shape on the far side of the cabin. He ran towards it, his clothes dripping water across the floor.

'Barbara?'

Her face was white and still. The cloth wrapped around her body was stained with dark blood. Too dark.

'You woke up last time,' he said. 'You've got to wake up this time.'

Silence. Water dripping on the floor, the rumble of the wheel on the road.

Then: a faint human whisper.

Ian felt a surge of hope. He reached down, put his hand near her mouth. For a moment, nothing. Then he felt a slight, warm movement of air against his fingers. He moved his hand to her neck to take Barbara's pulse.

Weak, but steady.

'She's in shock,' he said aloud. 'And she might be bleeding internally.'

He looked around him frantically for a moment; then realized he was looking for a telephone.

A telephone, to call for an ambulance, on a land-yacht in the middle of a Venusian storm, thirty million miles and three billion years from the nearest human hospital.

Jellenhut, he thought. Jellenhut had healed his burns. Jellenhut was bud-mother. Jellenhut would know what to do.

He raced across the cabin and scrambled up through the entrance. His ankle hurt, but not too badly: probably a mild sprain, some tiny part of his mind noted. Rest it, but don't let it stiffen up.

On the deck the rain was unabated, a hotter-than-comfortable showerbath that you couldn't turn off. A long flicker of lightning illuminated the washy deck, the dripping rail, a wide, sloping road running with water, and the steep slopes of hills on either side, glossy with run-off. Heavy in his drenched clothes, Ian ran under the sail, to see Jellenhut and Trikhobu hauling at ropes, five-handed.

'All east!' shouted a Venusian voice, with an edge of panic in it. 'As much east as you can!'

'Jellenhut!' called Ian.

She ignored him, hauled harder at the rope. Ian suddenly realized that Nohik-imaden was hanging over the stern of the land-yacht, each of his hands gripping a long triple rope attached to the wheel mounting. The deck began to slope.

'Jellenhut! I need your help!'

'Ian! Over here!' shouted Jellenhut in reply. 'Add your strength to the pull!'

'Barbara – ' began Ian, then realized he could hardly hear himself speak. The sound of the rain had got louder – no – that wasn't it –

He turned round, and saw a wall of white water, filled with fragments of rock and small branches, towering well above the masthead. He just had time to realize how impossibly close it was before it hit them.

11

Orders to Kill

Kintibi Jofghil wasn't in a good mood. The conversation with Mrak-ecado had taken so long that he'd had to finish his speech in the rain, and he was pretty sure that no one had heard the end of it. It was all the Doctor's fault. Jofghil had always known that the fungus-topped alien was up to no good. Why hadn't anybody listened to him?

The rain was still drumming on the shutters of the window; the mosses on the walls slept. It was so dark that one of the guards had lit a lamp.

'So he's still alive?'

The squadsman who had been given responsibility for the Sou(ou)shi communication device twitched his eye-stalks in acknowledgement.

'The Sou(ou)shi detected heliogram-like signals from an emergency escape device. They concluded that the Doctor had somehow managed to survive the passage through the upper air.'

'But they're sure he hasn't succeeded in sabotaging the sky-ship?'

'They detected it in time, they said.'

Jofghil felt the tension in his skin ease slightly. He didn't like to imagine what would have happened if the vast Sou(ou)shi ship had fallen out of the sky on top of them. He glanced at Mrak-ecado, but the old Philosopher seemed almost asleep, three of his eyes closed.

'Did they say where this emergency escape device was?'

'Sisikhigu's Beach.'

Jofghil opened the mouth facing a larger, darker,

squadswoman who stood silent, eyes pricked, in the west corner of the office.

'Lighibu: how many people will you need, to be certain of killing the alien before he reaches the city?'

Ian was fighting the current, and losing.

A hundred yards ahead of him, the cabin of the land-yacht projected from the water, the masts with their bedraggled remnants of sails above it. He was swimming as hard as he could, but they kept getting further away. The water was as thick as soup, and almost as hot; Ian could feel the blood pounding in his head, the sweat forming on his face and body. If he didn't drown, he reflected, he would probably die of heat-stroke.

A wave broke over his face, filling his mouth with soapy-tasting water. He spat it out, coughing. As his eyes cleared, he saw a shape in the water ahead of him.

A rock.

A huge, muddy green rock – with eyes.

It was Jellenhut.

Ian dipped his arms into the thick water, pushed it back with all his strength. He wasn't sure whether he was making forward progress or whether Jellenhut was simply swimming towards him, but she was getting closer. A star-shaped hand closed over each of his, yanking him forward with bruising force. He landed in a pool of foamy water on her back, saw the heavy rope securing her two rearward legs. It stretched above the surface of the water back to the land-yacht; he could see the figures of Trikhobu and Nohik-imaden, up to their mouths in water, hauling at the other end of it with the full weight of their bodies.

He and Jellenhut started to move towards the land-yacht, rather quickly. Ian slapped one of Jellenhut's legs, shouted, 'Well done!' then remembered another, more Venusian response and hugged her around the base of the eye-stalks.

By the time they reached the land-yacht, the water

level was below the deck rail; streams of brown muck were sluicing off the deck. Trikhobu was alone at the rail; Ian could hear Nohik-imaden rushing about on deck. His new knowledge, Inikhut's memories, told him that the crewman was unshipping the support boom. The land-yacht was already teetering, and without the boom it would fall over as soon as the water dropped below the bottom of the hold.

Jellenhut jumped aboard; the impact knocked the wind out of Ian, and he coughed. Only when he was almost lifted off Jellenhut's back by the heaving of her lungs did he realize that the Venusian must have been holding her breath for the duration of the rescue.

He jumped down, landed up to his knees in warm brown sludge. He'd kicked off his shoes in the water, and now regretted it; as he started to walk, sharp stones bit into his stocking feet. He'd also shed his jacket; the remainder of his clothing was a muddy, burned, torn mess. He realized it wouldn't be a bad idea to follow Barbara's example and learn to wear a Venusian belly-wrap.

Barbara!

He started towards the cabin entrance, moving as fast as he could through the clinging goo. The cabin must have filled with water – she would have drowned –

She was sitting on the edge of the doorway, her clothes and her face covered in mud, her legs trailing in the water that still filled the cabin. She looked up at his approach, smiled.

'I wasn't much use as a guard. Sorry.'

It was a moment before Ian worked out what she was talking about; too much had happened since the time of that agreement in Jellenhut's hut. When he'd worked it out, he kneeled down beside her and put an arm around her shoulders.

'I'm just glad you're alive.'

She looked at him with eyes that would barely stay open.

' 's better than being dead,' she muttered. Then her

head crashed onto his shoulder. After a moment Ian realized that she had fainted.

He pulled her up, laid her out on the deck. There was less mud here than lower down, but the ooze still came up to Ian's ankles.

There was a heavy squelching sound behind him; he turned, saw Jellenhut.

'Is she alive?' asked the Venusian simply.

'She was talking to me a minute ago.'

Jellenhut extended an eye-stalk, examined Barbara's body. When she pulled back the wrap Ian turned his back, though he wasn't quite sure why, in the circumstances.

'She's losing blood again,' said Jellenhut. 'Find me some clean water; I'll try to change the bandage.'

Ian squelched across the deck, winced as his foot caught a sharp stone. Nohik-imaden was talking with Trikhobu. Ian caught the words, ' – have to stay put until the globeroller comes past tonight.'

Tonight! thought Ian. He knew that was far too late. Barbara needed help now.

From Inikhut's memories of sailing, Ian knew that there would be clean water in the hydraulic balance system; the tap, made of silver-black chitin, was at the bottom of a pipe that looped over the cabin roof. It was muddy, but the water that came out of it was clean. A goldenwood bucket was half-full of slime; after sluicing it out twice, Ian decided it was clean enough – it would have to be. The land-yacht was already groaning dangerously on the booms as its weight shifted.

He squelched back across the deck. Nohik-imaden caught his free arm.

'Next time you drain the balance system,' he hissed, 'tell me about it first.'

'Sorry,' said Ian. 'I'm trying to save Barbara's life.'

But Nohik-imaden was evidently immune to sarcasm; he simply hissed again and let Ian go with a push that caused him to spill some of the precious water.

'We need to find some help,' Ian told Jellenhut when he returned with the water. 'Nohik-imaden's more concerned with the state of his yacht than with Barbara.'

'There's a village near here. Over the top of that hill somewhere.' She waved to the east. 'We always used to envy the clansmen there, they were officially Bikugih citizens. They could get the subsidy.' She paused. 'And no Death Inspectors, of course.'

She took the bucket and got to work on Barbara. Ian couldn't very well help seeing her body now; Jellenhut could only bring three hands to bear at a time, and needed him to hold the dirty dressings. This was no time for prudery.

The wound was at the top of Barbara's right breast; it looked nasty, and deep. When Jellenhut removed the old dressing, blood began to flow; fast, foamy, bright blood; too much of it. Jellenhut clamped the wound shut with her hand and passed herself a clean dressing. With a shock, Ian recognized a strip of his sister Pihellihut's belly-wrap.

Inikhut's sister, he corrected himself.

Inikhut's identity was nested inside his own: it required no effort on his part to think of Jellenhut as his bud-mother, and very little effort to think of Barbara as alien. He began to realize how Barbara must have felt for the last couple of days.

Jellenhut tied the dressing around Barbara's chest, pulling it tight enough to make the skin on the uninjured left side whiten. Barbara's body jerked and she gave a faint moan of pain. Jellenhut froze for a moment, then moved her eyes closer, carefully replacing the bloodied belly-wrap in such a way that only clean parts of the cloth were near the wound.

Ian became aware that Trikhobu was standing behind them, her writing-claw unsheathed, scribbling something.

'Ian says we should go and find help,' said Jellenhut, using the mouth facing Trikhobu. 'I agree. We need healing salve, a flask of blood-clotting agent, needles and thread to stitch the wound. I know a village nearby. Will you watch over Barbara whilst we are gone?'

Trikhobu twitched acknowledgement, still scribbling away.

Ian glanced down at Barbara.

'I don't know whether you can hear me, Barbara,' he said. 'But we're going to get help for you. Medical help.'

Barbara's eyes half-opened.

'Take a gun,' she said. 'Or five.'

Then her eyes shut again.

Legdhitreb Brignontojij of the clan Rastwet examined the blue box with care. It was barely as high as he was: on hoof-tip he would have towered over it. At a pinch, one squadsman could carry it on his back. Brignontojij wondered how anyone, however diminutive, could travel between worlds in it. Where did the power come from?

'It must be magic,' he said, mostly to himself. '*Anteyon* power, psi-power. Something of the sort.'

Nosgentanreteb, his assistant, twitched his eye-stalks respectfully.

'They say it appeared in a cloud of light, sir.'

Brignontojij looked at the glass lamp on the top of the box, the alien script on the sides. It was all very well for the Presidor to say 'destroy it'. If only Brignontojij knew what it was for – what it *meant* – then perhaps he might . . .

He looked above him, where the tall silver columns of the trees seemed to be perpetually toppling beneath the after-storm clouds rushing through the sky. He tried to imagine what it would be like to travel through the sky himself, and failed.

'Perhaps we could burn it,' Nosgentanreteb suggested.

'It might explode,' said Brignontojij, briskly dismissive, even though the same idea had occurred to him only a few minutes before.

But it was true: it *might* explode, with all the energy of

something that travels unimaginable distances. It didn't bear thinking about.

Experimentally he reached out with one leg. On the face of it, a few good kicks should do for the thing; it looked incredibly flimsy, rather like the sort of box you kept your belly-wraps folded in. But when his hoof made contact, nothing gave. He put a second hoof against the box, pushed with all his strength. The box tilted – tilted more – slowly fell, and hit the groundmoss of the Silver Ride with a dull thud. Brignontojij twitched an eye-stalk at Nosgentanreteb and kicked the fallen spaceship vigorously.

His hoof bounced off.

Nosgentanreteb had a go. He kicked out several times, with increasing vigour. For the last kick he pointed his hoof, jumped down with the full weight of his body. His ankle crumpled, and he drew in his belly with pain.

'No good, sir,' he reported.

'I'd gathered that. Are you all right, Nosgentanreteb?'

Two of Nosgentanreteb's hands were exploring his injured ankle. 'Nothing is broken. I'll be recovered in less than a red-to-violet, sir.'

Brignontojij noticed that a small crowd had gathered in the Silver Ride. They were keeping a respectful distance, but their eye-stalks were craning forward with open curiosity. He had half-decided to shout at them, threaten to withdraw their boarding rights for the Sou-(ou)shi ship – anything to get rid of them. Then he noticed a squat stranger in boatsman's yellow.

He had an idea.

'Hey, you! Boatman!'

The boatman gaped slightly, then took a step forward. Rain-wet moss squelched under his feet.

'We might need your help.'

The boatman advanced another few steps, gaping wider.

'Is yours a seagoing boat?'

The boatman advanced a few more steps.

'Three pyramids if you want to put that on it,' he said, darting an eye-stalk towards the blue box.

Brignontojij hesitated. The Presidor had said nothing about expenses.

'Not more than one.'

'Two and two cubes.'

'Two.'

'Done.' The boatman dipped a hand expectantly. Brignontojij fished in his ankle-bag and paid, then turned to Nosgentanreteb. 'Is your leg functional?'

Nosgentanreteb flexed it experimentally. 'Yes, sir.'

'Are you able to carry the craft?'

Nosgentanreteb looked at the box with a resigned expression and began unravelling a length of rope from around the top of his belly-wrap. With precise movements he retied it in a series of loops around his legs, leaving two long, trailing ends.

Between them, Brignontojij and the boatman lifted the alien ship; on the second attempt, they managed to get it in position on Nosgentanreteb's back. The top, the piece with the glass lamp, projected a little, but Nosgentanreteb assured them he would be able to walk. He insisted on tying the knots himself: four loops around each end of the box, joined by a large five-pointed bow. When he had finished, his skin was flushed blue with effort. The crowd, Brignontojij noted, were swaying with appreciation, as if they had been watching a gymnastic competition.

'Let's go,' he said, and set off at a slow trot. Nosgentanreteb shuffled by his side, the boatman followed.

'Efin Kallenhu's the name,' he offered. 'Clan Diarhini. I keep my boat at the Crenihilgen end of the harbour.'

Brignontojij waved a vague acknowledgement, but kept three eyes firmly fixed on the blue box. It didn't seem to be doing anything, which was a relief.

He wondered how far out to sea they should go before dumping it.

* * *

Jellenhut walked ahead of Ian in silence. She would make a few long strides up the slippery hillside, then stop, waiting for Ian to catch up. Ian struggled on, through the sodden mud liberally sprinkled with stones, past wiry blue bushes that hissed at him and tried to grab his legs as he passed.

'My feet hurt,' he said.

Jellenhut had done her best, wrapping more strips of Pihellihut's belly-wrap around them, tying it in place with strips of pleated chitin. It was better than walking in his socks, but not much. The material was lumpy, the chitin strips chafed his skin, and he kept losing his balance on the rough ground.

'How much further?' he asked Jellenhut.

When she winced – her eye-stalks curled, her mouths snapped shut – Ian realized that he had been speaking with Inikhut's voice. Both times.

'Sorry,' he said. 'I didn't realize that I was remembering.'

Jellenhut did not reply. From his new knowledge of Venusian body language, Ian could tell that she was suppressing powerful emotions: her skin was flushed blue, her mouths sealed tight. He looked up at the ragged grey clouds, which were still spitting occasional drops of warm rain, wondered what it was like to lose your children, your family, everyone you knew. What it was like to have them killed by the police of your own country. He realized, with a shock, that Jellenhut could not go home; she no longer had one.

'Jellenhut?' he asked aloud. 'Could you live in Bikugih? When all this is over, I mean.'

Jellenhut stopped short for a moment.

'How would I do that?'

'By going there, getting lodgings, finding a job – ' Ian trailed off. Inikhut's memories warned him that what he was saying made little sense in Venusian.

'I have no clan in Bikugih. No one to lodge with or to work for. I have no clan anywhere now.' She paused, looked three-eyed at Ian. 'Do not concern yourself with my future, Ian Chesterton of the clan Earth. It is not in your keeping.'

She strode forward once more; Ian struggled to keep up. He wondered if his sympathy was simply irrelevant to Jellenhut. He decided to try a different approach.

'It's not just the part of me that's Inikhut that feels sorry for you, Jellenhut. I understand what it's like to be cut off from my people.'

Jellenhut slowed down to let him catch up, but didn't stop. They had now reached a wide path surfaced with flat stones – no, thought Ian, a *narrow* path; it was only wide in human terms. Jellenhut's knees brushed the grabbing-bushes on either side, making the semi-plants wriggle and seethe.

'The Doctor – the one who brought us here, in his ship – isn't of the same people as us. He comes from – well, we think he comes from – well, we're not sure where he comes from, but it isn't our world.' Ian paused for breath. He wasn't sure whether he had Jellenhut's attention or not; she seemed fully occupied in brushing away the branches of the grabbing-bushes. 'The point is, he isn't able to take us home. Or at least, he says he isn't able to. Barbara and I have to live in the TARDIS; we don't have any choice about where we're going to end up. We've had some fantastic adventures – I've seen and done things I could never have seen or done on Earth, not if I'd lived to be a hundred. But it's not having the choice.' He paused, remembering Barbara's wound, the caked blood around the edges of it. 'Sometimes we get near to our home, to the right place or the right time, so near you could almost touch it – '

'This Doctor; is he a good or a bad person?' Jellenhut asked suddenly.

'Good,' said Ian; then, surprised at the swift certainty of his own reply, he qualified it: 'Basically good, but bad-tempered, mischievous – sometimes I don't trust him.'

'Be thankful that you have fallen in with a person who

is "basically good",' Jellenhut replied, as though the rest of Ian's words had not been spoken. 'There are many worse fates. If you really wish to return to the time and place you call home, I have no doubt that your friend will find a way, in time. Meanwhile, I think you should enjoy your "adventures". It is better to see many things than to see few.' She paused, seemed to think for a moment, then added: 'When you are older, and you tell the stories of your youth to your own nephews and children, you will see that you were enjoying them all along.'

The path was widening now; ahead, Ian could see a steep slope, the path snaking down. A few stone buildngs were visible but the floor of the valley was lost in a grey haze. Beyond, a chain of low black mountains rose, their tops hidden in the cloud. A shaft of sunlight struck one of them, making the slope green; in the greenness, something glinted.

A whole world, Ian realized, for the first time. I'm the first man on Venus, he thought; and Barbara's the first woman. In fact (he smiled at the memory), of the two of us she got there first, by a few seconds. Both of us three billion years before the Americans or the Russians or whoever in their rocket capsules and their silver suits.

'It's a pity it won't all still be there, in my time,' he said aloud. 'Humans and Venusians could learn a lot from each other; we're so different and yet – '

He broke off, realizing that Jellenhut was too far ahead of him to hear. He ran to catch up and saw that the bud-mother had stopped outside a stone building. Two other Venusians came out of the doorway, put a net over her –

A net, black fibres, pulling tight –

Ian jumped, pulled out his dart gun. It seemed to fall into his hand more easily now; before he could think, he was running forward, shouting, 'Let her go! Let her go at once or I'll shoot!'

One of the Venusians dropped behind Jellenhut; the other dropped to one side, back into the doorway. A black object flew through the air towards Ian. He dived to the ground: too late. Something fibrous and stinging wrapped itself around his body, began to bite into his skin. He pushed against it, felt fibres break; but others formed, began to tighten around his arms, his legs, his neck –

A red mist filled his eyes. He tried to claw the net away from his throat, but his hands wouldn't move.

The red mist turned grey. A roaring noise filled his ears.

I can't die now, he thought. It's impossible. I've just made a resolution to enjoy myself.

But he lost consciousness anyway.

Lighibu was glad that the rain had stopped. She could see clearly the length of the road now, all the way to Kuj Point. She scanned it continually, using three eyes in rotation so that no section went unwatched for more than a few heartbeats. Her other two eyes roved around the flat, mossy landscape on either side of the road, along the low ridge of the Kujinhi hills, even checking the green, choppy sea for boats.

She couldn't afford to miss the target.

Reports from further along the coast had said he was on his way, walking along the cliff-tops. Lighibu had wanted to go forward, kill him there, at a safe distance from the city, but the Presidor had overruled her. 'Let him get to the city,' he'd said. 'Then we can make sure of him.'

Lighibu signalled to the members of her Five, to confirm that they were still in position: Bufihil, the look-out on the top of the red stone tower of Bikugih gate; Porijineg, behind the diamond-seller's stall; Efenihu and Jerekarnijli in the low trees to the east of her; Nekedeju crouched down by the side of the road, cloth spread in front of him as if begging.

They weren't going to give themselves away, or make any open show of force: that might make the target wary. And they couldn't afford to do that.

For the twentieth time at least, Lighibu checked her weapons. It seemed strange not to be carrying a dart gun, even though she knew the alien was immune to them. She had a flint knife on each ankle and smaller diamond-bladed knives above her knees, disguised as body jewellery. There was a net-launcher strapped across her back, and a pouch of cuttershells hidden under her belly-wrap. She flexed her arm, practising a cuttershell throw, then recalled the chalk drawing of the alien. If she aimed for the neck of its single eye-stalk, and threw hard enough, she should be able to take the stalk off in one go. If it was unable to see, they should have a better chance.

Provided it lets us get that close. Lighibu shuddered uneasily.

Patches of sunlight moved across the road, picking out *kigfih*-drawn carriages and larger, family wagons pulled by *grifharji*; the bright sails of land-yachts bellying out in the strong breeze; and groups of travellers on the hoof, many with packs of possessions roped to their backs. All of them were coming into Bikugih to assemble for boarding the Sou(ou)shi ship. Lighibu had been at the rollerport when the shuttle landed, so she knew how big the ship was; even so, she found herself wondering how all of these people would get on board. The Presidor had said it would take a night, then the Sou(ou)shi would move on to Inarihib, Martahig, Conorihib, Burjianit, Ujannonot, and the High Sweet Lands, covering the whole world in less than a tenday.

A day after that, they would begin to disembark, on a new world. Never taking her eyes off the road, Lighibu wondered what it would be like. Would there be trees and groundmoss, *ghifghoni* and *nijij* and *cajingu*, or things like them? Or would a 'new' world be empty, just sea and stone, like a beach?

A flicker of light in Lighibu's south eye; Bufihil, the tower look-out, was signalling to her:

'Target sighted hill ridge.'

Every muscle in Lighibu's body tensed. She swung four

of her eyes to the ridge, keeping the fifth on Bufihil's position. She slid a monocular in front of one of her eyes and immediately saw the bipedal figure striding along the road. She could even see the smudge of white fungus on its head.

'Confirm target,' she signed back to Bufihil.

She kept the monocular trained on the alien, conscious of every breath through each of her mouths.

Me, she thought. Just me and my Five. If we succeed, then our city, our whole world, is saved. If we fail –

Then somebody else will probably do the job, she thought, with an involuntary eye-twitch towards the city walls and the heavy weapons squads behind them.

But best not to think about that. Best not to consider failure, and the consequences. There was a job to do. *The target will be allowed to pass into the net. As soon as he is past you, you will destroy him.*

Her east eye still trained on the alien, she discreetly signalled to her Five to check their weapons.

12

Venusian Underground

Jellenhut looked down at Ian with her one free eye-stalk. His face had lost that alarming shade of blue, but the marks the holding net had made on his neck were a dark, unnatural-looking red. The fibres were still drawn tight around the rest of his body, black lines against his pale body-wrappings. His arms were pinned to his sides; the skin of his hands, already damaged by the fire, was peeling.

'How dare you!' said Jellenhut, addressing the two clansmen in red belly-wraps who stood a body-width away, hooves arched slightly on the red and grey tiled floor. Both had guns drawn. 'We are on our way to collect medical supplies for this alien's clan-sister, who is injured. You have no right – '

The wider and heavier of the two clansmen broke in: 'Rights are not in question. We are not acting on behalf of any city or any law.'

His voice echoed from stone walls. Even the ceiling was stone, Jellenhut noticed, heavy and grey, bare of plaster, undecorated by any moss. Behind the guards, the floor was lower, and she could see a large circular doorway which opened into a darkened tunnel. She could not see the doorway through which she and Ian had been carried a few moments before: stone, she realized, must have rolled up and covered it.

Her belly tightened.

A slight wind blew out of the tunnel; it felt cool – deliciously cool, almost cold. To fight the feeling of comfort that the coolness gave her, Jellenhut pulled her legs and arms against the constraints of the net, felt the pain as the fibres bit into her skin.

'Where are we?' she asked, keeping her voice sharp and angry. 'And what is your authority, if it is not that of any city?'

Ian groaned, screwed up his face for a moment, then tried to sit up. Jellenhut hushed him, managing to wriggle one of her hands far enough away from her body to rest a finger-petal on the fungus-like substance above his eyes.

The guards, she noticed, were exchanging hand-signals.

Finally the tall one spoke again: 'You are in the territory of the Volcano People.'

A shock went right through Jellenhut's body. She had tbought she would never fear anything again after losing her children, but she felt fear now.

The Volcano People. The warrens. The warrens from which there is no escape.

'You are to meet our Commander,' the guard went on. 'Transport will arrive shortly.' As he spoke, the ground began to tremble.

An eruption, thought Jellenhut, her belly tightening once more. There's going to be an eruption of fire. That's what the Volcano People do.

A hot wind began blowing through the chamber, picking up fragments of dust, even small stones, and whirling them about. Wood banged against wood somewhere, the sound getting louder; it seemed to come from the tunnel entrance. Jellenhut craned her single free eye towards it, looking for the tell-tale flicker of flames.

A golden glow appeared in the tunnel, resolved itself into two lamps, glowing like a night-beast's eyes. The roaring sound became so loud that it almost burst Jellenhut's eardrums; stones bounced off her skin and dust flew into her eyes. Reflexively, she half-closed the hoods, reducing her vision to a blur.

A thing as large as a fallen tree burst into the chamber, its sides glowing with unnaturally bright lamplight. The thing made a terrifying shriek like something dying, then stopped with a ground-shaking thud only a leg's length from the guards.

Jellenhut felt the wind slacken, the dust settle. She opened her eyes wide again, and saw that the thing was a huge cylinder, made from plates of dull purple chitin.

Ian made a sound. Jellenhut swung her free eye around, watched with concern as he began to shake, his solitary mouth making a strange barking sound. Suddenly, she realized he was laughing.

The guards stared at him four-eyed, as puzzled as she was.

'I didn't know the Piccadilly Line ran this far,' said Ian at last. 'Jellenhut, ask them if this one stops at Leicester Square.'

The target was surrounded by children, which was a problem. It appeared to be showing them magic tricks: Lighibu could hear their shouts of delighted laughter, and caught the occasional flash of coloured cloth behind the crowd of jumping bodies.

The alien couldn't have chosen a more effective shield, she thought. To get rid of the children, we have to come out into the open; which means we lose the element of surprise. I suppose Bufihil could risk a shot from the tower, but if she missed –

The alien was close now, almost within jumping distance. Lighibu could hear its voice, though she couldn't quite make out its words above the noises of the road and the babble of the children. She felt a rising sense of panic. If it got inside the walls –

Then she had an idea.

'Hold fire,' she signalled to her Five.

She left her position by the side of the road, walking north into the crowd of children.

'Alien!' she called.

The pale, fungus-headed beast turned its sunken eyes to look at her.

There was no choice now but to go on.

'I have important news for you. Something you must know before you enter the city.'

Her Five must be wondering what she was doing, thought Lighibu. She could feel five sets of eyes trained on her, weapon hands ready, as she pushed her way through the now-silent children towards the alien. She hoped they trusted her enough to realize she wasn't really going to betray them.

Close. Closer.

The alien watched her, and the mask of flesh around its eyes wrinkled.

Closer –

Now!

She leaped forward, drawing three flint knives in the same movement. The alien started to fall back, to one side, but it wasn't going to be fast enough.

'STOP!'

Lighibu heard the shout, and thought, it's one of the bud-mothers. Doesn't understand. At the same time she corrected her jump to compensate for the Doctor's movement, extended a hoof, folded it into a killing point.

There was a child in the way. About seven years old, Lighibu guessed, even as her body wrenched itself to a stop, all five hooves on the ground.

The child, terrified, leaped clear over Lighibu's eye-stalks and landed south of her. A body-width to the north, the alien was half on the ground: its legs had collapsed. The child must have pushed it, Lighibu realized.

'Everyone stand clear!' she yelled. Children scattered in all directions. Someone shouted 'Stop!' again, but Lighibu took no notice. The alien was struggling to get up.

Don't give it a chance.

Lighibu lifted three legs clear of the ground and pivoted on the other two, ready for a killing roll.

'No! Stop!'

The voice was closer this time; Lighibu saw that it came from an elderly clansman in Philosopher's robes. She hesitated, lowered her body into a crouch. The alien was getting to its feet.

'I have orders from the Presidor!' the Philosopher shouted. Two hands fished clumsily inside a belly-pouch, produced a piece of paper which indeed had the golden-wax seal.

With a shock, Lighibu recognized Jilet Mrak-ecado, special adviser to the Presidor, most senior of the Night Councillors.

'All hold fire!' she yelled to her Five, in case anybody didn't realize what was happening.

The alien was walking past her; within easy striking distance. He turned his eyes to examine her for a moment, and said quietly, 'Thank you.'

Somehow, Lighibu didn't feel afraid.

'And thank *you*, my old friend,' the Doctor was saying to Mrak-ecado.

There was a pause. Venusians clustered around, eyes craning forward; Lighibu noticed Efenihu and Jerekarnijli among them. Somewhere, a *kigfih* snorted three times, its chitinous face-membranes clicking.

Mrak-ecado spoke at last:

'Alien known as the Doctor, honorary citizen of Bikugih, I place you under restraint of the Night Council on charges of treason against the citizens and Council of Bikugih, the penalty amounting to death.'

There was another pause. The sun came out, flooding the scene in a searing golden light. The road began to steam.

'I'm sorry, my old friend,' said Mrak-ecado softly to the silent alien. 'It was the best I could do.'

Ian had always considered the London Underground to be an uncomfortable method of getting around, but the Venusian Underground, he decided, was much worse. There were no grab-handles, no seats, no nothing. Just a tube without windows, lit by dim star-shaped lamps. The lamps on the outside had been brighter. The 'train' repeatedly accelerated and decelerated, and every few minutes it would stop, sway about for a bit, then drop through what felt like several yards of empty space and land with a bone-shaking thud; if it hadn't been for one of the guards pinning his stomach and legs to the floor with a couple of hooves, Ian would probably have been knocked senseless. The Venusians themselves didn't need anything to hold on to; their huge bodies barely crammed into the narrow space. It had taken several minutes for the guards to load Ian and Jellenhut, and several more for them to contort their limbs sufficiently that both of them could fit into the compartment with their captives. The enclosed space now smelled of ammoniacal sweat, and was astonishingly hot. Ian's raw skin burned.

He wondered how fast they were going, and how far. His watch hadn't worked since the fire; he tried to count the seconds, muttering, 'Miss-iss-ippi one, Miss-iss-ippi two,' but he lost track every time a hoof dug into his belly or a sharp movement of the 'train' banged his head back against the floor. In the end he gave up.

He wondered about Barbara. Whether Trikhobu and Nohik-imaden had gone looking for him, leaving her on her own. Whether a globeroller had come. Whether she was still alive.

Perhaps he could ask Jellenhut. Hadn't the Doctor said the Venusians were slightly telepathic? He tried to wriggle round so that he could see her, but the guard's hooves only pressed harder against his stomach and his legs.

The compartment began to shudder, and seemed to tilt forward: they were slowing down again, more rapidly than usual. Ian noticed the guards' eye-stalks waving about as if they were expecting something; sure enough, when the 'train' stopped, there was a loud, chitinous *snick* and the door fell open.

The light from outside was dull red; the air was hot and

smelled of sulphur. Ian had a sudden unnerving memory of a story he'd read about a train whose last stop was hell; everyone who was still aboard when the train arrived was one of the damned. He tried to dismiss the notion as fanciful but, as his ears recovered from the racket of the journey, he could hear a constant, low rumbling sound. He found himself thinking of squashing snails when he was a boy, of killing Venusians just hours ago. Of all the other sins in between.

The guard nearest the door was peering out. He spoke in a low voice to his comrade.

'Commander's here.'

The Devil? thought Ian. He imagined a Venusian with red skin and horns.

Rough Venusian hands lifted him clumsily. Carried between two guards, Ian emerged into a cloud of sulphurous steam. He coughed convulsively, his lungs suddenly as raw as if he'd had bronchitis for a week. His eyes itched and watered. He saw the dim shapes of three Venusians standing in front of him, heard a voice giving brisk orders, felt himself carried forward towards a bridge – surely it wasn't glowing red? He tried to protest that he wouldn't survive such heat, but only managed to start himself coughing again; then he was over the bridge, and realized that its red glow was reflected from the sea below.

A sea of magma. It seethed, bubbled, sent up gouts of yellow fire.

Ian coughed again, and again, and again, was unable to get his breath, and almost lost consciousness.

There was a faint pneumatic hiss, a rumble of rock in motion. The air became cooler, darker, cleaner.

Another hiss, another rumble.

Ian's lungs began to work properly again; his eyes began to clear. He saw a Venusian in front on him in a flame-red belly-wrap. Muscles corded on the arms and legs, the eyes were a startling sun-yellow. Behind him, an arched passageway covered in painted plaster led away into an indefinite distance.

'I am Mrodtikdhil, Commander of Volcano People,' the figure told Ian briskly. 'I'm sorry about the long journey. We have to keep the Command Warrens both secret and defensible. The idiots from the cities might interfere with our work otherwise. You are the Doctor?'

Ian shook his head. 'Ian Chesterton. But I'm of his – well, I'm travelling with him.'

'Good,' said Mrodtikdhil, clearly unperturbed. 'We need your help. It is a matter of vital importance to the survival of Venusian civilization.'

Oh no, thought Ian. Not again.

Jofghil couldn't remember a time when he'd been so angry. The time when he had failed in his attempt to be elected to the Night Council? Possibly. But he'd had Mrak-ecado's support then, someone to share his anger with, someone to help him get back at them. This time the old Philosopher himself was the target of Jofghil's anger.

He stared in disbelief at the order, sealed with his own gold seal on behalf of the Night Council, signed in his name with Mrak-ecado's blood. He looked up again at the heavy-set squadswoman who had brought it.

'Lighibu: where is Jilet Mrak-ecado now?'

'With the alien. They went to the harbour with the rest of my Five as escort.' She hesitated. 'The order specifies that the alien should be imprisoned on Rurif Island.'

Jofghil re-read the order.

'A trial?' he said. 'A trial is ludicrous. There isn't time. Everyone is leaving. The alien might pull some trick or other. It might escape.'

The squadswoman made no comment, merely waited, her eyes high, her legs braced. Beyond her, thin, hot bars of afternoon sunlight filtered through the shutters and wavered along the wall, setting the green and blue mosses twitching hungrily. A single spot of light fell on a tiled panel calibrated with the hours of the day. Focusing two eyes on the clock, Jofghil realized that it was almost exactly a day since Fefirhi Trikhobu had brought him the news of her father's death.

One day, and so much had happened. Two lots of aliens, one good, one evil; a total change of policy – even of belief; a new world to go to; and now Mrak-ecado's apparent betrayal. If it was a betrayal. If it wasn't, what could Mrak-ecado be thinking of?

The squadswoman was still waiting. Jofghil focused on her and spoke three-mouthed.

'Send a heliogram to the harbour, broadcast general addressed to Mrak-ecado. Tell him to come here and report to me at once. And just in case, go down to the harbour yourself and fetch him if he's not already on his way.'

'And the Doctor?' asked Lighibu.

Jofghil flattened his eye-stalks. 'What about him?'

'Are we to kill him, as originally instructed?'

Jofghil hesitated. Perhaps he ought to speak to Mrak-ecado first. If the old Philosopher felt so strongly –

No. Mrak-ecado might be old and wise, but he wasn't Presidor. Jofghil knew that he couldn't risk the future of every Venusian for the sake of an old clansman's friendship for an alien.

'The order is confirmed,' he told Lighibu. 'Kill the Doctor as soon as you have sight of him.'

The ventway was at least a mile high, Ian decided. Perhaps two. He had to crane his neck to see the tiny white disc of sky at the top. The movement made the fibres binding him cut into his shoulders; it felt like they were drawing blood. He tried to ignore the sensation.

'The last time I saw something like this,' he said, 'I was trying to blow it up. The Daleks were going to use it to destroy the Earth.'

'Who are Daleks?'

Ian looked down, winced; forgot he was tied up and tried to rub his shoulder, winced again as the net fibres cut into his arm.

'You're lucky, if you don't know what a Dalek is,' he said to the big Venusian. 'Believe me, you're better off not knowing.'

'There are always things it is better not to know,' agreed Mrodtikdhil.

It occurred to Ian that he hadn't yet spoken at any length to a Venusian who hadn't turned out to have a philosophical turn of mind. He just wished they weren't so keen on kidnapping people in order to expound their philosophies.

He looked around him again, at 'ground level', where three slanting ventways almost as wide as the main one sloped away into the Venusian crust. A faint, salty breeze blew out from one of them; it was surprisingly cool. Jellenhut and the two guards stood at a respectful distance across the wide stone pavement, well out of earshot.

'I suggest you get on with this urgent matter that we need to discuss,' he told Mrodtikdhil. 'My friend Barbara needs help. She may die. I must go back – '

Mrodtikdhil interrupted him, speaking slowly, emphatically, with all five eyes on Ian.

'There was an old clansman who lived in the dead mountains above the dead city of Cracdhalltar. His name was Kontojij. He had a special art, unique to the people of his former city, called *huyaot*. He could see into the future. He took readings daily for us, and his information was invariably reliable. This morning, when we heard of the arrival of the Sou(ou)shi spaceship, we sent a messenger to find out what readings this Kontojij had made today. The messenger found that Kontojij had been killed. Killed horribly, beyond hope of remembering.'

A pause. Ian became aware of a distant clicking of rock, as if someone were tapping stone with a stone hammer.

'Somebody didn't want you to see the future,' said Ian after a moment's thought.

Mrodtikdhil twitched his eye-stalks in acknowledgement.

'Unfortunately for them, Kontojij had already made a reading, and recorded the results.' The Commander drew a cylindrical message pod from a lip-pocket. 'We found this in the belly-pouch of a *ghifghoni* which accompanied our messenger on his return. It states that Kontojij saw many people dying – perhaps everyone in the world. It states that "two-legged, two-armed aliens" were involved.'

Another pause. Mrodtikdhil's huge yellow eyes surveyed Ian, as if confirming the count of his legs and arms.

'But that's ridiculous!' said Ian. 'The Doctor and I would no more kill your people than – than – ' He found that he couldn't think of a sufficiently absurd comparison. He just knew that the Doctor could not possibly be anything to do with it. Whatever 'it' was.

Mrodtikdhil was still watching him five-eyed. Ian became aware that his own voice was echoing, again and again, fainter and fainter, from ever further up the giant ventway. He must have been shouting.

'There have been at least seventy-four confirmed sightings of the Sou(ou)shi aliens,' said Mrodtikdhil. 'They are also two-legged and two-armed. They have a ship as large as a city. You, as I understand, have a much smaller ship and there are only three of you. Furthermore, you arrived by invitation to the funeral of Jikugihi Dharkhig. The Doctor was well known to that clansman, and others, and has never shown any enmity towards Venusians before. On the grounds of probability alone, I am more inclined to suspect the Sou(ou)shi. But you must accept that this does not mean that I can trust you.'

Ian thought for a moment.

'Barbara said the Sou(ou)shi were creepy,' he said. 'And the Doctor was going to investigate them.' He looked up at Mrodtikdhil; the Venusian still had four of his five eyes craned forward, almost within an arm's length of Ian's body. 'But if the Sou(ou)shi are trying to kill you, what can you do about it?'

'We could destroy the Sou(ou)shi ship,' said Mrodtikdhil.

Ian stared at the Venusian. 'How?'

'I'll show you.'

Mrodtikdhil picked Ian up, none too carefully, and slung him across his back. Ian felt the net cut into him; blood ran down his arm.

'It would be a lot easier if you let me go,' he said, but the Venusian was already trotting across the platform, holding Ian down with three hands. He noticed the guards following with Jellenhut, still keeping their distance.

They passed through a high stone gateway decorated with red and yellow tiles, into a stone passageway with bright-coloured frescoes on the walls. The design was of volcanoes in eruption – more reds and yellows – with fields of blue flowers growing out of the clouds of smoke. Tiny Venusians with tiny, diaphanous rotor blades sprouting from their bodies pollinated the flowers. Further on, larger flying Venusians became visible, sporting painted rotors. Ian found himself wondering whether Venusians ever had been able to fly, or whether it was just wishful thinking.

At length they reached a blank stone wall. Mrodtikdhil reached out, and twisted a wooden knob back and forth a few times in what was clearly a practised combination. With a loud hiss and a rumble of stone the wall rolled down into the floor, revealing a huge space filled with light. As they advanced into the chamber, Ian could see that the light came from hundreds, maybe thousands of *brakud*-oil lamps fastened to the walls. In between the lamps were diagrams, each several yards square, showing tubes and valves and chambers, covered in arrows and neatly labelled calculations. But far more startling was what hung in the middle of the chamber. It was shaped like a boy's glass marble, and it was about the size of St Paul's cathedral. As his eyes got used to the scale, picked out the details, Ian realized what it was.

It was a model of a planet.

The surface details were shown in pale, washy colours; the core glowed. In between were pipes: a network of pipes: big ones; small ones; vertical ones; horizontal ones; picked out in a rainbow of colours. They ran across the two continents, underneath the oceans and out through the volcanoes. There were other details – fine threads and nodules, which Ian realized were corridors, tube tunnels, and chambers like the one he stood in.

'The original object was preservation of the species,' commented Mrodtikdhil, lifting Ian three-handed from his back and carefully placing him on the ground. 'We planned to inject volcanic dust into equatorial orbit, thus partially shading the planet from the sun's heat for a time. The system was due to be set off within the next generation, if we could persuade enough of the surface people to join us.'

Ian opened his mouth to say something – perhaps that he didn't believe it would work – but Mrodtikdhil went straight on:

'We could however use the system now. It would still be almost entirely effective, and the debris might damage or destroy the Sou(ou)shi ship. This is where we need your advice. What are our chances of destroying the ship in this way? Is it worth the risk to the remaining surface dwellers?'

Ian looked round the chamber once more, struggled to concentrate through the buzzing in his head, the pain in his limbs, and Inikhut's memories which were prompting him to yell 'Mii-i-ma!' at the top of his voice. He noticed for the first time that the cathedral-sized model of the globe was truly floating, apparently unsupported in mid-air. What held it up? Antigravity? Electromagnetism? Psi-force? What powers did this new, technological group of Venusians have access to?

'I don't know,' he said at last. 'I think you know more than I do. The Doctor might be able to help you.'

Mrodtikdhil seemed to think for a moment.

'The Doctor. Yes, it was always the Doctor himself who helped Jikugihi Dharkhig. Perhaps he can help us for a change.' He swivelled two more eyes to Ian. 'Will you bring the Doctor to us?'

'I don't know – I'm worried about Barbara.' It was true; but Ian also wasn't sure whether he could trust Mrodtikdhil. He had no way of knowing whether the big Venusian was telling the truth.

'We will send help for Barbara,' said Mrodtikdhil. 'Your friend the bud-mother will show us the way. Will you help us?'

Still Ian hesitated, aware that above all else he wanted to be with Barbara, to make sure she was all right, that she wasn't in pain, that she would live. He reminded himself that the Doctor might be in danger too; but somehow that threat didn't seem quite so substantial. The Doctor would find a way out of any danger he was in; he always did. And Barbara might be *dying.*

He remembered the Doctor's comments about the TARDIS, how it was more steerable 'this far back'. He wondered if he and the Doctor could use the TARDIS to rescue Barbara. He was sure that the medical facilities on board the ship would heal her far faster, and more reliably, than Jellenhut could.

'Very well,' he said at last. 'I'll go to find the Doctor. But we may need to use our ship, the TARDIS.'

'The one that can travel in space and time?'

Ian nodded.

Mrodtikdhil extended a hand towards Ian.

'It seems as if we will have to trust you after all,' he said quietly.

There was a slight click of bone and a long, gleaming writing-claw emerged from the wrinkled skin of one of the finger-petals. It was sharpened; the blade glinted in the light of the *brakud*-oil lamps. The claw came closer, until the tip was touching one of the strands binding Ian.

Carefully, the Venusian began to cut him free.

* * *

Barbara looked at the knot of green moss wriggling in the centre of the ceiling and decided she was alive.

She had been eating flowers. She remembered it: little blue ones. They'd tasted sharp and sappy. That was when she'd thought that she might have died and gone to Heaven; she didn't know much about what Heaven was supposed to be like, but she remembered thinking that it might be the kind of place where you ate flowers.

'Hello,' said a familiar voice, deep and rumbling, like something big frying in deep fat. 'How are you feeling?'

Barbara propped herself up on one elbow and gazed at the big green alien squatting by her bed. She had a momentary feeling that she ought to be afraid of big green aliens, that she ought to scream or something, but the effort of sitting up had made her too tired to bother.

'Hello, Trikhobu,' she said, remembering the name quite suddenly, as well as the odd fact that this particular alien was somehow her daughter. 'I'm feeling a bit weak.'

'I'm not surprised. Since sunrise you've been overdosed, concussed, blown up, had a hole kicked in you and nearly been drowned; and it's still an hour and forty-three fifty-ninths to sunset. Do you normally have this kind of day?'

'There was a time when I didn't,' said Barbara muggily. A vague memory of several rows of several attentive little human faces rose up in her mind. 'But lately it seems to be happening to me a lot.' A thought occurred to her. 'Where's Ian?'

Trikhobu's skin flushed with blue blood.

'He – er – went for help. But he didn't come back.'

Barbara grinned despite herself. 'Pretty much as usual, then.'

She forced herself to sit upright, ignoring a feeling of dizziness and interesting pains from various parts of her body.

'Where are we?' she asked.

'The globeroller *Absolute Acceptance*. They seemed quite

keen to help you. I think they thought you were one of the other aliens, the Sou(ou)shi.'

Barbara glanced around the cabin. All the moss grew in knots; all the knots were wriggling, as if trying to untie themselves. There was a small round window, shuttered with slats of red chitin.

'Hmm. Inarihibi ship, isn't it?' she observed, drawing on Dharkhig's memories. 'What happens if the Death Inspectors get aboard?'

'I don't think they will.' Trikhobu glanced at a notepad covered in scribbled calculations. 'The odds were very much against it from the start, and we're almost in Bikugih now.'

Barbara relaxed slightly. At least they were going in the right direction. Once they got to Bikugih, she could meet up with the Doctor, find out what was going on, find Ian, get out of here.

Though she would be sorry to leave Trikhobu.

'Why was I eating flowers?' she asked.

Before Trikhobu could answer, a Venusian in a crisp white belly-wrap appeared in the doorway of the cabin, eye-stalks politely curled in the *highir* pattern.

'I'm sorry, ma'am, but we have to declare all aliens aboard the ship before it will be allowed into Bikugih.'

'Declare?' asked Barbara.

The clansman looked embarrassed.

'There's some kind of problem, apparently. There are three rogue aliens – ' He broke off, suddenly, all his eyes staring at Barbara. 'Excuse me!' he yelped. 'I think – ' There was a clatter of hooves as he scuttled off down the corridor.

Barbara stood up on the bed, and discovered it was a blue-and-white check belly-wrap. 'No beds on Venus,' she muttered to herself. Mechanically, she began folding the cloth around her body. She found her shoes and stepped into them.

There were sounds of shouting from outside, and heavy hoof-steps on the ceiling. Trikhobu, agitated, hopped towards the doorway.

'What are we going to do?'

Barbara shrugged. 'Try to get up on deck. Try to get off the ship, Try to find the Doctor.' She felt a sudden flicker of fear when she said the last words. Three rogue aliens, the steward had said. What if the Doctor had already been captured?

Well, there was no time to worry about it now. She pushed past Trikhobu and hauled herself up into the corridor. Her injured chest burned in protest and a yellow mist filled her eyes.

The corridor was empty. To the left, Barbara could see the bottom of a staircase and something that looked like daylight.

'Come on Trikhobu, quick!'

Her friend jumped up beside her with a thud that almost knocked Barbara off her feet. They started towards the staircase.

Barbara quickly became aware that she barely had the energy to walk; her legs were wobbling under her as if the joints were made of rubber.

I was *badly* hurt, she realized.

When she saw that the height of the treads on the staircase was about six feet, she gave up and asked Trikhobu to carry her. She watched the pentagon of sky get closer, saw the eye-stalks craning over the edge.

'Trikhobu, I think we'd better – '

But it was too late; Trikhobu was already jumping up the last step and on to the deck.

There were about ten squadsmen forming a tight circle around them, each with a gun in one or two hands and three or four very sharp-looking sticks in the others. They also had heavier weapons on their backs: stone harpoons, catapults, and something sharp and shell-like which looked as if it could cause a lot of damage quite easily.

'I'm one of the good aliens,' said Barbara weakly. 'Honestly I am.'

They ignored her. A hand moved slightly, to improve its grip on one of the throwing-shells. Barbara became aware of how hot the sun was, although it was quite low in the sky.

'She is a good alien!' exclaimed Trikhobu. 'She's my friend!'

'I'm sorry, Fefirhi Trikhobu, but you have been misinformed. This alien is dangerous. Please stand aside and allow us to kill it.'

'No!' yelled Trikhobu. 'I'm staying here!'

A buzzing noise filled Barbara's head.

I can't faint now, she thought. If I'm going to die, I want to at least know it's happening.

'Fefirhi Trikhobu, we must insist – '

The sun went out.

Barbara looked up, and wasn't particularly surprised to see the huge grey bulk of the Sou(ou)shi ship filling the sky. Dim blue light played over the ravines and the rims of the craters.

Her head seemed to clear a little.

'You see,' she said to the leader of the posse. 'My friends have come for me.' She sat up.

– and suddenly she was falling, impossibly incredibly falling away from the deck. She felt Trikhobu's arms reflexively tighten, hands closing on her arms, trying to hold on to her, but it was no use: she was wrenched out of their grasp, she was dropping, dropping upwards towards the Sou(ou)shi ship, the wind buffeting her ears. She saw the canvas of the globeroller's sails rushing past her, frantically tried to grab it, but it was too far and she only set herself spinning. She saw Trikhobu in mid-air behind her, whirling like a sycamore seed. The Venusian hit the canvas of the mainsail and slid along it, scrabbling for a grip. Barbara tried to call out, but her friend was too far away. She cleared the top of the mainsail; saw the streets of Bikugih, oddly dark and lifeless, turning above her. Air screamed in her ears, forced her head, her arms, her legs back. She could scarcely breathe.

Now she was facing the Sou(ou)shi ship. Already it seemed closer; she could pick out details, boulders, cracks in the ravened surface.

She wondered if she would still be alive when she hit it.

13

Trials of Conscience

The boat jumped about in the heavy swell like a nightfish on its mating day. Gobbets of hot, salty spray whipped through the air, stinging Brignontojij's skin. He scratched at it irritably, keeping three eyes on the alien's blue box, ready in the catch-net. The thing slipped and twisted in the ropes, clunking and scraping against the rocks they'd put there to weigh it down, for all the world as if it were trying to escape.

Brignontojij waved a hand at Nosgentanreteb; the squadsman and the boatman Kallenhu started turning the handle of the winch. The net slowly lifted above the deck, swaying dangerously; when it was high enough to be clear of their bodies, Kallenhu locked the vertical winch and started to wind the horizontal one. The crane turned, swinging its burden out across the rail and over the water. Brignontojij raised his arm, ready to signal Nosgentanreteb to release the net.

Suddenly Kallenhu craned four eyes to the south.

'Boat ahoy!' he shouted.

He locked the winch and jumped over Brignontojij to take the wheel.

Brignontojij looked to the east, caught a glimpse over the blue-grey waves of a low, black galley, its banks of oars chopping hard at the water.

'Heading straight for us!' shouted Kallenhu.

Belatedly, Brignontojij wondered whether he ought to have rustled up a larger escort for this job. A couple of Fives would have been useful in this situation.

But on the other hand, who could possibly – ?

Another glimpse of the boat: he saw a clansman in Philosopher's robes, shouting something.

'. . . not destroy . . . changed . . .'

Then, abruptly, the boat was alongside, oars still clashing with the water. There was a thud of wood on wood; the galley tilted, and for a moment Brignontojij was looking down at the oarsmen in their pit, their legs clenched around the oars. Then, with another thud, the galley righted itself.

'Sir!' Nosgentanreteb pointed at the deck awning of the other boat. Brignontojij saw, to his horror, an alien.

– like a giant stickwalker with white fungus on its eyestalk –

In an instant he'd drawn all five of his guns; Nosgentanreteb had done the same.

'The orders have been changed!' shouted the Philosopher. 'The TARDIS is not to be destroyed.'

Brignontojij swung one of his guns to cover the speaker.

'I'm sorry, honoured Philosopher, but I must assume you are in thrall to the alien. Please allow me to continue with my task as ordered by the Night Council.'

The Philosopher waved his arms about irritably and said, 'No! No! No! I *am* the Night Council, you idiot.' He reached into his lip-pocket, withdrew a piece of paper with the gleaming gold seal. 'The orders have been changed, haven't you heard anything I've said? We want the TARDIS – the alien's craft – in Bikugih, for examination. The alien is to be given a fair trial.'

Brignontojij examined the alien and the Philosopher in confusion. The alien looked up, caught his eye for a moment. The Philosopher shuffled across to the alien and began speaking quietly. Brignontojij watched for a moment, caught the word 'escape'.

He didn't hesitate. He leaped across the space between the two boats and landed, cuttershell-knife drawn, an arm's length from the alien.

The alien and the Philosopher stared at him. There was

a moment's silence. The deck heaved slowly. Brignontojij saw the eye-stalks of one of the oarsmen, just above deck level, peering at him curiously.

The stickwalker-alien stood up.

Brignontojij fenced forward with the knife.

'There's no need to be alarmed, squadsman,' said the alien softly. 'My friend here – because he is my friend, and for no other reason – was offering me the chance to take my craft and leave Venus with my companions.'

The Philosopher's arms started to wave about wildly. 'Doctor, I beg you – '

'But I'm afraid I will not be accepting the offer,' the Doctor went on, ignoring the interruption, and keeping his odd, stapled-in eyes on Brignontojij. 'I have every faith in Venusian justice,' he went on. 'Particularly that of the Night Council of Bikugih. I am sure that, if the truth is told, this matter will be resolved, and my companions and I will be able to travel on with our names vindicated and our consciences clear.'

'My old friend, please.' The Philosopher was speaking two-mouthed, his arms and legs twitching with emotion. 'Believe me. This escape is the only way.'

Brignontojij looked at the two of them: the frantic Venusian, the calm alien with his eyes turned away from his friend. He looked at Nosgentanreteb on the other boat, at Kallenhu with his legs gripping the wheel. To the south, he saw the Sou(ou)shi ship, like a new range of mountains rising above the horizon.

Abruptly he came to a decision.

'Nosgentanreteb!' he shouted. 'Secure the alien's ship. We're going back to the harbour to get this sorted out.'

Barbara's fall began to slow down at about the same time that she realized she was freezing to death. Her hands and feet were numb, and she was fairly sure the blue colour in her fingers was real and not some effect of her blurred vision. The wind felt like it was cutting pieces of her face away whole. Barbara hadn't really thought about what frostbite meant before; now she was beginning to wonder if it was the last thing she would ever think about.

The landscape beneath her – and it was unmistakably a landscape at this distance – was like the surface of the Moon. She was directly above a crater, a creased, flat-bottomed bowl about a mile across. Blue light played across the rock, but she had little hope of warmth from that.

With an effort, Barbara turned her head to face 'upwards' to Bikugih. The city was dark, a dim fingerprint in chitin on a flat plain. To the north, the sea glinted.

A delicious sensation of warmth spread around her back, and the rushing of the wind faded from her ears.

Not long now, she thought. To her surprise, she didn't seem to be afraid any more. She decided to keep her head facing the sea: at least the last thing she saw would be alive.

'Hello Barbara.'

Voices. That's it, then. Let's hope they're real ones. Let's hope there's a heaven to go to.

'We are sorry to have temporarily delayed your death in this way. We regret any inconvenience we may have caused you.'

Startled, Barbara twisted her head around, saw nothing except the crater and the blue light. The warm sensation in her back spread to her legs and arms, accompanied by pins and needles. She massaged her face: it began to sting.

'It was necessary to save your life because of the Doctor.'

'Oh,' she managed to say. Her voice sounded croaky, but manageable. 'I – ' she began, but the voices had more to tell her.

'We have analysed the mind patterns of the Doctor, and we regret that we have found him to be evil.'

Barbara looked down and realized she was quite close to the crater floor. But she wasn't falling any more; she was drifting down, as if she weighed barely anything at all. The air was quite warm, and her hands and feet were beginning to hurt in earnest.

'What's evil about the Doctor?' she asked, since the voices had been silent for a few seconds.

A single voice spoke in reply: 'He suffers from the habit of compassion. It is a dirty habit, leading to many unnecessary survivals.'

'I don't think compassion is – ' But again she was interrupted.

'It is necessary for the Doctor to die. In order to persuade him to do so, we plan to make use of his unfortunate habit. We understand that you are one of the species that experiences pain when physical damage is suffered. We intend to cause you pain in the hope that the Doctor's compassion will make him co-operate with our desire to kill him.'

The air around Barbara now seemed to be luminous: faint, momentary shapes formed and re-formed constantly. Slowly, the ground came up to meet her. It occurred to her to struggle, but her body would barely respond; it was as if she was wrapped in a blanket.

'Again, we regret the inconvenience this will cause you,' said the voices soothingly. 'Please have our assurance that as soon as our objective is achieved, you will be allowed to die without any further delay.'

There was a hole in the crater floor; Barbara drifted into it. She had a brief glimpse of rock walls, then a door closed above her and she was floating in darkness.

She expected to land, but she didn't. For a few moments she floated there, faint after-images of the crater walls dying in her eyes.

Then the pain began.

After a while, she started to scream, but it didn't do any good.

The heavy-weapons squads were in place along the length of the quay and the wide, flat tops of the main harbour walls. The sun was shining in the narrow piece of sky between the black limb of the Sou(ou)shi ship and the sea; its light gleamed off the goldenwood barrels of flamethrowers and the thick hafts of the explosive harpoons. The points of reflection moved steadily as the weapons slowly turned, tracking the boat carrying the alien. From her own position on board a commandeered fish-chaser at the harbour entrance, Lighibu couldn't see the boat, but the angle of the guns told her well enough where it was.

Not far away.

The Presidor was standing beside her on the green-painted deck of the chaser, four of his eyes craned towards the open sea.

'Any word from Mrak-ecado yet?'

He looked nervous, Lighibu thought. His mouths were tight, his belly drawn up. If he had been in her Five she would have told him to stand down until he felt more relaxed.

'Nothing,' she told him, adding, 'You would be safer on the wall, Presidor. People may hold their fire because of your position here.'

The Presidor stared at her, three-eyed. The low sun emphasized the wrinkles in the skin along his eye-stalks, made him look older than he was.

'I need to talk to Mrak-ecado,' he said. 'I need – ' He broke off. Lighibu had an awful feeling that Jofghil had been going to say 'his advice'. Hardly appropriate when he'd just made a rousing speech declaring the Philosopher to be a traitor and a criminal.

'We should go forward,' said Jofghil abruptly, with the mouth facing not Lighibu, but the sea.

Lighibu hesitated for a moment. The instruction didn't make any sense. In the open water, the galley carrying the alien could easily avoid them; and if they did succeed in catching it, then the heavy weapons in the harbour would be useless. Even if they were in range, the two boats would present only one target.

'Forward! We need to meet them in open water!'

With an inward popping of hands, Lighibu signalled to Bufihil, who was acting as pilot.

The squadswoman released the bulb of hormones that woke the four nightfish sleeping under the belly of the boat. Thinking that their mating-waters were close, the fish went into a frenzy of swimming. The chaser rose in the water, sweeping forward into the waves. Spray flew from the bow, tingled on Lighibu's skin. For a moment, despite the danger of the moment – or perhaps because of it – she felt a cool, clear exhilaration. This was the way to live. Five legs braced against the dance of the sea, the evening wind in her mouths, the taste of salt and sea-moss. She wondered whether the place where the Sou(ou)shi were taking them would have sea and wind and spray like this; wondered, too, whether she really wanted to go with the aliens, or whether she would rather face the End here, in this light, in a world she was part of.

Efenihu's voice broke her reverie; the squadswoman was shouting and pointing at something from the cabin-top. Lighibu followed her gaze, saw the black galley, with Brignontojij's commandeered fishing boat beside it. She didn't need to tell Bufihil what to do; the pilot had wrestled the wheel round two-legged before Lighibu would have been able to frame an order. The chaser heeled, water surged alongside, the hull creaked under the strain of the nightfish-harnesses.

Jofghil lost his grip on the deck, whirled round on one hoof, arms and legs scrabbling, slammed into the wheel-house wall.

Idiot! thought Lighibu. You shouldn't be here.

We shouldn't be here.

The deck levelled as they straightened course; Lighibu saw the galley only five *ojotti* away, still making for the harbour entrance.

'Weapons ready!' she yelled.

'Don't kill Mrak-ecado!' shouted the Presidor.

'I've no intention of killing anybody if I can avoid it,' said Lighibu crossly.

The distance between the boats was now about three *ojotti*, no more than twice the length of the big galley. Lighibu could see Mrak-ecado and the alien standing close together in the bows.

With her south eye, she saw Efenihu readying her arms to throw a cuttershell.

'Hold your fire!' she ordered, then jumped to the bow of the chaser, where there was a speaking-horn. She fitted her forward mouth to the wood.

'Mrak-ecado! We have orders to kill the alien and to place you under arrest. Please give way.'

The Philosopher's voice drifted back.

'. . . who?'

'From the Presidor himself.'

'. . . disagree . . . fair trial . . . Doctor needs a chance to reconsider.'

Reconsider what? thought Lighibu. Whether he's going to destroy Venusian civilization? Suddenly, she remembered the gentle eyes of the being she had almost killed on the road to Bikugih, eyes that had borne her no malice, eyes that had known instantly that she had only been obeying legitimate orders; and she knew, without any doubt, that the Doctor could not be about to destroy Venusian civilization. Someone, somewhere, was making a mistake.

The galley was alongside now, about an *ojotti* away, passing the chaser at trotting pace. Jofghil pointed at the alien staring at them from the bow, started shouting:

'Kill it! Kill it! Kill it!'

He was jumping up and down like a child asking for meat.

'Kill it!'

Lighibu saw Efenihu and Jerekarnijli raise their arms to throw; Bufihil, with the harpoon, crouched into the trigger position.

'*Hold – your – fire!*' bawled Lighibu, with all five mouths.

Everyone froze, even Jofghil. The stern of the galley

slowly passed them. Lighibu noticed Mrak-ecado signalling the oarsmen to stop.

She took three short jumps along the deck of the chaser, stopped in front of the Presidor.

'In the event of two members of the Night Council having a disagreement, the correct procedure is for a full meeting of the Council to be held. I would respectfully suggest that you call such a meeting as soon as possible.' She nearly added 'before all that ridiculous weaponry you've got at the harbour burns us out of the water' but thought better of it.

Jofghil stared at her, three-eyed. Lighibu could see the galley slowly turning in the water astern, Bufihil doping the fish and pulling the wheel around so that the chaser would stay within hailing distance.

Finally Jofghil said, 'I'll discuss it with Mrak-ecado.'

Lighibu felt her skin relax, the blood flow back into her belly. For some reason, the Presidor sounded almost as if he were pleased. After a moment Lighibu realized why.

Someone had told him what to do.

Therinidu's workshop smelled of leather and smoke. On the white plaster walls hung the dark, blunted star-shapes of Venusian shoes. A *brakud*-oil pressure lamp hissed on one wall, its parabolic mirror casting a golden light on Ian's legs as the shoemaker herself examined his feet.

The makeshift shoes that Jellenhut had made were already in tatters, and Ian's feet were bruised and aching. Mrodtikdhil, reluctant to allow any delay, had offered to detail a squadsman to carry Ian on his back; but Ian had insisted that he wanted to be able to use his own feet.

'Are you sure you don't want the hooves made up?' asked Therinidu, reading the distance between the back of the heel and the ankle from a yellow cloth tape measure. The markings on the tape didn't seem to be at regular intervals, but Inikhut's memories assured Ian that this was normal.

'I didn't have any hooves,' he told her. 'I've never had them.'

'How did you walk, then, without damaging the flesh of your foot?'

Therinidu seemed genuinely curious. She had measured every conceivable dimension of his foot: big toe to heel, big toe to ankle, ankle to little toe, little toe to big toe. She had used a device resembling a circular fan to measure the angles of various joints. She had asked about bone structure and watched him walk across the floor and back.

'I wore shoes,' he said. 'Leather uppers, hard leather soles. I suppose the soles would be pretty much the same as hooves, come to think of it.'

The Venusian twisted an eye to look at a pile of uncut leather lying against the far wall.

'I'll use a double thickness,' she said after a moment. 'I knew my father's hide would come in useful one day.' She walked across and pulled a thick, brown, wrinkled skin from the bottom of the heap, bracing two legs against the others to stop them from toppling over.

With a shock, Ian realized that the shape of the hide was unmistakably that of a Venusian. Inikhut's memories didn't seem to think anything was wrong, but even so –

'Your father?' he said aloud.

Therinidu turned two wide purple eyes to him, twitched the lashes.

'It may as well be used now,' she said. 'If the Commander's plan goes ahead, this whole place will burn tomorrow.'

Ian watched as Therinidu threw the hide over a tent-shaped cutting bench, drew a diamond knife and, apparently without consulting anything except her memory, began making a series of careful incisions. After a moment she lowered a couple of eyes until they were almost touching the leather, drew a second knife and began working two-handed.

Ian padded across to the doorway and looked out. The

guard, Keritiheg, was still there; Ian could see his hooves at eye-level, the bottom of his red belly-wrap, other Venusian hooves beyond, clopping on the pentagonal cobbles. Lifting himself by the arms and peering around Keritiheg's legs, he could see the whole of the vast dimly lit cavern that Mrodtikdhil had casually referred to as a 'pressure chamber'. Knobby, tree-sized mosses grew on the walls, partially disguising a spiral thread which ran on and on, narrowing slightly, into a misty, darkened distance. Shacks made of leather or wood were scattered around the chamber, with the cobbled roads winding between them. Nearby, some children were standing around a water fountain, washing themselves, jumping and squealing.

This whole place will burn. He imagined all the shacks empty, the children gone, a wall of fire scouring the chamber. He wondered how the displaced Volcano People would take to life on the surface. He wondered what the surface would be like with a billion tons of dust in orbit, filtering out the sunlight. Would it snow?

Ian heard the hollow thud of a wooden hammer behind him, turned and saw Therinidu working five-handed and five-eyed. One shoe was already taking shape: a curved, pleated shield of leather over a flat sole.

There was a clatter of movement behind him; a hoof tapped him on the shoulder, making him jump. He turned, saw it was Mrodtikdhil. He moved aside, allowing the Commander to jump down into the room.

'Are they ready yet?' Mrodtikdhil asked the leather-worker, his voice edged with impatience.

'Two red-to-reds,' replied Therinidu without looking up or pausing in her work.

Two red-to-reds: five or ten minutes.

Another clansman jumped down through the doorway, making the room crowded. The Commander introduceed the newcomer as Ruribeg, the Volcano People's agent in Bikugih. While Therinidu continued with her work, the Commander twitched impatiently and Ruribeg swung an ankle-bag from one leg to the next, catching it each time on the ankle-claw, never once touching it with his hands. Ian remembered Inikhut playing that game as a child.

There was a faint, strange, '*Chff*' sound. Puzzled, Ian looked around, then saw the *ghifghoni* nestling against one of Ruribeg's hips. Three of its small green eyes returned his gaze.

'He's my lucky charm,' said Ruribeg, scratching the little flyer under the belly with a spare hand. 'He was in Afhighid Kontojij's keeping.'

'He carries the message,' Mrodtikdhil said without taking his eyes off Therinidu and her work.

'What message?'

'The message from Kontojij,' Ruribeg explained, pulling a smooth chitin cylinder from the *ghifghoni*'s belly-pouch.

Ian nodded to himself. It made sense: carry a copy of Kontojij's message so that the Doctor could judge the situation for himself.

Ruribeg put the message pod back in the flyer's pouch and resumed his game of ankle-catch. There was a silence, broken only by the hiss of the lamp and the soft clopping of hooves from outside.

'They're ready,' said Therinidu suddenly.

Ian took the shoes, still warm from the moulding. There were no laces. He had some trouble pushing his feet into them, but once he had they fitted perfectly. He walked up and down the room a couple of times.

'Best pair of shoes I've ever had.'

Therinidu gaped warmly, stuck out her tongue in friendly salute.

Ruribeg had already jumped back out of the doorway. Mrodtikdhil followed, almost pulling Ian with him.

'The tube's ready to go,' he said. 'We can't afford any more delay; you will need to ride.'

As he clambered up on to the Commander's back, Ian asked if there was any news of Barbara.

'They won't even have got there yet,' said Mrodtikdhil briskly.

He set off at a trot along the path; Ruribeg and Keritiheg followed. Almost at once they began to descend into the rock, high blue-painted walls rising on either side. Small windows and doors were built into the walls at irregular intervals. They were far too small for Venusians, and Ian puzzled about them until a tiny child, younger even than Jellenhut's youngest, poked a leg and a couple of eye-stalks out of one of the entrances and made a series of faint squeaks.

'We let them practise with digging-machines as soon as they're born,' said Mrodtikdhil. Then, as if to himself, 'We'll have to make sure they're all out of there before we burn.'

Ian had a sudden, absurd image of five-year-old humans being given quarter-size bulldozers to play with. And, somehow, not demolishing their parents' houses. Venusians were *different*, he realized. It wasn't just a matter of having five eyes and five legs.

Abruptly a roof closed over the path; though, paradoxically, the illumination grew brighter. Frescos appeared on the walls: bright, whirling designs of air and sky and leaves. The path began to descend steeply, became a staircase – a Venusian staircase, of course, with eight-foot treads. Ian was almost thrown off Mrodtikdhil's back as the Commander bounced down the steps two at a time.

At the bottom of the stairs the tube vehicle was ready and waiting. It didn't really look much like a tube train, Ian reflected; it was only the noises it made, the hisses and clicks, and the environment – the tunnels, the stone platform – that made it seem familiar. It was more like a gigantic, perfectly cylindrical butterfly pupa. Looking closely, he could see that the dull purple chitin was indeed made up of overlapping plates, as if some dragon-sized insect had grown the pod and was maturing inside it.

Mrodtikdhil touched a knobby protrusion on the chitin, and a door fell open with a loud hiss and a clatter of chitin on stone. Ruribeg and Keritiheg got in; Mrodtikdhil wished them good luck, then lifted Ian three-armed and dumped him unceremoniously on the floor between them.

The door slammed before the Commander had even said goodbye.

Ian braced himself against the floor as the tube accelerated; when the worst of the clattering noise was over, and conversation became possible, he asked his companions whether they had been with the Volcano People all their lives.

Ruribeg replied, 'Of course. We were born into that necessity.'

Born into that necessity. Yes. Venusians talked like that all the time. 'It is necessary to . . .' 'The situation allows us to . . .' They didn't say 'I' very much; when they argued, it tended to be about the best way of doing things rather than who was right. Which probably explained why it was safe to put children who could barely speak in charge of digging machines.

'Our clan has been of the Volcano People since the beginning, for twelve hundred generations,' offered the guard over the clattering of the tube.

Ian thought he must have misheard. He did a hasty multiplication, then said, 'You mean that you've been building this lot for forty thousand years?'

Ruribeg twitched his eye-stalks in assent.

'The planning began earlier than that, of course,' he said. 'In the time of the Gardens.'

'Earlier – ?'

Ian swallowed.

'How old is the oldest clan?' he asked Ruribeg.

Ruribeg and Keritiheg looked at each other three-eyed for a few moments.

'Bikugih is the oldest *surviving* clan,' Ruribeg said eventually, a spare hand scratching the little *ghifghoni* under his belly. 'But the first clan to have written records, if that's what you mean, was Dhallenidhall; they existed for over a hundred thousand generations.'

Ian swallowed again. He was talking to two representatives of a species that had invented writing more than three million years ago. He had an absurd impulse to get down on his knees and beg them for something: wisdom, perhaps.

The tube began to slow down, juddering slightly; the noise made talking impossible. When it stopped, Ian asked how long Venusian civilization would continue if the Volcano Project succeeded.

'Three hundred generations,' was the immediate reply.

'You mean to say that you've spent forty thousand years building something that will only give you an extra ten thousand years?'

'Would it have been better if we had not done it?' asked Ruribeg.

Ian couldn't think of an answer to that. He sat back, shut his eyes and tried to rest, but the jolting movement of the tube, the constant acceleration and deceleration, the sheer discomfort of his damaged skin in the hot atmosphere, kept him awake.

'How long before we reach Bikugih?' he asked after a while.

There was no reply. Ian opened his eyes, saw that Ruribeg's eye-stalks were limp, the eyes milky. There was a red line around the centre of the Venusian's body, just above the mouths. As Ian stared, the top half of the body started to slide backwards. Blood and pieces of inner organs boiled over the rim of the exposed underside and spilled onto the floor. The lower legs fell outwards in a star pattern, gushing blood.

What kind of weapon – ? thought Ian. He shouted for Keritiheg, but there was no response. The blood and body fluids from Ruribeg flooded across the floor, staining Ian's trousers. The *ghifghoni*, displaced from the Venusian's hip, began flying around the top part of the tube, screeching.

Ian became aware that the tube was shuddering violently. One of the *brakud*-oil lamps crashed to the floor and went out. At the back, Keritiheg's body slumped and parted into two horizontal slices. A dark gap appeared in the walls of the tube, revealing stone walls rushing past.

It occured to Ian that he should keep his head down. He crouched as near to the bloodied floor as he could; his eyes started weeping from the ammoniacal stink. Suddenly the *ghifghoni* dived for Ian, landed on his shoulder, dug its claws in with its rotors still whirling.

There was a huge thud, and the whole floor of the vehicle rippled, throwing Ian into the air and forward. It was followed by a series of similar impacts; with each one, the top half of the tube separated further from the floor, until with a screaming sound and a flood of sparks it fell away. Ian heard the *ghifghoni* screech, once. One of the lamps exploded, making a brief fireball somewhere behind Keritiheg's body. Then something huge and heavy caught Ian in the back, lifted him into the air, and plunged him down into darkness.

Kintibi Jofghil settled himself in the goldenwood framework of the High Dais of the Presidor of the Night Council, trying not to scratch himself on the sword-edge rubies set on the outside of the wood. He had done that on the very first night he had presided over the Council and had been forced to get a bandage; he had never forgotten the shame of it.

The shutters had been opened, and the last rays of the sun shone in through the painted glass of the Great Window, filling the Chamber of the Night Council with yellow evening light. The light was not quite even: distortions in the glass made faint whorls of shadow that draped themselves over the goldenwood rings of the seats and the roughened stone of the floor. The dome had been folded back as well, but where the blue of the sky should have been there was the dark, cratered landscape of the Sou(ou)shi ship. Two shuttles were visible, moving slowly downwards, glinting in the sun.

Jofghil let one of his eyes follow them for a moment, then returned all his attention to the alien in the Trial Seat.

The Doctor was squatting on the inner edge of the wooden ring, his eyes alert. As the members of the Night Council came in he twitched his fungus-topped eye-stalk at several of them, as if greeting old friends.

Rather to Jofghil's surprise, Mrak-ecado had agreed to give his evidence. 'I only wanted to give my old friend a chance,' he'd said. 'There might be some innocent explanation for the *huyaot*.'

Jofghil watched Mrak-ecado twitching uncomfortably in the wooden ring of his Council seat, and wondered whether the old Philosopher had thought of an innocent explanation yet.

When all five by five of the councillors were seated, Jofghil began the Accusation.

'Alien known as the Doctor, you are accused of plotting to destroy all civilized life on Venus, possibly by means of sabotaging the ship belonging to the alien people known as the Sou(ou)shi, possibly by other means. There is evidence against you from Jilet Mrak-ecado of the clan Poroghini, Member of this Night Council, and from the aliens known as the Sou(ou)shi. Do you accept this Accusation or do you wish to question it?'

The Doctor stood. One of the whorls of shadow cast by the ancient glass of the window fell across his eye-stalk, making his skin look pebbled, decaying.

'I wish to question it,' he said quietly. 'Firstly I would like to know the nature of the evidence from the Sou(ou)shi, and how it was obtained by this Council.'

Jofghil was ready for this one.

'The Sou(ou)shi have testified that you attempted to set a destructive force in place aboard their ship. They stated that this force would make it impossible for them to carry out their intentions with regard to us, and might prove a danger even to them. They advised us that you should be neutralized in order to prevent further disruption to our mutual co-operation.'

The Doctor's face creased.

'That's exactly the sort of thing they would say, I'm afraid.' He paused, looking around at the members of the Night Council. 'They're not lying, they're just playing with other people's assumptions about the truth. When I first visited the Earth, many years ago, I had the misfortune to meet someone who called himself a marketing manager. He sold something poisonous, or perhaps it was dangerous; I'm afraid I can't remember what it was. But he sold a lot of it. He didn't tell lies, either. He explained it to me: he made people associate this thing he was selling with something good, something they really wanted – and then they bought it. Most of them died, of course, sooner or later. Funnily enough, there was a law at the time which said that he had to tell the truth about this thing – had to say that it was likely to kill people. And they *still* bought it, because it was associated with something clever or attractive. It always truly amazes me, how blind people can be to deliberate evil.'

Jofghil's eye-stalks flattened. What was the alien rambling on about? A marketing manager was somebody who managed a market and saw that all the shopkeepers had adequate space and that everybody got a fair return. What was this about selling something? And deliberate evil?

'Alien, I must ask you to keep to the point. Time is short. The members of this Council wish to join their clans aboard the Sou(ou)shi ship, and the vessel will not be here for long before it goes on to other cities.'

'The point is that the Sou(ou)shi are misleading you!' The Doctor was almost shouting. 'Every Venusian who boards that ship will die. Don't you see?'

There was a silence. Several of the councillors stirred, as if getting ready to ask questions. Jofghil decided to forestall them. The trick was too obvious for him to allow debate about it.

'I don't see anything,' he said, 'except someone who is lying to protect himself.'

'That is a prejudiced remark,' rumbled Mrak-ecado.

'The alien is making prejudiced remarks,' replied Jofghil tartly. He wasn't going to let the old Philosopher run the show either. 'Do you wish to hear Jilet Mrak-ecado speak his evidence?' he asked the Doctor.

The Doctor twitched his eye-stalk, said, 'Yes, I'm very much afraid I would.'

Jofghil heard Mrak-ecado's belly-wrap scrape against the wooden ring of his seat as the flesh underneath it reflexively tightened. His entire skin seemed to shrink, his arms and eyes twitched. But he stood up, slowly turning three eyes to the Doctor.

'I'm sorry, old friend; I had hoped it wouldn't come to this,' he began.

He detailed the message he had received from Kontojij, its description of the *huyaot*, the images of Venusians dying.

'Kontojij said there were no objects visible, only the deaths. No objects except "a blue box with a flashing light on the top" which, he says, appeared "in the curving space with the people who were dying, as if it were producing the force that was rupturing their bodies".' As Mrak-ecado spoke, he withdrew a scrolled piece of paper from his north ankle-bag and spread it out two-handed. To Jofghil's amazement he jumped out of his seat and offered it to the Doctor.

'Here, old friend. Argue against it if you can.'

The Doctor had been staring fixedly at Mrak-ecado all the time the Philosopher had been speaking; now he continued to stare, barely glancing at the paper in his hand.

'I should have thought it was obvious,' he said. 'Another Sou(ou)shi trick.' But his voice sounded weak, uncertain. There was a long silence.

Finally the Doctor looked down at the piece of paper. He pulled the glass objects that hung round his neck over his eyes and examined it closely. Once he muttered, 'Old friend, surely you do not believe the Sou(ou)shi to the extent that you would consider it necessary to – '

But he did not complete the sentence.

At last he looked up at Mrak-ecado, silently handed the paper back. The Philosopher was blue with emotion.

'I accept the evidence,' the alien said shortly, and sat down.

Mrak-ecado stood in front of him for a long time, then stepped slowly back to his seat. He was trembling.

Jofghil noticed that a fuzzy swathe of yellow light was all that remained of the light from the window: the sun was setting outside. He decided that the show had gone on long enough.

'If the evidence has been accepted, then the Council must make a decision,' he said. 'Councillors, please indicate to what extent you feel the Accusation is true.'

There was a brief hesitation, then the arms started to rise. A few of the Councillors only raised three or four arms, but most raised all five.

It was enough.

Mrak-ecado's arms remained folded across the top of his body; two of his eyes remained on the Doctor, and both the Doctor's on him.

'The decision of the Council is clear,' said Jofghil. 'The alien known as the Doctor is likely to carry out the actions described in the Accusation. For the safety of the people of Bikugih, and that of all other Venusians, it is necessary to prevent this. The alien has exceptional psi-power, this much is clear; and, if his escape from the Sou(ou)shi ship is to be taken as evidence, he seems to be capable of extraordinary manipulations of the physical world, almost amounting to magic. Therefore I feel, as I have felt from the beginning, that the only way to prevent him from killing all of us is to kill him.' Jofghil couldn't help gaping a little with his spare mouths as he said the words. But they were true: their logic was impeccable. 'Does any Councillor disagree?'

Mrak-ecado's arms twitched once more, but he said nothing.

'Squadsmen!' called Jofghil. 'Take the alien from the Council Chamber and execute the decision immediately!'

A Five of squadsmen stepped forward from the shadows at the fringes of the chamber, their hooves clicking on the stone. They lifted the Doctor out of the Trial Seat and led him away. He didn't resist, but his eye-stalk turned as he left the Chamber so that his gaze remained on Mrak-ecado.

Somehow his eyes frightened Jofghil.

'Make sure he doesn't get away this time,' he ordered the squadsmen. 'Make sure he dies. Please. For all our sakes.'

Book Five

The Burning Sky Hour

14

Boarding

Podsighil was afraid of the pentaclaviphonium player. He looked like a monster, with all his wooden pipes and chitin bells and valves and keys and scaffolding. And the noise he made was frightening too: *whoom-phah-CLANG, whoomphah-CLANG-CLANG.* Podsighil buried her eyes in Vivi's leg, but she couldn't bury her ears.

'Get *off*, Podsi. I need to keep up with mother,' rumbled Vivi.

'Don't like the noise!' wailed Podsighil.

'Never mind about the noise, we have to get on the spaceship.'

Podsi felt herself being lifted off the ground as her sister loped four-legged across the hard stone of the roller-port. Bejewelled legs and double-wrapped bellies rushed past; Podsi realized all of a sudden that they were right in the middle of the marching band. There was the double-bubble player with her coloured glass towers full of frothing water, *plink, plink, gubble-gubble plink.* The five-drummer went *bom-bom-bom-bom-bom*, and then the big drum above his eye-stalks went *b-BOM-BOM!* The cogwheeler went *click-clock-clickety-clock*. The barrel-pipes hooted, the inflatable horns roared.

This is better, thought Podsighil. As long as we stay away from that pentaclaviphonium.

Ahead she could see the thing that Vivi said was a spaceship. It looked like a big budling made out of chitin, squatting down on one belly. The sun gleamed off its top legs; at the bottom, light shone out of its mouths. Podsighil wondered how the light got down from the top to the bottom.

'It's a miracle!' she shouted, remembering something that her bud-mother had said earlier. 'Miracle! Miracle!'

'It'll be a miracle if we ever find mother again in this crowd,' said Vivi, picking up Podsighil two-handed and dumping her on her back.

Podsighil looked around, suddenly anxious again. 'We've lost bud-mother?' she asked. She cast her eyes around wildly, making the crowd, the rollerport, the marching band, the spaceship all into one big blur. 'Bud-mother!' she shouted.

'Don't worry, we'll find her. She's going on the spaceship with us.'

But Podsighil was not to be comforted. 'Bud-mother!' she shrieked. 'Bud-mother! Bud-mother! Bud-mother!'

'Podsi, it's all right – '

'Lost! Lost! LOST!' Her eyes were flat against her hips now; tears were running down her sides and into her mouths. 'Lost bud-mother!'

Blurrily she saw a yellow, wrinkled hand reach out and touch her on the lips.

'Don't worry, little one. I'm sure your sister will find your bud-mother when you get on the spaceship.'

Podsighil inspected the newcomer, blinking her eyes rapidly to clear the tears. She was old, dressed in a faded green belly-wrap. Her three eyes were a watery grey-green, and they looked down on Podsi with warmth and kindness.

'Lost bud-mother!' pronounced Podsighil, but with less conviction. This clanswoman *was* a bud-mother, or had been, once.

'Yes, but you'll find her again. Don't worry about her now. Think about how wonderful it's going to be, how exciting. A whole new world! What are you going to do when you get there?'

'New world?' asked Podsighil, suddenly suspicious. 'A new world full of aliens?'

'There will be plenty of space for us, I think,' said the clanswoman. But Podsighil could tell that she wasn't sure.

Suddenly Podsighil remembered her birth: the dark water, the blaze of light, the blood. The sorrowful voice saying, 'The bud-brother won't live.'

Won't live. Wontlivewontlivewontlive –

'We're going to die!' she shrieked. 'We're going to die we're going to die we're going to – '

But Vivi was walking again, towards the open mouth of the alien spaceship.

'Be quiet, Podsi,' said her sister. 'We're not going to die. We're just going somewhere new. Now think how you've offended that nice old clanswoman – '

'We're going to die!' bawled Podsi with increasing conviction. Eyes were curling towards her; curious, concerned.

'It's all right, it's just that we can't find our bud-mother,' she heard her sister explain. 'She's upset.'

The crowd parted for them, the ramp came closer.

'No!' shrieked Podsighil with all the force of her lungs. 'We're going to die!'

'We are not!' shouted her sister, speeding up to a canter. The ground was tilted beneath them, and rang with a sound Podsighil had never heard before.

'We're going to die!' she screamed. Then she just screamed and screamed and screamed, as the alien light closed around her body like teeth.

Ian didn't know how long he'd been walking. He hadn't collapsed yet, so he assumed that it was less than twelve hours; and he couldn't remember when he'd started, so he assumed it was longer than thirty minutes. Any length of time in between seemed possible.

He'd searched the pockets of his battered trousers for a lighter, a flint, a match, anything that would let him see where he was going. One of the Doctor's famous everlasting matches would have been ideal. But there had been nothing, not even a handkerchief.

The *ghifghoni* gripped his shoulder tightly. At first it had made the occasional faint *chff*; now it was silent.

'Don't give up, old boy,' he told it. 'We'll get there if we just keep walking.'

The stone rang under his feet, as smooth and level as a London pavement. More so. Ian wished that there were cracks in the stone, loose pebbles, anything which would make for change or difference. Markers, or some sort of regular divisions. He wished he'd thought to count his steps. Then at least there would have been some way of judging how much ground he'd covered. Not that it was any use knowing that when he had no idea of where he was going.

'Just keep walking, that's what we've got to do,' he told the *ghifghoni*, though he was fairly sure that it was asleep.

At first he thought the light was an hallucination. He so much wanted to see a light, he reasoned. Yet there could be no light; not appearing suddenly like that; unless –

He became aware of the breeze blowing in his face, warm and stale and smelling of stone.

The light grew brighter, was accompanied by a clattering noise.

Ian felt a sudden shout of panic. A train! He tried to cram himself against the side of the tunnel, but it was hard to get a grip on the smooth stone.

The sound got louder, the light brighter, the rushing wind faster. The *ghifghoni* took off, shrieking.

The train looked like a disc, a bright red disc with a corona of golden lamplight. But as it grew closer, Ian could see a flaw, a misshapen piece hanging away from one side.

The side of the tunnel where he was standing.

He started to run across; as he did so the misshapen piece resolved itself into a door, half-way open. He caught a glimpse of two green Venusian eyes hooked round the jamb.

There was a shout, a click, and the air filled with sparks

and the smell of burning chitin. Ian scrambled up the side of the tunnel, slipped, fell.

The train hit the stone floor with a massive thud, and stopped six inches from his body.

Ticking chitin, creaking wood, echoes chasing themselves up and down the tunnel, then silence. Slowly Ian picked himself up.

A Venusian eye was watching him from the narrow gap between the door of the train and its frame.

'Alien! Have you got the *ghifghoni*?'

Ian blinked.

'Ruribeg and Keritiheg are dead,' he said.

'The *ghifghoni*! With the message!'

Ian looked around and saw the *ghifghoni* waddling towards him across the lamplit stone, its long shadow slowly getting shorter as it walked. Suddenly it seemed to realize that it had his attention; with a loud squawk, it took off and gyrated towards him, landing five-clawed on his head.

'Ouch!'

'Has it still got the message?' asked the voice from the train.

Ian reached up, felt around the little flyer's belly. He found a pouch with the smooth chitin cylinder within. He nodded.

'Now get aboard the capsule, please. We need to get to Bikugih.'

'Ruribeg and Keritiheg are dead,' said Ian again. 'The tube capsule just fell in half – and their bodies – '

'We imagined as much when you did not arrive. It is the *nenetif*. The fibres of its web are so thin that they cannot be seen, but they will cut through anything. You are fortunate not to be awaiting remembering yourself; your small height must have saved you. Now please – '

Hands reached out, pulled Ian in through the door. The *ghifghoni*, disturbed, sank its claws into his scalp.

He slapped at it. 'Stop that!'

The Venusian who had been speaking put Ian down on

the floor, pulling the door closed behind him with a third hand whilst taking the message pod with a fourth. Ian recognized the guard who had travelled with Jellenhut. Then, as he stepped to one side, Ian saw Jellenhut herself.

'Bud-mother!' He ran to touch her lips.

'Ian of Earth,' she said, returning the gesture. 'It seems we are to adventure together some more.'

The guard was tapping at a large black box covered with buttons of various shapes; with a jolt, the capsule started to move, in the opposite direction to that which it had come.

'Did you find Barbara?' asked Ian.

Jellenhut lowered her eye-stalks.

'I'm sorry, my friend. They'd gone – to Bikugih, apparently.'

'There was some sort of incident at the rollerport,' the guard added. 'She vanished.'

'I'm sure she's safe,' said Jellenhut hastily. 'But your friend the Doctor is on trial for his life.'

'What!?' Ian put his head in his hands, forgetting the *ghifghoni* which fluttered off with an annoyed squawk. Why did things always get like this?

'That's why we need Kontojij's message. To convince the Bikugih Presidor that the Doctor is not likely to be the real threat. We need the Doctor alive.'

The black box which the guard had been tapping earlier suddenly issued a loud wooden thud. The guard pressed it to his mouth, which struck Ian as odd until he remembered that a Venusian's ears were located in the upper lip.

The box clicked and rattled for a few seconds; then the guard put it down, rather suddenly.

'I'm sorry, Ian of Earth,' he said. 'But the Commander has just received a message from Bikugih. We are too late. The Doctor has been executed.'

Vivojkhil was furious with Podsi.

She'd been playing up for the whole journey on the

shuttle. When she'd finished screaming that they were going to die, she'd seen the view out of the huge curved windows and started on a variation: 'We're going to fall! We're going to fall and die!' Several people had shushed her, and looked at Vivojkhil with annoyed curves of their eye-stalks. Vivojkhil had flushed blue with embarrassment.

Now that they'd arrived on the ship, and there was some chance of finding the rest of the clan, Podsi had taken to wriggling. First she would shove herself into Vivojkhil's belly, then she would jerk away, then upwards, then down.

'Podsi!' said Vivojkhil. 'For the clan's sake, stop it! I can't walk properly with you wriggling like that.'

She gazed around the huge chamber. It was at least twice as high as the shuttle, and filled with a vast crowd of people. They milled around, eye-stalks waving; one after another would stand up on the tips of their hooves to see where they were. Sou(ou)shi, riding in their finned vehicles, rode above the crowd, pointing and speaking in their soft voices.

Vivojkhil wasn't high enough to see anything at ground level except the top of something that might be a ramp in a direction she thought was west; though her direction-sense seemed confused up here.

She pushed herself up on hoof-tip, caught a glimpse of something she thought might be a bud-mother's green belly-wrap –

Something banged against her legs.

'Podsi!'

But the little one was gone, scurrying through the crowd, squealing 'Bud-mother!'

For an instant Vivojkhil was tempted to leave her. Let someone else find her, return her to the clan. But then she thought of facing her bud-mother and having to tell her that she'd lost her clan-sister.

She set off at a canter, swerving between people.

'My sister! Podsighil! Stop her!' she called.

She saw the yellow-skinned old bud-mother, who hand-signalled, 'Where?'

Vivojkhil indicated with her eyes the direction her sister had taken, and at the same time saw the little one galloping up a narrow ramp.

'Podsi!'

But Podsighil either didn't hear or didn't take any notice. She carried on to the top of the ramp, vanished into a dark passageway.

Vivojkhil saw one of the Sou(ou)shi.

'That passageway,' she gasped. 'Where does it go?'

The Sou(ou)shi followed her gaze with its alien eyes.

'Dangerous,' it said. 'Not permitted. This way, please.' It put its golden-fuzzed body between Vivojkhil and the ramp. Vivojkhil jumped over it, galloped up the ramp, and into the passage.

The walls were bare rock, receding into darkness. Podsi was nowhere in sight.

Lighibu was proud of her Five. She didn't think that one of them – except possibly Bufihil – knew why they had been ordered to save the Doctor's life, but they had obeyed the orders without question. No debate, no philosophical points, no contrary visions. They had, quite simply, trusted her.

It was a pity that they might have to die for it.

It had been simple enough to snatch the alien away from Brignontojij's squadsmen; they were slow, careful, heavy-weapons people who should never have been given the job of guarding the alien in the first place. Lighibu had gone in, got the Doctor on her back and gone before anyone had even had a chance to cry 'Treachery!' Anyone who'd tried to stop her on the way out, she'd simply gabbled, 'Has to be removed from the Council Chambers – Presidor's orders,' wondering each time how many oaths she was breaking.

Too many.

Once she'd reached her Five, assembled at the top of

South-west Grand, she'd handed the Doctor to Bufihil and shouted, 'Relay! Confuse pursuit! Harbour!'

And her Five had obeyed.

She glanced at them now, trotting down Ujannonot Street. Porijineg had the Doctor, who was sitting cross-legged, his arms around the base of her eye-stalks, his clear, intelligent eyes darting around, taking it all in. Jerekarnijli was running point; Nekedju was far ahead, checking the route was clear; Efenihu and Bufihil were off the sides, invisible, confusing the pursuit.

That was the theory. But it was a bit difficult to confuse pursuit with an alien riding on your back, and Lighibu knew it.

She looked at the grey faces of the houses passing by, then at the still-distant sea ahead. In truth, she wasn't really afraid of Brignontojij's squads; her Five had been dodging through the streets for almost a middlechange now and there was no sign of close pursuit. And she was almost sure he'd deliberately held his fire when she'd rescued the Doctor. But the Sou(ou)shi –

She made herself tip an eye upwards, at the black landscape that had taken over the sky. She wondered for a moment how she could ever have been fooled. It was obvious, surely, that that lifeless mountain wasn't going to take anyone anywhere. It was a death-trap. Why didn't the Presidor realize? Were people that desperate to escape?

Blue light stirred in the shadows of the landscape above. Lighibu felt her belly tighten, and curled her eye away from the ship.

Don't think about it. Don't attract attention. Concentrate on the job.

She looked again at her comrades, trotting casually, now switching the alien smoothly from Porijineg's back to Jerekarnijli's, for all the world as if it were a training exercise.

Yes, thought Lighibu. A training exercise. We're just practising taking the alien back to his ship so that he has a chance to thwart the Sou(ou)shi's plan to kill everyone in the world. Just practising. In case we ever have to do it for real.

She risked twitching an eye at the shadow in the sky, and hoped she was fooling it.

'It's a lightless signalling device,' explained the guard, who'd introduced himself as Soneghil. 'It works the same way as heliograph apparatus, but you can't see the light. It contains – ' Soneghil lowered his voice, though Ian was sure that Jellenhut, only feet away at the other end of the tube capsule, could hear anyway ' – *electric circuits*. Made of *metals*.'

Ian nodded. It would have to, if it was a radio, which he supposed it was.

'You press this symbol here – ' Soneghil indicated a star-shaped piece of wood ' – to send. You can only send straight down the tunnel; you code the name of the person you wish to address, so *Mrod – tik – d – hil*, like that.'

Ian was rather surprised to find that he recognized the syllabic code; he wouldn't have expected a village-child like Inikhut to be aware of it. But apparently he'd been taught heliograph signals, which used the same code, quite literally at his mother's knee; hoof-taps on the ground: *In – i – k – hut; Jel – len – hut*.

The 'lightless signalling device' rattled with the acknowledgement from the Command Warrens.

'Alien to recover space-and-time vehicle,' signalled Soneghil. 'Will return to your quarters and assist us.'

Ian almost smiled. He would be lucky to be able to get into the TARDIS without the Doctor, let alone assist the Venusians with it. And even if he did, by some miracle, manage to get into it, get it to work, find Barbara alive –

Then they were going to go, to Earth, anywhere on Earth, anywhen, just as long as there were human people around them. A normal human place, where they could lead normal human lives.

The tube swayed, forcing him to grab hold of Soneghil's

arms to stay upright. It began shuddering, slowing down; finally it stopped with a sharp jolt.

'We're here,' said Soneghil, pulling at a catch on the wall to open the doors.

It was a long way up; Jellenhut carried Ian. At last they emerged, into twilight, a ring of blue sky around the horizon, and the dark shadow of the Sou(ou)shi ship above. One of the craters on its surface caught the last rays of the vanished sun, making a ragged, oversize crescent.

Blue light danced around it.

Ian looked down, away from the unhealthy sight, and saw that he was standing on a sandy headland. Tall, knotted strands of moss stood waist high. A hot wind blew from the sea. Below, Bikugih harbour was spread out, a deep blue lake filled with white boats. The TARDIS stood in a pool of lamplight on the quayside, instantly recognizable, a rectangular box in a world of pentagons.

Half the Bikugih army appeared to be encamped around it. There were squadrons of cutter-throwers, harpoonists, infantry in trenches with things that looked very like mortars. And more were arriving, from several directions. Even from this distance, Ian could hear the shouting of orders and the massed rumble of hooves on stone.

'I think they're expecting us,' said Soneghil. 'Have you any suggestions, Ian of Earth?'

'None,' said Ian grimly. 'None at all.'

At first Barbara thought that she was hallucinating. Its skin green-black in the dim blue light, the Venusian child was standing on a stone ledge some six feet below where Barbara floated, helpless, in mid-air. All five of its eyes were turned towards her, and it was piping, 'Please alien help find bud-mother! Please! Alien! Help!'

Why should I see a Venusian child? thought Barbara. Why not Ian, or the Doctor? Why not the TARDIS?

'Please! Alien! Help!'

I'm the one who needs help, thought Barbara. Why am

I hallucinating someone who wants help from me? But even as she thought about it, another crippling wave of pain moved down her back, drowning out every other sensation.

When it subsided, becoming a mere burning agony in her belly, the child was still there.

'Please! Alien! Help!'

Perhaps it *is* real, thought Barbara. She tried to say, 'Help me!' but no sound came out. She struggled to clear her throat, was rewarded by racking pain in her arms and shoulders, then a long, blinding agony in her head.

When it lessened a little, the child was gone.

'Help me,' moaned Barbara aloud, her voice hoarse and rasping but audible. 'Help me.'

But she was too late: there was no response.

After a while, the pain came back.

Fefirhi Trikhobu stared three-eyed at the waves breaking along the shingle, her other eyes following the slow, implacable rise of Sou(ou)shi shuttles from the city to the ship above.

She had never been so miserable in her life. Yesterday, when her father Dharkhig had died, she had been sorry, she had mourned; but he had led a long and glorious life, and he would be remembered.

Today, her friend Barbara had been snatched away by her enemies, and Trikhobu had been able to do nothing about it.

Worse, no one had believed her.

While she was still hanging from the sails of the globe-roller, scrambling down hand-over-hand, afraid that at any moment she might fall to her death, she had been screaming at the assembled squadsmen and crew: 'Don't you see? They've taken her because she was our friend! They are the enemy, not Barbara! It's the Sou(ou)shi we have to fight!'

And all the time thinking about Barbara falling, falling impossibly into the sky. Never to be remembered.

When she had got down to the deck they had arrested her.

She had managed to get herself released, had galloped all the way to the Presidor's Apartments, then, hearing of the trial, to the Chamber of the Night Council. Only to hear that the Doctor had been executed.

She had come down here, then; to be near the sea; to be near the Doctor's craft. In case the remaining alien, Ian, turned up again. In case she could be any help.

Trikhobu turned an eye to the harpoonists' emplacements, which hid her view of the TARDIS. She had tried to approach that way once already, only to be told to keep back from the 'dangerous artifact'.

If that was what they believed, she thought, it was all over. They would dump the TARDIS in the sea, they would all climb aboard the Sou(ou)shi ship, they would all be killed.

She stared at the waves breaking, at the shuttles rising, at the points of the tall harpoons silhouetted against the sky.

Irresistible forces.

She thought of Barbara again. She thought of all her people. Her father's people. Her world.

Falling into the sky.

Never to be remembered.

Lighibu knew she'd made a mistake when she saw the lights.

It was too late to stop Bufihil, who was carrying the Doctor; she was already around the corner of Jonikhil Street, silhouetted against the glare of the pump-lamps. Lighibu could hear the creaking of the bellows that fed the blue-white *brakud* flames.

She signalled Porijineg and Jerekarnijli to halt, then trotted forward.

As she looked at the rows of harpoons, cuttershells, catapults and fire-throwers defending the Doctor's ship, Lighibu remembered something that her instructor had told her when she had first joined the hand-to-hand squads: 'Everybody will make mistakes in their life. This is natural, to be expected. The difference when you are a fighter by trade is that your mistakes will cost lives: yours, or somebody else's.'

She stared at the heavy-weapons squads, aware that they were staring back at her. She couldn't see Brignontojij anywhere; not that he would have been in charge of a force this size.

There was the unmistakable click of harpoons being readied for firing; someone had given a hand signal.

The next instruction would be to fire.

Lighibu measured the distance between her and the Doctor's ship.

A trained Five against heavy weapons. It had been done; battle of the Puri'pinidhall, wasn't it? She tried to remember the tactics number.

Another serried click of harpoons, this time to the south.

She took a deep breath. For a moment she doubted whether her Five would obey her; then she was ashamed of herself for doubting.

'Five!' she bawled. 'Manoeuvre Three-Four-Four! Now!' Each Five had their own number code; the squadsmen facing them wouldn't know whether they were going to attack, run or surrender.

But as Lighibu had expected, they didn't take any chances. Even as Bufihil leaped into the air, her body shielding the Doctor, the harpoons started flying.

Trikhobu started moving as soon as she saw the Doctor. She ran up the slope towards him, shouting, 'No! No! Don't kill him!'

No one appeared to take very much notice. Weapons clicked. Someone shouted something. Harpoons and cuttershells whistled through the air. An arm, detached from its body, spun skywards, jetting blood. Trikhobu felt her stomachs heave.

There was a sudden explosion of light as a shell caught the *brakud* pump-lamps; curtains of flame spread through the air. There were screams, the smell of burning flesh.

'No!' shouted Trikhobu. 'No! No! No!' But it was happening. It was happening and she couldn't stop it. The outer ranks of squadsmen, nearest her, were calm, but their weapons were trained on her body.

She ran back down to the waterfront, leaped onto the beach, into the sea, heedless of the danger of wild nightfish. The water was hot, and the salt stung her eyes. She pushed on, half-swimming, half-walking, her breath tight in her lungs, until she judged she was roughly level with the TARDIS on the quay. There was no beach now, only surging, treacherous water.

Just in time, Trikhobu saw the squadswoman in the water ahead of her, gun raised.

'Friend!' signalled Trikhobu frantically, with her free hands. 'Ally!' Though in truth she had no idea which side the squadswoman was on.

But the gesture seemed to be enough: the squadswoman leaped from the water, cleared the high wall. Half-blinded by spray, Trikhobu saw a burning cuttershell fly out over the water.

She braced her legs against the shingle, ducked her body under the water to let buoyancy do some of the work, and jumped.

Hooves scrambling on the edge of the wall, she saw the Doctor standing in front of the TARDIS, his body jammed between two clanswomen. One of the clanswomen had part of an arm missing, and a gash across one side that was sending out splashes of purple arterial blood; the other was dead, half her belly missing.

As Trikhobu watched, squadsmen climbed on to the bodies, long diamond knives ready, and drew their arms back to strike.

Trikhobu jumped forward, almost landing on top of the Doctor.

'In the name of Dharkig!' she shouted.

The squadsmen hesitated, their knife-arms only a body's width from Trikhobu and the Doctor.

Trikhobu took a breath, declaimed three-mouthed: 'I am Fefirhı Trikhobu of the clan Poroghini, chosen as daughter of Dharkhig the Acceptor. In the name of my much-honoured father I say you must not kill this alien.'

The squadsmen still hesitated, eyes wavering. The Doctor stepped forward and put his key in the door of the TARDIS.

'Thank you, my dear,' he said quietly.

Somewhere in the smoke of the battlefield, a clansman began to scream in pain.

'Squadsmen!' came a shout from the east. 'You have your orders!'

The TARDIS door opened; light spilled out.

'Look! It's getting away!' shouted someone.

'I say she's an imposter!'

'Kill them!'

From the TARDIS came the Doctor's voice: 'I think you'd better get in with me.'

Trikhobu pitched herself onto one side, careful to keep her injured arm off the ground. She drew her legs in, rolled into the TARDIS doorway.

Stuck fast.

'Fetch a dart gun! Kill her now!'

The nearest squadsmen suddenly came to life, stepped forward and plunged their knives towards Trikhobu. She parried the blows with her free arms, felt warm blood flowing.

'No! I am Trikhobu! You can't kill me!' she shouted, though she knew that they could, and would.

Inside the TARDIS, the Doctor was tugging at her other arms, pulling as hard as he could. It was no good.

A knife plunged towards Trikhobu's belly, but stopped as the owner died, arms rigid, eyes bulging. Trikhobu saw an irontip dart protruding from the dead clansman's hip, saw the gun in the hand of the injured squadswoman he had been standing on.

The body tipped sideways, rolled away. A harpoon flew through the air, its wire singing; somehow it glanced off the TARDIS and clattered over the wall.

The injured squadswoman braced her legs, gaped slightly.

'For justice,' she mutterd. 'And Bikugih.'

She jumped, three shins forward, directly at Trikhobu. The impact knocked Trikhobu through the door and across the floor of the TARDIS; before she could right herself she collided with a six-sided object which had a worryingly metallic look. The entire ship shuddered. She scrambled to her feet, shaking, and gazed four-eyed at the huge interior space of the Doctor's vehicle.

With her fifth eye, she saw the injured squadswoman's legs convulse, her eyes fill with milk-of-death.

'No!' she yelled.

'Too late, I'm afraid, my dear,' said the Doctor. He strode to the six-sided object and pressed a switch.

The door of the TARDIS began to close.

Ian hadn't realized there was a battle going on at first. The flights of harpoons and cuttershells, the Venusians rolling through the air, had seemed more like a rehearsal, even a dance. Even when the lamps had exploded, he'd thought for a moment that it was planned, a moment of drama in the tableau.

Then he'd seen the Doctor riding a Venusian through the flames, and evidently still very much alive.

Ian had started running straight away: down the steep side of the headland, tripping and stumbling, avoiding the impossible Venusian-sized 'stairway'. Jellenhut had caught up with him, offered him a ride; by the time he'd dissuaded her, convinced her to keep back, the lights were all out. He could see Venusians jumping, weapons flying, bursts of flame.

He ran along the causeway towards the harbour, peripherally aware of Venusians shouting, pointing. Something sharp and dangerous skittered across the stone near his feet. He could see the TARDIS ahead, its light flashing –

– *its light flashing* -

– and the familiar sound, filling the air, shaking the ground –

The TARDIS dematerialized.

Ian stopped, his chest heaving, sweat prickling on his face.

'Doctor!' he breathed.

It was impossible. The old man wouldn't leave them behind – he wouldn't leave them to be killed by the Venusians and the other aliens and –

Face it, he has.

Ian bunched his hands into fists, rammed them together.

There was a chitinous click behind him.

Ian turned, saw a Venusian with a harpoon launcher across his back. He ran to the left, almost collided with a second armed Venusian.

'Over here!' shouted a voice. 'We've got one!'

Weapons piled up on every side. Weapons with sharp edges. Ian looked desperately around him, saw that he was completely surrounded. The Venusians were almost climbing on top of one another in their eagerness to bring weapons to bear.

'Alien known as Ian, assistant to the Doctor,' boomed a military voice from somewhere out of sight. 'We propose to kill you. Do you have anything to say?'

15

Losses

Vivojkhil stared, four-eyed, at the blank wall of rock that marked the end of the passageway.

'Podsi!' she called softly; then gave way to panic again and shouted, 'Podsi! PODSI!'

There was no response.

Vivojkhil flattened her eye-stalks. She was certain that there had been no forks in the passage; it had simply curved down and down and down, uniform grey rock lit by a dim blue light.

I should never have come so far, she thought. Now I'll have to go all the way back. Podsighil must have gone down a different corridor. Or perhaps she got back on the shuttle. Someone's bound to have seen her. The old clanswoman will help.

Vivojkhil heard hoofsteps behind her. With a cry of relief, she started up the passage.

She realized her mistake when the alien came into view. It didn't look like the Sou(ou)shi who were directing the people leaving the shuttles above. A faint blue light emanated from its fuzzy skin, and sparks danced in its eyes. It was probably just doing that because it was dark, thought Vivojkhil. But it frightened her all the same.

'This is not an area where it is safe for your people to be,' said the Sou(ou)shi. 'Why are you here?'

'I'm – it's my clan sister – she ran down here – I can't find her – '

'You are separated from one of your own?'

'Yes, her name's Podsighil, she's only little – '

'You need not worry about being separated. You will all be in the same place very soon.'

'But I need to find her now!'

There was a pause.

'It is possible for me to take you to the place where you will all meet, so that you will not suffer the pain of separation any longer. Would you like that?'

'No,' said Vivojkhil. 'It's Podsi I'm worried about. She'll be very frightened. Can't you help me to find her?'

Another pause.

'It would be better if you were taken to the place where you will all meet soon.'

The alien was not large; it was no bigger than the one who had ridden on Vivojkhil's back that morning, but it seemed to be blocking the entire passageway. The blue glow emanating from its body had brightened.

Vivojkhil felt her belly tighten with fear.

'Please,' she said, 'I need to return to my clan. Please let me pass.'

There was another pause, longer than the first two. Vivojkhil's belly clenched tighter and tighter, until she wondered if she was going to be physically sick with fear.

Then the alien stepped aside.

Vivojkhil galloped up the corridor as fast as she could.

'The fact is, my dear Trikhobu, I'm very much afraid we're lost.'

The Doctor was standing by the six-sided thing he'd called a console, the one that she'd rolled over on her way in. His face was wrinkled with disapproval.

'Lost?' echoed Trikhobu blankly, trying to control a feeling of inner panic. She had assumed that, once the Doctor was in the TARDIS, he would be able to solve all their problems; or, at the very least, save his friends. It had never occurred to her that he might not even be able to steer the ship.

But they'd been travelling for over a middlechange already, and all that the strange box-window on the wall had shown were places Trikhobu had never seen before: a bubbling swamp (poisonous, according to the Doctor), a yellow, half-lit desert (oven-hot) and an expanse of water covered in mountains of ice (too cold, the Doctor had said, though Trikhobu found it hard to see how it was possible for anything to be too cold). Nothing had been even remotely near the Sou(ou)shi ship, which was where the Doctor said he wanted to go. She suspected that none of them had been on Venus at all.

She curled an eye to examine her bruised hip, wondered if she had somehow broken the TARDIS by rolling over the console on her way in. She didn't dare to ask.

The Doctor was speaking again, his eyes on the console. Perhaps he was speaking to himself, Trikhobu thought, but she listened anyway.

'I had expected that the dimensional stability would be greater in this part of the continuum but it seems that, once one has made any kind of contact – '

He looked up at her with his two strange eyes that both faced in the same direction.

'We may not be able to get back.'

Trikhobu felt her belly tighten. She imagined what would happen to her people if they failed to return. She imagined what would happen to *her* inside this box full of metals and alien sounds. She might die in here, of starvation if nothing else.

The TARDIS shuddered as it landed with a jolt.

'Well, we've arrived, ' said the Doctor. 'Let us see what we can see on this occasion.'

With an effort Trikhobu controlled her panic and looked at the box-window. The latest view appeared to be a starlit night; at least, Trikhobu could see the stars. She couldn't, however, see the ground. She stepped closer to the window, but still no ground appeared. She banged her bruised leg on the four-legged wood-and-cloth sculpture that stood near the console, grunting in pain.

'If I could just see the land,' she said. 'I might be able to recognize it. I've travelled quite a lot – Inarihib, Ujannonot, the High Sweet Lands.'

The Doctor again turned his single eye-stalk to look at her. 'You haven't travelled as much as I have, my child. I'm afraid we're a long way from the High Sweet Lands.'

Trikhobu flattened her eye-stalks humbly.

'We aren't on Venus any more, are we?' she asked. Her voice sounded oddly hollow.

The Doctor ignored the question.

'The first thing we need to know is when are we? The second question – a related subject, but most definitely the second question and not the first – is where are we?'

'Shall I go outside and have a look?' offered Trikhobu.

'You can't go outside,' said the Doctor. 'There's no air.'

'No air?' She was puzzled. 'How can there be no air?'

The Doctor made a tutting noise.

'My dear Trikhobu, there are lots of places in the universe that don't have any air. And they are vastly greater in number than the places that do.' His fingers moved over the console. The terrifying metallic clicks that resulted made Trikhobu's belly clench once more.

'But we've got to get home!' she shouted suddenly, two-mouthed in despair.

'I'll do my best, Trikhobu, I promise you that. I want to get back to Barbara and Ian as much as you want to get back to your people. And believe me, I don't wish to abandon the Venusians in their time of peril. But I can't promise – ' He broke off as the glowing central column of the console began to rise and fall again. The floor shuddered and the air filled with the roaring noise of the TARDIS in flight.

Like a *grifharji* in pain, thought Trikhobu. Like a *grifharji* when it is dying.

' – any more than I could promise Barbara and Ian,' the Doctor was saying. 'The TARDIS just isn't very easy to direct, and that's all there is to it.'

So it isn't my fault, thought Trikhobu. It's always been like this. Which means –

Which means that it will be subject to –

Trikhobu felt a sudden surge of hope. She pulled her notepad out of her lip-pouch and started to make some calculations.

When he had been alive, Inikhut had wanted to meet the Presidor of Bikugih. He had wanted to see the power, the glory, the fineweave cloths of office.

Now that he was dead, he had met the Presidor in the flesh, and he wasn't disappointed.

Ian could feel the Venusian child's awe even through his own gut-wrenching uncertainty. Inikhut wanted to squat down, to say, 'Oh honoured one; greatest and most revered one – '

Ian quelled the impulse. It would look like begging, and begging wouldn't do him any good.

The Venusian officer who'd said, 'He'll be more useful to us alive,' and thus saved Ian's life, was standing next to the Presidor; they were exchanging hand signals, but too rapidly for Ian to read. Somewhere behind him, Jellenhut stood under guard. The message capsule was in the Presidor's north hand, unopened.

Suddenly Ian realized that the Venusian in blue Philosopher's belly-wrap standing behind the Presidor was the Doctor's old friend Mrak-ecado. He felt a surge of relief: at least someone was on his side. It seemed incredible that only a day ago he had suspected the old clansman of poisoning Barbara and the Doctor.

'Philosopher!' he called.

Mrak-ecado was already looking at him with three eyes; at the sound of Ian's voice they curled towards him, indicating polite interest.

But Ian noticed that Mrak-ecado's skin was strained tight and flushed with blue blood. The Philosopher made a hand-sign: 'Nothing.'

Ian frowned. What did he mean, nothing? 'I can do nothing to help you'? Or 'Say nothing'? And why was he so upset?

The Presidor had finished his silent conversation with the officer; now he turned the message pod over in his hand, popped it open, pulled out the scroll and read it. Ian watched, conscious of the restraining arms of the guards on his, of the steady beating of the sea against the shingle behind him. It was almost dark; above, the Sou(ou)shi ship emitted a faint blue glow.

Suddenly the Presidor spoke, with the mouth that faced Mrak-ecado.

'I need to see the message that you received from Afhighid Kontojij.'

Mrak-ecado seemed to hesitate for a moment, then drew a scroll from one of his lip-pouches and handed it to Jofghil.

The Presidor held the two scrolls, one in his north hand, one in his west, read them both together. A spare eye curled interrogatively towards Ian; another towards Mrak-ecado.

'How do you explain the differences?' he asked, with his west mouth, which faced neither Mrak-ecado nor Ian.

'If you let me see the messages – ' began Ian.

'The aliens must have some secret means of communication. They must have copied the message and then amended – ' began Mrak-ecado at the same time.

All Jofghil's eyes swung round to the Philosopher, who stopped speaking abruptly in mid-word.

'You have not read the new message. How do you know that one is an amended copy of the other?'

Mrak-ecado flattened his eye-stalks.

'I'm sorry, Presidor. I am merely assuming that the alien's message seeks to contradict what Kontojij – '

'It is not the alien's message! It is signed by Kontojij! And furthermore it is complete – yours is the partial copy. Apart from that, the two are almost identical. Are you trying to tell me that your copy – cut and then stitched together again – is genuine, and a whole, uncut scroll is the fake?'

As Ian watched in bewilderment, Mrak-ecado crouched down, his eye-stalks quivering. Ian had never seen a Venusian make that gesture before, but Inikhut's memories told him it was one of intense humiliation.

'There is an explanation,' said Mrak-ecado at last. His voice was barely audible, mere breath. 'But it is not one that I wanted to give.'

Ian noticed that the Venusians behind him were standing up on their hoof-tips, craning their eyes to get a look at the action.

'If you, the alien and I could go somewhere alone,' Mrak-ecado went on, 'then I will explain my conduct.' He waved his eye-stalks around for a moment, then pointed out a *juldihaj*, a low, brown mushroom of wood and chitin which stood at the junction of one of the city roads and the quay. 'We could go there.'

Jofghil looked at the two message scrolls again. His free eye met one of Mrak-ecado's.

'Very well.' He twitched a hand at Ian's guards. 'Bring him.'

'No!' said Mrak-ecado. 'Alone. The three of us. I will vouch for the alien.'

'I promise on my belly that I will do you no harm,' said Ian; then realized to his embarrassment that he was mouthing the formula from a Venusian children's game.

It seemed to suffice. Jofghil twitched his hand again, and Ian was released. They set off for the *juldihaj* in the dimming light, Mrak-ecado in the lead, Jofghil following, Ian bringing up the rear. The crowd parted for them.

Mrodtikdhil opened his eyes, looked at the pattern of lava flows curling around the rim of his desk. He raised his eye-stalks to look at his Councillors.

'And the sub-Dhallenidhall caverns are not cleared?'

He knew he was asking the question again just for the sake of asking it, to make the time longer, to give them all more time –

'They received the message late, Commander.' The

councillor flattened his eye-stalks. 'There was a problem with the signalling device.'

The Commander twitched acknowledgement, opened the mouth facing a clanswoman who stood with a notepad in her west hand.

'Any more news from the surface?'

'The embarkation is proceeding, Commander. More than sixty per cent of the population of Bikugih are aboard the alien spaceship now, according to Panhidkhil's estimate.' She paused. 'I must urge you to make a decision, honoured one.'

Yes, thought Mrodtikdhil. But you are not the one who will have to live with the consequences of that decision. The deaths in the sub-Dhallenidhall. On the surface. In the ship, if the ejected rocks succeed in destroying it. Or all our deaths, if they don't and the aliens come after us.

He looked at the *dihilribi* mosses on the walls, opened the mouth facing a third councillor, a small, aged clansman with yellowing skin.

'The valves are set? Reversed?'

'As you ordered, my friend. Reversed at seven by four-two-two and eighteen to twenty five on the Chain.'

'And you agree with my analysis? That the ejecta will move north?'

'Yes. But I cannot say whether they will hit the ship. None of us can.'

'You see – you don't even know if it will work,' said a fourth clansman, also small and with yellowing skin. 'My old friend! I beg you!'

Mrodtikdhil took a breath before turning to a fifth councillor, who had a signalling device pressed against her upper lip.

'And the other alien, the Doctor?'

'It appears he has now left Bikugih in his ship, but it is not known whether he intends to assist us, or whether he has left Venus altogether.'

Mrodtikdhil twitched acknowledgement.

'Keep in contact with Soneghil. If the alien reappears, let me know at once.'

He snapped his eyes upright, tapped a hoof on the floor.

'We will wait for one middlechange; then we will hold a vote. In that time you must decide how many hands you will raise for the possible destruction of our world.

'And may the Fires consume us all if we are wrong.'

Pown(ow)ri stared at the mm'x crystals and wondered what was missing. The sculpture looked the same, and yet – out of the corners of his eyes – there always seemed to be less of it.

It disturbed him.

He reached out with his mind and touched the overmind of the Set, seeking strength and comfort; but it could give him little. The Set was weak now, awaiting the coming feed.

Food! Pown(ow)ri's stomach trembled at the thought of it. Saliva rushed to his mouth. Food! Gobbets of warm, trembling, blood-thick flesh –

There was a sound: a whisper. Rhythmic. Getting louder.

Was it coming from the sculpture?

Louder still. A pulsating roar, filling the air.

A blue shadow appeared in front of Pown(ow)ri, thickened. He took a step back, then, ashamed of his fear, stepped forward again.

The shadow became a blue box with a white light flashing on top of it. The roar echoed down the passageway, ended in a solid thud.

Matter transit, thought Pown(ow)ri. And not of Venusian design – only four faces to the box.

He informed the Set and received a confused response culminating in a question: 'The Doctor?'

The door of the box opened, and Pown(ow)ri saw that it was indeed the Doctor. Pown(ow)ri stared. He still didn't know how the alien had survived the destruction of the shuttle; now he appeared to have escaped execution at the hands of the Venusians.

The Doctor stared back at Pown(ow)ri for a moment, then looked over his shoulder into his ship.

'I really think it would be best if you stayed in the TARDIS, Trikhobu. Quite aside from the difficulty of getting you through the door, I don't think you would be safe.'

Puzzled, Pown(ow)ri wondered how the Doctor could possibly have a companion inside his tiny ship. Was it a dwarf species? An artificial intelligence of some kind?

But the name had sounded Venusian.

'Don't you agree?' said the Doctor suddenly. He was facing Pown(ow)ri again.

'What are you asking me to agree to, Doctor?' said Pown(ow)ri carefully.

The Doctor's face creased up, and for a moment Pown(ow)ri thought, with a surge of hope, that the alien was ill. Then the Doctor put his hand in front of his mouth and began to giggle.

'Did you hear that, Trikhobu? Pown(ow)ri is worried about what we might want him to agree to!' He straightened up, facing Pown(ow)ri again. 'I rather think that it is us who need to be careful what we agree with you, and not the other way around.'

He stepped out of the door, shutting it carefully behind him.

'What I need are the answers to two questions. One: who betrayed the Venusians to you? And two: where is my companion Barbara?'

Pown(ow)ri smiled. The Doctor might have escaped two attempts to kill him, but his reactions remained predictable.

The third plan would work.

'I'm sorry, but I can't answer your first question,' he said. 'The matter is confidential, as I am sure you can appreciate. But I am able to inform you that your companion is in our safe custody. We are subjecting her to extreme but non-damaging physical pain, and will continue to do so until such time as you give the required permission for us to kill you.'

The Doctor nodded gravely. 'I thought it would be something of the sort. Ah, well. Thank you for the information, Pown(ow)ri.' He opened the door of his ship and stepped inside.

Startled, Pown(ow)ri shouted, 'Wait! Did you not understand our terms?'

The Doctor looked through the door once more, a broad smile on his face.

'I quite understand them, Pown(ow)ri. But I'm afraid I don't agree with them. I will apply my own remedies. Goodbye.' His head disappeared inside the ship and the door began to close behind it.

Pown(ow)ri's body tightened with anger. This Doctor might prevent the whole feed! Without thinking, he jumped forward, pushed through the closing door, knocking the alien aside. Stopped for a second, and stared at the huge space he had entered.

Some kind of dimensional trick, he decided.

Then he saw the Venusian.

Saliva rushed to his mouth again. Suddenly he saw a way of solving the problem of the Doctor and satisfying his hunger all at once.

He advanced towards the Venusian, who retreated, her belly retracting with fear. Pown(ow)ri curled his hands and pushed out the long, gleaming claws.

'Give me the permission to kill you, Doctor,' he growled. 'Or I will kill this one. Now.'

The inside of the *juldihaj* was dark. Mrak-ecado scuttled around the wooden platform and lit a single lamp by pulling on a cord. The flame wavered, brightened; the Philosopher's long shadow formed over the water in the pool.

Jofghil splashed into the water, squatting down so that his mouths were immersed; Mrak-ecado slid in to join him. Ian sat on the platform, his knees drawn up against his chest, feeling like he had as a child when he had watched his parents have a 'serious discussion' – uncomprehending, and a little afraid.

Jofghil brought a single mouth above the water line, spoke.

'Very well, old friend. What is your explanation?'

Ian realized that the Presidor was afraid too. He was staring three-eyed at Mrak-ecado, who crouched low in the water so that it washed around the base of his eye-stalks. After what seemed a long interval, the Philosopher surfaced and spoke five-mouthed.

'This is something that I believe,' he said formally, then went on: 'The Sou(ou)shi are not evil. It is true, as Kontojij says in the part of his message that I removed before showing it to you, that it is they who will kill us all, who will drink our minds – '

'True!' squawked Jofghil. 'And you knew it?'

'And I knew it. My friend, I invited them. I gave them permission.'

Jofghil sprang upright in the water, splashing Ian on the platform. *'What!?'*

'I gave them permission because they will remember us.'

'Remember? But you have said they will kill – ' Jofghil trailed off.

'I gave them permission because they will remember us for ever. I have said they are not evil. They will do as they have promised. They will take us to another world: the world of memories – the world that we all go to in the end. And we will stay there, not die when this world dies.'

Jofghil had been backing away from the Philosopher, step by step, as the latter had been speaking. His mouths were sealed tight, his skin a livid blue.

'No,' he said weakly. 'It won't work. It can't work. You have lost the balance of your mind, clan-uncle.'

He scrambled up on to the platform. It shuddered

under his weight, almost pitching Ian into the water.

'I am sorry but I must fetch the guards – this must be stopped at once – '

Mrak-ecado stood up too, to his full height, towering above Ian with his eyes almost brushing the wooden beams of the roof. Water dripped from his arms, his belly cloth.

'My friend! Please try to understand!'

But Jofghil was edging towards the door.

Mrak-ecado turned to Ian.

'Chesterton of the clan Doctor! Please! Make him understand! I made him Presidor because he was a fool, because he wouldn't see what was being planned, but he must understand now – if you in your wisdom speak – '

'I'm not wise,' said Ian quietly. He stared at the shoes that had been made for him in a couple of minutes, thought of the three million years that Venusian civilization had existed. 'But I think you're wrong,' he said eventually.

Jofghil had reached the door: Ian could hear the rattle of the catch behind him.

Mrak-ecado reached into a lip-pouch, drew out a bright, many faceted crystal.

'Clan-nephew! Look!'

Ian felt a sudden, certain premonition of danger.

'This is a predicting-crystal, clan nephew. The same as that which Kontojij would have used. We will perform a *huyaot*. Here, now. You will see that I am right.'

Ian glanced over his shoulder, saw Jofghil frozen by the doorway, four eyes staring at his clan-uncle.

'Go!' mouthed Ian. 'Go now!'

But Jofghil didn't understand.

Ian saw his own shadow forming as the room filled with blue light. He turned to see the crystal glowing as brightly as an electric torch. Sparks of light were drifting in the air around it.

Ian stood up, pushed past the apparently hypnotized Jofghil and tried to lift the catch on the door.

It wouldn't move. He pushed at the door, put his

shoulder to it. It was no use. Blue light glowed around it, bonding it shut.

He turned again and saw the blue sparks coalescing into humanoid figures. They walked slowly across the water, their feet below the surface. As they rose onto the platform, Ian dodged, running around the pool.

'Stop them!' he bawled at Mrak-ecado.

'The permission has been given,' said the Philosopher. 'I cannot prevent them following their desires now.'

Jofghil screamed. At the last moment, he tried to jump aside, but one of his legs stayed behind, wrenched away at the socket. Blood jetted from the wound. Four-legged, the Venusian started to scuttle around the platform. The Sou(ou)shi figures abandoned the leg, advanced on him. Their heads seemed huge; long, curling canine teeth reached down over their chins. Pieces of skin began to fly away from Jofghil's body, whirled around the room, flapping, dripping blood, in an obscene parody of flight.

Ian tried to dive forward – to do something, to save something, to escape – but met the massive barrier of Mrak-ecado's body. Two long Venusian arms wrapped themselves around his torso and legs.

'I am sorry, Chesterton of the clan Doctor,' said the Philosopher. 'But, as you have admitted, you are not wise. It must end now.'

One of the two Sou(ou)shi figures turned from Jofghil and began to cross the water. It was huge now, its head almost brushing the ceiling. The mouth was a snout, lips curled back, the teeth like tusks, dripping saliva. The flesh had become real, solid behind the supporting blue glow: Ian could smell it as it came nearer. The predator stink of rotten meat.

The thing growled, deep in its chest. Its eyes glowed. Fragments of blood and flesh orbited around it.

It reached out for him.

16

Deceptions

Trikhobu stared three-eyed at the advancing alien, her belly clenched with terror. Its head seemed to have grown bigger: huge teeth were sprouting from the jaws. With her remaining two eyes Trikhobu looked for a means of escape, but there was nothing large enough to hide behind and all the doors she could see were too small for her to pass through.

'Trikhobu!' the Doctor shouted. 'Push him out of the door!'

'But the claws – they're metal – '

'They won't hurt you, Trikhobu. Not in here. They're psi-weapons, you see.'

Trikhobu decided there was nothing to lose. She braced herself against a wall, fitting three hooves into the round depressions, and kicked out with her other two legs.

The hooves bounced off. The alien staggered backwards for a moment, then recovered its balance. It looked startled, but unhurt. Before Trikhobu could recover from her surprise, it pounced.

Claws raked along Trikhobu's skin. Jaws closed around the base of her eye-stalks.

Nothing happened.

The Sou(ou)shi bit harder, clawed and kicked.

Trikhobu felt the kicks, a little, but the teeth and claws made no impression.

'They're not real, Trikhobu.' Amazingly, the Doctor was walking towards them. 'They're just an illusion. He can't hurt you with them as long as you stay in the

TARDIS, and he isn't strong enough to hurt you without them. Now if you follow my instructions – '

Even through its blood-lust, the alien seemed to have realized now that something was wrong. It turned and snarled at the Doctor, lashed out with a long, clawed hand. The Doctor didn't even flinch: Trikhobu was sure that the claws went straight through the flesh of his face without touching it.

'Walk to the door, Trikhobu. Hold on to him – don't let him go.'

Trikhobu wrapped three arms around the alien and, holding it as if it were an angry child, walked around the console to the door.

'Now, on the count of three, put him down on the floor and, before he has a chance to move, kick him as hard as you can.'

The Sou(ou)shi was struggling violently, biting and clawing, but all it was able to do was make Trikhobu's arms ache with the strain. Its body seemed to have diminished once more, was now no bigger than the Doctor's.

'One,' said the Doctor, 'two – THREE!'

Trikhobu threw the alien into the doorway, kicked with all her strength. The body of the alien flew out of the door, but stopped short with a hand on the jamb. Incredibly, it began to pull itself forward again.

'His psi-defences seem to be working perfectly well, unfortunately,' observed the Doctor. 'Try again whilst he's outside – but he careful, he *can* hurt you there.'

Without giving herself a chance to think about it, Trikhobu jumped at the Sou(ou)shi in the doorway, this time folding her hoof into a point. The alien's arm lashed out; claws passed within a finger's breadth of her skin. The hoof made contact, sending the two-legged body flying.

Then Trikhobu's own body struck the doorframe, knocking the breath out of all her lungs at once. The TARDIS swayed, righted itself.

The Sou(ou)shi had landed in a heap of glowing crystals. Blood was flowing from its chest.

'I've hurt it!' said Trikhobu. 'I think I might have killed it!' She remembered a phrase her father had once used: 'killing anger'. Shame burned inside her.

Inside the TARDIS, the Doctor was walking over to the console, his cane ticking on the floor.

'It can't be helped, Trikhobu. He was, after all, trying to kill you.'

'But – '

The Doctor closed a contact, and Trikhobu found herself pushed back inside the TARDIS as the door closed.

'Now, my dear, if you would be kind enough to apply that tracking formula of yours again. This time the person is a child called Vivojkhil, and the co-ordinates were – let me see – '

Trikhobu reached down, pulled the green notepad out of her lip-pouch, glanced at the four-dimensional matrix formulae she'd scribbled with such hope only a middle-change ago.

Her hand felt curiously numb as she bared her writing-claw.

Mrak-ecado screamed as the Sou(ou)shi closed its jaws over his leg.

'No – NO! I am not ready yet – you promised me I would be the last – that I could honour – '

'You have given your permission,' hissed the Sou(ou)-shi. 'It is not appropriate for you to rescind it now.'

The Venusian jolted back, pushing Ian at the monster. The Sou(ou)shi picked Ian up, flung him down onto the platform. Ian winced as his battered hands scraped on the wood.

Mrak-ecado screamed again. Blood spattered Ian's borrowed belly-wrap as he crawled towards a door at the back of the platform. There was a notice on the door: 'Jokhil Beribuhi of Yoniji welcomes you to this place of cool waters, which has been provided by his clan for fifteen thousand, two hundred and five generations. If refreshment is required, please ask the one who stands behind this door.'

Behind Ian, Mrak-ecado was struggling, his throats making a bubbling, squealing sound. The platform jounced, cracked, tilted sideways, flinging Ian against the door. To his surprise it swung open, pitching him into a darkened room.

Run, he thought; but for a full second his legs wouldn't move. Then, at last, seemingly in slow motion, he pushed himself upright, began to run.

Blue light filled the room. There were tall glass cylinders filled with brown powder, stacks of white chitin bowls, ceramic tiles on the floor. Ian looked for an exit, saw an archway leading to an upward-sloping ramp. But when he tried to run towards it, his legs ceased to respond. They remained stiff, unmoving, as if they were cased in plaster.

Frantic, Ian pushed at his calves with his hands, chopped at his knees, but nothing happened.

There were heavy footsteps behind him. The sense of paralysis spread to his arms, his neck. Ian tried to turn around, could not.

Hands the size of dinner plates closed over his chest; long claws met in a cage over his ribs. Ian felt his body being lifted into the air. He saw the *juldihaj* pool again. Jofghil, his eye-stalks thrashing, was desperately trying to raise himself on his one remaining leg. Blood bubbled from his throats.

'We are sorry, but it is not appropriate for you to leave at this stage,' growled a huge, deep voice from somewhere above Ian's head. 'We have business with you which needs to be completed.'

It was the yellow-skinned old clanswoman who had found Podsi.

'She was just sitting by herself, telling a story about falling down a hole and speaking to an alien.'

She tickled Podsighil's leg, and the child woke up, turning a sleepy eye towards Vivojkhil.

'Found an alien. Floating in the air. Talked to her,' she said solemnly, then added, 'Want to go home now.'

Vivojkhil examined the child with one eye, letting the other four rove over the huge, crowded chamber. Another shuttle had just arrived, towering above the eye-stalks of the crowd. Its ramps were lowering slowly to the ground. Goldenwood-coloured trios of Sou(ou)shi were waiting to give directions to the new arrivals.

Suddenly Vivojkhil realized that one of her eyes was staring directly at her clan-sister Anaghil.

Anaghil saw her at the same moment; they both waved. Anaghil beckoned.

Vivojkhil quickly thanked the old clanswoman, giving her name and clan so that hospitality could be claimed in return; then she picked up the sleepy Podsighil and set off through the crowd.

For a moment she lost Anaghil again in the crush of bodies; then she caught sight of her bud-brother Durfheg and clan-brother Kigihij. She ran towards them quickly, before anything else could happen.

'We thought you and Podsi had been left behind!' said Durfheg. 'Bud-mother instructed us to wait here in case you came up on the next shuttle.'

'We are to meet at the place-with-grey-water,' said Kigihij helpfully.

'What happened to you?' asked Anaghil, pushing her way between two clansmen.

'Podsighil got frightened at the rollerport, then when we got up here she fell down a hole or something and I got lost looking for her.' Vivojkhil decided not to say anything about her encounter with the Sou(ou)shi; her panic of a few moments earlier seemed silly, childish. Everything was all right. Of course it was. Her clan-siblings and everyone else wouldn't be so calm, so happy, if there was anything wrong.

Anaghil was giggling.

'Podsi! Always Podsi!'

She clicked a hand across the little one's leg; this time Podsighil didn't wake up. She must have tired herself out, thought Vivojkhil.

They started to walk towards the main exit, which was easy enough since it was the direction in which everyone else was moving. As they got closer, the crush of hooves and legs and belly-wraps thinned and Vivojkhil saw that there was no single doorway, just a long series of stone arches through which shone a pale grey light.

They walked through the nearest archway and Vivojkhil gaped.

A new world lay before her. A grey lake, trees, *beghi* paddies, hills, another lake –

'Is this all for us?' she said.

'Bud-mother says it's only for one and a half tendays,' said Anaghil. 'Then we get a whole world.'

As they descended the slope towards the lake, Vivojkhil became aware of a deliciously cool breeze. Kigihij led the way towards a stand of *bosifghal* trees by the lake; they walked for a moment between the thick trunks.

Durfheg leaned over and tapped one of them; it made a curious, un-wood-like sound.

'Artificial,' he said. 'They built them.'

Vivojkhil thought about it.

'I suppose they had to. They would hardly have had time to grow any.'

'Not far now,' said Kigihij. Then he suddenly stopped, his lips sealed tight to reveal his ears.

Then Vivojkhil heard it too. A deep, rhythmic roar. Getting louder.

Her fear came back. She remembered Podsighil shouting 'We're going to die!' as they'd boarded the shuttle – the blue light in the eyes of the alien in the passageway –

Something was shimmering on the path below them like a heat mirage. A blue box with a white light flashing on top of it. It thickened, and the roaring got louder; then, with a final thud, it was there.

Vivojkhil braced her legs to run.

The door of the blue box opened and the alien stepped out. Not a Sou(ou)shi, but the same fungus-topped alien who had ridden on Vivojkhil's back that morning.

Podsighil opened her eyes, said, 'Alien! *Friend* alien!'

Anaghil took a step forward; Durfheg took a step back.

'Go to the beginning and start again,' muttered the alien, turning his stapled-down eyes to look at Vivojkhil, Anaghil, Durfheg and Kigihij in turn. 'Yes indeed. And it works every time. I really think Fefirhi Trikhobu has suggested an excellent new approach to the problem.'

'Can we do anything to assist you, honoured one?' asked Vivojkhil politely.

Before the alien could reply, Podsighil bounded out of Vivojkhil's arms and ran across to him, snuggled herself around his legs.

'*Friend* alien!' she proclaimed loudly.

'Ah – yes, my child, very kind of you to say so,' said the alien, patting her somewhere near the eye-stalks. He looked up at Vivojkhil again. 'I'm looking for my companion, Barbara. I don't suppose you know anything about her?'

'Friend alien in cave!' said Podsighil.

The Doctor patted her again. 'Quite so, my dear.'

'Barbara? Does she look like you?' asked Durfheg.

The Doctor considered for a moment. 'Well, near enough, I suppose. It really is most important that I find her. From what I hear, the Sou(ou)shi have got her, and that would be terrible. Terrible.'

Vivojkhil shuddered at the word 'terrible'. She suddenly realized that this conversation was very, very important.

'In cave! Wouldn't talk to me!' said Podsighil.

'Shut *up* Podsi,' said Vivojkhil.

'We haven't seen any stickwalkers – sorry, any aliens with two legs – except the Sou(ou)shi, honoured one,' said Durfheg.

The Doctor tutted, turned his head to face the open door of his ship.

'Trikhobu, the children don't know anything. We'll have to try a different location. Work out the tracer formula for Barjibuhi and the Rocketeers.'

Podsi's hand reached up and tugged at the cloth around the Doctor's belly.

'Podsi!' shouted Vivojkhil and Anaghil, almost in the same breath.

The Doctor looked down; Podsi looked up.

'In cave,' she said. 'Alien friend in cave.'

The Doctor stroked the flesh beneath his mouth, screwed up his face. He crouched down so that his eyes were level with the child's.

'What cave, exactly?' he asked. 'Where?'

It was then that Vivojkhil noticed the Sou(ou)shi, standing in deep shadow between two of the false tree trunks. In the darkness, she could see the blue glow of its eyes.

It had taken Jofghil and Mrak-ecado a long time to die.

The blood had stained Ian's new shoes and the hem of his borrowed belly-wrap. It had run into the water of the pool, splattered the windows of the *juldihaj*.

Ian had banged on those windows until his fists were raw, but he had made no sound and the glass had remained unbroken. He had shouted at the dim forms of the Venusians he could see outside, but although some of them were looking directly at the window, it was clear that they saw nothing, heard nothing.

Jofghil was now little more than a skeleton. One of the Sou(ou)shi sat amongst the bones, methodically crunching them as if they were sticks of celery. The other was still tearing gobbets of flesh from Mrak-ecado's corpse. From time to time it looked up and glanced at Ian, as if making sure he was still there. Its head was huge, the jaws long and sabre-toothed, the eyes as big as saucers.

Suddenly it spoke: 'Our business with you has become

urgent. We would like your assistance.'

'Assistance?' Ian was incredulous. He would have laughed, but laughter would have been inappropriate in the face of so much blood.

'We should point out,' began the other Sou(ou)shi, spitting out a mouthful of bone fragments, 'that both of your companions are on board our ship at present. We have set in motion events likely to result in their deaths. These events could however be terminated, and all three of you allowed to leave freely, in the event of your deciding to assist us.'

Ian stared at the monster hunched over the bloodied skeleton, its jaws wide. He swallowed.

'What do you want me to do?'

The first Sou(ou)shi spoke again.

'We have a difficulty with the Venusians who live underground. They have built a device intended to cause a series of volcanic eruptions. We believe you know about this.'

Ian nodded.

'We have received information to the effect that they are likely to activate this device soon.'

The Sou(ou)shi broke off to renew the attack on Mrak-ecado's corpse; its companion took up the thread.

'The device may render the planet's surface habitable for some time, thus reducing the number of Venusians available for us to eat.'

'It would be difficult to hunt them all down on the planet's surface,' observed the first Sou(ou)shi.

'There is also a possible danger to our spaceship. Therefore we would like you to signal to the leader of the underground people, with the authority of your friend the Doctor, advising him not to operate the device.'

'We would like you to do this now,' added the first Sou(ou)shi, standing upright. Its head was at least ten feet off the ground. Blood and fragments of flesh and bone covered its skin. 'We will escort you.'

The blue light in the room dimmed, died. For a

moment Ian stared at blackness, then a hand caught his arm.

The door opened and he found himself being marched through it by the two Sou(ou)shi, now a perfectly ordinary size and shape, their pale fur clean of blood.

The Venusians outside muttered, stirred, their bodies a single dark mass in the dim evening light.

'Your Presidor and the Philosopher do not wish to be disturbed,' said one of the Sou(ou)shi. 'But it has been decided to remove this alien to a place of restraint. We will do this for you.'

The crowd parted for them, a wall of dark Venusian bodies on each side, topped by curious eyes. Ian stared at them, amazed. Coudn't they *see*?

He looked over his shoulder at the *juldihaj* and saw clean windows, a single dim lamp. He looked down at his blood-spattered belly-wrap, saw blue light dancing over it, hiding the evidence.

He wanted to shout, 'They're evil, they're deceiving you, they're going to kill you all.' But he thought of the Doctor and Barbara, and said nothing.

They left the quayside and started up the steep slope to the headland, the Sou(ou)shi picking their way with care on the damp soil. Ian heard a scuffle of hooves on stone behind him, heard Jellenhut shout, 'I will support him! It is my duty! He is my friend, who helped me to remember my children!'

Someone muttered a reply, then there was a shouted order: 'Let her go if she wants to.'

Hooves pounded on the soil.

'Ian of Earth! What has been decided?'

Ian said nothing. He was ashamed even to look round.

'Is there anything I can do? Can you not speak?'

No, thought Ian, I can't speak. There's nothing to say. How can I tell you that I've decided to betray your entire species for the sake of my friends?

One of the Sou(ou)shi turned its head.

'Stay back, please. The alien is to be kept in isolation.'

Ian heard Jellenhut's hooves hesitate, stop. He visualized her eye-stalks waving in puzzlement, but still could not bring himself to look around. Instead, he stared at his feet, protected by the dancing blue light of the Sou(ou)shi, treading down on Venusian soil. Left, right, left, right, left, right. They seemed blurred, unreal, as if they were under water.

After a while, Ian realized that this was because his eyes were full of tears.

Walking gingerly on his shorn feet, Kantihif Havteg advanced down the path between the artificial trees. Ahead, a blue lake lay amongst grey *beghi* paddies.

'The lake isn't real either,' said Barjibuhi, behind him. 'The water is cold, and it only comes up to your mouths. And look – !' The older clansman kicked at the soil on the path, revealing that it was no more than a coating of crushed clay, hoof-deep, over bare rock.

'I don't see that it matters,' said Havteg mildly. 'I'd have been quite happy to live in a hermit's cell for fifteen days if it meant going to a new world.'

The leader of the Rocketeers huffed.

'Well, yes, I suppose so. But it's all so shoddy. When I think how much care we took over our rockets – '

Havteg realized he wasn't going to hear anything new, and stopped listening.

He was disappointed in Barjibuhi; in all the Rocketeers. As soon as he had been released by the Presidor, Havteg had rushed to the rollerport to see the miracle of the Sou(ou)shi ship; once aboard, he had straight away sought out his comrades. He had expected talk of the wonders of Sou(ou)shi science: the silent shuttles, the vast ship, the artificial environment within. Instead he had found Barjibuhi and Mrithijibu cursing the aliens for refusing to let them have a guided tour of the engine chambers, and a cluster of others moaning about the colour of the sky.

'I still wish they would share some of their science with us,' Barjibuhi was saying now. 'Show us how to travel between worlds for ourselves, rather than just treating us as passengers.'

'Perhaps their science is so far beyond ours that there is nothing that can be explained,' said Havteg.

Barjibuhi stopped short, three eyes on Havteg.

'Are you saying we're stupid?'

It was Havteg's turn to stop, brushing the soil with his shorn feet.

'No – not exactly. But I'm not sure I believe that Venusians are – ' he hesitated, choosing the word carefully ' – *suited* to certain kinds of science.'

Barjibuhi huffed again, shut his mouths in a tight line.

'Let me explain further,' said Havteg. 'How long have the Rocketeers existed?'

'A thousand and ninety-seven generations. You know that as well as I do.'

'And have we ever built a rocket – even a small one – that flew as high into the air as this ship can?' As he spoke, Havteg remembered the shuttle flight, the sun shining through the window, the land stretched out below, a dark carpet rippled with mountains. It was a sight he had dreamed of since he had been old enough to dream.

'No, we haven't,' Barjibuhi was saying. 'But it doesn't mean we can't. We were working towards it. With help – '

He broke off, suddenly, pointed with an cyc towards the lake.

Havteg looked, saw the gleaming craft with the three Sou(ou)shi in it skimming an arm's length above the water, approaching them rapidly.

'Perhaps they've changed their minds about the engines,' said Barjibuhi.

The craft reached the shore of the lake, began climbing the path. It stopped no more than a bodys-width from Havteg and Barjibuhi.

The Sou(ou)shi started to speak immediately, all three at once.

'A problem has arisen. You have heard of the alien

called the Doctor?'

'We've had dealings – ' began Havteg cautiously.

But Barjibuhi broke in: 'Heard of him? He's the burner who told the Acceptancers to destroy our rocket base!'

'You can identify him?'

Only one of the Sou(ou)shi was speaking now; the others were turning their single eye-stalks round, left to right, right to left, searching.

'Havteg can,' said Barjibuhi, without waiting for Havteg to speak. 'He almost had the burner once.'

'Good. Our problem is that the Doctor has boarded our ship against our will, and damaged one of our people. We have every belief that he intends to prevent the fulfilment of our mutual project by any means possible. Unfortunately, although the Doctor is a threat both to you and ourselves, our moral code prevents us from killing him at this time. We wondered if you would be in a position to render assistance.'

'Er – ' said Barjibuhi.

'You want us to kill him?' asked Havteg.

'We cannot ask you to do that, but we should point out that such an action would be of immense benefit to the mutual interests of the Sou(ou)shi and the Venusian people.'

Havteg considered. Somewhere in the distance he heard children shouting, playing. Our future, he thought. That's what's important. I have no choice but to help.

'Where is the Doctor?' he asked the Sou(ou)shi.

'Not far from here,' said one of the aliens, turning its single eye-stalk to look behind it. 'Not far at all.'

'Up here? Are you sure, Podsi?'

'There was a hole!' said Podsi, pointing with an eye at a blank stretch of rock on the floor of the passageway. 'Just *there*!'

Vivojkhil swung an eye to the Doctor.

'Eminently possible, child,' he said. 'Now let me see.'

He stepped forward, prodded the rock with his cane.

Nothing happened. He crouched down, ran his hand over the surface.

'Hmm – yes, I think so.' Still crouching, he turned so that his eyes faced Podsighil. 'Now, little one. If you could step forward and stand just here – '

Podsi waved an eye-stalk at Vivojkhil, another at Anaghil, a third at Durfheg, a fourth at Kigihij.

'Go on,' said Vivojkhil. 'Do what the alien says.'

Podsi trotted towards the spot indicated by the Doctor. As she reached it, he tapped the ground with his cane once more. The rock silently parted, and the little one dropped from sight.

Anaghil rushed forward. 'Podsi!'

'Told you there was a hole.' Podsi's voice echoed slightly, as if she had fallen into a large cavern.

The Doctor rubbed his hands together. 'Just as I thought,' he said. 'They're making it easy for us.' Then he stepped forward and vanished into the hole.

It was Vivojkhil's turn to step forward. She peered over the edge, three-eyed, and saw a sloping passage, the Doctor's back.

He looked round.

'Come on, follow me, all of you! There's no time to lose.'

Ian recognized the smell of Venusian blood as soon as he walked out of the lift chamber. Then he saw it: pools on the stone platform, fragments of flesh and bone adhering to the walls and to the sides of the tube vehicle that was still parked there. The 'lightless signalling device' stood in the middle of the platform. An area around it had been meticulously cleared of all traces of the carnage.

Somehow that made it worse.

'Why?' asked Ian, turning to the nearest Sou(ou)shi and grabbing its shoulders. 'Why did you kill Soneghil? He was no threat to you.'

'He refused to send the message,' said the Sou(ou)shi calmly.

'The one who spoke to him was hungry,' added the second Sou(ou)shi. 'We are all hungry.'

Ian hit the Sou(ou)shi across the face. It pulled its body out of his grasp with surprising strength; Ian almost toppled onto the blood-messed stone.

'What is the difficulty? Mrak-ecado gave permission for us to eat all Venusians, jointly or severally. Surely it is not your place to object to this?'

Ian raised his fist again, then put it down. Violence was no use: he knew that he would not be able to hurt the Sou(ou)shi, slight though they looked at the moment – and they might easily trick him into hurting himself. None of which would bring Soneghil back. Besides, there were Barbara and the Doctor to consider.

Sweating, trembling, Ian turned to the Venusian signalling device. It was switched on, tapping out a faint message: '*Ack – know – ledge – Ack – know – ledge –* '

Ian pushed the 'transmit' key, signalled, '*Mrod – tik – d – hil*'.

The response came back instantly: '*Send*'.

Ian hesitated for a moment, trawling Inikhut's memories for a syllabic code for his own name, Ian.

It was then that he realized he couldn't do it.

He could almost hear the Doctor's voice: 'How many Venusians are there living? And how many of us? Do you truly think we have the right to sacrifice them in order to save ourselves?'

But Barbara –

He wouldn't let himself think it.

His hands trembling, his body hunched over the device to hide it from his Sou(ou)shi guards, he started to signal: '*Doc – tor – Go – vol – can – o – now – Go – vol – can – o – now – Go –*'

I'll probably be buried in here when it happens, Ian thought. Killed by a rockfall or something. If not I'll give the Sou(ou)shi permission to kill me or, better still, do it myself.

The alternative – living alone on an alien world where

he had let his friends be killed – didn't bear thinking about.

'*Go – vol – can – o – now – Go – vol – can – o – now –* '

Were they never going to answer?

One of the Sou(ou)shi stepped forward.

'What is the response? Will they cease their operations?'

Ian didn't reply, just kept tapping the key.

'*Go – vol – can – o – now –* '

'Ian! We must be advised at once of the response.'

Ian stopped keying and turned to face the Sou(ou)shi, wondering what he could say to give himself more time.

Then the ground began to tremble.

This time Barbara was sure it was an illusion.

The Venusian child was there again, but this time the Doctor's head was floating next to it, unsupported in mid-air. His cane was whisking above his head, quite near to Barbara's feet. She could hear the swishing sounds quite clearly.

A very detailed illusion, she thought. Shame the Doctor hasn't got a body.

Then there was a burning pain in her jaw which quickly spread over the whole of her skull and in rivers down her back. Barbara curled up, tried to scream, couldn't.

When the pain receded, the illusion was still there. The Doctor had a body now: he was standing on the back of a smallish Venusian, which seemed to have too many legs, all tied into improbable knots. His cane was still swishing through the air.

Abruptly it connected with Barbara's leg.

It hurt: but that didn't surprise her, because everything hurt at the moment.

'Barbara!' said the Doctor's voice. 'You must listen to me! Hold on to the cane!'

A talking illusion, thought Barbara. Well, it had to

come. She wondered when the Sou(ou)shi would just let her die.

'You must hold on to the cane!'

Without really thinking about it, Barbara reached down and grasped the end of the cane. That hurt, too: rivers of pain ran up her arm, pooling in her chest.

The cane began to pull, and that hurt more. Barbara held on, felt herself being turned head over heels, dragged down towards the rock ledge where the Doctor and the Venusians stood.

I'll hit the rock, she thought. I'll go right through it.

But she didn't. She impacted softly with the leathery flesh of a Venusian. It didn't hurt, although it stung a little.

The Doctor had an arm around her shoulder.

'There! Are you feeling better, my dear? Neural amplification fields can be very uncomfortable, I know.'

'N-n-neural w-what?' muttered Barbara hoarsely.

'Takes the body's own nervous activity and sends it back to your brain. It results in a massive feedback loop in your nervous system, of course.'

'Oh.'

A muffled Venusian voice spoke from below:

'I can't hold on much longer.'

The Doctor dropped down, pulling Barbara with him.

'Through here, Barbara. I'm afraid there isn't time for you to rest yet.'

Yellow lights danced in front of Barbara's eyes. After a moment, she realized that these *were* illusions. Through them, she saw small Venusian bodies scrambling around in near-darkness.

'Alien! Now we've got two!' squeaked a Venusian child.

The Doctor struck an everlasting match, and Barbara saw that all the Venusians present were children.

'Durfheg! Vivojkhil! I'd be grateful if you could carry Miss Wright for me.'

Venusian hands lifted Barbara's body, hooves clicking

on stone. She began to feel sick.

A pool of dim light appeared above them. The baby Venusian scampered out of it, still squeaking. 'We've got two aliens! Two!'

Then Barbara came out into the light. She was in a passageway, surrounded by Venusians.

'Hello, my friends,' she said. 'I am honoured to see you all.'

The Doctor stepped out by her side.

'Ah,' he said, 'Kantihif Havteg. I'm pleased to meet you under more auspicious – '

A heavily built clanswoman in the belly-wrap of the Inarihibi Death Inspectorate pushed forward. She grasped hold of Vivojkhil with two legs and physically threw her aside. She raised two hands, each carrying a long stone knife.

'No!' shouted the Doctor. 'There must be some – '

A Venusian hoof flashed out; somehow, the Doctor dodged, dropping to the ground.

'Aliens friends! Friends!' the little one was bawling.

Barbara caught a glimpse of two Sou(ou)shi standing behind the Venusians, their eyes glowing like blue lamps.

'Get the children out of the way,' someone said. 'Then kill the aliens.'

A yellow mist rose up in front of Barbara's eyes. She knew that there was something she had to do, something vitally important, the only thing that could save them now.

But she couldn't remember what it was.

The mist thickened.

17

Detonations

Ian knew that there was only one thing he could do, so he did it.

He rushed straight past the Sou(ou)shi and started to scramble up the stairway to the surface. It was harder to climb than it had been coming down: the treads were almost five feet high. Blood ran from his hands as they gripped the edges of the steps; the welts on his arms and neck pulsed thickly. He felt sick and dizzy, but the thought of the Sou(ou)shi behind him and the pressing need to see what he had done drove him on.

They were waiting for him at the top, and four of the Sou(ou)shi were with them.

The ground was shaking violently now. Small pebbles jumped out of the soil, clicking together and rolling around. A deep rumbling filled the air.

The Sou(ou)shi still had their normal form, but their eyes glowed with blue fire. The Venusians swayed on the unsteady ground, taking aim as best they could with their various complicated weapons.

'Alien! You have killed our Presidor and betrayed our world!' shouted one of the Venusians. 'We can show no – '

'Kill him!' screeched the Sou(ou)shi in harmony. 'Kill him now!'

Behind them, the northern horizon glowed red with fire.

Dharkhig stood up and surveyed his people. They were crowded into a narrow stone passage, shouting, confused.

Someone that Dharkhig didn't recognize was holding a struggling child.

'Kill them!' shouted an alien voice. 'Kill them now!'

Another alien surveyed Dharkhig from the west, its eyes curiously calm and knowing.

The Doctor. Of course.

It was time to speak. Dharkhig only had one mouth in this strange alien body, but he spoke three-mouthed anyway.

'People of Bikugih, people of Inarihib, people of the High Sweet Lands! Listen to the words of Jikugihi Dharkhig of the clan Poroghini!'

The crowd seemed to hear him: gradually, there was silence. A gun was raised, knocked down by another hand. Dharkhig surveyed them five-eyed, then set his eyes in the *didhabhir*, the proper position for speaking. Maybe the crowd saw that, maybe they did not.

'I have always taught you that we should accept our fate,' he began, then paused before continuing: 'I am ashamed.'

He had their attention now: every eye in his sight was turned towards him.

'I am ashamed because you did not understand me. I am ashamed because I did not notice when you did not understand. You accepted your fate because you had no choice – and I, in my arrogance, thought it was because I was telling you to accept it.

'I apologize. I failed you in my duty as Councillor and Presidor; as speaker for the Venusian people I failed you. The proof of this is around us now: the ship of the Sou(ou)shi.

'You would never have believed it for a moment, if you had truly accepted the End. You would have seen it for what it was: Death on the prowl through the space between worlds, Death that feeds on life. It was obvious enough.

'I should have spent more of my time warning you that there were such things. But I did not always listen to the right advice.'

Dharkhig permitted himself a glance at the Doctor, a twitch of an eye-stalk. The Doctor shook his head, in that gesture of the negative peculiar to his kind: I do not blame you.

'It is too late now for me to listen, but it is not too late for you. Listen!' He was speaking five-mouthed now, with all the force of his breath and mind; and he knew, from the brightening in their eyes, that many of those in the crowd were hearing it that way.

'You who are aboard this ship must make the sacrifice, now, for the sake of those who remain on the surface of the world, and still have a chance to live. You must rise up against the Sou(ou)shi. You must destroy them, you must destroy their ship, *and you must accept the death without remembering that follows*.'

A faint, squeaky, alien voice called out, 'No! She is distorting the truth! We will remember – '

A clansman leaped into the air, kicked out: the Sou-(ou)shi's head snapped backwards, and its body dropped.

Dharkig knew then that he had won, knew even before the second Sou(ou)shi was kicked down and a chain of hand signals began to spread the news to the crowd beyond sight and hearing.

He permitted himself one last glance at the Doctor, who nodded and said, 'Goodbye, my friend.'

Then Dharkhig let go, and Barbara's body dropped to the ground, empty of consciousness.

All around, the battle was beginning.

Ian staggered on the shaking ground, almost fell through the entrance to the stairway. Around him, the Venusians crouched and dipped their eyes against the glare from the sea.

A plume of yellow-white flame was rising from the northern horizon; to the south Ian could see a huge column of black smoke filled with slowly tumbling rocks. The rocks were glowing red.

From the corner of his eye, Ian saw a Venusian galloping towards him.

'He has caused this violence! Kill him!' shrieked the Sou(ou)shi.

The Venusian was close now. Ian tried to jump to one side but a violent shock threw him to the ground. Before he could scramble upright again, the Venusian was standing over him. Ian tried to roll aside, but the belly descended, pushing him into the soil –

– the belly? That wasn't a way to kill anyone! Then he recognized the green cloth of the belly-wrap.

'Jellenhut!' he shouted, but the sound was lost in the air-tearing sound of the explosions.

Jellenhut too was shouting; Ian, pressed to her belly, a foot from one of her mouths, caught the words 'no harm'. He doubted that any of the others could hear anything.

Then he noticed that one of them was making hand signals. He looked up, saw that Jellenhut's hands were also dancing. Ian couldn't understand the whole code, but he recognized the words 'accusation', 'responsibility' and 'evidence'.

He would have laughed, if Jellenhut hadn't been sitting on his chest: with their planet blowing up beneath them, the Venusians were holding a formal debate on whose fault it was.

'We should be taking cover!' he shouted, but no one heard.

Then he saw the Sou(ou)shi.

They were fifteen feet high, with huge, serrated jaws, four arms ending in triple scimitar blades, legs like iron pistons. They looked more like praying mantises than anything humanoid. Ian suspected that he was seeing their true form for the first time. They arched themselves forward, jaws and arms extended over their chosen prey. Blue light flamed around them, drowning even the glare of the eruptions.

Ian knew it would be no use to shout. He jabbed an elbow into Jellenhut's belly, pointed.

She looked, saw, reared up in warning.
It was too late.

Pown(ow)ri knew that he was going to die.

His body was too badly damaged to support the Change; without the Change, he could not feed; without the food, he would die. With luck, his mind would be captured by the Set, and he would live on forever within it. If the Set itself survived.

He watched his blood trickle down his chest and join the pool of fluid on the floor. One of those strange crystals floated in the pool, enigmatic as ever, its shape indefinable. He stared at it for a moment, wondering if he could somehow stay alive by deciding what shape he was seeing.

No.

He closed his eyes and, with an effort, renewed contact with the Set.

The ship was in chaos.

Somehow, the Venusians had been warned. And the Venusians were big animals, well armed and very well organized. They had killed a lot of Sou(ou)shi before they could Change, and even the Changed ones were not invulnerable. Phalanxes of killers from the command rooms were cutting their way through the Venusian chambers now, using metal swords, projectile weapons and blasters, but they were suffering losses. The Sou(ou)shi would win in the end, but it was a war, not a slaughter.

And outside –

Pown(ow)ri linked with the ship's sensors, felt dust, pumice and small rocks pounding the shell. In the distance, huge, hot columns of ash and dust were rising from the planet's surface. Rocks the size of small mountains were tumbling above the equator, some on courses which intersected –

Pown(ow)ri felt a shock which sent fresh blood running from his chest. He once again renewed contact with the Set.

'We need to move the ship!' he told them. 'We are in danger!'

But the Set did not respond: all Pown(ow)ri received was the heightened input of Changed eyes, the taste of flesh, of blood, the painfully pleasant screaming of dying minds.

'We need to move the ship!' urged Pown(ow)ri, with all the force of his weakened mind.

'Kill! KILL!' came the response. Blasters flared, swords cut, blood flowed.

'We must move the ship!'

'KILL! KILL!'

'Move the ship!'

'KILL! KILL! KILL!'

Anaghil led the way because she was the fastest. Then came Kigihij, with Podsi tucked firmly onto his back. Durfheg and Vivojkhil took the rear, carrying Barbara and the Doctor respectively.

The TARDIS seemed to be a long way away: twice they had dodged battles, terrifying scenes of scattered limbs and bloodied corpses. Durfheg had been sick, and now he was running with vomit staining his belly-wrap.

Vivojkhil had a moment – just a moment – to wonder what had happened to her bud-mother and the rest of her clan, to wonder who would look after Podsi and the others if they survived, to wonder if it was worth surviving.

Then Anaghil shouted, 'There it is!'

Vivojkhil looked and saw the TARDIS in the middle of a ring of armed Sou(ou)shi, all in their giant, killing form. There was a glint of metal and fire flicked out. The soil under Anaghil's feet boiled into flame, revealing bare rock. She barely tumbled backwards in time.

'That way!' shouted the Doctor, pointing back the way they had come. Vovojkhil obediently started to move, only to see Kigihij's legs explode into flame.

He screamed, once.

Miraculously, Podsi jumped clear; Vivojkhil saw Anaghil's arms lift the little one.

Kigihij screamed again as the flames rose up around his body.

The Sou(ou)shi were approaching.

The Sou(ou)shi had killed three or four of the Venusians before the cuttershell throwers had found a way of killing them, slicing through the neck below the protective armour. Then it had been over in seconds.

Ian watched as the squadsmen tentatively approached the twitching, headless corpses, then retreated again as the arms reached up for them. Blue light moved everywhere.

Then it was suddenly gone.

Ian scrambled out from beneath Jellenhut's belly, looked up at the sky.

A rock the size of a mountain was tumbling through space with slow, apparently silent grace. As Ian stared, it ploughed into the side of the Sou(ou)shi ship. Cracks spread from the point of impact. Ian caught a glimpse of something that might have been normal daylight from within, then the gaps filled with fire.

'Barbara and the Doctor are in there!' he shouted, pointing.

The cracks in the ship widened. Pieces of glowing rock skipped across the cratered surface like pebbles over water, sending up explosions of flame every time they touched.

Jellenhut was saying something: probably she was shouting with the full force of her lungs, but all Ian heard over the continuing roar was a scratchy whisper:

' – must take cover – '

Stones were falling out of the sky; they glowed red, and hissed when they hit the ground.

Ian pointed at the ship, now clearly disintegrating.

'Barbara!' he shouted. *'Barbara!'*

Pown(ow)ri felt the pain of continued impact through his link with the ship's sensors. He felt systems die as walls broke apart, he felt fire move through drive chambers and power units.

He coughed blood, felt a strong, hot wind blow over his body. The crystals around him rattled and hummed.

The ship, like his body, was damaged beyond repair, and he knew it. But if only they would move it, he thought. If only they would move the ship away from these boundaryless crystals, these shapeless, shape-changing, other-dimensional colours.

If only they would move the ship away.

If only they would –

'Move the ship!'

Pown(ow)ri felt a shock of realization in the Set as the walls of the Venusian chambers cracked. He opened his own eyes and saw a wall of fire and ash moving towards him down the passageway.

Just before he died, he felt the ship move at last.

Vivojkhil stared at the Sou(ou)shi. They were swaying uncertainly, their huge, clawed hands trembling.

'They're moving the ship,' said the Doctor from his position cross-legged on her back. 'It should keep them busy for a while. Run to the TARDIS, quickly.'

Vivojkhil looked at Anaghil, who was staring five-eyed at her bud-brother's smouldering body.

'To the TARDIS,' she repeated. Then she noticed that the ground was shaking.

'Quickly!' urged the Doctor. He pointed with his cane, and to her horror Vivojkhil saw that there was a hole in the floor of the world, a wide crack like a river of night. As she stared, fire boiled up out of it. The ground began to shake more violently.

Vivojkhil needed no further urging: she bolted for the TARDIS at full gallop. The Doctor held on, gripping her neck painfully.

Abruptly, she was falling.

Falling upwards.

The ground dropped away beneath her; ahead, the

TARDIS tumbled through the air, rotating slowly.

Her eyes waving wildly, Vivojkhil saw that the other members of her clan were also tumbling through the air.

'No gravity,' said the Doctor, as if she had asked for an explanation.

To her horror, she saw one of the huge, killing Sou(ou)-shi drifting nearby. Its claws flashed out, raked Durfheg.

He convulsed and died.

'My bud-brother!' yelled Vivojkhil.

The Doctor reached down and touched her lips.

'I know, my dear, but we must reach the TARDIS or it will be the same for all of us.'

A fierce, hot wind had started to blow; the far wall of the chamber had vanished behind a wall of fire. Green and black motes were dancing in front of the flames. With a shock, Vivojkhil realized that they were clansmen, dying.

The TARDIS was closer now. The door was open, and Vivojkhil saw to her amazement the long green arms of a Venusian reaching out from it, the hands sweeping the air, finger-petals wide open.

'Grab my arms!' shouted a clanswoman's voice.

Vivojkhil wasn't near enough, but the Doctor suddenly stood, jumped from her back, sailed towards the TARDIS, landed in the doorway within the web of arms.

His voice drifted across the wind: ' – very long time since I did *that* – '

The wall of fire was closer: its heat was hurting Vivojkhil's skin. She saw the female alien's body drifting past, grabbed hold of it.

But in her other eye, the TARDIS was receding. She saw Anaghil and Podsi hauled to safety by the unknown clanswoman.

She thought for a second, then looked at the female alien. The eyes were closed, but the mouth was open. There was blood flowing in the flesh around her mouth, making it red. She was probably alive.

Vivojkhil kicked her legs to set her body spinning, hurled the alien towards the TARDIS.

She almost missed, but the arms protruding from the door managed to snatch her. Vivojkhil watched them struggle against the screaming of the wind. A rock tumbled past, momentarily obscuring her view of the ship: when it had passed, the alien was gone but the door was still open.

The wall of flame was very close now.

'Go!' yelled Vivojkhil, though she knew that they couldn't possibly hear her over the roaring of the wind.

A piece of burning debris – perhaps it was a tree trunk – caught the TARDIS and sent it spinning rapidly, end over end.

'Go!' yelled Vivojkhil again.

Flames blocked her view. A searing pain encased her, tearing away her breath.

The flames cleared. Through blurry eyes Vivojkhil caught a glimpse of the TARDIS, tiny now and still tumbling, silhouetted against a vast mass of white-hot rock. She couldn't see whether the door was still open.

'Bud-mother, I go to join you,' she muttered.

Then the flames returned.

Ian clung to the rim of the stairway, stared at the tiny form of the Sou(ou)shi ship, turning end over end near the southern horizon.

Below him, somewhere, Jellenhut was shouting something over the constant thunder of the eruptions: ' – to operate the tube pod – assist – '

The ground was shaking as if it were the skin of a drum; Ian could barely keep his balance. Fragments of burning grit fell out of the sky.

The Sou(ou)shi ship started climbing; Ian felt a surge of hope. If they could still control it –

Then he saw the yellow-white flare bursting out of the ship, the rocky shell disintegrating, the red-hot fragments tumbling slowly away from it.

There was nothing left that he could see: no core where anyone might be alive.

He stared at the fragments, stared at them until they faded into the red-and-black chaos of the sky. Then, slowly, step by step, he began to descend the stairway.

18

Victory and Defeat

'The particle density in the equatorial orbits is still considerably higher than predicted,' said Ian, glancing up from his report to the huge, creased bulk of Mrodtikdhil. 'The dust from the Sou(ou)shi ship has spread over a band from thirty degrees north to forty-five degrees south, most of it well above any significant atmosphere.'

The Commander's eye-stalks twitched. 'How long will it remain in orbit?'

'At least as long as the volcanic ejecta; possibly twenty to thirty per cent longer.'

Mrodtikdhil began scribbling something on a notepad. While he worked, Ian looked around the office and saw the tiny amber buds peeping out from the mosses on the walls. They were being allowed to seed; as a celebration, Mrodtikdhil said. The new strain of *dihilribi* would be called *sihakih*, or Victory.

The Commander tore a page off his notepad, spoke:

'By my calculations, the increased cooling factor should give us at least an extra hundred generations of life before the End. Do you agree?'

'I'm not so familiar with that formula,' said Ian. 'Frankly, I thought I'd leave that side of it to you. But yes, you're bound to gain some time.'

The Commander gaped at Ian. 'I'm most grateful to you for your assistance. Your knowledge of orbital mechanics and upper atmospheric densities has proved invaluable as an aid to the monitoring process.'

'Thank you,' said Ian formally. 'The honour is mine.'

Mrodtikdhil shuffled the papers and notepads on his desk around for a moment, then tapped the floor beneath it with a hoof.

'It is necessary for me to see the Inarihibi delegation, to make preliminary plans for the repossession of the city. If you – ' He gestured to the door.

'Of course.'

Ian bowed, in lieu of squatting, and left the Commander's office. He knew why Mrodtikdhil had been so keen to dismiss him: his presence as an advisor was deeply resented by the Inarihibi.

And not only the Inarihibi. The Venusians who lived in the warrens had become markedly xenophobic. Ian didn't blame them; after the Sou(ou)shi, all aliens must seem bad. And he knew that few Venusians understood the details of what had happened – that there had been two sets of aliens, that Ian had always been on their side.

He looked cautiously around him as he walked down the passageway, his hand near the dart gun at his waist. He jumped when a Venusian appeared from the shadows, but it was only Jellenhut.

'Ian of Earth, I have news for you.'

Ian's heart jumped, as it always did at the word 'news'. Even after three weeks, he heard the roaring sound of the TARDIS in every silence, in every creak and groan of the slowly settling rock around them.

Jellenhut must have seen his reaction, for she said, 'Not that, Ian. I'm sorry.' She paused. 'They have recovered the tube terminus under Bikugih where we left the squadsmen and the others.'

Ian remembered: scrambling aboard the tube pod with Jellenhut and two squadsmen. The ground shaking, dust falling from the ceiling. The door closing. His hands on the signalling device, keying frantically. The little *ghif-ghoni* squawking on the floor, oblivious to the crisis. At last, the pod beginning to move. Somehow reaching Mrodtikdhil's command centre intact.

The other squadsmen left behind.

'Two of them were alive,' said Jellenhut. 'Brignontojij of Rastwet and Nosgentanreteb. They survived by eating the bodies of those who died.'

Ian opened his mouth to express horror; recalled just in time that in Venusian terms this was a good thing.

'Honour to the survivors,' he said formally.

He wondered if he would ever get used to the Venusian way of thinking. Inikhut's memories were fading now, incorporated into his own only where he'd had a use for them; several times in every day, something like this would happen and his mind would scream 'Alien!'

He walked with Jellenhut to their quarters – actually Ian's quarters, provided by Mrodtikdhil, together with a guard for the door. But Jellenhut insisted on squatting in the outer chamber, eyes alert, 'watching for you'.

As they passed the guard Ian noticed, as he had noticed for the last tenday, how thin Jellenhut was becoming. The bones of her legs and the twin hinges that supported her jaws were clearly visible through the shrinking flesh.

'Bud-mother, you should eat more,' said Ian for at least the fifth time.

'I eat all I need,' replied Jellenhut, settling on to her belly. It was her usual reply.

Ian paced round the room, looked at the stone walls, the twitching mosses, the *ghifghoni* asleep in the wooden cage he had built for it. Khobu, he had called him: Venusian for 'hope'.

False hope, he thought.

'You can't starve yourself like this. I won't let you.'

There was a long pause. At last Jellenhut said, 'I go to join my children. You know that, Ian of Earth.'

Ian circled the room again, his fists clenched, struggling to think of a way of persuading his friend to stay alive.

'Look, Jellenhut,' he said at last, 'I know you feel that you failed your children by running away. But if you had died with them, would they have been remembered? Would any of us?'

Jellenhut was silent.

'I mean to say,' Ian went on, 'I failed the Doctor and Barbara by signalling to Mrodtikdhil as I did when I knew they were aboard the ship. They died, probably, because of what I did. But if I had done anything else, all of your people would have died at the hands of the Sou(ou)shi. That's what I tell myself when I feel like you do: the Doctor may be dead, Barbara may be dead, I may be dead, but the Venusians are alive because of what we did.'

He stopped, out of breath, his face flushed and sweating.

'I did not know you were planning to die, Ian,' said Jellenhut quietly.

'Eh?' Ian turned and looked at her. All five of her eyes were on him. 'I'm not. Not in the near future, anyway. I'm helping Mrodtikdhil with the planning. It's amazing what you can do when you have the outlook of a different civilization. There's crop rotation to tell him about – I don't know how your people ever managed without it – and I'm working on the construction of a microscope – '

But as he spoke, it all sounded hollow, without meaning: the empty shell of a life. He saw from the set of her eye-stalks that Jellenhut thought so too.

' "I may be dead",' said the Venusian softly. 'You should be aware of the words in your own mind, Ian.'

Ian opened his mouth to object, then realized he *had* said the words.

'I didn't mean – ' he began, then thought of the years speaking to Venusians, walking in ashy Venusian fields, participating in the endless Venusian philosophical debates.

The years. Never seeing a human form: a man, or a woman –

He sat down on the floor, put his head in his hands.

The *ghifghoni* woke up, and gave a warning *chff*. Ian glanced up at it, puzzled. Glanced at the doorway.

Then he heard it.

The sound was unmistakable. This time it wasn't the rock settling. He could already see a faint glow in the air above Jellenhut's head, and as he watched, the blue shape thickened in the air between them.

The guard rushed in through the doorway, weapons drawn; but Jellenhut must have made some sign to him, for he stopped, lowered his cuttershell, and merely stared five-eyed as the TARDIS materialized.

Ian too stared, hardly able to believe that this time, at last, it was real. But there was the flashing lamp; there were the words 'POLICE BOX' in white on blue; there were the instructions for the use of the telephone.

After a short interval, the door opened, and the Doctor stepped out.

'Ah, Chesterton. Just the man we've been looking for. I wonder, could you possibly help us to get Fefirhi Trikhobu through the door of the TARDIS?'

As Ian continued to stare, Barbara appeared behind the Doctor, smiling.

'If you and your friends here were to pull,' the Doctor went on, 'and the rest of us pushed from the inside, I'm sure we could manage – '

Stifling a giggle, Barbara slipped past the Doctor and stepped towards Ian, her arms extended. She was wearing a new white dress, and she had acquired a sun-tan. There was no trace of her injuries.

Ian took her hands, looked at her face for a moment.

'Where – ?' he began.

'It's a long story.' Barbara shrugged. 'I'll tell you later, when – '

There was a clatter of tiny hooves and a small Venusian scurried around the Doctor's legs.

'We're home!' she squeaked. 'Anni! Vivi! We're home!' She leaped sideways, saw Jellenhut, froze for an instant. Then stepped forward, one hoof at a time, eyes askew.

'Bud-mother?'

'I'm not – ' began Jellenhut, then stopped. Her eyes

waved between Ian, the child, the guard, and the Doctor, who was peering at the situation with interest around the side of the TARDIS. 'I can't – ' she began again.

The little one tilted her body upwards, raised three arms in a begging position.

'Bud-mother?'

Jellenhut reached down with two hands and picked up the child, snuggled it against her belly.

'We're home!' squealed the child comfortably. 'Home! Home! Home!'

From inside the TARDIS, another voice: 'Podsi! Podsi! Where – '

A larger child clattered into sight, squeezed past the Doctor.

'Podsi – oh!'

She stopped, squatted to address Jellenhut.

'Rhibu Anaghil of Trijhi, honoured one.'

There was a silence, broken by the click of the Doctor's cane on the stone floor as he moved around the TARDIS for a better look.

'There is authority in the Laws of Being for a change of clan, in certain circumstances,' he observed to Jellenhut.

There was a sound from inside the TARDIS: a leathery creak of skin. Ian turned to look and saw a large Venusian child pushing her way through the door, turning onto her side to do so. Ian stepped back to let her roll out; as she fell back on to her feet he noticed that there was something odd about her skin. It was wrinkled, a bare, pale blue-green around the knees, the lips and eye-stalks. Only three of her eyes seemed to be working properly.

She walked slowly, stiffly, around the TARDIS, squatted in front of Jellenhut.

Ian turned to Barbara.

'What happened to her?'

'Vivi was burned when the Sou(ou)shi ship exploded. We had to go back to pick her up. That's why we've been so long, because Trikhobu's calculations went wrong after that, and we ended up on – '

'But I got it right in the end!' said a voice from the TARDIS door.

Ian stared, saw the mouth and two eye-stalks of an adult Venusian.

He let go of Barbara's hand, stepped forward, stuck his head inside the TARDIS door. He looked from one side of Trikhobu to the other, from top to bottom of the door.

He started to laugh.

'What's so funny?' asked Barbara.

'But how – ?' began Ian, then broke off and doubled up, his whole body shaking with laughter. 'How did she ever get in?'

Ian's shirt was stuck to his back, and sweat was still running down his face.

It was all very well the Doctor standing around waving his cane, saying that they'd had no trouble on somewhere-or-other, they'd had this machine and had managed to get Trikhobu in and out of the TARDIS twice. It was even less use his going to the console and prodding at switches that altered the internal configuration of the door, but had no effect whatsoever on the outside.

It had taken over an hour to get Trikhobu out of the TARDIS.

Ian wiped the sweat from his eyes, walked across the room to Jellenhut. She was alone apart from Podsi – the two older children were with Trikhobu outside, saying goodbye to Barbara. The Doctor was sitting splay-legged against the side of the TARDIS, looking hot and bothered, for all the world as if he had done a large measure of the work.

Jellenhut turned an eye and a hand to Ian, reached out and gently grasped his neck.

'Our custom,' said Ian with a slight smile, 'is to shake hands.'

He extended his own and, after a small pause, Jellenhut took it, the finger-petals reaching almost to his elbow.

'Farewell, Ian Chesterton of the clan Earth,' she said.

'You have been a good friend to me. May you enjoy many more adventures.'

'Oh, I don't think we'll have many more adventures. You see Trikhobu's developed this formula for moving the TARDIS to someone's position at any time, based on a known – '

As he spoke, Barbara jumped down through the doorway of the chamber. She stopped to wipe at the tears on her face, then waved a piece of paper at the Doctor.

'Trikhobu says that this ought to find my mother in January 1965 – '

The Doctor stood up, looked from one to the other of his companions. 'Ah, yes,' he said. 'There was something I wanted to ask you about that.'

Ian and Barbara looked at each other. Barbara spread her hands, palms up.

'You see, I thought we might make a couple of little stops on the way. I asked Fefirhi Trikhobu if she would be kind enough to calculate a course for us to reach Susan's wedding – now I'm sure you'd like to go – and before we do that we need to pick up some gold.'

'Gold?' asked Barbara.

Ian glanced at Jellenhut.

'Many adventures,' she said drily and, in an astonishingly human gesture, winked.

The Doctor was still chattering on.

'Gold for the wedding ring of course! Now, Trikhobu's method only works for tracking people, so naturally I had to think of someone I know who has worked with gold, preferably in its native state – ' He broke off, glancing from Ian to Barbara and back again. 'Have either of you ever heard of Aristea of Alexandria?'

'No,' said Ian and Barbara together, then glanced at each other and grinned.

'But I think we're going to.'

Epilogue

Dawning

In the days when her father had been alive, Trikhobu would never have believed that there were so many children in the world.

They galloped across the ashy ground between the blocky shapes of the new houses; little ones, big ones, medium-sized ones, all of them shouting and jostling and jumping. Their hooves sent up plumes of grey dust as they ran; their belly-wraps were caked with ash.

Suddenly one of them shrieked, 'Fefirhi Trikhobu!'

Thirty sets of little eye-stalks curled to look, and then the whole pack of children swerved like a flock of *ghifghoni* and galloped towards the spot where Trikhobu stood, jumping over the new, green wetmosses and soakfruit bushes that had been planted to mark the middle of the street. Within a few moments they were all crowded around her, climbing over one another in their eagerness to have sight of her, batting at each other with arms and eye-stalks, and all of them shouting at once.

'Honoured Trikhobu!'

'Tell us about the Doctor! Tell us about Ian! Tell us about Barbara!'

'Were they magicians?'

'Did they fly down from the sky?'

'Did you really go to another world in their ship?'

Trikhobu craned her eyes at the low grey sky in a gesture of unwillingness, but the children weren't fooled; after a moment she gave in.

'Very well, I'll tell you.'

Trikhobu spoke for almost a middlechange: she told

the children about Barbara and the funeral meat and the Magnetologists' firecracker; about the arrival of the Sou(ou)shi; the chase after Ian in the land-yacht; the battle with the Death Inspectors; Barbara's injuries and the storm; the moment when Barbara had fallen up into the air and she, Trikhobu, had almost fallen with her; about the battle at the harbour; the flight in the TARDIS with the Doctor; the TARDIS's arrival on the Sou(ou)shi ship, and her own fight with Pown(ow)ri; and finally how Vivojkhil and her clan-siblings had rescued Barbara, whilst, far below in Bikugih, Ian had deceived the Sou(ou)shi to save the Venusians.

' – and so the world was saved because of the virtue and honour of the Doctor and his companions,' she finished, using the familiar formula she had used a twenty-five of five times. 'May they be remembered until the bones of time are cracked.'

The children gaped, thanked Trikhobu and offered her the hospitality of their clans. Then, slowly, the children dispersed, began chasing themselves home along the dusty street.

But Trikhobu had almost forgotten them; she was staring at the sky, where she supposed that the Doctor and Barbara and Ian still were, somewhere, somewhen. She remembered something that Jellenhut had said after the TARDIS had left: 'Barbara and Ian will return to their home one day; but the old one knows no necessity but travelling, always travelling.'

Until the bones of time are cracked.

Trikhobu wondered how long that really was, and whether she could calculate it. She got out her notepad, unsheathed her writing-claw and began scribbling.

After a while, it began to rain.

They had lost.

They had lost everything.

They had lost everything and they were happy.

What joy! For the prey to turn predator! To feel the splintering of bone, the boiling of blood in vacuum, the searing pain of bodily death! Even the storm of anger they felt at the interference of the Doctor in their game was a joy, a deep joy from the bottom of their souls. They cared! For the first time since they had run on those long-ago plains, they cared about something! They wanted him dead so badly.

They assessed their situation.

They were drifting, bodiless, through space. They had managed to consume the minds of some of the Venusians that had died with them, enough to sustain them for a short journey, but not for a long one. There was no returning to the second planet: the pressure of the solar wind pushed them inexorably outwards. Their only hope was to steer, to somehow find a safe haven.

Then they remembered the third planet. The oxygen sky, the primitive life.

The life that would not always be primitive.

They controlled their drift, allowing themselves to slip into the magnetosphere of the young world. Down through the painful storms of the ionosphere. Down to the surface. Below, into the shelter of the rock.

They welded themselves to the rock, bonded the structures of their minds to the interstices of crystals. Slowed their consciousness down to conserve their precious energy. Shut down their thoughts, one by one, until they only knew one thing.

They were waiting to be found by something they could eat.

They were waiting to be found.

They were waiting.

Available in the Doctor Who – New Adventures series:

TIMEWYRM: GENESYS by John Peel
TIMEWYRM: EXODUS by Terrance Dicks
TIMEWYRM: APOCALYPSE by Nigel Robinson
TIMEWYRM: REVELATION by Paul Cornell
CAT'S CRADLE: TIME'S CRUCIBLE by Marc Platt
CAT'S CRADLE: WARHEAD by Andrew Cartmel
CAT'S CRADLE: WITCH MARK by Andrew Hunt
NIGHTSHADE by Mark Gatiss
LOVE AND WAR by Paul Cornell
TRANSIT by Ben Aaronovitch
THE HIGHEST SCIENCE by Gareth Roberts
THE PIT by Neil Penswick
DECEIT by Peter Darvill-Evans
LUCIFER RISING by Jim Mortimore and Andy Lane
WHITE DARKNESS by David A. McIntee
SHADOWMIND by Christopher Bulis
BIRTHRIGHT by Nigel Robinson
ICEBERG by David Banks
BLOOD HEAT by Jim Mortimore
THE DIMENSION RIDERS by Daniel Blythe
THE LEFT-HANDED HUMMINGBIRD by Kate Orman
CONUNDRUM by Steve Lyons
NO FUTURE by Paul Cornell
TRAGEDY DAY by Gareth Roberts
LEGACY by Gary Russell
THEATRE OF WAR by Justin Richards
ALL-CONSUMING FIRE by Andy Lane
BLOOD HARVEST by Terrance Dicks
STRANGE ENGLAND by Simon Messingham
FIRST FRONTIER by David A. McIntee

The next Missing Adventure, to be published in November 1994, is *The Crystal Bucephalus* by Craig Hinton which will feature the fifth Doctor, Tegan, Turlough and Kamelion.